AUTUMN SKY

AUTUMN SKY

a novel by

GALE SEARS

Covenant Communications, Inc.

Cover image © 2004 by David Sandberg

Cover design copyrighted 2004 by Covenant Communications, Inc.

Published by Covenant Communications, Inc.
American Fork, Utah

Printed in Canada
First Printing: August 2004

10 09 08 07 06 05 04 03   10 9 8 7 6 5 4 3 2 1

ISBN 1-59156-586-3

ACKNOWLEDGMENTS

Thanks to Eloise James and Bertie Larson for enchanting walks in their orchards; to Annette Overson for all things equestrian; and to Annette Capner and Darla Isackson, who were part of the original serendipity. Love to my mother for bringing me peanut-butter sandwiches to sustain me as I wrote my first stories in the "Larch"; and to my family and friends who are astonishing in their encouragement, love, and help.

For George, who has always believed in me.

CHAPTER 1

Alaina Lund stepped out of the quiet farmhouse into the midnight chill. Her ears began to ache from the cold immediately, and she covered them with her gloved hands as she ran toward the orchard. The grass made a strange crunching sound under her feet, and she looked down in horror to see the once pale-green blades now frozen black. *No! Please. Not frost this late in March. This is impossible!* She raced past the barn, now coated a ghostly white. *We're going to lose everything!* A gust of wind howled past her, and she hunched lower trying to maintain her speed, but the ground was hard and crusted with a thin spray of ice and her feet kept sliding from under her. She cried with frustration as she struggled to get to the suffering trees.

She heard the sickening sound of cracking wood and knew it came from the apple orchard. Straining to see through the dark, she caught the pale reflection of tree branches covered in silver hoar frost. She stumbled closer as another crack beat against her eardrums. *No!* She saw the snap of a branch shake the tree as it crashed to the ground. Iced in delicate decay, the lacy apple blossoms jingled like softly breaking glass as they hit the earth. The stars shone brilliant white in the cold obsidian sky, but they gave no warmth, no hope. Alaina stared into the endless darkness. *Why was God doing this? Why would He destroy such beauty?*

She willed her feet to move and ran to the trees. She could hear them moaning as the merciless wind shoved against their frozen branches. *What can I do?* Paralyzed by such cruel devastation, Alaina allowed frantic thoughts to clamor uselessly in her head as she stood clenching and unclenching her hands. *Help me! I don't know what to do!*

Through the din, Alaina caught the sound of her father singing, and her heart jumped. *Where is he?* She yelled out to him, but her voice was thin and raspy. *There! His singing again! Or is it the wind?* She turned wildly, searching for him. If he were here, everything would be all right. If he were here, this suffering would stop. Hundreds of grinding cracks pounded against Alaina's ears as branches began falling in deafening surrender. Fear kept her shackled in place, surrounded by the gruesome destruction. She had to move! Find her father! She had to run! But she could not run. She tried to scream, but the sound was torn away in a howl of wind, and she felt her legs break under her like splintering wood. She fell slowly down—down to the hard, unyielding ground. The final thing Alaina saw before darkness was her father standing over her, his face white as death.

"Laina! Laina!" Her sister Eleanor's soft voice called to her from far away, and Alaina struggled to open her eyes. Everything was gray—the walls, her bedspread, the sky out her bedroom window. "Alaina, are you sick?" Eleanor's voice sounded worried. "Can I get you anything?"

Alaina opened her eyes wider and rolled onto her back. "What happened?"

"You were moaning in your sleep. Are you all right?"

Alaina sat up. "Did we have a freeze?"

Eleanor, a pale shadow in the gloom, reached down and took her hand. "I don't think so. Just rain."

The sick feeling of her dream diminished, and Alaina sat back against her pillow.

She felt Eleanor shiver. "Here, get in bed with me. Is Kathryn still asleep?"

"Nothing wakes her up," Eleanor replied, climbing gratefully into the warm bed.

"What time is it?" Alaina asked, yawning.

"Early. Sun won't be up for an hour."

The girls snuggled down into the covers and lay quietly, listening to the soft hiss of rain.

"Did you have a bad dream?" Eleanor finally ventured.

Alaina sighed, "Oh, Elly, it was terrible. I don't remember it all, but the trees were frozen, all the blossoms just frozen black, and there was wind, and it was so dark." Alaina felt a chill move down her spine. "All the trees were breaking."

"Breaking?"

"The branches were just breaking off."

Eleanor pressed closer to her sister. "That couldn't really happen, could it?"

Alaina hesitated. "No, probably not. Not like in my dream anyway." She sifted through the images. "Father was there."

"Well, that was good."

But Alaina remembered the chalky white of her father's face. She shivered, and pulled the covers closer to her chin. She hated when her dreams felt like warnings.

"What else happened?" Eleanor asked sleepily.

"I don't remember much more. I think I fell down, but I don't remember."

"Well, it was just a dream," Eleanor replied.

"Right. Just a dream."

Eleanor was quiet after that, and Alaina was sure she'd drifted off into peaceful sleep, a sleep Alaina envied. She closed her eyes against the gloomy light, but she could not expel the dreary sound of rain pelting on the roof or untie the knot of dread that had settled in her stomach.

When the first rays of sunlight pushed against the black rain clouds on the eastern hills, Alaina slipped out of bed, dressed, and went to the orchard to check the trees. As she walked the path to the groves, she felt the chill of the rain-soaked air, and looked quickly for evidence of frost or ice, but saw no signs. She lifted her eyes to the apple trees and watched as the soft, pink glow of sunrise brushed the clouds and spilled down into the orchard. If imagination could have taken her to the rich silk bazaars of China or the Paris countryside in spring, she would have refused going. To her, the green March hillsides east of Sutter Creek reminded her of Eden, and no exotic temptation would drag her from the place. She belonged in the California foothills and was perfectly content to occupy her time with life and work on her father's farm.

She moved into the chill shadows of the apple orchard, surveying the trees and noting the rich brown mud caked on her boots. She smiled. Mud was a good sign. Placing her hand against the moist bark of the nearest tree, she ran her fingers lightly up the branch to the swelling buds, where life sang in the March coolness, rumbling deep into her arms and shoulders.

"How does it look, daughter?" Samuel Lund called as he hoofed his way through the wet of the hillside.

Alaina turned to watch her father's approach. His body was tall and angular, and his movement across the grassy hillside was confident and powerful. Her legs were long at eighteen, yet she knew she'd never match his stride.

"The signs show well," she answered confidently. "No frost, only good wet rain."

"Never heard of good dry rain," he teased, coming to stand beside her. "Maybe in Arizona they have good dry rain, do you think? Maybe New Mexico."

Alaina gave her father a sidelong glance. "I meant wet as in liquid—not frozen. You're just jealous because I was first to be among the trees this morning."

He tugged at her thick braid of hair. "Jealous? Yes, I am. I am indeed." He studied the opulent buds as he spoke, admiring the Master's workmanship. His strong fingers moved deftly within the maze of branches as he walked from tree to tree. Alaina followed closely, watching her father's competent inspection. After a time, the lines at the bridge of his nose softened and he turned to her with a smile. "We'll check the pears next, but all should be well. No frost; only good wet rain," he repeated. Samuel Lund patted his daughter's arm and moved off into the grove, humming one of the hymns he loved.

Alaina looked to the acres west of their house and marveled at the pearly fluff of pear blossoms. Spring frost and hail were feared enemies to such a delicate creation, but even now the air was warming as the sun crested the hilltop, and she felt the dread of last night's dream unravel. She smiled and sighed. She loved their farm: a long swath of meadowland drenched with blue and white lupine, California poppy, and yellow buttercup; a rise of rolling hill covered in apple trees, and on an even higher ridge, oak trees and tall pines—ever green against the blue sky. Alaina smiled as she thought about rays of pale morning sunlight brushing the Methodist church tower in Sutter Creek, and shimmering on the windows of the Main Street shops. To her the small towns of the Sierra foothills were magical, tucked away like gold coins in a velvet purse. In the quiet of her mind, she measured the perimeter of her life: Pine Grove, Jackson, Sutter Creek—noisy boomtowns of the California gold-rush days that in sixty years since had softened into placid hamlets for farm supply and mercantile stores. There were still foundries in Sutter Creek, but overall farm families had replaced the gold-fevered drifter. The region had lost much of the spicy grit-edged spirit of the '49ers, although their independent brio still flared up in grandchildren and great-grandchildren. Now, "invention" and "industry" were the watchwords of the new century, and many a town doctor could be seen driving one of Mr. Ford's new horseless-carriage inventions.

Alaina pushed the errant wisps of dark hair back from her face and sucked air deep into her lungs. This morning, even breathing was a prayer of gratitude. She would not leave this hillside for a thousand mornings. She would live on air, water, and sunlight. She shoved her boots down into the mud and lifted her face to the rain-soaked sky. As she closed her eyes, she could feel the moisture in the air sparkle against her skin

"Hey ho! Trouble here, Fancy!" Her father's voice came clearly through the morning stillness, brushing away her rambling thoughts. She smiled. Obviously there wasn't too much trouble; otherwise, her pet name would have been forgotten. She remembered the first time her father had given her the endearing title. She was five years old and had climbed into the lower branches of one of the apple trees. She'd been there for some time when her father had found her.

"Here you are, Miss Alaina. Your mother and I have been looking for you."

"I had to come talk to the apples."

He'd smiled at her. "Really?"

"Yes. They weren't getting very big, so I had to talk to them."

A surprised look flashed onto his face. "So, you're the magic person who makes our apples so big and beautiful!"

She remembered blushing—the first time she could recall—and nodding her head.

Father had laughed and put her up on his shoulders. "You're just full of fancy, little one. Full of fancy." She smiled as she remembered him being her galloping steed all the way back to the house.

"Alaina Lund?"

She jumped, realizing she'd been daydreaming again. "Coming, Father!" She hurriedly pulled her boots from the mud and moved toward the sound of her father's voice.

The smell of nature intensified as she moved into the grove. It was the smell she loved above all others. The scents of warm spice cake, fried bacon on cold mornings, or McPherson's lilac soap were meager charlatans to this smell, which brought peace to her heart and elation to her soul. She'd once heard Pastor Wilton preach a fiery sermon about denouncing the world, but she never would. Never with mornings such as this spilling over with the fragrance of dirt after the rain, and last season's leaves gone to soil. She'd be sorely disappointed if, when she died, she found that heaven did not smell like her apple orchard after a rain. She figured it would, because if God made the world, then He made the smells too, and this must surely be His favorite.

She moved through several rows of trees and caught the blue of her father's shirt as he moved along the top of a small ridge. Thinking of his call to her, she was proud of the trust her father showed in her as they worked the orchard together. Most men would have passed the female child in preference for a younger male offspring, but Alaina's brother James was lazy and not willing to work the orchard.

Alaina pushed her pace to legitimize her father's confidence. His back was to her, and he seemed to be concentrating on something at his feet. Alaina tried to anticipate the trouble as she made her way among the trees. All care had been taken in pruning and arresting bore infestation, and the winter cold had been sufficient for a good set. But given the direction of Father's attention, the problem might not be with the trees at all. Her mind was a jumble of possibilities when she finally reached his side.

"Now see here, daughter," Samuel Lund barked before Alaina had time to catch her breath. "This mad rush of water is likely to wash away half my fruit trees and the family relief house if you don't get it dammed up properly."

"*Your* fruit trees?" Alaina retorted, noticing the quick spark in her father's green eyes. "Hmmm. Well, if they're *your* fruit trees, then this must be *your* wash, and I'll gladly fetch *your* shovel, so *you* can dam it up, or divert it, or whatever you think is best for *your* property."

Samuel let out a snort. "Where in the world did you learn such impertinence, young woman?"

Alaina only smiled.

"I suppose we'll need to divert it," Samuel replied after taking a moment to compose himself. "Looks like another douse of rain tonight."

"Divert it? Won't that be a lot of work?" Alaina questioned, trying hard to keep a smile off her face.

Samuel Lund caught his daughter's eye in a stern reproach. "Hard work never hurt the two of us before. If it must be done, then it must be done."

"I suppose you're right," Alaina answered, sighing dramatically. She turned abruptly and started walking in the direction of home.

"Whoa now! Don't go for shovels," Samuel called, moving quickly to catch up with her. "I'll get them."

Alaina stopped abruptly, a wicked grin playing on her lips. "Oh, I wasn't going for the shovels. I was going for James Allen."

"What in the world for?" Samuel asked with suspicion.

"So he can help you with the digging," Alaina replied simply.

"And where will you be?"

"In Sutter Creek with Mother. Don't you remember? She said today we would be going into town for things."

"Things? What things?"

Alaina held back a giggle. "Things. You know—store goods, oil, a new washboard, clothespins."

"Clothespins! I have to deal with your lazy younger brother all morning so you can help your mother buy clothespins?"

Alaina laughed outright. "Why, Father! What would Mother say if she heard you talking about her pride and joy like that?"

Samuel Lund grunted. "She can buy clothespins anytime."

"No. Today is the day." Alaina flipped her long skirt and started off down the hill. "I'll send James up with the shovels."

"You hate shopping," he called in a last-ditch effort.

"I do not," she countered. "Besides, I have to drive the wagon." She heard him grunt, then mumble something under his breath. She so enjoyed teasing her father, and she regretted the loss of their morning together as much as he did. But there was no possibility of her mother consenting to her missing proper women's chores in order to dig in the dirt.

Alaina tried to imagine her mother with a torn skirt or dirt under her nails, but somehow the picture wouldn't stay. Alaina looked down quickly to check her own nails. *Goodness! These will never pass inspection.* She'd have to make a stop at the rain barrel before entering her mother's domain. She took another look at her gentle hands and slender fingers and saw them every inch her mother's. She flipped them over defiantly, palms up. *Well, the calluses are mine,* she thought. She knew as the firstborn daughter she'd grown to be her mother's frustration—abandoning her dolls at three and refusing to learn sewing or knitting. She didn't mind cooking or wearing skirts, but her cooking was always spicy, and her skirts were always plain.

Her mother's high-class ways would have to be passed on through her younger sisters Eleanor and Kathryn—or perhaps through her brother James. Alaina chided herself for such a mean thought. It wasn't James's fault that Mother kept the strings tight on him. She knew part of that was her transgression. Elizabeth Louise Knight, of the wealthy Los Angeles Knight family, was not about to let any of her other children follow the headstrong, non-accommodating ways of the firstborn. Alaina knew that she and Mother had always been at odds with each other, especially since she'd started working in the orchard with Father, a task Mother didn't consider women's work. Of course, neither Mother nor James cared much for the orchard anyway. Alaina thought that sad and wished James would break away and learn the things Father could teach him, for he was, in looks at least, very much Samuel's son: dark hair, green eyes, and a long, easy gait. James was also very strong for sixteen, and Alaina often wondered why her father didn't insist on him spending more time doing farm chores.

As Alaina stepped from the wet hillside grass onto the dirt road, she could see Kathryn by the mud pond pitching stones at the ducks. Kathryn was a very peevish nine-year-old who looked down on all her older siblings. She spied, and sulked, and told such fibs that it was all Alaina could do not to get down the Holy Bible and thrash her with it. Kathryn was decent to only two people, Mother and Father—Mother because Kathryn idolized her, and Father because he treated her kindly, much more kindly than Alaina thought she deserved.

Alaina figured that Mother turned a blind eye to the little churl's deplorable behavior because Kathryn was the aristocratic beauty of the Lund children. It seemed, as the last child, she had acquired all the physical glory from both sides of the family. Kathryn had vivid blue eyes (a shade deeper than Alaina's own sky blue) and chestnut brown hair that shone in the sunlight like a newly brushed colt. She was the only child to receive that gift of Mother's beautiful hair, and took great pride in sitting on her bed every night brushing through her long curls a hundred times, much to the envy of her two older sisters. Alaina often consoled herself by thinking that while she and Eleanor were quite plain creatures, they had been blessed with Father's joyful character. Kathryn's personality, on the other hand, most resembled that of Great-Uncle Milburn Lund, who'd run off with his neighbor's wife, robbed two hardware stores, and slugged it out with a sheriff in Iowa before being shot in the leg and brought to justice.

As Alaina neared the house, she heard a pained squeal from Kathryn. She grinned. *Well, little sister,* she thought gleefully, *the ducks have a right to defend themselves.* She moved carefully around the side of the house to the rain barrel. She knew the morning would be much more peaceful if Mother didn't see her in this "unladylike" condition. She was just about to dip her hands into the cold water when the back porch door suddenly opened. Alaina sucked in her breath and prepared for a stern reproach.

"Hi, Laina!" came a bright and comforting voice.

Alaina relaxed noticeably. "Morning, Elly," she whispered, motioning for Eleanor to be secretive. "Where's Mother?"

"Kitchen," Eleanor replied, closing the door carefully behind her. "Don't worry, Mother's deep into dishes." Eleanor flopped down on the wood box. "How's the orchard? Did we have any frost damage?"

"Nope. Only rain. Father will check the pears, but all should be well." Alaina splashed her hands gingerly in the icy water.

"Oh, goodness! That must hurt," Eleanor said, wincing. "If Mother wasn't in the kitchen, I'd fetch some warm water off the stove."

"I'll be all right," Alaina replied. "We Lund women are tough."

Eleanor started to whoop, but caught herself. She whispered gleefully, "Well, you're tough, and I'm exquisite."

"Another new word, Professor Eleanor?"

Eleanor smiled broadly. "It's my new word for the week."

"I see," Alaina replied, smiling at her sister's dear little character. "Well, Professor, I need you to do something for me, but you'll have to be sneaky and fast."

"Sneaky and fast?" Eleanor echoed. "Oh sure, that's me. Sneaky, fast, and exquisite."

Now it was Alaina's turn to stifle a laugh. "I need you to bring me my blue skirt with the white trim."

"Is that it?"

"That's it."

"That's easy!" Eleanor answered, jumping up. "Where should I bring it?"

"The storage shed."

"Will do!" Eleanor answered with military crispness. She gave a grand salute and disappeared back into the kitchen.

Alaina smiled, her heart filling with affection for the skinny snip of a girl. She thought of herself at fourteen and knew there was no comparison. Eleanor had a tenderness that she'd never possess, a way of seeing the best in everyone, even in the most despicable of characters. At an age when most other children were desperately concerned about themselves, Eleanor looked outward. Admiring her sister's character always made Alaina reflect on her own shortcomings. After a moment's thought, she vowed to be more generous in her feelings for James and Kathryn, no matter how hard it would be.

"What are you doing?" Kathryn snapped as she slipped around the corner of the house.

Alaina jumped, splashing water down the front of her skirt. "Kathryn, you little monster!" she scolded without thinking.

"What did you call me?" Kathryn asked, glaring. "What did you say? Did you call me a monster? Mama said you weren't to call me names anymore!"

"Calm down, Kathryn. I didn't mean it. You just frightened me."

A determined scowl fixed itself on Kathryn's face. "I'm telling Mama what you said. And . . . I'm telling her that you got mud all over your gray skirt."

Alaina gritted her teeth. In the last three minutes she'd been in the presence of saint and sinner. She liked the saint much more, but the sinner had to be dealt with here and now, for it was obvious that Kathryn was in a dark mood from being pecked by the duck, and was eager to see someone else in pain.

"Well, go ahead," Alaina replied nonchalantly. "Tell Mother about the skirt. She won't care. You see, Kathryn, I've been out working this morning, not running around throwing rocks at Mother's prize ducks, like someone I know." She calmly went back to scraping the dirt out from under her fingernails.

Kathryn stood perplexed for a moment, and Alaina held out fleeting hope that she'd outsmarted the little fox. But then the wheels turned in Kathryn's head and the next cog fell into place.

"You still called me a monster!" Kathryn said, stiffening. "And I'm telling." She turned and raced to the back porch door, yelling in her most wounded voice, "Mama! Mama! Alaina called me a fat, ugly monster!"

As she took off running toward the front porch, Alaina thought of several other appropriate names for her youngest sibling. When she hit the porch steps, she stopped, untied her muddy work boots, and left them sitting on the ground by the bottom stair. Then she bounded up the rest of the stairs, stripping off her skirt as she went. When she reached the landing, she stepped out of the muddy flannel skirt and shoved it under the wicker table by the front porch swing. She looked quickly through the parlor window to check for Mother and the little monster, and seeing only friendly inanimate objects, snuck in the front door and darted up the stairs. She met Eleanor, blue skirt in hand.

"Wh—What in the world?" Eleanor stammered.

"Change of plans," Alaina whispered, gently pushing her confused sister back into the sanctuary of their bedroom, where she quickly shut the door and slipped on her clean skirt. As she was trying to button the last of her buttons, there was a purposeful knock at the bedroom door.

"That's Mother," Eleanor whispered. "Here, let me help."

Another knock. "Alaina Kay Lund. I need to have a word with you."

Alaina hated it when Mother used her full name. She always made it sound so stiff and bitter. "Coming, Mother," she responded, quickly checking her reflection and smoothing her skirt. Eleanor gave her an encouraging smile.

Alaina opened the door and offered her mother her most innocent face. Mrs. Lund looked straight into the eyes of her oldest child and walked stiffly into the room. "Eleanor, I need to speak to your sister."

"Yes, ma'am," Eleanor said, rising. "I have to finish sweeping the floor in the parlor." She touched Alaina's arm lightly as she passed by, and offered a wink of encouragement. Alaina felt the sudden impulse to follow her out of the room, but instead she smoothed her skirt and tried to feel eighteen and not eight, which was difficult with Mother silently scrutinizing every movement.

Mrs. Lund hesitated a moment, then spoke firmly. "We seem to be having a problem again with name-calling." Alaina lowered her head, knowing better than to respond. Her mother continued pointedly, "We seem to think that name-calling is an appropriate hobby for a young lady with manners." She sighed. "Alaina, must I remind you again of that quality of patience which seems to be so lacking in your personality?"

Alaina's eyes wandered from her mother's black shoes to her own uncovered feet. Ugly water stains ran the entire distance around her new tan stockings. She calmly tucked her toes under her skirt and glanced up to see if her mother had taken any notice, but her mother's eyes were intently watching her daughter's face. "Have you anything to say, Alaina?"

Alaina took a deep breath. "She startled me. I didn't mean to call her a name; it just slipped out."

"I see. And what if Pastor Wilton startled you? Would you also call him a fat, ugly monster?"

"Just monster."

"I beg your pardon!" Mrs. Lund queried, a distinct edge to her voice.

Alaina stammered, "No! No! I don't mean I'd call Pastor Wilton a monster! I only meant that I called Kathryn a little monster, not a fat, ugly monster. She exaggerated the whole incident. She always does that."

Mrs. Lund held up a graceful hand to stop Alaina's excuse. "I often wonder who is older, you or Kathryn."

Alaina set her jaw.

"All I require from you," Mrs. Lund said in a warning tone, "are apologies. One to me and one to Kathryn."

Alaina swallowed, trying to unclench her teeth. "Yes, ma'am. I'm sorry."

"I hope that I will not have to speak with you again about this flaw in your character."

"No, ma'am."

"As our eldest child, your father and I expect you to set the example for the others."

Alaina thought that an impossible task, but only answered, "Yes, ma'am."

Mrs. Lund walked to the window and pushed back the wooden shutters. "It is a lovely morning, so may we put this unpleasantness behind us? James has the wagon ready, and I would like to leave shortly, without further incident. Is that possible?"

Alaina was grateful for the change of mood. "Yes, ma'am. I'll put on my shoes and be ready right away."

"And brush your hair a bit," Mrs. Lund instructed as she moved to the door. "And don't forget your hat."

"Yes, ma'am."

When she heard the door latch click into place after her mother's departure, Alaina breathed a sigh of relief and flopped back onto the bed, amazed at the slight reprimand. Could it be that Mother was finally seeing past Kathryn's princess face? Alaina found that unlikely. Perhaps it was just that on such a beautiful morning, Mother thought harsh words and punishments were unwelcome intruders. Whatever the reason, Alaina was grateful. She would have a morning and afternoon in town, and James would be home doing what he dreaded most—working.

Alaina sat up. *James*! She hadn't sent James to Father with the shovels. She jumped up and ran to the window. James was at the front of the house affixing the hold-back strap to the wooden shaft of the wagon. She opened the window and called down to him. He looked up slowly, shading his eyes against the morning sun. "What do you want?" he growled in his newly acquired baritone.

The annoyed edge in his voice made Alaina bristle, but she bit her tongue. "Father wants you in the orchard this morning. You need to take up shovels and the pickax." Alaina stopped, knowing what would come.

"What for?"

"Because he has work for you."

James yanked on the tug strap with more force than was necessary, making the roan horse shy sideways. James patted the horse's flank to calm it. "I have to stay with the wagon."

Alaina was just about at the end of her patience. "You can go up as soon as Mother and I have left for town." She quickly drew her head inside the room and slammed the window shut, not wanting to hear any more of his muttering. She found her shoes quickly, brushed through her hair, and shoved the blue straw hat on her head. She hated wearing hats, but a proper young lady would not dare to be seen in town without one (as Mother always said), and since she did love going to town, she never made a big fuss about it. She snatched her short cloak out of the closet and her leather gloves from the dressing table, then headed downstairs. Eleanor met her when she reached the front hallway. "Is everything all right? Are you in much trouble?"

Alaina smiled at her younger sister's protectiveness. "Actually, she wasn't very angry at all. Maybe she's getting tired of Kathryn's mischief."

"Do you think so?" Eleanor asked in disbelief.

Alaina laughed and took Eleanor's hands. "No, but we can always hope." They both laughed. "Good luck with Kathryn," Alaina added, pulling on her gloves. "I certainly wish you could come with us."

"Me too," Eleanor said wistfully. "But I'd hate to think what disasters Kathryn would cause if left to herself. She'd probably blow up the relief house."

Alaina laughed hard as she opened the door and stepped out onto the front porch. James had already helped Mother into her seat and had loaded the box of linens for the church raffle. Alaina hurried around to the driver's side to climb up. James only pretended to help her as an excuse to give her a hard pinch in the soft flesh of her arm. Alaina pulled away and lifted herself into the seat. "Don't help me!" she hissed, glaring at him. "And don't forget your responsibility to Father."

She took up the reins, undid the brake, and gave Friar Tuck a light slap on the rump. "Walk on, Tuck!" she said firmly. As the eight-year-old gelding started forward, Alaina gently rubbed the sore spot on her arm. What a brat James could be. Just because he was angry about having to help Father, did he have to take it out on her? It was the age-old flogging of the messenger. Of course, James probably assumed it was her idea that he be set to labor, and so felt justified. Alaina suddenly smiled. The vision of James working was worth one small pinch. She clucked reassuringly to Friar Tuck and sat up straighter in her seat.

She knew, however, that her brother's vindictive behavior was mostly prompted by envy. She and James had never been very friendly siblings, but since Alaina had taken over his job of driving mother to town, she'd felt an increasing menace in his attitude. Well, it wasn't her fault that the sixteen-year-old had been distracted by Mr. Drakerman's daughter, Lois, and had run the wagon into a big gully. It was the only time Alaina had seen her mother lose her temper with him, and the remembrance brought a knot to her stomach. She also thought of the similar tongue-lashing she'd receive for any such blunder, so she pulled Friar Tuck to a slower pace and increased her vigilance. Father had spent many weeks wearing down Mother's resistance to Alaina taking up the manly responsibility of driving to town, and she was not about to lose the privilege because of negligence.

Mother seldom talked during the two-hour ride into Sutter Creek, so Alaina used the welcome solitude to enjoy the beauty of the day, taking in the wondrous sights and smells of the land all around her. As she did so, Alaina turned the wagon from the curved track that ran through their property, and onto the main road. A stately row of pines bordered Cold Creek Road as it slipped over the crest of Morris Hill and down into the valley beyond. On its way to meet up with the Kit Carson track, the road would pass the Drakermans' apple farm, the

Simpsons' property, and Crazy Granny's house. New people had bought the land bordering Granny Pitman's to the south, and would start fixing up the old dilapidated farmhouse the first of June. Alaina had heard rumors that the family had six children, with a boy just about her age. She hoped the rumors were true, as there were so few young people in the county. She would enjoy going to a dance at the church and not having to be partnered with clumsy Markus Salter. Markus was a fine enough fellow off the dance floor, but when the band started up, he seemed all elbows and clomping feet.

The day was already warming as the sun lifted toward the tops of the trees. The rain the night before had soaked the ground, so Alaina was careful to avoid mud holes. She was confident of Friar Tuck's surefootedness, and over the months of driving in sleet and frost, she'd learned to have confidence in her own abilities as well. She re-adjusted her grip on the lines and gave Tuck an encouraging tap on his rump, vowing that this ride into town would be as uneventful as all the others had been.

As they started the climb up Morris Hill, Alaina turned in her seat to look at the farm and the white, wood-framed house nestled among the oaks and pines. She gloried in the sight of the pear trees in bloom and the waiting apple trees on the hill. Her father was a wonderful farmer and a wonderful man. Everyone liked him, even Crazy Granny Pitman, who let him bring food supplies right into her kitchen. No other person had stepped foot inside her creepy house for the twenty years since her husband had hung himself in the attic. Of course, the hanging part was town legend, which Father said was hogwash.

Suddenly a slice of cold wind left over from winter's icebox cut down the hollow, shaking the pines and forcing the women to grab for their hats. Alaina scowled at the frigid interloper and pulled her cloak tight, holding the lines with one hand.

"We should have worn our heavier coats," Mrs. Lund said stiffly, shoving her hands deeper into her muff. "This is going to be a miserable trip into town."

Alaina didn't respond, praying the prophecy would prove untrue, and groaning as her uncovered ears began to ache. Then, just as suddenly as it came, the wind was gone, changing direction up to the higher elevations where snow still lingered in the shadow of massive granite cliffs.

"See!" Alaina said, brightening with the warmth of the sun on her back. "We're tougher than that old gust. He'll blow himself out before we reach Pine Grove."

Her mother sat up straighter and adjusted her hat. "I'll want to stop by the church first."

"Yes, ma'am," Alaina responded cheerfully. The cold feeling of before melted away, and she actually felt like singing. Then again, she didn't want Mother reprimanding her for such inappropriate behavior, so she kept still and stored up all her gaiety for her meeting with Joanna Wilton, the pastor's daughter and her best friend. They had met the summer of 1901, when they were worldly-wise women of six and attending vacation Bible school for the first time. Their first encounter had been at the arts table where Joanna, with her strawberry-blond curls and starched white pinafore, was modeling clay into ugly snakes and icky bugs. Alaina was delighted, and soon the two were producing creatures at a furious pace. When Mrs. Thayer, their Sunday School teacher, had questioned the religious significance of all these lower forms of life, Joanna responded without hesitation, saying they were one of the curses Moses dumped on Pharaoh. Alaina hadn't understood one word of the explanation, but it sure seemed to hush up Mrs. Thayer. The frosty teacher had stood a moment, squint-eyed and frowning, just waiting for the twosome to break into mischievous giggles. When they didn't, she shook her head at them and turned away to oversee the less spirited of her little flock. Just after she'd left, Alaina pretended to gobble up the bugs and snakes, sending Joanna into joyful fits of laughter. They had been friends ever since.

Alaina was hoping that Pastor Wilton's wife would invite her and her mother to dinner. It would be heaven if she and Joanna could sneak away and gossip to their hearts' content, or perhaps they could go window-shopping, or over to see Dr. McIntyre's new automobile. She was spinning a dozen wonderful plans when an unknown horseman came galloping up over Morris Hill. Alaina held firm on the lines, squinting her eyes in an attempt to make out the general age and form of the rider.

"My goodness!" Mrs. Lund commented. "Someone seems to be in a hurry."

"I wonder if somebody's in trouble?" Alaina questioned.

"Well, I do not recognize that horse or that young man," Mrs. Lund responded.

Alaina stopped squinting and wondered if perhaps she should set her vanity aside and get glasses.

"I think it is just some hay-headed boy from Pine Grove, out to prove what a fool he is," Mrs. Lund continued. "He ought to be severely scolded."

Alaina did not respond. The rider was close enough now for her to see that he was indeed a young man—a very handsome young man. She felt her throat tighten and her face flush. *Oh, please don't stop,* Alaina prayed. *Please just ride by. We won't care if you aren't neighborly. We won't care a bit.* Suddenly she hated her plain face and her stupid blue hat. She wanted Joanna's strawberry-blond curls and anyone else's face. *Oh, for heaven's sake,* she chided herself, *no sense getting flighty over a perfect stranger who will probably rush by without even a wave.* She sat up very straight and attended to the horse and wagon. *At least he'll be impressed with how well I handle this rig,* she thought proudly. *That is, if he has time to notice anything at the furious pace he's going.* She figured she'd give him just a stiff nod as he passed by, yet, within moments, she found herself pulling up the reins and setting the brake, for it was obvious that this stranger—this very handsome stranger—had every intention of being neighborly.

"Hello!" the rider called warmly as he pulled his horse to a stop on Mrs. Lund's side of the wagon. He removed his hat and ran his fingers through thick chestnut-brown hair. Alaina saw a slight smile at the corner of her mother's mouth. "I'm Daniel Chart," he declared. "My family bought land just about a mile down this road. Are we going to be neighbors?"

Alaina felt like her stomach was filled with mine tailings, and she knew if she tried to talk she'd sound just like Crazy Granny Pitman. Luckily, the graces of her mother's proper upbringing were not undone by Daniel's overwhelming charm.

"Indeed we are, Mr. Chart. I am Mrs. Lund and this is my daughter, Alaina."

Alaina glanced up and caught Mr. Chart's bright smile full in the face. She felt a summer's warmth rush into her cheeks, and she busied herself with her gloves, trying hard not to bite her lip. Again, Mother unknowingly came to her rescue.

"My husband's name is Samuel, and our farm sits half a mile up the road, Mr. Chart. You can barely see the house through all the trees." Mother turned and pointed the direction.

"What a beautiful location," Daniel complimented, standing up in his stirrups. "A bit of heaven on earth."

Alaina looked back toward the farm and knew he was not exaggerating. She liked him now for more than just his face.

"Do you have brothers and sisters, Mr. Chart?" she asked bravely.

"Why, yes, Miss Lund. I have four brothers and one sister. I am the oldest."

"I'm the oldest too," Alaina ventured in a soft voice. She was surprised she had any voice at all.

"Well, you have my understanding sympathy." He smiled.

Alaina smiled back, unable to remember any other words in the English language. She brushed a wisp of hair out of her face and smiled again. If he kept looking at her with those warm, brown eyes, she would probably start crying, or worse, laughing.

"And what are your parents' names, Mr. Chart?" her mother asked with mannered efficiency.

"My mother's name is Edna Anne and my father's name is Fredrick Robinson, ma'am."

"Not Chart?"

"No, ma'am. My mama married Mr. Robinson some nine years ago. My youngest sister, Rebecca, is their child."

"I see," Mother said, nodding her head. "You were the man of the house when your father passed away."

Daniel hesitated. "Well, Mr. Chart did not pass away, ma'am. My mother divorced him."

Mrs. Lund's back straightened noticeably, and Alaina involuntarily yanked on the lines, causing Friar Tuck to knock into the shaft. The wagon jolted and Mr. Chart's horse danced sideways. It was a dismal moment, and Alaina wanted to hide under a rock. Again Mother took control. "That really is very unfortunate, Mr. Chart."

"Yes, ma'am. Thank you," he answered flatly.

"Now, Mr. Chart, if you will pardon us, we have errands to complete in town," Mrs. Lund stated, a polite smile brushing her mouth.

"Of course," the young man said, putting on his hat and turning his horse.

Alaina was upset by the abrupt change of mood and wanted desperately to lift the grayness of the moment. "You really should ride down and meet my father, Mr. Chart. He's out in the back orchard and would love to make your acquaintance."

The very handsome young man smiled at her gratefully, a touch of animation returning to his face. "Thank you, Miss Lund."

"Just be careful he doesn't put you to work," she warned with mock gravity.

This time his smile was complete. "A little work might make a better man of me," he answered with a tip of his hat. He turned his horse and headed off in the direction of the Lund property.

Alaina doubted that anything could make him better than he was. Her hands felt hot as she pushed off the brake and gave the command to "walk on." As the wagon started moving to town, she had the strong desire to turn in her seat and watch the disappearing figure, but she kept to her work and tried to calm the tight feeling in her stomach.

"It was wrong of you to invite Mr. Chart to our farm, Alaina," Mrs. Lund said icily, her face stoic.

"But I . . ."

"I know you had all the best intentions, but you are very naïve and do not understand the unfortunate situation of his home life."

Alaina hated it when her mother spoke to her as though she were still a little girl, but she knew better than to argue. "Yes, ma'am," she answered without emotion.

"A very unfortunate situation," Mrs. Lund repeated, shaking her head. Alaina waited for her mother to say more, but Elizabeth Knight Lund was keeping her own company, and the journey continued in silence.

Alaina kept her mind busy by remembering every detail of the encounter so she could share it with Joanna: the way he sat his horse, the color of his hair, and how he tipped his hat. Mr. Chart seemed a thing of wonder far more mysterious than anything her imagination could create. A tinge of conscience nudged her thoughts as she recalled the look on Daniel's face when her mother had politely but firmly ended their conversation. Alaina hoped sincerely that he'd taken her advice and ridden out to meet her father. Perhaps then there'd be a chance for her to make a new friend.

The sun came from behind a cloud, warm and comforting on her back, and she urged Friar Tuck to a canter. Mr. Chart's smile had been soft and genuine in spite of her plain face and ugly blue hat. The memory of his brown eyes made the breath catch in her chest.

"Watch your pace!" Mrs. Lund snapped. "We are not running a race!"

Alaina reluctantly slowed the horse to an approved trot, contenting herself with thoughts of her afternoon with Joanna and the fun they'd have talking about the handsome Mr. Chart. Indeed, Mr. Chart's smile alone could fill an afternoon.

CHAPTER 2

James Lund knew how to impress a girl, especially a girl like Lois Drakerman—physical prowess. He stripped off his shirt, confident of the warm April sunshine, and picked up the hay fork as though it were a familiar tool. Lois had come up the hill on the big gray workhorse to fetch home her little brother, Christian, but it was obvious as she looked toward the barn that she hoped for a distraction. When she saw James move into the barn, she pulled hard on Dragon's lead rope, urging the big horse off the track and into the side pasture. Dragon was prized for his strength and endurance, not his promptness in following new commands, so Lois countered his reluctance with a booted kick.

James watched the girl's actions through a knothole in the barn door and smiled at her predictability. He went deeper into the coolness of the barn and moved a couple of grain bags, waiting for Lois to call for him. He heard the clop of Dragon's hooves on the hard ground in front of the barn and the soft "whoa" of the rider.

"Hello? Anybody in there?" she hollered at the barn door.

James chuckled to himself. "Nope, nobody in here! Everybody's up at the house."

Lois giggled, then cleared her throat. "James Lund! You stop teasing me and come out here."

"What for? I'm busy working."

"Don't make me laugh. Now come out and help me down off this horse."

James shoved open the big barn door and stepped out into the sunlight. "Well, I suppose there's no sense in you breaking your legs." He slipped on his shirt and moved to the side of the docile gelding, reaching up his hands for the girl. She slid into his arms without hesitation. James kept his hands on her waist after her feet hit ground, and Lois didn't try to break away.

"You sure are skinny," James remarked with a wicked smile.

"Am not!" Lois replied hotly, pushing his hands away. "Jeb Parker thinks I'm absolutely perfect, so you just keep your stupid opinions to yourself." She reached up, took ahold of the lead rope, and turned the big horse in the direction of the house.

"You're not going already, are you?" James teased.

"And why shouldn't I?" she answered curtly. "I came to pick up my little brother, and I don't see him around here." She moved on in the direction of the house, her braids bouncing.

"You just want to hurry on up to the house so you can see our new worker."

Lois stopped the big horse and turned quickly to face James. "What new worker?" she asked anxiously, forgetting for the moment to mask her youthfulness.

"The handsome one my dad just hired on."

"Oh, James Lund! You stop teasing me."

"I'm not. He did hire somebody to help with the trees."

"Yeah? And I bet he's fifty years old and ugly as a post."

"Bet you he's not."

"Bet you he is."

"A kiss or a quarter."

"What?"

"If he's around twenty and handsome, I get a kiss; if he's not, you get a quarter."

Lois smacked Dragon on the rump to get him moving. "Come on, Dragon, let's get ourselves away from this madman." She gave James a wicked look and moved away toward the house. "You'd better get back to work or your daddy might just hire another ugly farmhand to take your place."

"Boy, are you ever gonna be mad when you have to pay up on your bet," James called after her. He hooted loudly when she tossed her head and stumbled over a shallow ditch. He leaned the hay fork up against the barn and followed her. The day called for mischief and he wasn't about to deny it.

* * *

April in the Sierra foothills was the reconfirmation of all life. The rolling hills shrugged off the scorch of the previous summer and brought forth green grass that was food for the soul. This April the air was especially mild and soft against the skin. Rarely did a cool breeze blow down from the mountains, and the usual spring rain was almost nonexistent. June would be feverish, and July scorching, but April was worth all the other months combined.

Alaina stood at the sink in the stuffy kitchen, chafing at the "proper women's work" she'd been assigned and dreaming of the beautiful outdoors. She hated being cooped up inside, and she hated washing draperies; indeed, she hated every aspect of spring cleaning, yet spring cleaning was something Elizabeth Knight Lund did every April without exception. Alaina vowed that when she had a home of her own, spring cleaning would be done in February or November—dreary months when no one relished being outside much anyway.

Alaina scooped up a large wad of drapery and set to scrubbing with a vengeance. She envied Kathryn, who had been assigned to check duck-egg clutches by the pond, and Eleanor, who was outside beating carpets. The half-opened window, through which she peered, did not give her enough expanse. She wished not only for space, but for wings.

Her mother entered the kitchen purposefully and laid the last of the drapery panels across the back of the chair. She moved to the sink and placed her hand on Alaina's arm. "Not so forcefully, Alaina. The material's not burlap."

Alaina didn't answer, but relaxed her hands and treated the soft fabric with more consideration. Mrs. Lund sighed and moved back into the pantry to resume her organizing, while Alaina's longing gaze wandered again to the scene outside the kitchen window. The fresh green of the hillsides and the dark green of the pines wonderfully complemented each other, while the fringe of apple trees on the hilltop, in full lacy bloom, looked like frivolous girls in pink and white petticoats. She knew that legions of industrious bees were pollinating the pippins, winesaps, and their own special brand—the King Davids. Her father had crossed a Jonathan and an Arkansas Black to produce one of the prize apples in the region.

"Be sure and rinse those draperies twice," her mother called from the pantry.

"Yes, ma'am," Alaina answered automatically as she felt her throat tighten and the sting of tears pinch the corners of her eyes. "Don't be stupid," she muttered to herself. "People don't cry over laundry." But even as she said the words she knew she wasn't crying over laundry. Her heart ached as she gazed at the emerald of the hills. She wanted to be out there, out in the orchard with her father. She'd been his trusted helper since she was twelve years old, and now he'd brought in someone else to take her place—some no-good drifter, down on his luck and hungry, some stranger who'd been begging for work down in Sutter Creek. She twisted the drapery into a knot. Why did her father have to take pity on him? Even now, this unknown person was standing under the canopy of blossoms listening to Father's rumbling voice as he talked tenderly about the trees. She twisted the drapery again. How could her father abandon her to the isolation of the house? Tears rolled over her rounded cheeks, and she wiped them away with the back of her soapy hand.

"Alaina, are you daydreaming? I do not hear much work going on out there."

"I was watching a hummingbird outside the window. I didn't want to frighten it."

Mrs. Lund came out of the pantry carrying several quart jars containing discolored fruit. "Alaina, please try to keep your mind on your work."

"Yes, ma'am."

"After you're finished with those draperies, you're to go out and make up the back room in the shed for the new worker."

Alaina tensed.

"Is there a problem?"

Alaina pulled the plug in the sink and watched the dirty water drain away. "No, ma'am."

Mrs. Lund set the jars on the sideboard and went on giving instructions about the cleaning requirements and what bedding to use, but Alaina heard only droning. Her mind was fixed on a morning several years earlier when the trees hung with glowing ripe fruit and she sat up in the branches listening to a bird sing, weeping for the beauty that surrounded her.

"Alaina . . . Alaina!" The sharp tone of her mother's voice cut into her meandering thoughts and brought her back to soggy draperies. "Have you heard a word I've said?"

"No, ma'am. I mean, yes, ma'am! I'm . . . I'm just not sure what bedding to use."

Elizabeth Lund pursed her lips and took a deep breath. None of her other children caused her this amount of frustration. When she spoke, it was deliberate and a bit louder than her usual proper tone. "Two sheets, the gray blanket, and the double wedding-ring quilt. Did you understand that?"

"Yes, ma'am."

"Well then, finish up those last two panels and get to it." She gave her daughter a "get busy" look and moved back into the pantry.

Alaina sighed and walked over to the stove to retrieve the hot water. Mechanically, she set the huge kettle on the sideboard near the sink, plugged the drain, and pumped in well water until the sink was half full. Then she lifted the heavy kettle and poured in the hot water. Her face flushed with the scalding steam, and she wiped her forehead on her dress sleeve. At the moment, she felt just like one of those poor slum girls in New York, forced to work day after day in grimy, rat-infested sweatshops. She remembered when her favorite teacher, Miss Johnson, had shown the class photographs from a book called *How the Other Half Lives*, and Alaina knew she would fit easily into any number of the dismal pictures of servitude.

She finished the last panel quickly and left the lot in the sink for Eleanor to hang out later. She wished desperately that she could swap jobs with her tolerant younger sister, for she was definitely not pleased with having to set up the back room for the new worker. Alaina didn't want the stranger here, usurping her place and working in the groves with her father. Surely Mother knew how painful it was for her to see this man taking her place in the fields? As Alaina knelt at the linen chest, she decided that this was Mother's lesson on proper place. As she gathered up the bed linens, she tried to think of subtle but effective ways of making the usurper feel unwelcome. She wanted to put tacks in his bed or cayenne pepper in his water pitcher so he'd pack his bags and head back to Idaho or Utah or wherever it was Mother said he'd come from. The indignity of the whole situation scraped her nerves like a boar-bristle brush, and she had trouble keeping her mind on her task. On her way out she stubbed her toe on the quilt chest and cracked her elbow on the door frame; so by the time she headed across the yard to the usurper's new living quarters, her temper was boiling and sputtering like a pot of chili.

On their way in from the duck pond, Kathryn and little Christian Drakerman met up with the scowling and muttering Alaina as she made her way to the shed. They took one look at her hurricane expression and ran in the opposite direction. Kathryn may have held the title of Lund family fighter, but she was no fool, and poor little Christian Drakerman could be intimidated by a frown.

With one foot, Alaina pushed open the sliding door to the shed and met the cool escape of air with resignation. Standing quiet for a moment, she allowed her eyes to adjust to the shed's dimness, then hefted the heavy bedding in her arms and moved toward the back of the small building. She adored the smell of leather, grain, and the last of the winter-stored apples—opulent smells that swirled together in the opaque shadows and made her smile in spite of her sullen demeanor. This little kingdom had been one of her magic childhood places, with nooks for disappearing during hide-and-seek, an opera house for singing, and a schoolhouse for learning her letters under Father's patient care. Whereas storerooms belonging to other farm families might be cluttered eyesores, this one, captained by the hand of Samuel Lund, was orderly and enchanting.

The door to the back room was ajar, and Alaina maneuvered her way through the opening and into the small cubicle. Sunlight wedged its way through the narrow west-facing window, making the six-by-eight-foot room bright enough to cause Alaina to blink when she entered. She moved to the single wood-framed bed against the wall and tossed down the bedding. The bed had a crisscross rope support upon which lay a very thin mattress. Alaina grinned at its meager appearance and hoped it was also lumpy. Of course, James had never complained about it, and he slept here almost every night during the hot summer months. She still might have to resort to tacks.

Alaina glanced quickly about the room to assess how much time she'd be held prisoner cleaning it. She noticed with restiveness that a dull film of dust coated everything. In fact, a fine tawny powder had been sent spiraling into the air when she'd thrown down the blankets, and she moved to shove open the window and give the grit a means of escape. A soft April breeze blew across her face, and Alaina chafed anew against her unjust sentencing. With a sulky growl, she propped open the door to the room and went out to gather the cleaning articles. As she secured the rags and shaved soap, she thought that this lazy drifter ought to be cleaning his own room.

She had been down at the Drakermans' when her father had brought the fellow in from town. Eleanor said he seemed like a nice, quiet young man; Kathryn said he looked like a bank robber; and James said only that he looked like he could do a lot of work. In this instance Alaina actually agreed with Kathryn. Her imagination conjured several horrible crimes that surely would have made him a fugitive from his native land.

Alaina glared down at the bucket of cold water she'd just pumped from the well and decided not to temper it with any hot. If he didn't like her cleaning methods, he could just clean it again himself. She tersely dusted off the bed frame, the windowsill, and the top of the small table with the cold, clammy cloth. She unfolded the sheets and blankets and halfheartedly arranged them on the scrawny mattress. Lastly she dumped the mucky water over the floorboards and out through the open door. She was so intent on dispatching her duty quickly that she didn't notice the stocky figure standing at the room's entrance. Alaina looked up with a start, realizing she'd sloshed a sizeable amount of water over the stranger's well-worn boots.

"Oh! Oh, my goodness! You frightened the wits out of me!" Alaina stammered.

"I'm sorry," the stranger said simply, shaking one foot and then the other. "I wasn't even sure I was headed in the right direction."

Alaina regained her composure, feeling a gnawing coil of resentment winding itself around her civility. "Well, if you're the new hired hand, then this is your room. I've just finished cleaning it."

The young man didn't seem to take offense at Alaina's biting tone. "That's very kind of you. It looks nice. Real homey."

Alaina bristled at the young man's soft features and easygoing familiarity. She shook back her wild dark hair, making sure not to offer him one welcoming look. "Do you know where my father is?" she asked, her tone brusque.

"I believe he's gone to the house. I was sent to find my room."

"Well, you've found it, Mr. . . . ?"

"Erickson. Nephi Erickson. And you have to be Samuel's oldest child, Alaina."

How dare you use my father's given name, Alaina thought hotly. She fixed her most disdainful look on him (a look she'd often seen her mother use to great effect) and pulled herself up to her full height. She compared her straight carriage to the strangely named vagabond's sloping shoulders, and felt vastly superior. "I think it would be appropriate if you addressed my father as Mr. Lund and myself as Miss Lund."

A look of pained embarrassment stamped itself onto the young man's face. "I . . . I'm sorry. I didn't mean to talk out of place."

Alaina felt a rush of regret, but covered it by picking up the bucket and rags and handing Nephi the broom. "You are forgiven. Maybe they just do things differently where you come from."

"Maybe so," he answered quietly. He kept his pale blue eyes averted, poking the broom absently at the toe of his boot.

Alaina hesitated, wanting to say more—wanting him to say more—but she had obviously put him in his place and had discouraged any further conversation with the "grand lady of the manor."

All she wanted to do now was escape with the few meager strands of aloofness still left to her. "Do you mind doing the rest of the sweeping up?" she asked with a slight touch of repentance in her voice.

"No, of course not," he replied eagerly, his eyes still unable to meet her gaze. "I would have been glad to do the whole thing myself."

Alaina resented the sting of chastisement she felt. "Don't be silly, Mr. Erickson. We take good care of our hired help." She gave out a forced little laugh, but there was no mirth in it, and the young man did not laugh with her. She brushed past him with as much dignity as she could posture, hurrying gratefully to the big sliding door and the clean smell of the outside. She couldn't remember acting so rudely to anyone in her entire life. She knew she was far from being a compassionate or saintly person like Eleanor, but she had never intentionally hurt another person's feelings like she'd just done to the young man from out of state.

She had just about decided to go back and apologize to the sandy-haired newcomer when she saw the apple trees in bloom on the hill-side and felt again the hard coil of resentment snaking into her mind. Perhaps it would be better if she left things the way they were. There really was no place on the farm for an extra pair of hands, and the sooner Mr. Erickson realized that, the better.

Alaina turned resolutely and moved back toward the big house. Apple-blossom breezes caressed her unkempt hair and played gaily about her skirt, persuasively applying for a frolicsome companion, but Alaina had bitter feelings to occupy her time, so the moment passed and the invitation was withdrawn.

CHAPTER 3

Although spring had started out dry, the final weeks of April and the first part of May 1913 went on record as the wettest the California foothills had experienced since records were kept. Hardly a twenty-four-hour period escaped rain. If the clouds broke up in the day, a storm would pass through during the night. If an evening were dry, by morning the rain would be coming down in buckets. Old-timers spent a good deal of time comparing the current downpours to prior ones; fruit farmers imagined mold and spores thriving in the soggy soil, and root rot killing off new plantings by the acre; and their wives lamented that no tender shoot in their vegetable gardens would survive the drowning.

Crazy Granny Pitman dragged a rowboat into her front yard, giving the community ample fodder for gossip and spurious comment. The name "Mrs. Noah" began circulating, and some of the school children made up a rhyme:

Mrs. Noah built a boat.
Into that she put her goat.
When the rain was two feet deep
She put in her horse and sheep.
When the rain was two feet more,
She put in some chickens—four.
When the rain was six feet deep,
She floated away down Sutter Creek.

Kathryn relished that she could recite the whole thing by heart, and so did many times a day, to her oldest sister's irritation.

Alaina had had enough of the persistent dampness. It was May now, and May was supposed to be the tail end of the wet season, with the majority of days being sunny and mild. She was tired of wet soaking the bottom of her skirts, of mud on her boots, of clammy sheets and blankets. The dreary days began to seep into her already cranky demeanor, and she found herself venting her ire on any chore given her. This morning she'd been sent to muck out the chicken coop. It was a chore on which she could release a lot of frustration: one, because it was such a filthy job, and two, because it was a job normally slated to James, who was at school doing year-end exams. Alaina found it interesting that Mother was usually so clear on what constituted men's and women's work *except* when she saw the need to teach obedience or humility.

Besides all the other reasons to be out of sorts, Alaina was tired. She'd been haunted by the dream again—the dark vision of the frozen trees and Father's ghostly face. The vivid nightmare often came to her as it had the first time, resurrecting feelings of fear and helplessness, but last night another image marked itself into the dream, a shadowy figure that wandered among the trees, whispering words she couldn't understand. She never saw the man's face, but dread followed her through the night, and she woke with a headache.

Alaina pushed the hat off her head, and continued work with a vengeance. She raked the polluted straw into a pile at the center of the coop, praying all the while that James failed every one of his exams. She growled at the ping of rain on the tin roof, and was so intent on her cross feelings that she didn't hear Father's approach.

"Don't scare the chickens, Fancy. They won't lay for a week."

She turned quickly. "Oh! Sorry. It's just such a dreary chore."

He smiled knowingly. "On another dreary day."

"Yes, sir." She began raking again.

"Well, that's why I've come to rescue you."

She looked at him expectantly. "Really?"

"Yes. I'm off to check the status of the pear crop, and I need your help." He picked up the flat-nosed shovel and began moving muck from the pile out to the wheelbarrow. He called over his shoulder, "If that's all right with you."

It had been a month since she'd been invited to work in the orchard, and she was too amazed to hope her father really meant what he'd said. When her father returned, she snapped out of her daze and began working with intent.

"And where is Mr. Erickson?" she asked casually.

"I sent him to start difking around some of the apple trees."

Alaina raised her eyebrows. "In this wet?"

A smile played at the corner of Samuel Lund's mouth. "Yes. And don't look so smugly pleased about it."

"I'm just surprised James didn't clamor to stay home from school and help."

Samuel Lund shook his head. "Alaina, that clever tongue will get you into trouble."

Alaina smiled and thought about Mr. Erickson's difficult task. Difking was hard work under the best of circumstances; it entailed using the horse and a shallow plow to dig up grass and weeds to a certain circumference around each tree. In this boggy condition it would be a miserable job.

"We had to get started. Weather's held us back as is."

"Of course. I agree," she answered placidly.

"Our job won't be much of a picnic either," Father reminded, winking at her as he took another shovel full out to the wheelbarrow.

The melancholy which had pressed down on her all morning lifted in an instant—the ghostly image of her father's face replaced by the warm smiling countenance she now saw. Father was right. Working out in the orchard again would not be a picnic; it would be heaven!

The rain was heavy as they walked toward the pear trees, now in full shiny leaf. Alaina moved silently beside her father, not caring one jot about her rain-soaked coat and hat or the chill in her fingers. She was once again her father's helper, and the thought of working among the pear trees gave her day a cherished brightness.

Narrow compared to the apple trees, and much more delicate, Bartlett pear trees were becoming famous in the Sierra foothills, with wondrous groves flourishing as far east as Placerville. Alaina was proud of her father's foresight in being one of the first in the Sutter Creek area to champion the showcase crop, although the early-blooming trees were a worry. They were lucky to have had a fairly mild March when the pears were in full blossom. A few bitter nights had concerned Samuel, but he was confident that this would be a banner year for his Bartletts, yielding close to six hundred bushels.

The rain stopped, and Alaina could hear her boots squishing in the boggy soil. "Stupid rain," she muttered.

Her father chuckled beside her. "It could be worse, Fancy."

Alaina's stomach lurched as unwelcome images of her nightmare intruded into her thoughts. "You're right. Of course, you're right," she answered quickly. "I need to count my blessings."

"Yes, indeed!" Samuel Lund responded. "My cup runneth over!"

"With all this rain, it can't help but run over," Alaina responded.

Samuel laughed heartily. "Now, Miss Alaina, be careful about twisting the word of God."

They walked on together in companionable silence as droplets of water fell from tree branches and swirling gray clouds maneuvered overhead. Alaina felt the loneliness and betrayal of the past several weeks being lifted from her shoulders.

"Father?"

"Yes."

"Is . . . how is Mr. Erickson working out?"

"Very well. I like him. He has a farmer's heart and know-how."

"Then his family are farm people?"

"Nope. Business of some sort, in Salt Lake City."

"Salt Lake City. That's a long way away. What's he doing way out here?"

"Don't know, really. He's rather tight-lipped about that. I figure a man has a right to his privacy." He paused. "You haven't spoken much to him."

Alaina felt the gentle if unintended reprimand in her father's words, and fumbled to find an excuse. "There hasn't been much opportunity."

"Hmm." Samuel crouched down and pulled up a clump of grass, examining the mud at the roots. "I've tried to convince your mother to let him sit with us at table, but . . ." His words trailed off as he began walking.

Alaina knew what her mother's response to such a request would be. Those who were hired help were servants, and as such, ate in their own quarters or had a plate at the table when the family was done eating. Mr. Erickson preferred to eat in his own room, leaving his tray on the back step for one of the girls to fetch in for washing.

Alaina didn't care where he ate, and she really wasn't interested in getting to know him or his background. Her only motive for asking questions was to see if her father had any misgivings about hiring this unknown drifter. Mr. Erickson had disrupted an agreeable working arrangement Alaina had come to treasure, and even though Father needed her help at the moment, there was no guarantee this chance would last, as Mother seemed insistent that her eldest daughter stay indoors and attend to proper women's work. Still, there was always so much to be done on the farm, especially during the spring and fall—apple thinning alone took weeks of intensive labor, and all hands were required. Alaina prayed her usefulness would not be set aside. She slapped the water off her hat and hurried to catch up with Father, masking spiteful feelings in innocent inquiry.

"So . . . he's been a help to you?"

"Nephi?"

"Yes."

"He's an honest worker."

"Nephi's a strange name, isn't it? Is it Indian or something?"

"Nope. It's a name out of their Mormon bible."

Alaina stopped. "Their what?"

Samuel turned to her. "The Mormons have a book that they consider scripture."

"Like the Bible?"

"Yes."

Alaina was stunned. She had never been confronted with something so strange. "Where'd it come from?"

"New York."

"New York?" Alaina's thoughts flew around inside her head, and her stomach felt sick. "Mr. Erickson told you that?"

Samuel moved close and took ahold of her arm. "Alaina, do you need to sit down? All the color's gone from your face."

She looked into her father's eyes. "A Bible out of New York? Have you ever heard of anything so strange?" Her father was silent. "Well, have you?"

"I don't know enough about it to make a judgment," he answered simply.

Her father's words brought her up short. Samuel Lund had always taught his children to study out new ideas and give them a chance to stand or fall by their own weight—but a Mormon bible?

"What I do know for sure is that Mr. Erickson is a good man. He may keep to himself, but I find no deceit in him. No matter how odd you may think his beliefs, I want you to treat him with respect. Can you do that?"

Alaina took a deep breath and faced her father squarely. "I can try," she answered, the words sounding choppy.

Father looked at her with raised eyebrows. "Alaina?"

"Yes, sir. I'll treat him with respect."

"That's my girl." He patted her arm. "Now, we have work to do."

Alaina nodded, and headed out in full stride toward the pear grove, making her father play catch-up.

"Once you've set your mind to something, Fancy, there's no stopping you," he complimented, coming to walk beside her.

Alaina smiled. The clouds broke in the west, and she rejoiced to see a swath of brilliant blue sky. She pushed thoughts of Mr. Erickson out of her mind and concentrated on the glorious work ahead of her. Questions for her father about the change in her place on the farm would have to wait. For now, life had resumed its natural order, and she meant to hold on to that for as long as possible.

Samuel shook water off the brim of his hat. "Here's hoping we don't find many black seeds."

"Or fire blight," she added. "I have my fingers crossed."

Samuel chuckled. "You'll work better if you keep them uncrossed."

Alaina flexed her fingers and moved with her father into the grove.

Peaceful hours enfolded the two laborers in a shared reverie as they spot-checked the crop. The rain had stopped for good, and, as it drew near three o'clock, Alaina discarded her hat and coat; climbing the tall ladders was hard enough in a long, heavy skirt.

She carefully examined the fledgling fruit for black seeds, which meant unpollinated blossoms and pears that would never mature. She also checked for fire blight, a devastating spore infestation brought on by too much rain. After hours of inspection, she found the trees to be amazingly healthy, and she knew that father was sharing in the same good news. She twisted from side to side to relieve the stiffness in her back, and climbed down the wobbly ladder to the ground. More blue was showing through the clouds now, and periodic sunlight danced its way to the ground, playing within the branches of the trees. Alaina's spirits lifted as she thought of sweet warm days without rain.

"Laina!"

She turned quickly to see Eleanor trudging across the alfalfa pasture on her way home from school. Alaina waved and yelled a greeting, smiling with the fond memories she carried of her daily mile walk to and from the Drakerman farm. The Drakermans' oldest boy, Warren, worked in the foundry, and for years had transported the children in his wagon into Pine Grove or Sutter Creek every day for their studies. She had loved her years at school: the smell of the books, the peer companionship, the teachers who opened her mind to an ever-expanding world. She supposed if she didn't become a farmer's wife she could always be an old-maid schoolteacher like Philomene Johnson. Miss Johnson taught and traveled and grew the loveliest roses in all of Alameda County—a good life indeed. But if Alaina were forced to honesty, she would have to admit it could not compare with working a farm. In her mind, working the land brought back a part of the original garden, and forever secured man's connection with deity.

Eleanor tromped tiredly into the grove as Alaina was shaking out her wet coat.

"Hi, Laina!" she puffed.

"Hi, Elly. Want a drink?" Alaina responded, handing her sister the canteen.

"Oh, yes! Thanks." Eleanor took a long drink and handed the canteen back. "What a day!"

Eleanor's face was flushed, errant wisps of hair escaped her braids, and her skirt was spotted with dirt smudges, indicating that she had indeed had a trying day.

Alaina smiled at her fondly and put an arm around Eleanor's slim shoulders. "Pretty bad, was it?"

"Oh, no! It was an infinitely fine day! My team won in kick ball, I passed my arithmetic exam, and Mavis Beck didn't make fun of my stitching in home craft."

Alaina chuckled. "My, that is an infinitely fine day."

Eleanor smiled, picking up her books and sliding her arm around Alaina's waist. "So, you've been working in the orchard?"

Alaina smiled warmly at the excitement in Eleanor's voice. "I have."

"How wonderful for you!"

"Well, Miss Eleanor, home from the drudgery of school, are you?" Samuel Lund asked seriously as he walked in long easy strides toward his girls.

"Never any such thing," Eleanor retorted, going to him for a hug. "It has been an infinitely fine day."

Samuel chuckled. "My, oh my. That's just the sort of day Alaina and I have had, isn't it, daughter?" He smiled at his helper, and took Eleanor's books. "So, will you tell me all about your infinitely fine day as we walk home to supper?"

"Of course!" she answered happily.

Samuel turned to his oldest daughter. "Are you coming, Miss Alaina?"

"Shortly. I need to find my hat."

"We'll see you at supper then."

The two moved off toward the house, Eleanor chattering excitedly as she recounted the events of her day. Alaina stood contentedly, watching after them until their voices faded from hearing. The stillness of the grove was a benediction, and she wanted to keep the feeling close and store it for future times. She looked around at the beautiful pear trees and wondered what the future held for her. Would she be able to continue working in the groves, or be confined again to the regiment of womanhood defined by her mother's narrow-minded upbringing?

Alaina shook back her hair and looked up to the patchwork sky. *Dear Lord, I know I'm asking for a miracle, but could you change my mother's heart into the heart of a farmwoman? Or, at least help her to know how I feel. I wouldn't be so angry with her if she'd only let me be what I want. Well, you understand. Oh, and make Mr. Nephi Erickson infinitely homesick for Utah. Amen.*

She retrieved her hat, blew a farewell kiss to the pear trees, and headed home to supper.

CHAPTER 4

Edna Chart Robinson understood clearly that divorce was not something easily considered in her day and age, for it indicated drunkenness or adultery or some other deplorable sin branded equally upon each partner. The failure of that sacred ordinance was the failure of both, and many a grass widow regretted breaking ties with a philandering husband because of what was suffered thereafter. Judging by the polite, icy distance kept by the "proper" folks of Pine Grove and Sutter Creek, it was a sentiment they shared. Edna Robinson was a quiet, industrious woman who didn't waste her time worrying about what other folks were thinking. She, her second husband Fredrick, and their six children had moved onto their property up Morris Canyon the middle of May, set up housekeeping in a small temporary shack, and started work planting a garden and beginning repairs on the large eight-room farmhouse. Although it was now nearing the last days of June, the only people that Edna and Fredrick could call acquaintances were Pastor Wilton, Samuel Lund, and Samuel's two older daughters.

Of course, those "proper" churchgoers figured that healing the sinner and bringing the fallen back to the fold was the holy man's job, and that visits by the Lund family were in the realm of neighborly duty. With those responsibilities taken care of, the sanctimonious could continue to keep their distance.

But Samuel Lund did not visit the Robinson place out of duty or responsibility. He visited because he thoroughly liked and admired Fredrick Robinson—a burly man of ready humor and common sense, who stood six foot six in his work boots and owned the handshake of a wrestler. The two men would take on one of the never-ending jobs around the homestead with such lighthearted camaraderie that a Calvinist would have been chagrined.

It was the first time Alaina had ever known her father to have a close friend. She smiled as she leaned against the gate and watched the two men heading out to mend fence posts. She knew she needed to get back and help Mrs. Robinson thin carrots, but for the moment it was nice to stand by herself in the warm morning sun and reflect on new acquaintances.

"Idle hands are the devil's workshop," Daniel Chart called out. Alaina jumped, knocking over the watering bucket, which clattered across the hard ground. Laughing, Daniel came to her side. "I'm sorry, I'm sorry," he said contritely. "I didn't mean to scare you."

His apology was sincere, and Alaina felt foolish and ungainly as she tried to compose herself and calm her breathing. She wished Daniel's rumbling voice and handsome face didn't have such an unsettling effect on her. Even after many shared conversations and weeks of being around him, she always felt the way she did that first time they'd met: her hands hot, her stomach knotted, her brain unable to remember the English language.

She stood up straight. "I . . . I." She forced her thoughts to stop tumbling. "I guess I was just daydreaming." Daniel smiled. Alaina liked that smile. "I was just thinking how well our fathers get along," she said, turning to hide the rush of color to her cheeks.

"Your father is a good man," Daniel returned.

It was the kind of thing she would expect him to say. Simple. Direct. Over the past weeks he'd amazed and charmed her with his unpretentious manner and lack of guile. Alaina had always suspected that people who were extremely good-looking always double thought, and double spoke. Daniel was a pleasant contradiction.

Suddenly Alaina realized that Daniel was chuckling.

"Oh! I . . . I was off again, wasn't I?" Alaina stammered.

"Yes, indeed, Miss Lund," Daniel answered, pushing the gate back and forth. "The way you meditate, I figure you'd do well as one of those monks over in China." He said it kindly, and Alaina laughed in spite of herself.

"Mama says I have the heart of a poet, and the head of a milk-maid. Whatever that means."

Daniel studied her face, noting the momentary wash of pain that tightened her attempted smile. "I think you just see things different from us commoners," he answered quietly. "Your mind, Miss Lund, holds galaxies."

It was the nicest thing anyone, aside from her father, had ever said to her, and she felt a warm tingle move through her arms into her fingertips. She also realized it made her feel confused, and more than a little embarrassed. She smiled timidly at him, and quickly changed the subject.

"I like your stepfather a lot, Daniel, although when I first met him I felt like running in the opposite direction. He was so big, I thought he'd have a temper to match. But now that I know him, I'd say he has the patience to last through a winter's freeze."

Daniel grinned broadly, and she saw a glint of merriment flash in his eyes.

"What? Did I say something funny? Is he terrible when outside people aren't around?"

Daniel laughed and shook his head. "No. He's the most gentle person I know. I've only seen him angry once, and that was at his wedding to my mama."

"Is it a dreadful story?" Alaina asked before she could stop herself. "Would you tell me about it—if it's not some dark family secret?"

"Well, it's not a secret, and really not much of a story," Daniel answered apologetically. "The whole thing took about two minutes."

Alaina raised her eyebrows, but didn't speak. She hoped her silence would encourage him.

Daniel took off his hat and fanned his face. "I was ten years old at the time. Ten years old, and always hungry. If there was food within two miles, then that's where I'd be. Anyway, after the 'I do' part of the service was over, I headed straight into the house to find the food. So my seven-year-old sister and me were standing behind the table eating everything in sight when my Uncle Matthias—that's my mama's brother—came in with somebody to get a drink of lemonade or something. Seemed to me Uncle Matthias had found his own stiffer drink elsewhere, and had guzzled quite a bit. He was talking in this loud obnoxious voice about the wedding and the food, and whopping this poor fellow on the back. Just about then my stepdad comes in. He takes one look at Uncle Matthias and his face gets sort of serious. He says, 'Well, Matthias, it seems you've been celebrating my wedding.'

"Uncle Matthias comes up to my stepdad, looks him right in the face, and says, 'Celebrating? Of course I'm celebrating . . . happy night, Fredrick. Our family is grateful . . . just so grateful that you were willing to take Edna off our hands.'"

Alaina's back stiffened. "Oh, he didn't say that?"

"Oh, yes he did. And even drunk as a skunk, there was no excuse for him saying it, and so Fredrick knocked him out cold. One punch, and Uncle Matthias never even felt the floor."

"Serves him right," Alaina said, kicking a dirt clod. "What a horrid thing to say."

Daniel smiled, and she suddenly felt as if a clasp had fastened on their friendship. She relaxed and smiled too. "Bet he had a headache when he woke up."

Daniel leaned closer to take her into his confidence, and Alaina felt the soft hairs at the back of her neck tingle. "Everyone was glad to see Uncle Matthias knocked flat. Two weeks later he moved to Elko, Nevada, and we haven't heard from him since."

The sound of an approaching horse made them turn.

"Now, who could that be?" Daniel questioned. "Maybe it's someone from town come to pay a visit." He gave Alaina a wink that eased her discomfort. She hated that the townsfolk were so pinched in their thinking. Even Pastor Wilton's wife avoided the Robinson homestead and insisted Joanna do the same.

"Looks like your farmhand."

"Really?" Alaina shaded her eyes and squinted.

Daniel chuckled. "Have you ever thought about glasses, Miss Lund?"

Alaina quickly lowered her hand. "I can see perfectly well, thank you," she said and gave him an imperious look that made him chuckle again.

"Of course you can."

"Well, I can."

"What color neckerchief does he have on?"

"Neckerchief?"

Daniel hooted. "You probably can't even see his neck!" He was laughing openly now. "Can you see the horse?"

Alaina wanted to hit him, but she broke into laughter instead. "Daniel Chart, you stop teasing me!"

"Ah, pride goeth before the stumble, Miss Lund."

"Weren't you on your way to help with fence posts, Mr. Chart?"

"And leave you to face Mr. Erickson alone? I wouldn't think of it. He's one of those Mormon boys, you know, so you and Eleanor better be careful."

Alaina's mirth fell away abruptly. "What in the world are you talking about?"

Daniel's soft lips curved into a smile. "Well, they practice polygamy, don't they? He may just snatch you two off to Utah for a double wedding."

A man had never insinuated anything so intimate to her before, and Alaina felt the flush of embarrassment from her fingertips to the top of her head.

Daniel noticed her discomfort and reached out to touch her arm in apology, but she stepped away.

"Alaina, I'm sorry. It was a stupid thing to say."

She could feel the heat on her skin and dared not face him. "Never mind . . . it's . . ." She looked up to see Mr. Erickson only twenty yards away. When Nephi saw her glance in his direction, he smiled and raised his hand to tip his hat.

Alaina wanted to run, but she could envision herself stumbling over the uneven ground, tripping over her cumbersome skirt, and ending up flat on her face in the dust. So she stood her ground like a Sioux princess.

"I'm really sorry," Daniel murmured as he moved past her to greet Nephi.

Alaina nodded. In the regaining of her composure, it was all she could spare.

Daniel walked purposefully toward the unexpected visitor. "Good day, Mr. Erickson."

"Good day, Mr. Chart," Nephi answered, climbing off Friar Tuck and offering his hand.

Daniel took it, and smiled warmly.

Nephi nodded his head at Alaina. "Good day, Miss Lund."

"Mr. Erickson. What brings you here?"

"Your mother sent me to fetch you and your father home."

"Is anything wrong?"

"I don't know, miss. I brought the post from town, and shortly after she sent me to find you."

"My father is there." Alaina pointed to the edge of the clearing where Samuel and Fredrick were working. "Go fetch him, and I'll get Moccasin."

Nephi remounted his horse and rode out into the field. Alaina turned and headed for the paddock to get the mare ready for riding. Daniel was beside her.

"What can I do to help?"

"Please tell your mother I won't be able to work with her in the garden today."

"I will, and I'll go ahead and get Moccasin saddled."

"That's not necessary."

"I want to." He lightly touched her elbow and took off at a powerful run.

Alaina wanted to forgive him straightaway, but she couldn't. It was more than just the embarrassment. She was upset that he'd say something so judgmental about someone else. He hated the unjust treatment of his mother, and yet here he was ridiculing someone he hardly knew. As she walked, her skirt caught on a sticker bush, and she yanked it free. *Oh, what do I care? Maybe I'm making too much of the whole thing. Daniel is a good person. He just made a mistake.*

When she reached the paddock, Daniel had the saddle on the sturdy Appaloosa, and was cinching up the girth.

He continued working as his words tumbled out. "I'm so sorry, Alaina. It was uncalled for. I like Nephi. I think he's honest and a very hard worker. Just because his beliefs are strange, it's not something I should hold against him."

"I know, Daniel. We all say things we wish we could take back."

He looked her square in the face. "I do wish I could take it back."

There was such remorse in his eyes. How could she stay angry with him? But before she could speak, they were interrupted again by the approach of Friar Tuck, this time carrying Mr. Erickson and her father.

Nephi pulled the horse to a stop beside the fence, and Samuel Lund quickly dismounted, coming over to put the bridle on Moccasin. Alaina could usually read the emotion on her father's face, but at that moment she couldn't tell if it was frustration or fear.

"What do you think happened?" she asked quickly.

"Don't know," Samuel replied. He managed the bit into Moccasin's mouth, securing the brow band as Daniel finished with the saddle. Samuel moved to the side of the horse and swung himself up. "Thanks, Daniel."

"Hope everything's all right, sir."

"Thank you, son. Alaina, you ride with Nephi. I'm going ahead." He turned the horse out of the paddock and gave the mare a slight heel poke. Moccasin responded immediately.

"But I'll go with you!" Alaina called.

Her father did not respond as he rode away. There was silence as the three watched the horse and rider disappear down the road. *How can I ride home behind a stranger?* Alaina thought in a panic as Nephi took his foot out of the stirrup and reached out his hand for her. She glanced at him quickly, and then back down to the ground. *The more I make of this, the more embarrassing it'll be for me. I'll act as if it's nothing.* Alaina put her foot defiantly into the stirrup and took Mr. Erickson's hand. He pulled her up, and she grabbed the back of the saddle, settling herself on the rump of Friar Tuck. She could not look at Daniel for the scarlet in her face.

"Please, let us know if you need anything," Daniel said sincerely.

Alaina cleared her throat. "Yes, we will. Thank you."

Friar Tuck started off at such a pace that Alaina had no choice but to hold on tightly to Mr. Erickson. She had ridden behind Father or James many times, but never behind a stranger—and a stranger who was a young man only a few years older than herself. She wondered if she should grab the material of his shirt or place her hands on his sides. What was proper? *Oh, Alaina Lund, you're being a goose.*

Nephi slowed the horse to a walk. "Probably more comfortable for you if we take it a little slower."

She relaxed her hands. "Yes, thank you."

They continued on in silence.

Alaina brushed a wisp of hair from her face. "You've no idea what my mother wants, Mr. Erickson?"

"No, miss. Sorry. She keeps her own company, that's for sure."

Alaina smiled. "Yes, she does. That's because it's proper, and everything my mother does is proper."

Nephi did not respond, and Alaina sat straighter, trying to think of something to say to ease the awkward silence. It was Nephi who finally spoke.

"I don't quite figure her for a farmer's wife."

"My mother?"

He cleared his throat. "Sorry. It's not my place to speak out like that."

"It's all right, Mr. Erickson. She probably wouldn't mind if you said that right to her face. It would be a compliment."

"She doesn't want to be on the farm?"

"No. She came from a very different background. My Grandfather Knight was a rich businessman in Los Angeles."

"Then how in the world did your mother and father meet?"

"My Uncle Cedrick in San Francisco. He's a banker. My father went to him for a loan to buy the farm. Cedrick is married to my mother's sister, Ida." Alaina paused, amazed at how she was chattering on, but she continued. "Anyway, Uncle Cedrick admired my father straight off and invited him to dinner at his house. Well, my mother was up from Los Angeles staying with them, and that's where they met."

"And they took to each other right away?" Nephi asked.

Alaina shrugged. "I guess so. They married about a month later."

"A month?"

"Yep. Grandpa Knight was real angry. My mother got disowned, or disinherited, or something."

"How terrible for her," Nephi said softly.

Alaina was surprised by the tenderness in his voice.

"Still, I can't imagine her not loving the farm," he added.

His voice drew her thoughts into the sunlit orchard with its rich smells and peaceful solitude. Her heart ached with the missing of it. She was allowed to help for a short time during apple thinning, but it was obvious that this outsider had usurped her position as Father's indispensable helper in the groves. Her rising resentment brought silence between them once more, so Alaina focused her thoughts on

Mother's anxious summons and the clomp of Friar Tuck's even pace. She was pulled from her reflections when Nephi began speaking again.

"It must be hard for her."

Alaina leaned forward. "I beg your pardon?"

"To leave all that behind. To come from her family and the city to a wilderness."

"I wouldn't call our farm a wilderness, Mr. Erickson," Alaina protested.

"Oh, of course not! It's just that . . . well, my . . ." He hesitated and cleared his throat. "My mother wouldn't let my father give up the hardware business in Salt Lake for anything. Some women like the city."

Alaina was surprised at his eagerness for conversation. Since he'd started work two months ago, they'd only exchanged a few words in passing. Perhaps he was nervous or lonely. Alaina felt a twinge of guilt as she thought about how she'd treated him.

"Were you born in Salt Lake City, Mr. Erickson?"

"I was."

"And are your father and mother still there?" she pushed, hoping for a bit more information about his past.

"They are," he answered in a low voice, and she felt his body tense beneath her hands.

"Hmm." It was obvious that family was not a comfortable subject, and Alaina bit her lip against all the other personal questions popping into her head. She waited for a moment, then asked simply, "Is it nice there, in Salt Lake City?"

"It's beautiful, but . . ." He hesitated. "It was time for me to be out on my own."

There was silence once again, and this time it seemed Mr. Erickson would not revive the conversation. Alaina was sure an intriguing story lay under his hesitation, but Mr. Erickson kept silent as the enchanting June afternoon slid away in the uncomfortable stillness, and she was glad when they finally reached the house. Nephi helped her down off the horse and tipped his hat to her without comment. As she headed up the front steps, he found his voice.

"I'll put Friar Tuck away."

"Thank you, Mr. Erickson." Alaina reached the front door, where she stopped, unsure of the bad news that might be waiting on the other side. Her hand trembled on the doorknob, and she took a deep breath.

"I hope there's no real trouble," Nephi offered kindly.

"Thank you." Her tone was flat, and she moved into the house without thinking to look at him.

Nephi stood staring at the closed door for a long moment, then turned and led Friar Tuck in the direction of the barn.

CHAPTER 5

Alaina was suffocating. It was the Fourth of July, and she had been wearing black for a week. She hated black. It brought out the darkest color of her hair and made her skin look like aspen bark.

"In mourning we shall wear black, and there will be no argument."

The memory of her mother's clipped edict made her bristle all over again. She vented her frustration on the braid she was putting into Kathryn's hair.

"Ow! You did that on purpose!"

"I did not. It would help if you sat still."

Kathryn rubbed the back of her head and dislodged several pieces of hair. "I'm sitting as still as I can in this hot dress. I hate this dress!"

For once Alaina and her youngest sibling were in agreement.

"Why do we got to wear them?"

"*Have* to wear them," Alaina corrected.

"Why?"

"Respect."

"For Aunt Ida's dead husband?"

"Yes."

"We didn't even know the old coot."

Alaina laughed before she could stop herself. "He wasn't a coot, and he wasn't old."

"Older than Dad."

"Only a few years."

"That's old."

"Hmm."

"Aunt Ida is Mother's sister?"

"Yes." Alaina picked up a black ribbon and began tying it at the bottom of Kathryn's braid.

"Older sister?"

"Yes."

"Aunt Ida and Uncle . . . ?"

"Cedrick."

"Sounds like a butler's name."

Alaina held back another laugh. "He's not a butler, but he and Aunt Ida have a butler."

"Really?"

"Yes, and maids and cooks."

"Are they rich?"

"Very. They live in a big house in San Francisco."

"Have you seen it? Aunt Ida's house?"

"Once, when I was a little younger than you." Alaina laid the brush on the dressing table. "We went for a visit."

"But you've never seen Grandpa and Grandma's house?"

"Grandpa and Grandma Knight?"

"Yep."

"No. They live far away in Los Angeles. Besides, they want nothing to do with us," Alaina rambled on without thinking.

"What do you mean?" Kathryn asked, craning her head around.

"Oh, nothing. Never mind. Sit still."

"Why don't they want nothing to do with us?"

"*Anything* to do with us. They just think we're an ignorant farm family."

Kathryn turned back around and sat quietly. After a time she sighed. "Poor Mother."

"Why do you say that?" Alaina asked, tugging on Kathryn's braid.

"Well, because she married into an ignorant farm family and she lost all her money."

Alaina growled. "Oh, Kathryn, for heaven's sake, keep quiet!"

"No! I want to talk about Mother's family. So, Grandpa and Grandma Knight still want to see Aunt Ida?"

Alaina didn't answer.

"So do they? Do they?"

Alaina growled again. "Yes! Aunt Ida married well," Alaina pointed out, a note of irritation in her voice. She was losing patience with Kathryn's meaningless questions—difficult enough to endure in mild weather, let alone in this wretched heat.

"I want to marry well," Kathryn said dreamily.

"I'm sure you do."

"Don't you?"

"What?"

"Want to marry well?"

"I want to marry a good man and live on a farm," Alaina stated simply.

"Well, I want a big house, and a butler, and a cook, and servants. I bet Mother would like to live in a house like that again. I bet she misses it."

Alaina pressed her lips together, trying to keep herself from saying something that would get her into trouble.

The bedroom door opened, and Eleanor came in. She looked tearful, which was unlike her usual bright demeanor.

"Elly? What is it?" Alaina asked with concern.

"Mother says we have to wear our black to the celebration picnic, or not go at all!"

Kathryn burst into tears. "Everyone else will have on their summer white. I hate Uncle Cedrick! I don't care if he is the richest man in the world!"

"Kathryn!" Alaina and Eleanor exclaimed, exchanging surprised looks.

"Well, I do hate him!"

Eleanor came to sit beside her distraught sister. "Kathryn, you can't hate someone who's dead."

"Why not?"

"Because . . . because it's not polite," Eleanor pointed out.

Kathryn jumped down from the bed. "I don't care about that. He's up in heaven wearing summer white, and I'm down here in this stupid black dress!" She stomped out of the room and slammed the door. Alaina and Eleanor gazed at the door for a moment, then burst into laughter. Alaina put her hands over her face to try to calm herself. It would never do for Mother to hear them laughing. Gaiety of any kind was not allowed while you were in mourning—even if it was for a rich old coot you'd only seen once and who didn't care a twig for you or your family.

Eleanor's giggles were subsiding. She undid the top two buttons at her throat and fanned herself with her skirt. "It's too hot for laughing."

Alaina poured water into her washing bowl and replied, "It's too hot for anything." She soaked a cloth, wrung it dry, and handed it to Eleanor. Eleanor shook it and placed it at her throat.

"Maybe I won't go to the picnic this year," she said sullenly.

This was definitely not like Eleanor. "Elly, you love the picnic! You always win at the races and eat the most watermelon."

"I wouldn't race this year even if I wasn't wearing black."

"Why not?"

"It just seems juvenile."

Alaina smiled. Little Elly was going through that melancholy point in life when she didn't want to participate in childish games and such, but wasn't confident enough for adult responsibilities.

"Well, we can sit together in the shade and look regal."

Eleanor handed back the cloth. "I'll just look sweaty."

"You will not. We'll just sit and converse with all the cute young gentlemen."

Eleanor squinted her eyes. "All the cute young gentlemen?"

"There are a few in Sutter Creek."

"Two."

Alaina laughed. "Eleanor Lund!"

"Three, if you count Daniel Chart, but he'll spend his time talking to you. Four if you include Nephi Erickson."

"Mr. Erickson?"

"You don't think he's cute because you find him different."

"He is different."

They heard footsteps approaching the bedroom door, then a stiff rap and the door opened. Mrs. Lund stepped purposefully into the room.

"Girls, I want chores done early today. Mr. Erickson will be taking us to town several hours before the picnic. Alaina, your father wishes you to ride in with him later."

Alaina, who had not been paying very close attention, looked up quickly. "Just me?" she asked, a bit too eagerly.

Her mother's stern look made her dim the brightness of her expression.

"Yes." Mrs. Lund turned and motioned to her younger daughter. "The garden, Eleanor."

"Do you know what he wants?" Alaina questioned.

"I do not," came the flat reply. "Eleanor?"

"Yes, ma'am." Eleanor stood up and moved to the door.

"Alaina?"

"Yes, Mother?"

"Eggs first. I need two dozen for the picnic. And do not let your mind wander while you dust." She moved out of the bedroom with Eleanor following.

Alaina's sweet sibling paused at the door to offer a look of eager surprise. "Wonder what he wants?" she whispered.

Alaina shrugged. "I can't guess."

"Eleanor!"

"Coming, Mother!" And she was gone.

Alaina wanted to yelp for joy, but she didn't dare. She took a quick look in the mirror and shook her head. How odd to be doing chores in her stiff black crepe skirt. How odd to be wearing black at all when she felt just the opposite of mournful. A solitary ride into town with Father was its own celebration.

Defiantly she pushed up the sleeves of her black blouse, wondering why Mother kept to all the archaic social rules of her spoiled youth. She wasn't living in Los Angeles or San Francisco. She lived on a beautiful farm in the barely tamed foothills of California, where a person wore black on the day of the funeral, and only then if they were actually attending. Uncle Cedrick had been buried five days ago, and this meaningless show of sympathy would go on for another sweltering week. *But I don't care!* Alaina suddenly decided. She could wear sackcloth and ashes today and it wouldn't dampen her spirits.

Alaina wound her braid into a bun and pinned it at the back of her head. She didn't even care if the maddening heat subsided by the evening's festivities. She would wish cooler temperatures for everyone else, but she would be happy no matter what the weather.

Morning chores occupied her thoughts well past ten when Father called a stop. Mother served a light meal of cold pears and pork on hard rolls. Afterward, the girls cleaned the kitchen, and Mrs. Lund supervised the men as they loaded the wagon with dishes, cutlery, and a makeshift table for the family's picnic. They also loaded hand-sewn articles for the church bazaar; two bushels of corn, a salted ham, and two dozen hard-boiled eggs for dinner; and finally, an old settee for the auction.

Kathryn had refused to help with kitchen chores, for which Eleanor gave her a bitter scolding. Kathryn was so taken aback at being reprimanded by her normally genial sister that, instead of running to tattle, she sulked in the barn, bemoaning her fate to the sympathetic milk cow until it was time to go to town. She came sullenly across the yard in answer to Father's call, kicking dirt and refusing to look anyone in the face. She didn't even smile when Father patted her head and lifted her into the wagon.

Alaina was sure the stiff black clothing was making everyone irritable and wished they could all revolt against Mother's tyranny. Visions of the French Revolution kept coming into her mind, complete with banners flying and guillotine blades dropping. Poor James sat grudgingly on the front seat of the wagon looking uncomfortable in his black Sunday pants, stiff white shirt, and black necktie, while next to him was Mr. Erickson in soft cotton pants and a light, tan summer shirt.

Alaina moved to Mr. Erickson's side of the wagon and handed him a canteen of water, which he took with a smile and a thank you. She looked up at him to reply, and was caught by the icy blue of his eyes. She glanced down quickly at her boots, hoping he didn't see the slight lifting at the corners of her mouth.

She kept her eyes lowered when she handed James his canteen, trying to clear jumbled thoughts and chiding herself for such a silly reaction to a pair of blue eyes, especially Mr. Erickson's blue eyes. When she gave Mother, Kathryn, and Eleanor their summer parasols, she willed her mind back to the excitement of the day's possibilities. She would spend the whole afternoon with her friend Joanna, visiting with old friends from school, eating ice cream, and enjoying the patriotic parade. Perhaps the handsome Mr. Chart would join them in their revelry. And, if that weren't enough joy for one day, she would be riding into town with Father.

Alaina came out of her daydream when she realized Eleanor was shouting and waving to her as the wagon moved away from the house.

"Bye, Laina! Bye! See you at the picnic!"

Alaina smiled and waved enthusiastically. It seemed the excitement of the Fourth of July celebration had finally caught Eleanor in its fervor, and Alaina was glad for it.

"Bye, Elly! See you soon!"

Mr. Erickson turned in his seat to look at her, and Alaina immediately dropped her hand. She glanced over at Father, who was standing quietly with his hand shading his eyes, watching the receding wagon.

"I do think Tuck could pull a barn if I asked him to," he commented, his voice full of pride.

"I believe he could," Alaina answered, watching the magnificent animal pull the wagon steadily.

Father looked over at her and smiled. "You love this farm, don't you, Fancy?"

Alaina felt emotion catch in her throat, but her words came out steady and true. "I do."

He turned his face away from her to watch the wagon. There was an unreadable look on his face, and Alaina felt a chill of apprehension move across her skin. She noticed tiredness in her father that she'd never seen before. She rebuked the feeling into submission, owing his paleness to the miserable heat and having to wear a starched white collar and necktie.

Samuel took out his neckerchief and wiped his forehead. "Another scorcher. Seems like this year we're being tried by flood and fire."

Alaina scoffed. "Well, it doesn't help being trussed up in these monkey suits."

Samuel laughed at the churlish look on her face, which brought a flush of color to his own cheeks. "I don't think you could get a monkey to wear one of these."

Alaina now joined her father in laughter, amazed at his disparagement of Mother's proper upbringing. It was a mystery to her how her parents had ever decided on a life together. She knew the story of their meeting, her mother being sent to San Francisco to care for her

Aunt Ida as she'd convalesced from pneumonia, and Father having been so taken with the mannered Miss Knight at supper that he'd secured work at the produce mart in order to court her. Alaina knew the how and when, but not the why. Why had two people from such different backgrounds decided to spend their lives together? Why had her mother said yes to a proposal after only a month of courting? Why had her father asked after only a month of courting? Perhaps it had been getting on toward fall, and Father had trees to plant.

Alaina shook her head as possibilities tumbled around in unending resolutions. She knew her parents cared for each other, for she had often seen them walking the farm together, holding hands and sharing whispered conversation. And didn't Father give Mother a gift every month? Every month without fail since Alaina could remember. But, in spite of that, it must have been a disappointment when the newly married couple had arrived at the farm and she made clear the duties to which she would and would not tend. She would never be a Mrs. Drakerman or Robinson, who labored side by side with their husbands in the glorious work of farming, nor would the proper Mrs. Lund ever experience the contented peacefulness after the hard work of harvesting was complete. Perhaps her mother knew a tiny bit of that feeling when she brought in the garden, but even then the majority of the work fell to the children. Alaina had never understood her mother's disdain for the land, but, as Father seemed perfectly content with his wife's company, it was something Alaina rarely considered, and so their marriage continued to be a mystery to her, a mystery that she was glad needed no solving in her near future.

"Well, let's ready the horses, what do you say?" Father's words brought her back to his side, and she smiled up at him. "I think there's ice cream waiting for us in town." He winked at her and put on his hat.

"Ice cream?"

"And blueberry pie." He turned and headed for the barn at such a pace that Alaina had to race to keep up. "I guess you'll have to ride Titus," he teased.

"Have to? I love Titus!" Alaina answered indignantly, catching her father's smile and smiling back at him. Father knew how much Titus meant to her. She was two when the colt was born, and they had grown up together in mutual affability. At sixteen, the horse had put in years of useful labor. Other farmers referred to old horses as hay burners, she supposed because they ate more than they gave back, but Alaina disagreed. Their handsome bay had sired Friar Tuck, as well as a dozen other foals in the region—sturdy horses that gave meaningful service and companionship. He had pulled plows and wagons, carried people thousands of miles, and listened patiently to all of her child-hood woes. He was of great worth to the Lund family, and would be, Alaina hoped, for many years to come.

Alaina sighed when they reached the coolness of the barn, and although she knew the temperature difference was only a few degrees, it was a welcome refuge from the devilish sun. Titus came immediately to hang his head over the slats of his stall, pawing the ground and snorting a welcome. Alaina smiled. Was it a welcome, or a request for the carrots she had in her pocket? She gave the giant horse his treat and went to get the saddle, all the while speaking to him in a tender voice. Titus flicked his ears this way and that to catch every sound.

Father called to her from Moccasin's enclosure. "I thought we'd take the Morganson track into town. It'll take us longer, but it should be a bit cooler down through the hollow."

She stopped cinching Titus's saddle, brushing damp hair from her face. "Good idea."

"We'll ride to Granny Pitman's first and take her some potatoes, then catch the track from there."

Alaina smiled as she thought about her father's attachment to the scrappy little recluse. "You won't mind if I stay outside, will you?"

"It'll probably be a good idea," Samuel chuckled.

Alaina circled Titus, checking his legs and hooves, and placed a canteen of water in her saddlebag as Father secured the twenty-pound sack of potatoes behind Moccasin's saddle. They finished their prepa-rations in silence, then led the horses outside into the heat. Titus snorted and shook his head.

"I agree," Alaina said, putting on her broad-brimmed straw hat. Titus looked at her and flicked his ears. "Here now! It may be ugly, but it keeps the sun off my head."

Titus tried to take a little nibble of the hay-colored brim, and Alaina playfully swatted at his nose.

"Maybe he wants one for his own head," Samuel observed, giving her an amused wink.

"Well, I'll buy him one in town!" Alaina yelped, as she jumped away from the horse's persistent attempts to snatch the hat off her head.

Father chuckled as he shut the barn door and secured the latch. "Are you two going to play games all day," he teased, swinging himself into the saddle, "or are we going to town?"

Alaina gave Titus a good-natured tug on his mane and lifted herself onto his back. The gentle horse shook his head again, gave a kick with his back leg, and took off at a trot before Alaina had time to give him a command.

"I always said that horse was the most patriotic animal on the farm," Father hooted. "He just can't wait for the parade and the speeches!"

Alaina slowed Titus to a walk and sang him "Yankee Doodle" until Father caught up. The foursome moved side by side out the main gate of the farm and onto Cold Creek Road, where the horses' hooves kicked up the powdery dirt, leaving a fine cloud of dust behind. Alaina was glad they weren't taking the main road into Sutter Creek. Morganson track meandered its way around the knolls and hollows of the farmsteads east of Pine Grove, where stands of oak trees clustered along creeks fed by natural springs. Here, even in the hottest summers, one could find refuge in the shade, green grass, and small meadow flowers.

Alaina adjusted the brim of her hat to block out more sun and hummed a few lines of "Yankee Doodle." She thought ahead to her time in town and smiled. Joanna might be fresh and alluring in summer white, Mother's scrutiny might have to be endured, and Mr. Erickson might try and join in with her group of friends. But Alaina decided that no matter what, she was going to turn it all into a delightful day of adventure. As Philomene Johnson always told her students, "You can look down and see mud, or up and see stars."

CHAPTER 6

The parade began at four after a volley of rifle fire and a blast from the town cannon. The oppressive morning heat had actually dissipated during the previous two hours, sending people out of stores and shaded back gardens to watch along the parade route. Shops and houses displayed large American flags, and miniature copies of that patriotic symbol were carried gaily about town by youngsters and the aged alike. Alaina pushed aside one of these flapping menaces that came near to poking out her eye.

"Oh, Alaina, I'm sorry!" Joanna Wilton giggled. "I can't seem to remember to not get carried away and wave my flag in your face." For a moment Alaina's lifelong friend fixed her with a look of contrition, then turned abruptly as a cheer went up from the crowd. "Oh, look, Alaina! It's the hook-and-ladder boys!" Joanna waved her flag off to one side and cheered for the strong young men of the fire brigade.

After them came the Knights of the Assyrian Cross—a scientific, philosophic, and literary fraternity whose fun-loving and charitable endeavors were appreciated by all. The men usually paraded in some sort of costume, and this year was no exception.

"My father's joined the buffoons this year," Daniel Chart informed them as he nonchalantly took a place behind Alaina.

"And why aren't you out there with him, Mr. Chart?" Joanna asked teasingly.

"I didn't want to make a mule of myself, Miss Wilton."

"So you think your father is a mule?"

"Actually, he's a pig."

Before Joanna could react, the group came into view, accompanied by laughter, clapping, and hoots from the parade goers. Fifteen grown men marched in perfect formation, their faces covered in papier-mâché animal faces: Markus Salter's father—a large man with a limp—was an elephant; thin Mr. Greggs from the post office was a monkey; and, yes indeed, Fredrick Robinson was a pig. It was hard to pick out the identities of the rest of the goats, roosters, and dogs, but the crowd cheered enthusiastically.

At one point the menagerie broke ranks and ventured over to bray, cluck, or bark at the audience, causing the little children to squeal with delight and the delicate ladies to pretend horror. One young billy goat became very forward with Joanna, tickling her into a fit of giggles until a more level-headed cow finally came to drag him away.

"I think Jim Peterson has a fondness for you, Miss Wilton," Daniel said, smiling as he watched a rosy glow color her cheeks.

"Jim Peterson is a light-minded fool, Mr. Chart," Joanna answered in mock displeasure. "Besides which, I don't believe I asked for your opinion."

Daniel tipped his hat and gave her a wink, forcing her to turn and hide her giggles.

It was difficult for the crowd to calm down for the next group comprised of forty-niners and Civil War veterans. The eight old miners wore coarse blue shirts, carried picks, and rode proudly on a bannered hay wagon, while the military men, in their tattered uniforms, walked beside the wagon in quiet dignity. One officer carried a picture of George Washington, which brought tears to many eyes and caused Argus Bell, the foreman at the foundry, to wave his hat and yell out, "First in war, first in peace, and first in the hearts of his countrymen!" A grand cheer went up from all those standing by, and Joanna started crying.

Next came the carriages carrying the county and local officials and their wives. People were polite, waving and calling out greetings, but in truth, everyone was waiting for the chief attraction—the float of the states, pulled by six magnificent draft horses. When it came into view, the spectators were not disappointed.

Joanna waved her flag madly. "Oh, look! Look how pretty it is this year! Doesn't Lela look stunning?"

Lela McIntyre, draped in yards and yards of silver tulle, stood regally in the center of the float, holding a scroll which read "Goddess of Liberty." Her hair, done up in the old Gibson style, was crowned with an enchanting wreath of garlands, while surrounding her were forty-eight little girls dressed in summer white, each wearing a pink sash proclaiming the name of a different state.

"My, we are a big country," Joanna exclaimed. "Oh, and look at the little Carson twins! Aren't they adorable?"

Six-year-old Josephine and Grace Carson sat on higher tulle-covered haystacks, proudly representing the two newest states, Arizona and New Mexico, admitted to the Union in 1912. Their sashes were a slightly darker pink, and while all the little girls wore garlands in their hair, Josephine's and Grace's were festooned with flowers and ribbons.

The parade ended with Mr. Turner's brass band playing "The March of Victory," while Joanna indulged in another flurry of flag waving. "I just love our parade!" she sighed happily.

"We can tell," Daniel remarked good-naturedly. "And how about you, Miss Lund? Did you enjoy it?"

"I did," Alaina answered without much emotion.

"Hmm. Not very enthusiastic," Daniel remarked, moving out with the crowd toward the Miner's Hall.

Joanna put her arm around Alaina's waist and followed. "It's all right, Mr. Chart. Alaina is in mourning, you know."

Daniel raised his eyebrow but only said, "Of course, that answers it."

Alaina knew he didn't believe that Uncle Cedrick's death was the reason for her melancholy, but she didn't care. Her heart was aching with the message Father had given her on their way into town, and if the black clothing served as a mask for the true genesis of her misery and reserve, so be it.

When Mother said she had no idea why Father wanted Alaina to ride with him into town, she was not telling the truth. They had delivered the potatoes to Granny Pitman, who showed her gratitude by offering Father a drink of hard cider and sending her mangy dog Nimrod after Alaina. Alaina was a stranger Granny thought might be a bandit, and bandits had to be run off. Luckily, the dog had no teeth and his heart wasn't into the chase, so there was no harm done. In fact, Nimrod ended up lying on his back and letting Alaina scratch his belly.

She and Father laughed about that for several minutes after leaving Granny's property, after which they settled into a comfortable silence. But then it seemed Father's mood had changed. Alaina was content to absorb the sights and sounds of the warm afternoon, while Father seemed caught up in deep, worrisome thoughts. Several times she saw him glance at her, then look away.

At one point they stopped by the side of a small creek and dismounted to splash cool water onto their necks and faces, and let the horses drink. Alaina looked carefully at her father's features and saw again the tiredness she'd seen earlier.

"Alaina, I need to speak to you about something important."

She felt tightness in her chest, as the tone of Father's voice indicated a solemn message. He threw a couple of stones into the creek and let out an exasperated sigh.

"Come harvest time, you won't be helping in the groves."

Alaina lowered her head, as tears, unwished for, sprang into her eyes. "I . . . I . . . Is it something I've done?" Her voice faltered, and she wiped angrily at the tears washing down her cheeks.

"Oh, Fancy, don't cry," her father entreated tenderly. "It has nothing to do with your ability. You could run that farm all by yourself if need be."

"Then why?" she pleaded. "I've been your helper for a long time."

"I know you have, and . . ."

"Is it because of Mr. Erickson?"

"Mr. Erickson?"

"Has he done such a good job in taking my place?"

Father lowered his head. There was silence between them as Alaina struggled to gain control of her emotions and Father tried to find words to explain.

"You are a woman now, and you need to take more responsibility for duties in the house."

The words poured into her ears like poison, and she felt resentment welling up within her. This was Mother's doing. Mother was insisting that Alaina be forced into her proper woman's place, and Father was tied by conjugal commitment to honor her wishes.

"But I could do both. I would gladly do both. Mrs. Drakerman works the farm and still performs her household duties."

Father didn't reply. Alaina noted the drawn look on his face as he knelt down to splash more water on his neck, and something told her to hold her tongue, that this was just as difficult for him as it was for her. Compassion outran her swift temper and heartache, and she swallowed hard before speaking again.

"I'm sorry, Father." She stopped, fighting back the emotion. "I'll do what's asked of me. I'll honor your wishes."

Samuel stood up slowly and looked his daughter in the face. "You have been a blessing to me every day of your life, Alaina, and I thank you for obeying, especially when the reason doesn't make much sense to you. That shows me just how much character you have. I'm proud of you."

He came to her and brushed the tears off her cheeks. She looked up at him, and a slight smile touched the corner of his mouth. "And, who knows, Fancy? Things may change. Things change all the time . . ."

"Alaina! Alaina Lund, where are you today?" Joanna's voice sounded like crystal chimes fluttering far away.

Alaina's thoughts were pulled away from the green dell, and she found herself staring at Dr. McIntyre's automobile. She looked across the shiny hood to see Daniel Chart and Nephi Erickson in sociable conversation.

"Are you feeling all right?" Joanna questioned, shading Alaina with her parasol. "I bet it's dreadful in that horrid black dress."

"I'm all right. Just a little dizzy." As soon as the last word left her mouth, she knew it was the wrong thing to say to mother hen Joanna.

"Daniel Chart, did you hear that? Alaina feels dizzy. Perhaps you should find her a place to sit."

Alaina gave her friend a sidelong look. *Find me a place to sit? I am perfectly able to find my own place to sit.* But it was too late. Daniel was at her elbow, ready to guide her. "Good idea," he said. "I wasn't very excited about going into that furnace of a Miner's Hall and listening to boring speeches. Come on, Nephi, let's find these ladies some shade."

Alaina was mortified. Joanna Wilton was used to being treated like fragile china, and liked it. But it made Alaina feel awkward and foolish.

"Really, I'm fine," she protested, but no one seemed to be listening. As they headed toward the park where dinner would be served in an hour or so, they passed the baseball field where some of the younger children were pretending to run bases. Eleanor was just passing second when she noticed her sister being pushed along by Daniel Chart.

"Hey! What's wrong?" she called, changing direction and coming to her sister's side.

"Nothing," Alaina said, stopping and retrieving her elbow. "I just felt a little dizzy."

"Miss Eleanor," Daniel said, tipping his hat to the younger Lund sister. "Now how in the world can you be running out in the hot sun in a black dress?"

Eleanor colored for a moment, then stood up a little straighter. "We Lund women are tough, Mr. Chart, if it's any of your business."

Alaina broke into laughter, with Daniel and Nephi joining her after the initial shock. Joanna just stared, openmouthed.

"You're gonna catch flies, Joanna," Eleanor warned as she took Alaina's hand. "Come on, I've got the quilts laid down under the trees there." She pulled her sister along lovingly.

As they reached the shadows, Alaina asked admiringly, "Eleanor Lund! What's gotten into you?"

"Me? What happened to *you?* You never get dizzy."

Alaina sat down gratefully on the familiar worn quilts, about to share some of her sorrow with her younger sibling, when Joanna came up beside Eleanor.

"I've sent the boys back for drinks," Joanna announced, taking off her hat and fanning her face with it.

"Oh, good idea," Eleanor said. "I like it when the boys have to work."

"So, my friend," Joanna continued, ignoring Eleanor's childish remark, "are you feeling better?" She sat down gracefully next to Alaina, a concerned look on her face.

"I'm fine, Joanna. Thank you for being worried, but, really, I'm fine."

Eleanor lay down on the other blanket, a distance from the two older girls, and pretended to nap.

"It's so nice here in the shade," Joanna sighed, languidly lying back and looking up into the canopy of leaves.

Alaina took off her hat and lay back too.

"Wasn't the parade divine?" Joanna asked no one in particular. She brushed her hair out from under her head, where it fell in soft ribbons of strawberry gold on the quilt.

"It was nice."

"Nice? Alaina Lund! Daniel was right. Mourning or no mourning, you could be a little more enthusiastic. The states float alone was worth the whole parade."

Alaina smiled. "You're right, it was beautiful."

"Well, that's better."

They were quiet for a moment as they listened to the Methodist tower bell ring five o'clock.

"I wonder if Mr. Erickson was proud?"

Alaina turned her head. "What do you mean?"

"To see his state represented. Actually, I'm surprised the government let Utah into the union with that polygamy situation."

Alaina was silent. She knew of the "polygamy situation" because they'd studied it briefly in a history class, but she'd never thought about it affecting actual people.

"I'm just dying to ask Mr. Erickson if he knows any polygamists, but I'm sure he'd deny it. I think they're mostly embarrassed by it now," Joanna said in a knowing voice.

Alaina thought back to her one brief conversation with Nephi about his home, and she wondered if that was why he'd been unwilling to talk about his life there.

"Well, water under the bridge," Joanna said lightly. "And Mormon boy or not, I think he's very nice-looking."

Alaina was shocked. "You do?"

"Well, not as handsome as Daniel, but yes, very nice-looking. Have you ever noticed the color of his eyes?"

"Not really," Alaina said, staring upwards.

Joanna giggled. "Alaina Lund! You are such a liar."

"Joanna!"

"Well, you are. You might have to talk with my daddy about bearing false witness."

The girls, including Eleanor, were giggling so loudly that they didn't hear the approach of the objects of their gaiety. Alaina sat up abruptly when she heard a twig snap, the laughter catching in her throat.

"Oh! Oh, my!"

There stood Daniel holding a large glass container, and Mr. Erickson a few paces behind with the tin cups.

"We . . . we were just . . ."

"It's all right, Miss Lund. I promise not to tell your mother you were laughing," Daniel said, smiling.

All the girls were sitting now and regaining their composure, but Alaina found she couldn't stop looking at Mr. Erickson's sky-blue eyes.

"I'm glad you're feeling better," he said, handing Alaina a cup.

She muttered a thank-you, and then occupied herself tying a shoelace, relieved when Mr. Erickson moved on to give a cup to Eleanor and Joanna.

"Thank you, Mr. Erickson," Joanna said brightly.

"I would like it if you called me Nephi, Miss Wilton."

"Only if you call me Joanna."

Nephi offered a shy smile and nodded. "I'd be pleased to."

"Well, Daniel, why don't you and Nephi come sit with us for a spell, unless you have something better to do?"

Daniel chuckled as he sat down next to Alaina. "You'll have our undivided attention until supper."

"So, that's where we stand on the list—supper, then us."

"Actually, it's supper, baseball, then you."

"You're a scoundrel, Mr. Chart."

During this banter, Nephi positioned himself next to Joanna, with a view of Alaina.

"So, Nephi, how do you like California?" Joanna asked simply, turning her attention to the sandy-haired Mormon boy.

"Well, I haven't seen much of it, but I love this area. The high Sierras are a wonder. I came past Lake Tahoe on my way out, and I don't think there's any place to compare. Have you seen it, Daniel?"

"Lake Tahoe? I haven't, no," Daniel answered, pouring everyone a cool drink.

"Miss Lund?"

Alaina was caught by surprise. "Me? No. I've never been that far east, but I hear it's beautiful."

"Words can't really match it. It's tough to make a living there, or I'd have stayed."

"Really?" Eleanor broke in. "I hear they can get eight to ten feet of snow in one snowstorm!"

"Well, maybe I'd live here in the winter and live up there the rest of the time," Nephi replied.

"And how did you land in Sutter Creek, Nephi?" Joanna asked, sipping her drink.

"Poked my finger at a map."

Joanna choked. "You . . . you did not!"

Nephi smiled. "I did."

"Well, that was very brave," Joanna said.

"Or desperate," Daniel laughed.

Nephi smiled.

"And do you have plans to go back to Utah?" Joanna asked innocently.

"No," Nephi answered, shaking his head. He took a drink of juice. "No. Maybe someday, but right now I like it here."

Memories of her conversation with Father flooded back, and Alaina found herself clenching her jaw so as not to say anything spiteful. *"Come harvest time, you won't be helping in the groves."* Of course, Nephi's being on the farm had nothing to do with her restriction from the orchard, so her reason to wish him gone really didn't exist anymore. Mother's edict would stand, and not having Nephi to help would only place an unnecessary burden on her father. She was finding it impossible to sort out her feelings.

"Tell us about Salt Lake City," Eleanor ventured quietly. "Is it a city in the middle of a desert?"

Nephi hesitated, aware of Alaina's eyes fixed on him—of four pairs of eyes fixed on him. He wasn't used to being the center of attention, and it obviously made him uncomfortable. He took a deep breath.

"It's . . ." He cleared his throat. "It's not in a desert," he managed. "Well, not the kind of desert you imagine. There are these big mountains just east of the city—ten, eleven thousand feet high. The place where the city sits used to be pretty desolate—prairie grass and not many trees. But people have been planting trees ever since the pioneers arrived, so it's better now." He stopped, figuring his companions must be bored with his prattle about mountains and trees, and sure that they were secretly much more curious to hear about mob attacks and men with ten wives. He was grateful that good manners kept them away from those topics, as it was impossible to talk about faith or religious conviction without the proper setting or the mighty influence of the Spirit. He was also grateful they hadn't asked specific questions about his family, as it was a painful subject for him. His mother, the dearest woman in the world, was his father's second wife, and when the Manifesto set plural marriage aside, she'd had to change her life completely. She had accepted her new situation with faith and equanimity, only to be repeatedly maligned by the first wife without any intercession or reproof from Father. The injustice was some-thing Nephi could not forgive. When he'd stepped onto the train for California, he locked away his past, and set his interest in the future.

Daniel's voice brought Nephi back to the present. "I heard the streets in Salt Lake City are wide enough for four team of oxen to walk abreast," he added.

Nephi smiled. "That's true. The streets are very wide."

There was another lull in the conversation, and Nephi took the opportunity to change the subject.

"Do you play baseball, Daniel?"

"I do. And you?"

"I love the game. I was on a team back home."

"They play baseball?" Alaina broke in.

Nephi smiled. "Yes, Miss Lund, and we dance and play musical instruments, too." He said it good-naturedly, which eased Alaina's discomfort.

"I'm sorry," Alaina said softly.

"Never mind. I only get upset if people try looking for the horns on my head."

Eleanor snorted. "I never heard anything so silly."

It was Daniel who changed the subject this time. "Well, I think after supper, when the baseball game gets started, Nephi and I will help out the team, and you ladies should come cheer us on."

Joanna held out her cup for another drink of juice. "Only if you promise to dance with us at the dance."

Alaina saw the tops of Nephi's ears go red as he avoided eye contact with anyone.

"Of course, you'll have to go over to the creek and bathe first," Joanna added glibly.

Alaina now joined Nephi in his embarrassment. How could Joanna, the pastor's daughter, talk about something as private as men taking baths? It always surprised her that her friend was so comfortable with worldly topics. Maybe she knew Bible stories that were a bit bawdier than David and Goliath or Jonah and the whale. Alaina was glad when the conversation turned to farming, horses, and the building of the new high school—safe, boring topics that harmlessly filled up the time until supper.

Long tables had been built under the shade trees, and women from the Methodist Church's auxiliary began setting out food from home ovens, ice boxes, and cool dark cellars: ham, fried chicken, corn on the cob, tomatoes, potato pie, baked beans, lima beans, hot rolls, corn bread, pickles, applesauce, hard-boiled eggs, early-ripe pears, watermelon, rock melon, cakes, and pies. The bounty seemed endless. People gathered from all directions, chattering and happy. The Fourth of July was the grandest get-together of the year, and the folks in and around Sutter Creek, like folks in towns across the nation, endowed the day with thankful celebration.

Alaina's group of companions disbanded to find their families for supper, promising to meet up afterward for the rest of the evening's activities. Nephi helped Alaina and Eleanor carry the quilts to where Father had set up the low makeshift table at the far end of the field. It was a beautiful spot, close to a creek and shaded by a giant oak. Mother had covered the rough boards of the table with an ivory linen cloth and set out dishware and cutlery. Alaina looked around at the other diners who sat unceremoniously on blankets, with tin plates and cups. When would Mother ever bloom to fit her surroundings? Didn't she realize the spectacle she made of the family with her high-mannered ways? Alaina clenched her jaw against a swelling anger that made her chest ache.

Father caught sight of the threesome as they drew near the picnic area, throwing up his hand and calling a greeting. "So, the prodigals have returned!" he hooted. "And look! They've brought our chairs!"

Alaina chuckled at her father's exuberance, wondering if he'd had more than just the one hard cider from Granny Pitman. Most of the churchgoing men in the area spent their days in tough, back-breaking work and so felt justified in abandoning sobriety once a year. Father was no exception.

He gave Alaina a focused look, which carried a weight of worry, but she gave him a reserved smile and patted his arm.

"So Nephi, haven't I been blessed with the loveliest daughters in the world?"

"Father!" Eleanor choked. "That's not a proper question."

"It isn't?"

"No, it isn't."

"I'm sorry, Nephi, let me make it up to you—you must join us for the picnic," he insisted, swaying slightly as he helped Nephi fold the blanket and lay it at the side of the table.

Alaina caught the stern look that crossed Mother's face.

"I wouldn't want to intrude," Nephi answered, glancing in Alaina's direction.

"Perhaps he and James could sit together in the wagon," Mrs. Lund suggested. "The table will be a little crowded with seven."

"Nonsense," said Father, patting Nephi on the back. "There's room for all."

Mother, who would not make a public spectacle of her feelings, simply handed Kathryn another plate to set and made room at the foot of the table.

"So, here we are together on this good day . . . on this Fourth of July day . . ." Father boomed, bringing James forward and putting an arm around his shoulder. "And here is my son, James . . . and there stand my three lovely daughters . . ." Kathryn giggled at her father's odd behavior. ". . . And my good wife." Elizabeth Lund did not seem pleased by her husband's compliment. Samuel continued in a volume that had all the children holding back laughter. "Lord, thank you for a good crop, and a good helper, and this good food. Amen."

Alaina said "amen" with much too much mirth in her voice, which she covered by bowing her head.

"Here's your plate, Laina," Eleanor said, giggling. "I'll race you to the food!"

"Hey, wait for me," Kathryn whined, chasing after them.

"Walk, girls!" Mother's voice came sharply, and the three sisters slowed to a proper pace.

"Oh yeah," Eleanor whispered. "I forgot we were in mourning."

CHAPTER 7

Alaina figured their picnic would be awkward and silent, but she was pleasantly surprised. The men got into a conversation about automobiles, with James taking the lead on many points, while she and Eleanor talked about the building of the new high school and Philomene Johnson's trip to Italy. Before classes ended in the spring, the traveling educator had brought pictures of the marvels she would see in Florence and Rome. Eleanor couldn't get over the cathedrals and the artwork. Mother even participated in this conversation, remarking that she thought travel a frivolous way for Philomene to spend her inheritance.

After supper the dishes were returned to the wooden box for transport home, the table was taken apart and put back in the wagon, and James and Father were set to work carrying the settee to the Methodist church for auction.

Nephi thanked the family for a nice meal and excused himself to find Daniel. On his way out he passed Joanna, who was coming to find Alaina. "Hello, Joanna," he said, tipping his hat.

"Hello, Nephi," she returned, a marked lilt to her voice. "Will I see you later at the game?"

Nephi nodded and continued on his way, while Joanna moved into the Lund picnic area. "Hello, Mrs. Lund. Did your family have a nice picnic?"

"We did dear, thank you. And your family?"

"Yes, ma'am."

Mrs. Lund laid her apron on the side of the wagon. "Please excuse me, Joanna. I must go and help your mother with the auction." She turned to her daughters. "Alaina, remember to behave properly, and Eleanor, especially you—no racing."

Eleanor hung her head. "Yes, ma'am."

"And keep an eye on Kathryn."

Elizabeth Lund moved off in the direction of town, leaving the girls to their youthful endeavors.

"So, are we ready to cheer on the boys?" Joanna asked eagerly.

"I'd rather play," Eleanor answered, moving over to stop Kathryn from throwing rocks at the birds.

"Eleanor Lund, you're still a little tomboy! I thought you'd grown out of that," Joanna teased.

Alaina came immediately to her sister's defense. "Actually, I'd rather play too. It's boring to just sit and watch."

Joanna looked at her dear friend, smiled, and shook her head. "You always have had your own mind about things, haven't you?"

Alaina returned a sly smile. "I suppose I have, although I don't always get my way."

"Like having to wear black in the summer."

"I hate black!" Kathryn spit out as she came near the girls.

Alaina caught herself before she agreed.

"Well, the sun's going down, and it's much cooler than before," Joanna mothered. "In fact, I think it's going to be a delightful evening, so come on. I've set my blanket in a perfect spot to watch them slide home." She took Alaina's and Eleanor's hands, and led them cheerfully off toward the baseball field, Kathryn tagging behind.

The sky turned pearly saffron on the western horizon as the sun relinquished its station. It would be hours before dark, but Alaina could actually feel a stirring of coolness, and she undid her bun, letting her hair fall loose down her back.

"We're s'pose to keep our hair braided," Kathryn informed her errant older sister.

Alaina answered by shaking her hair into added freedom.

"Nephi ate supper with us," Eleanor informed Joanna as the girls ambled toward the crowd gathering around the field.

Joanna's eyes widened. "Really? I'm surprised your mother allowed that."

"I know, we were surprised too."

"Oh, for heaven's sake," Alaina scoffed. "It was just a picnic!"

Joanna gave her friend a skeptical look, but didn't reply as they maneuvered their way around growing numbers of spectators.

The teams from Sutter Creek and Amador City were a mixture of farmers, miners, shopkeepers, and civil servants. Markus Salter, at eighteen, was the youngest player on the Sutter Creek team, while the postmaster, Elijah Greggs, at forty, was the oldest. Rumor had it that before moving to California he'd been a pitcher on a team in Indiana, so he not only played, but was also the team captain.

As the girls seated themselves on Joanna's blanket, Alaina looked around for Daniel and Nephi. Markus Salter caught her eye and waved fervently. She smiled and waved back, then continued her search until she found Daniel in the outfield throwing the ball to Argus Bell. She finally spotted Nephi on the sidelines talking to Mr. Greggs. Alaina figured the captain was evaluating Nephi's familiarity with the game before trying him out in a position, but, curiously, he instead handed Nephi some sort of package and headed out for the pitcher's mound. Alaina watched as Nephi scanned the crowd of spectators, finally catching a glimpse of Joanna's strawberry curls.

"Oh, look, there's Nephi!" Joanna said, waving. "I wonder if he's going to play."

Nephi was moving in their direction, bringing the mysterious package with him.

"Well, how nice," Joanna commented. "He's coming to say hello."

Alaina was concentrating on the practice activities taking place on the field, so she jumped when Nephi came up and spoke her name.

"Yes, Mr. Erickson?" she said, steadying her voice. "What can I do for you?"

"Would it be difficult for you, Miss Lund, to hold this package until the end of the game?" He held the brown-paper-wrapped parcel in her direction.

Out of the corner of her eye, Alaina caught Joanna's crooked smile and immediately reached up her hand for the package. "Of course not, Mr. Erickson. Not difficult at all."

"Thank you." He turned back toward the field.

"May we peek inside?" Joanna yelled after him.

"I'll tell your father if you do," he called over his shoulder.

Joanna smiled. "Hmm . . . maybe he does have a little sense of humor." She took the package out of Alaina's hands. "I wonder what it is?"

"Give that back, you awful thing."

"Oh, I'm sure you're not just dying to know," she teased.

"It's none of our business."

"Look! It's from Salt Lake City. It's a box of some sort. Maybe his mother sent him salt-water taffy." Joanna shook the box. "Hmm . . . No rattle."

"Give it here!" Alaina scolded, taking the parcel back.

"I'd like to know what it is," Eleanor said, leaning around Alaina's shoulder to look at the postmarkings.

"Me too!" Kathryn chimed in, not content to be left out.

"Joanna Wilton, you're a bad influence, and no one is going to open this package, understood?"

"King George, spoiling all our fun," Joanna sulked playfully.

"You certainly are parsimonious," Eleanor added, using one of her "professor" words.

"Yea, possumous," Kathryn imitated.

Gales of laughter followed this pronouncement, and soon thoughts of the package were lost in the gaiety and the opening notes of "The Star-Spangled Banner." Mr. Turner's brass band stood near the pitcher's mound, playing expertly, while the opposing teams stood along the first- and third-base lines. All the team members wore their everyday clothes, but were distinguished by their caps—red for Amador City, and blue for Sutter Creek. Everyone sang the anthem with great emotion and cheered afterward, adding to the excitement of the day.

Alaina liked baseball and should have easily been able to concentrate on the action of the game, with Daniel playing second base and Nephi playing first, but her mind kept returning to the farm, awakening poignant images of home and its abundant surroundings: the fragile ivory petals of the rose-of-Sharon bush that grew against their front porch, green pears turning pale yellow in the summer heat, rough wooden crates stacked in the barn, and the pungent smell of the soil after a rain.

A cheer went up from the crowd, jolting Alaina out of her reverie. It was the top of the ninth inning, and Daniel Chart had just hit a long drive to left field, sending Nephi Erickson charging from first base, around second, and on to third. Joanna was cheering, calling out instructions, and overall not behaving like a pastor's daughter. Of course, Joanna rarely behaved like a pastor's daughter.

"Run, Nephi! Run! The left fielder has you covered!"

Nephi reached third base a moment before the ball slammed into the baseman's mitt, and the referee called the Mormon boy safe.

A cheer exploded from the Sutter Creek spectators, and although they seemed to be wary of Mr. Erickson's strange religious beliefs, his apparent athletic ability was not in question.

Alaina looked up to check the score, barely able to make it out: Amador City, 23 and Sutter Creek, 27. The gloam had faded into gray stillness, and the sky was turning inky over the eastern horizon. It was fortunate the game was almost over, or they'd be playing by moonlight.

"Your boyfriend is up to bat, Joanna," Eleanor teased, "and he'd better pay more attention to the pitcher and less to you."

Jim Peterson did seem to be focused on Joanna—making sure she was watching him as he stretched his back and took a few practice swings.

"Hey, billy-goat boy! Keep your eye on the ball!" Argus Bell yelled at him, laughing.

Many in the crowd chuckled, and Joanna turned a creamy shade of pink. Nephi, his base close to their blankets, glanced over at her, a wicked little grin pulling at his mouth.

"I'd keep my mind on the game if I were you, Mr. Erickson," she replied tartly.

It was good advice, as Jim Peterson cracked the first pitch—a line drive out past shortstop. Nephi bolted from the base and made it home standing, but Daniel wasn't so lucky. He rounded third with the crowd cheering him on, but his slide was mistimed and the catcher snagged the throw from the second baseman, tagging him out before his foot hit home plate. The Sutter Creek crowd teased him good-naturedly, even though his out retired their team. Daniel added to the camaraderie and fun by standing, dusting himself off, and giving a low bow to all the jeering fans. Alaina saw Mr. and Mrs. Robinson laughing at their son's antics, and she thought again what good people they were—a thought that seemed to be spreading throughout the community.

The score was now 28 to 23, and Amador City had one last chance at bat. It proved to be short-lived however, when, after two men had base hits, Markus Salter made a surprising high-fly catch in center field, and Daniel and Nephi stunned everyone with a brilliant double play which ended the game, sending the Sutter Creek fans into jubilation.

Joanna pulled Alaina to her feet, and, with Kathryn in tow, they joined the rest of the townsfolk flooding the field. Alaina could see that Nephi and Daniel were standing together, surrounded by base-ball enthusiasts who were smacking them on the back and eagerly shaking their hands. Suddenly she felt plain and awkward, and if it hadn't been for Joanna's persistent pulling, she would have gone back to stand on the sidelines, away from the clamorous crowd. Joanna would not let go, and Alaina soon found herself only a few feet from the popular pair. She noted that while Daniel loved the attention, Nephi kept glancing from side to side, obviously looking for a way to escape. Elijah Greggs came up to congratulate his star players, directing most of his attention to Nephi. Alaina was so close to the men, she couldn't help but overhear the glowing praise.

"You're a powerful player, Mr. Erickson, one of the finest I've seen."

Nephi glanced self-consciously at Alaina, then back to Mr. Greggs. "Thank you, sir. It was great to play again."

"Land sakes, boy, it's a shame we don't have a regular team for your talents. It must be that clean Mormon living. You outplayed everybody."

"Except me, of course," Daniel broke in, giving Nephi a slap on the back.

Nephi smiled broadly at Daniel, grateful for the interruption, and Alaina recognized a lasting friendship emerging between the pair.

She held out the package to him. "Congratulations on the win, Mr. Erickson."

"Thank you," he said, taking the parcel and fixing her with a broad smile.

"Well, he wasn't the only player," Daniel interrupted. "What did you think of our double play?"

Alaina chuckled. "Hmm . . . passable, I guess."

Daniel staggered against Nephi. "Passable? Our game-winning double play, passable? You are just too hard to please, Miss Lund," he said in mock disappointment. "I pity your future husband, I surely do."

Joanna overheard this remark and turned to him with a scowl. "Daniel Chart! What a mean thing to say, even if it is in jest."

But Alaina had a mischievous glint in her eye. "Who said I was going to marry, Mr. Chart? I may just travel the world like Philomene Johnson."

"And spend months away from your farm? I don't believe a word of it."

Alaina felt the wound reopen and looked quickly down at her feet, no longer enjoying being the center of attention.

"Hey, Alaina!" James called, pushing his way through the crowd to her. "We have to go."

"Go? What do you mean, go?" Joanna interrupted. "We still have the dance."

"Mother says we're not staying," he grumbled. "It wouldn't be showing Uncle Cedrick proper respect."

Alaina noted the sarcasm in James's voice, and inwardly applauded his small step toward independence. And though she too bristled at another command from Mother, she was glad for the excuse to leave. She'd been holding her smoldering emotions inside the whole afternoon, and she was tired.

"Tell her I'll be right there, James, and take Kathryn with you."

"Where's Eleanor?" James asked, looking for his other sister.

"I think she went off with her friends. You'd better find her, too."

James hesitated before leaving, reaching out to shake hands with Nephi and Daniel. "Great game! That last play was . . . well, it was . . . it was great."

Nephi smiled. "Thanks."

James stood staring at the farmhand as if seeing him for the first time. "Oh, sure . . . I . . . I didn't know you could play like that. The way you hit. Three home runs!"

Kathryn grabbed James by the cuff. "Come on! I want to go home."

"All right! All right!" James snapped, snatching his arm away. "Oh Nephi, Father says you can stay if you'd like. You can ride Moccasin home." James shook Nephi's hand one last time, then turned and moved off into the crowd, leaving the remaining companions to untie their plans.

"Perhaps we can get your mother to change her mind," Joanna offered hopefully. Alaina was silent, and Joanna shook her head. "Probably not."

"You can stay, Mr. Erickson," Alaina said, looking straight into his blue eyes. "Father gave you leave."

"Sure! You could ride home later with our family," Daniel added, attempting to lighten the mood.

Nephi looked steadily into Alaina's tired eyes. "Thank you, Daniel, but I think I'll head back."

"Well, isn't this just dandy!" Joanna growled. "Our one night to have fun together, ruined by . . ." She bit her lip. "Sorry, Alaina." She put her arm around her friend's waist. "This must have been a terrible day for you."

Joanna had no idea of the truth of her words.

"It's all right," Alaina insisted. "You and Daniel go have fun for all of us. Hopefully no other uncle will die before the harvest festival, and we can dance then."

Joanna brightened. "The harvest festival! I love the harvest festival!"

Alaina laughed at her friend's childlike ability to change moods. "So, we'll plan on harvest time, and, of course, I'll see you every Sunday."

"Well, that's a tonic at least," Joanna replied, kissing her friend on the cheek.

Daniel stepped forward. "I'll walk you to the wagon if you'd like, Alaina."

"There's no need," Nephi interrupted, turning to shake Daniel's hand. "The two of us are headed in the same direction."

Alaina was too tired to argue, although she would have preferred to walk with Daniel. She might have been able to share some of her sorrow with him, knowing he would understand. She could tell none of it to Mr. Erickson.

The last of the spectators were moving off toward the Miner's Hall, their voices murmuring through the night air, the first notes of music from the dance coming out to meet them. Joanna's head turned toward the sound, excitement momentarily brightening her face, then she looked back at Alaina with the appropriate melancholy.

Alaina smiled. "Go and have fun . . . really. Daniel, take good care of her." She was confused by the look on Daniel's face, which indicated the assignment would be more duty than pleasure. Yet he nobly offered Joanna his arm, giving her a wink.

"I suppose we have to follow the lady's command," he said teasingly. He then looked at Alaina as if no one else were present. "Will you promise me the first dance at the harvest festival?"

Alaina gave him a tired smile. "All right," she answered. If the day had been different, she would have felt elated and a bit overwhelmed by so much attention, but no amount of flattery could undo the knot of pain tied around her feelings.

"Good night, Nephi," Joanna was saying, as Alaina's thoughts came back to the baseball field. "It really was a wonderful game."

"Thanks for cheering us on," Nephi replied.

"Goodnight, you two," Daniel said, tipping his hat to Alaina. "Well, Miss Wilton, shall we go and shock your father?"

Joanna giggled as they moved off toward the town, leaving Alaina and Nephi alone in the dark. Alaina turned quickly and began walking toward the wagon, with Nephi striding to catch up. They walked together in awkward silence, neither eager for meaningless talk. Nephi had been aware all afternoon of Alaina's preoccupation with some personal pain. Many times he saw it wash across her face and haunt her blue eyes. He tried not to react when he noticed the bleak look, but he found it difficult. Her life had become meaningful to him and he wanted to talk with her and share her heartache. And while he knew they shared no bond that allowed him to intrude on her solitude, his heart pushed him into folly. He reached out and lightly touched her arm. "Alaina?"

She stopped abruptly and turned to him, looking at him curiously. "Yes?"

He swallowed, trying to keep the panic out of his voice. "I . . . I just wanted to know if you were all right."

"What do you mean?" A frown wiped away the curiosity. "Why would you ask that?"

"It's just that you've been rather . . . sad all day, and I wondered . . ."

"What, Mr. Erickson? You wondered what? If you could help me?" She felt frustration and embarrassment push their way into her chest.

Her temper surprised him, and he lowered his head. "I . . . I guess so." He had no way of knowing the floodgate of resentment he was opening.

"What do you know about me, Mr. Erickson?" Alaina spit out. "Do you know anything about what I want or what my life was like before you came here? Do you?" She kept her voice down, but the words were harsh and biting.

He was so unsettled by her anger that his mind scrambled for mending words. "I'm sorry, Alaina. I didn't mean to upset you. I just thought we could talk. Sometimes it's nice to have somebody to talk to."

She blinked at him in disbelief. She'd have felt so much better if he'd thrown her anger back at her, giving her a reason to go on pouring out her pain. She didn't know how to defend against his kindness. She growled in frustration. "I don't want to talk about it!" Tears coursed into her eyes and she turned away. "I just want to go home," she snapped as she walked quickly toward the wagon. She was tired of noise and people and gaiety. All she wanted was to get back to the farm and the quiet beauty of the orchard. She wanted the bone-deep satisfaction of work—of bringing in the harvest. She brushed the tears from her cheeks, her mind searching frantically for some way to ease the sorrow, and she remembered something her father had said: "*Who knows, Fancy, things may change. Things change all the time.*"

She slowed her pace and repeated the words in her mind over and over. Somehow they blunted the pain and offered her hope. For now, she would make that thought her saving grace.

CHAPTER 8

Samuel Lund was not one for fuss. He was a good-natured man, and often jovial, but he did not enjoy being the center of attention nor frivolous distractions which took him from needed labor. This July 24, as in previous years, he was spending the day working, allowing his forty-fifth birthday to pass by unnoticed.

Alaina and Eleanor had wished him well as they'd gone to milking, and Mother had served him raspberry preserves with his biscuits, but no other acts of celebration were needed. Besides, it was only a few weeks before the pear harvest began in earnest, and preparations were occupying Samuel, Nephi, and even James from dawn to dusk. Nephi labored with diligence and contentment in every job assigned him, and it was obvious Samuel trusted not only the boy's work ethic, but his opinion as well.

Alaina turned her thoughts to bean picking, glaring at the seemingly endless rows of staked plants with their abundant crop. She would be kept busy picking the rest of the afternoon. She pulled several beans from their stalks and put them into the canvas bag she had slung around her neck. She wasn't working with the trees, but at least she was outside. She adjusted her straw hat and took a drink from the canteen. Poor Elly was inside with Mother preparing beans for canning—a job which the three women would accomplish in the cooler temperatures of late evening. From mid-July through October, no one rested on the farm as the land put forth its abundance and demanded unceasing attention.

Alaina let her mind wander as her hands kept up the constant pattern of pulling beans and putting them into the sack. She thought about Philomene Johnson, Roman ruins, and monks in China. She wandered the halls of Aunt Ida's house in San Francisco and tried to remember what the different rooms looked like. She was thinking about the states float in the Fourth of July parade when she saw Mr. Erickson come around the side of the house and head in her direction. He carried something with him, and she wondered what brought him away from the groves in the middle of the afternoon. He looked up briefly as he approached, then at his boots. When he was near the edge of the garden, he stopped and tipped his hat.

"Good afternoon, Miss Lund. Have you seen your father?"

Alaina lifted the strap over her head and dropped the bag to the ground. "He's in the barn, Mr. Erickson, repairing drying racks." She saw him shift his weight and look uneasily in the direction of the barn. "Is anything wrong?"

He looked quickly back to her and shook his head. "No . . . no, I just want to . . . to wish him well on his birthday."

"How did you know it was today?"

Nephi smiled. "Actually, Kathryn told me all your ages and birthdays when I first arrived."

"She didn't!" Alaina choked.

Nephi noted her displeasure. "I'm afraid she did. Sorry."

"What a wretched child! She . . . she . . ." Alaina stopped herself abruptly, although she had several appropriate names on the tip of her tongue.

"I am sorry," Nephi said soberly. "Maybe she was just trying to be nice."

Alaina raised her eyebrows, and Nephi smiled with understanding.

"So, I guess I'll go find your father."

Alaina again noted the reluctance in his manner. "I'll go with you. I need to get out of the sun for a while." She figured her offer would put him at ease, but it actually had the opposite effect.

"I'll . . . well, I . . . well, of course, Miss Lund . . . if you need to get out of the sun." He turned and headed for the barn without waiting for her.

"I'll take these beans in to Mother and be right with you," she called at his back.

He waved over his head and kept moving. Alaina smiled at his odd behavior, wondering why he should be so nervous about wishing Father a happy birthday. She picked up the heavy bag of beans and lugged it into the kitchen. Eleanor and Mother stood silently at the sink, cleaning and snapping beans in preparation for their later job of canning.

Rows of shiny glass jars covered the table, waiting to receive the produce, and Alaina inwardly groaned as she imagined standing for hours filling each container.

"Hi, Laina!" Eleanor said brightly as Alaina set down the bag and removed her hat.

"Hi, Elly."

"It's hot out there, isn't it?"

"It's hot in here too."

"How many rows have you finished?" Mother interrupted.

"I'm on the third."

"Hmm." Mother wiped her hands on her apron and went into the storage room.

Alaina looked at the large pile of green beans on the drainboard and gave Eleanor a stern look. "You can stop snapping any time, Miss Elly."

"Well, you can stop bringing them in," Eleanor returned haughtily, then laughed at their banter.

Alaina smiled and gave her a hug. It was hard to believe that Eleanor would soon be fifteen. Alaina remembered when they were little girls, following Father around like ducklings whenever he worked near the house or barn; sneaking newly picked apples out of the crates; chasing salamanders back into the creek . . . so many shared adventures.

Mother returned from the storage room with a canteen, and Alaina busied herself with dumping beans into the sink. Mrs. Lund unscrewed the cap of the canteen and held it under the spout as she pumped water.

"I want you to take this to your father."

"Yes, ma'am."

"And a couple of dry biscuits," she ordered.

"Yes, ma'am." Alaina wrapped several of the morning's biscuits in a napkin, hefted the canvas strap onto her shoulder, and took the canteen from her mother. As she headed for the door, Mother's voice followed her. "Alaina, your hat."

Alaina put the canteen strap on her other shoulder, held the cloth full of biscuits in her teeth, and plopped her hat unceremoniously on her head. Another two rows of beans loomed in her future, and she chafed at the labor. It was not that she minded work—she liked to work, and to work hard, but some jobs paid better wages in fulfillment.

She dropped the bag at the edge of the garden and headed for the barn. She was sure her original reason for going was moot as Mr. Erickson would, by now, have delivered his birthday wish and be on his way back to the orchard. So she was surprised as she approached the barn to hear Mr. Erickson and her father talking and laughing. She pushed aside the large door to find them sitting on a hay bale, repairing chicken wire on the drying racks, and chatting away like two women at a sewing bee. Nephi stood up immediately when Alaina walked in, and Father followed suit, a bemused expression playing on his face.

"Hello, daughter! Is it green beans for supper then?"

Alaina groaned. "Oh, I hope not."

Father laughed at her sour expression. "Here, come have a seat by me and forget about beans for a spell."

"Gladly." She moved to one of the hay bales and sat down, handing her father the canteen and biscuits. "Mother sent these along."

"Two presents in one day? I am a fortunate fellow. Here, look at this book Nephi's given me—all the way from Salt Lake City." He held out a small black book, and she took it without thinking.

Nephi cleared his throat. "Well, sir, I'd better get back to work. I just wanted to wish you well."

"Oh, stay a minute or two. It's my birthday. Everyone can take a rest."

Her father's behavior was not typical, and she glanced up from the book to study his face. He was smiling, and he gave her a wink, but there was still that marked tiredness in his eyes—a worry to her. But this was always a busy season, and she needed to remember the near exhaustion she'd always felt at harvest time—the nights when supper was a burden, and sleep was the only redemption. She absently turned the book to glance at the spine, and a jolt of trepidation jumped into her brain. She looked up with unguarded emotion pinching the muscles of her face.

"This . . . this is . . ."

"The Book of Mormon," Samuel said evenly. "Mr. Erickson had it sent all the way from Salt Lake City." His warm glance encompassed the Utah boy, and Alaina saw their farmhand's shoulders relax and a smile touch the corner of his mouth.

"He also tells me that every year in Salt Lake City they have a big parade in my honor. Sit, Nephi. Sit."

Alaina quickly handed her father the book. "And you believe that?"

"Tell her, Nephi."

"Well, we do have a parade every July 24th," he said, settling back on the hay bale. "It's to celebrate when the first pioneers, Mormon pioneers, entered the Salt Lake Valley."

Samuel slapped his knee. "What do you think of that? A parade on my birthday!"

"I'm sure Grandma Lund knew nothing about it when you were born," Alaina said coldly.

Samuel laughed. "Well, of course she didn't, good Presbyterian woman that she was, but somewhere on the streets of Salt Lake a band might have been playing a Sousa march the same time I was having my first howl!"

Samuel and Nephi chuckled, but Alaina found none of it funny. She had a rolling ache in her stomach, and she wanted to yell at her father to throw the book away. Why would this interloper think they'd want anything to do with his Mormon bible, or his strange beliefs?

She pushed herself unsteadily to her feet. "I need to get back to work."

Nephi stood with her. "I do too, sir."

Samuel extended his hand, and Nephi took it. "Thank you for your thoughtfulness, son."

"You're welcome, sir."

"I will take a look at it."

Nephi simply nodded his head and moved out of the barn. Alaina stood still for a moment listening to the drone of flies, then turned to move out of the barn also.

"Is something troubling you, Alaina?" Father's voice came calmly and softly.

She stopped for a moment, her thoughts racing, then turned back to face him. "Why did he give you that book?"

"What do you mean?"

"Why did he send clear back to Salt Lake City for a book that he knew we wouldn't care about? A false Bible that means nothing to us?"

Samuel was quiet, and Alaina stood respectfully waiting for his reply. When he finally spoke, his voice was full of tenderness. "Maybe it's the same as if I wanted to share my love of the orchard with someone who'd never seen apple trees or walked among them while they were in full bloom. How do I share that with someone who's never felt what I've felt?"

Alaina's heart ached with the remembered images and smells of the orchard, and she felt tears pressing against her eyelids.

"How could I share that with them? I'd want to take them into the grove." Samuel stood silent for a moment. "I don't know, maybe Nephi loves this book for some reason, and he wanted to share it with me. Would you ask me to deny his kindness?"

Silence moved between them.

Finally Alaina looked up into her father's face. "No."

He smiled at her, then spoke gently, "Now, you'd better get back to the beans so you can finish before nightfall."

"Are you going to tell Mother about the book?" Alaina pressed.

"When the time is right," Samuel answered, going back to work.

Alaina scoffed. "No sense stirring up a hornet's nest."

Samuel looked at her. "Alaina, please don't be critical of your mother. It's not proper."

Alaina bit her lip. She hated being chastised by her father. His tone was always calm and his assessment always correct. It was true, it wasn't proper for a child to criticize a parent, but sometimes when bitter feelings needed an outlet, Alaina found it satisfying to pour them at Mother's feet. She shook the unkindness out of her head. "Sorry, Father."

Samuel smiled at her. "Not to worry, Fancy. We'll get it sorted out." He moved to her and patted her arm. "I think I hear beans calling."

Alaina smiled back at him, a weight lifting off her shoulders. "You could always come and help me."

He shook his head. "Nope, it's my birthday. No one is required to pick beans on their birthday."

Alaina let out a whoop. "What a big fat fib!" She turned to walk out of the barn, chuckling and shaking her head.

Father called after her. "Well, you get to tell big fat fibs on your birthday too!"

She stepped out into the afternoon sun feeling reassured. Why should she fret about a silly little book? Her father was a sensible man—one of the most sensible men she knew. She started humming one of Father's favorite hymns. No snake-oil salesman would bamboozle him. Father would read a page or two and dismiss it as a hoax, returning the book to Nephi and graciously insisting that the quaint but false book never be mentioned again. Perhaps Mr. Erickson's feelings would be so shattered that he'd leave, on foot, to hike the seven or eight hundred miles back to his home in Salt Lake City to rejoin the others of his kind. Maybe he'd arrive back on July 24th and they'd have a big parade in his honor.

Alaina snatched up the canvas bag, placing the strap around her neck and moving back into the garden to enthusiastically pick beans.

CHAPTER 9

Joanna was a beautiful bride. She stood on the front porch of the Lunds' farmhouse, turning in circles and letting Alaina inspect her fragile gauze dress for dirt or tears. Sewn carefully into the delicate white fabric were yellow satin rosebuds and tiny white pearls. Joanna's soft strawberry curls had been pulled up on top of her head and were encircled by a ringlet of flowers. She looked like an angel.

Alaina sat on the front steps as Joanna turned and thought about what an odd month September was for a wedding: still fairly warm, dry, dusty, and the height of the picking season. She brushed a bit of dirt from the hem of the fragile dress, and wondered where all the other people had gone.

Suddenly Joanna bolted into the house, slamming the door and causing Alaina to jump. She turned quickly to see what had frightened her friend and discovered Daniel Chart, Mr. Erickson, and Markus Salter approaching the house. They were wearing their work clothes, and each carried a bouquet of flowers. *Work clothes certainly will not do for a wedding. Where is Pastor Wilton? He needs to tell these men a thing or two.*

Markus walked up solemnly, handed Alaina the flowers, and tipped his hat. Then Daniel did the same, and lastly Mr. Erickson. She was angry and insulted. *Why are they giving me flowers? How can they mock me on Joanna's wedding day?* A hot dry wind blew open the front door, causing one of her mother's cherished vases to fall and shatter. Alaina stood quickly, dropping the flowers to the ground. *Where was everyone?* She heard the bell chiming in the Methodist church tower as another gust of scratching wind tore at the rose-of-

Sharon bush, ripping off the ivory petals and scattering them across the porch. She saw Father out by the barn, and called to him to come to the wedding, but the wind tore the sound out of her mouth and he didn't hear. He was leading Titus out to work in the groves, and she made up her mind to join them. Working would be much more sensible than attending a wedding. She smoothed her blue skirt with the white trim, placed her straw hat on her head, and followed Father. *No one is going to tell me what to do today. No one.*

Alaina woke with a terrible thirst and a headache. A dream. It had only been one of her dreams. She had fallen asleep in the porch swing, and the hot August sun had found its way around the protective shading of the roof to cause her misery. She sat up slowly, rubbing the back of her neck. Her eyes felt heavy, and there was a high-pitched ringing in her head.

The front screen door opened, and Eleanor emerged with two glasses of lemonade—with ice! Every Sunday when the family went in to Sutter Creek for church, they stopped at Thayer's Ice House to buy three large blocks of ice. One went into the icebox, and the other two into the root cellar. Ice was an elusive commodity, and the wasteful use of it to cool drinks was strictly prohibited. Yet sneaky Eleanor had somehow chipped off a few pieces and snuck them into their lemonade.

Eleanor gave Alaina a worried look as she moved out onto the porch. "Oh, good. If you weren't up by the time I brought these out, I was going to wake you. It's not a good idea to fall asleep in the sun."

"Thank you, Elly," Alaina answered gratefully, taking the cool lemonade and quickly drinking half the glass.

Eleanor shook her head. "Dehydration."

"What?"

"Dehydration. Your body doesn't have enough moisture in it."

Alaina smiled at Eleanor's newly discovered interest in the workings of the human body.

"You really should get out of the heat," Eleanor commanded.

Alaina chuckled. "And how do I do that?"

"Go sit in the root cellar for a little while," Eleanor answered in a practical tone. "If you recall, we did it all the time when we were little."

Alaina finished her lemonade, her head feeling better. "Well, I'm afraid it would be a tight fit now." She stood to stretch her back. "I know. Why don't we go up to the oak bower and stick our feet in Niagara Falls?"

"Oh! We haven't done that for a long time!" Eleanor answered excitedly. "I'll go sneak some gingerbread to take with us." Eleanor snatched up the empty glasses and bounded into the house.

Alaina was excited too. Their Niagara Falls was a cool place within a tangle of old oak trees, where sparkling spring water gurgled over a mossy cropping of limestone rock. The falls tumbled into an oval pool five feet across and three feet deep, surrounded by soft grass and, on occasion, wildflowers. It had been the perfect place for two little girls to sit, dream, and tell stories.

Father had chosen the acreage for their farm with great care—admiring not only the beautiful view and cooler temperatures, but also the abundance of water. Thirteen springs originated on the property, and there was sufficient groundwater to make irrigation unnecessary. Alaina remembered the delight she felt in second grade when Miss Johnson informed her students that the headwater for Sutter Creek was located on the Lund property.

She looked across the meadow to the beckoning hills, hoping the distraction of Niagara Falls would help dispel the nagging fragments of the dream: Joanna in a white gauze dress, the broken vase, the young men handing her flowers. The images made her feel agitated, and she was glad when Eleanor returned with the gingerbread and a spirit for adventure.

It was warm as the girls hoofed their way past the mown field of feed hay, through acres of heavy-laden apple trees, and up the hillside. August was always hot, but the daylight hours were shrinking, and soon autumn would bring welcome relief.

"Are you sure you're feeling all right?" Eleanor inquired, turning to look at her sister's face.

Alaina took a deep breath and nodded. "Fine. My headache's almost gone."

"Dehydration is very serious."

"Well, if I faint, I have you here to take care of me."

"Lucky for you," Eleanor pronounced.

After another ten minutes of walking, they reached their special place. They sat down immediately and began untying their shoes and taking off their stockings.

"Oh, it is so beautiful!" Eleanor said happily.

Alaina looked around at the hundred-year-old oak trees, the sunlight flickering through their sheltering leaves, and smiled. It was beautiful, and she felt a peace enter her heart that had been absent many months.

The cool water of the spring splashed along its rocky path into the pool, and Eleanor stuck her feet into the clear water, shivering with the temperature change.

"This feels good, Alaina. Hurry up! Put your feet in!"

Alaina followed her sister's orders, kicking a splash of water in Eleanor's direction.

"Stop that," Eleanor scolded. "We do not want to muddy this pool with a silly water fight." She reached down and flicked a handful of water at her sister, hitting her right in the face.

For the next two minutes water flew in all directions, amid giggles, shrieks, and name-calling. Finally the girls declared a truce and lay back on the grass to catch their breath and dry out.

"Markus Salter asked about you today in Sunday School," Eleanor said lazily.

"Asked about me?"

"Mmm-hmm. He wondered if you'd been invited to the Harvest Ball."

"That's months away!" Alaina scoffed.

"I don't know, maybe he wants to be first in line."

Alaina threw a pebble at her. "Oh, Elly, don't be a goose. And anyway, I was at Sunday School. Why didn't he just ask me in person?"

"Now who's the goose?" Eleanor chuckled. "Markus Salter is afraid of his own shadow."

Alaina sat up, exasperation stamped on her features. "Eleanor Lund! Markus Salter and I have known each other since kindergarten. We have been to several of the same dances, and we have even danced together."

Eleanor just smiled. "But he's never formally asked you to a dance, has he?"

Alaina went to say something, but her mouth just opened and closed.

Eleanor giggled. "See? Markus Salter, the beau."

Alaina found her voice, and another pebble. "Don't be silly. We are friends and only that."

"From your point of view."

"From any point of view." Alaina lay back down to indicate an end to talk about Markus Salter. She fished a small stone from under her back and threw it into the pool. She could never think of Markus Salter as a beau. He was a very nice fellow, and extremely good in science and anything to do with machinery, but they had been friends too long for it to go any further.

Alaina shifted her thoughts to Philomene Johnson and her fascinating trip to Italy. The schoolteacher had returned home the end of July, bringing pictures of the Coliseum, Saint Peter's, and the gardens at Tivoli; and no matter what Daniel Chart said, she *could* see herself touring that magical country—she would just have to go in the wintertime when work on the farm was minimal.

"Isn't this a great Sunday?" Eleanor said, breaking the silence.

"Hmm," Alaina answered dreamily.

"Chicken and dumplings for dinner, a trip to Niagara Falls, and even Pastor Wilton's sermon was sort of interesting."

"Elly!"

"Well, he has that low, rumbling voice that mostly puts me to sleep. I guess I stayed awake today because I didn't agree with what he was saying."

Alaina sat partway up. "How can you not agree with him?"

"I just didn't."

"But, he's been to school. He's studied all those things."

"So?"

Alaina sat up, at a loss for words. She'd never even thought about doubting the pronouncements of a priest or reverend, and here was dutiful little Elly stating flatly that she disagreed with something Pastor Wilton had said. She looked up to see that Eleanor was watching her closely. "So, what couldn't you believe?"

Eleanor put her feet back into the pool, and Alaina could tell she was trying to figure out how to explain her feelings. "He was speaking about the Holy Trinity, and it never makes sense to me. I've tried to see the idea—three in one, God as spirit, Christ as God on earth . . ."

"Well, it's a mystery," Alaina said.

"But it's not. To me, it's not," Eleanor answered, wiggling her fingers in the water. "I see three different people."

"People?"

"Yes."

"But God is spirit, Elly, not a person."

"I know that's what the church teaches."

"Then doesn't that make it true?"

"Does it?"

"Elly!"

"I love the church, I do, Laina. It teaches good things, like God's love for all of us. But, you see . . . that's the problem . . . I've never felt that if a child or some poor person on an island somewhere died without baptism, they wouldn't make it back to God's love, that it's already decided who makes it to heaven and who doesn't."

"But Wesley taught against that. He taught that all could be saved," Alaina countered.

"I know. But . . . Oh, I don't know how to explain it. If Wesley had questions, can't I have questions?"

"About what God is like?"

"Yes."

Alaina's headache was starting to come back. She'd always known her younger sister was smart, but until this moment the depth of her thinking had never challenged Alaina's ability to respond. She looked at Eleanor with a new respect, somehow understanding that the soft coating of childhood had melted before her eyes.

"Have you talked to Father about this?"

"No," Eleanor said, dribbling water onto her toes.

"He'd want you to. He would, Elly. Remember how he always says give everything a chance?"

Eleanor smiled. "That it will stand or fall of its own weight?"

Just then, Samuel Lund's voice came clearly through the grove, calling out his daughters' names. It was such a coincidence that both girls jumped and gave each other surprised looks.

"How odd. I wonder if he felt we were talking about him?" Eleanor asked in an amused tone.

Alaina stood up. "I wonder what he wants?" She circled her hands around her mouth and called out to him. He called back directly, indicating that he was coming to find them. Alaina sat down, placing her feet in the cool water and taking a drink from the waterfall.

"We can share our gingerbread with him!" Eleanor said excitedly, jumping up to find the package.

The serious scholarly thoughts of moments before melted into girlish expectation as Eleanor ran barefooted to meet Father. Alaina sat still, pondering her sister's spiritual insight and questioning her own feelings of spiritual contentment. She had never thought much about the things taught in Sunday School, accepting the stories with the simple faith of a child. And now that she was older, and a practical person, spiritual insights were set aside for everyday living: Would the winter be cold enough for a good crop? Would there be enough rain? Would the summer be too hot? An apple-scented breeze blew through the branches of the oak trees, making the leaves quiver, and playing for a moment with the wisps of hair around her face. She smiled. How could she be such a practical person and a daydreamer at the same time? She was glad for it, however, because daydreaming softened the realities of life.

"Hey-ho, Fancy!" Father called as he entered the bower and caught sight of her.

She held up her hand. "You can only stay if you know the password."

"Password?" Father stopped, and Eleanor moved beside him, winking at Alaina.

"Hmm . . . password, eh? Let's see . . . perhaps . . . Titus?"

Alaina and Eleanor were amazed. "How did you know that?"

Samuel chuckled. "It's been your password for everything since you were little." He ruffled Eleanor's hair and jumped the small creek to sit beside Alaina. "What a perfect spot on a hot Sunday afternoon."

"And we have gingerbread!" Eleanor announced proudly, showing off the small bundle.

"That's why I came. Hand it over!"

Alaina smiled as Elly opened the carry bag and handed Father the biggest piece of cake.

"Here, Laina," Eleanor offered. "You take the smallest piece."

"What?"

"Well, I need the bigger piece because I'm growing more than you."

Alaina laughed. "Maybe you're just greedy."

"Could be," she agreed, taking the bigger piece and sitting by Father.

Alaina looked out over the hillsides of the farm, blanketed with precious apple trees, and felt heaven wrap warmly around her.

"Where's everyone else?" Eleanor asked between bites of cake.

"Mother and Kathryn are napping, James has gone to visit Lois Drakerman, and Nephi and Daniel have taken a ride over to Pine Grove." He finished his gingerbread and took a drink from Niagara Falls. "And I'm here with my two lovely daughters," he added, splashing each with a handful of water.

"Oh, no!" Alaina commanded. "We've already had our water fight."

Father chuckled, sitting down and giving her braid a tug. "Then we'll just sit here in the shade and tell stories." He leaned his back against a gnarled oak tree and removed his hat. "So, what shall we talk about?"

There was a long pause, and Alaina was sure Eleanor was trying to pluck up her courage to talk about her Trinity question.

Father looked at both of them with a puzzled grin. "What's this? Normally, when the two of you are together, you chatter away like magpies."

Eleanor smiled. "I . . . I was just trying to think of the perfect Sunday story, and all I could think about was Miss Johnson's trip to Italy."

Father chuckled. "Well, I think that's a fine topic for Sunday conversation."

"You do?"

"Certainly. Where should we begin?"

Alaina and Eleanor exchanged a look of delight, and their precious time together flowed happily along, encompassing thoughts about cathedrals, artists and creativity, the Sistine Chapel, the Apostle Peter, and even the Italian countryside.

"Would you like to live in Italy?" Alaina asked her father.

"Italy? Hmm. It would mean leaving the farm, wouldn't it?"

"Well, you could grow grapes over there," Alaina teased.

"No. I believe I am content to spend all my days here," he answered, leaning his head back and closing his eyes with a sigh. "How nice for God to give us a day of rest."

Alaina couldn't think of a better time to bring up the subject of Eleanor's apostasy, and motioned for her to talk. Eleanor shook her head, and Alaina motioned again.

"Can I join this game, or is it just for girls?" Father asked, chuckling.

"How do you do that?" Alaina questioned, shaking her head.

"What?"

"See through your eyelids."

Father chuckled again, opening his eyes. "It's a gift you get when you become a parent. Especially when you become the parent of two sneaky girls. So, what's the secret? You want to live in Italy?"

"No!"

"You want to go with Miss Johnson on her next adventure."

"No . . . no . . . it's . . . well . . . Eleanor has a question." Alaina gave her sister a stern look that indicated it was her turn to talk.

"I don't believe in God," Eleanor blurted out.

Alaina blinked in surprise. That's certainly not the way she would have started the conversation. She glanced over at Father, but he was waiting patiently for Eleanor to continue.

"I mean, I believe in God, just not how we've been taught in Sunday School." She hesitated, and Samuel waited. "I mean, there has to be a God because of all the perfection in nature, and the universe, and the Sistine Chapel, but . . . well, I've never been able to see Him as some floating mass of spirit that can be everywhere at once." She stopped again, and Alaina tried to clear her head. She'd never spent much time thinking about it, but she really didn't see God as some floating mass of spirit either.

Father's voice came calmly and encouragingly. "How do you see Him, Miss Eleanor?"

She hesitated. "If we were made in His image, then wouldn't He look like a man?"

"You mean when He made himself flesh as Jesus?"

"No. I don't believe that."

Alaina was certainly glad Mother wasn't here right now, or she'd be dragging Eleanor off for a lecture from Pastor Wilton.

Father sat up a little straighter. "What do you believe?"

"I think Jesus and God are two separate people."

Alaina cringed, expecting Father to offer a stern argument to this blasphemy, but he seemed intent on allowing Elly a wider road to hell.

"You believe They are two people?" he asked calmly. She nodded. "And the Holy Spirit?"

"He's . . . that's . . . well, I'm not sure. He's a separate person, or spirit—maybe just the spiritual essence of God and Jesus . . . of Their love."

Samuel Lund laid his head back against the tree and sighed deeply. "Two people."

Alaina was sure he was trying to figure out a way to save his wayward child—trying to find the words to bring her back to the fold. When she looked at Eleanor's pale face, she knew Eleanor was thinking the same thing.

Alaina started to speak in Eleanor's behalf, but stopped abruptly, seeing something she'd never seen before—a tear running down the side of Father's cheek. She sat staring as he sighed again and looked directly at Elly's face.

"Out of the mouths of babes," he said softly, wiping the tear from his face and smiling warmly at his middle daughter.

"Are you angry with me?" Eleanor asked.

Father shook his head. "No."

"Do you think I'm going to hell?"

Father smiled. "No. I think you're an answer to prayer."

Alaina thought that was a strange thing to say, and Eleanor seemed perplexed by it too, but Samuel Lund wasn't finished saying strange things.

"I think you need to speak to Nephi."

"Nephi?" Eleanor questioned.

"His faith teaches something unique about the Trinity."

Eleanor stiffened. "Made up by Joseph Smith?"

Father chuckled and stood up. "I suppose that's in how you look at it. There's no harm in talk, Elly, only in a closed mind."

Alaina wondered how much "talking" Mr. Erickson had been doing since giving her father the Mormon bible on his birthday. She'd seen the two men on several occasions in earnest conversation, and now she knew it wasn't always about the farm. Surely Father was smarter than to believe any of that hogwash, yet here he was encouraging Eleanor to ask Mr. Erickson to share his beliefs about the biggest mystery of the Christian faith.

Father moved over and held out his hand to help Eleanor up. "He doesn't have horns, you know."

Eleanor narrowed her eyes. "I know that."

Alaina stood on her own, brushing leaves off her skirt and picking up her boots. "But they do have more than one wife."

"Yes indeed, they used to have more than one wife, and I can't imagine it," Samuel quipped. "It's hard enough to handle one woman . . . Could you imagine four or five?" He gave a frightened look that made Eleanor and Alaina laugh.

The sun dropped behind a bank of clouds on the western horizon, flooding the bower with a rich golden light. Samuel turned and looked out across the acres of fruit trees. "God has surely been good to me," he said, his voice thick with emotion.

Alaina wondered if he might cry again, but Samuel Lund put on his hat and spoke firmly to his daughters. "I hear a few chores calling to us before supper's on the table. Shall we get to them?"

Alaina knew there was one word for the difference between city Sundays and farm Sundays, and that was *work*. Some chores had to be attended to—rain, sleet, snow, or Sabbath.

Samuel headed off toward home, with his barefooted daughters following at a slower pace.

Alaina slipped her arm through her sister's. "Are you really going to talk with Mr. Erickson, Elly?"

"I am," she answered. "Father's right. There's no harm in talking."

Alaina stepped around a sticker bush and decided not to put in her two cents' worth. Eleanor wouldn't be taken in by Mr. Erickson's sales pitch. In fact, Eleanor would probably shame the Mormon yokel into silence with her impressive Bible scholarship.

The feeling of peacefulness she'd felt in the bower returned to her as she watched the ginger sun sink lower into the western sky. She called for Father to wait for them, then she and Eleanor raced each other—the winner to be declared Queen of the County Fair.

CHAPTER 10

Alaina had never thrown anything out of anger in her life. Now, in less than two minutes she'd tossed a harness, a currycomb, and a jar of saddle soap. She was angry, frustrated, and sad all at once. She stormed around the barn, flinging out biting words of resentment and causing Titus to stamp and snort. She felt lost and frightened. How could Father do this? He wasn't thinking clearly. Somehow Mr. Erickson had taken away his soul. She hated Mr. Erickson. Why had he come? Alaina kicked the tack box and started crying. She hated to cry. She stepped on the currycomb, snatched it up, and threw it hard against the barn door. It produced a loud, sharp sound, making Titus whinny in fright. A moment later the door was pushed aside, and Father stood framed in the pale morning sunlight. Alaina blinked as brightness poured into the dim interior. She stood shaking—her face smudged with dirt and tears, her fists clenching and unclenching.

"Alaina."

"I don't want to speak with you."

Samuel Lund stood quietly, unmoving as Alaina turned away to hide her tears. Titus made a comforting snuffling sound, which drew Alaina to him. She laid her cheek against his soft muzzle and cried.

The morning had begun normally: braiding Kathryn's hair; early egg-gathering and milking; table setting and bread slicing; the sun rising over the hillsides of the apple orchards, pouring like golden honey through the kitchen window and illuminating the day's possibilities. The family sat together in the same chairs as always, bowing their heads for prayer and thanking God for the goodness of their lives. Over breakfast, Father and James had discussed plans for the day's work. The last of the pears were being picked and sent off to Martell for shipment to San Francisco, and Alaina remembered the feelings of resentment she'd had toward James and Mr. Erickson for their inclusion in the satisfying work of the harvest. She still had those feelings as the plates were cleared from the table and Father brought out the scriptures to read the daily passage. Kathryn groaned and laid her head on the table—the same as every other day. Then came the words that would change everything.

"I'm reading this morning from the Book of Mormon."

Kathryn's head came off the table, and Mother sat as stiff as a statue.

"I have read it over these last few weeks and find it to be an amazing book—a good book."

Alaina looked at Father's large, work-worn hands gently placed on the pages of the open book, and forced herself to stay seated in her chair.

"I will read the words of Alma, an ancient American prophet."

Ancient American prophet? The only ancient people in America were the Indians. Prophets among the Indians? What is this book?

Father began to read, but Alaina heard only droning. Her thoughts were turned toward Nephi Erickson and the sorrow he'd brought into her life. Her feelings about him had softened over the past weeks as she'd watched him work. He was strong and capable, and whatever task Father gave him he took on with pleasure. It was evident that he loved the farm and valued Samuel Lund's goodness. Why then would this quiet outsider give her father a book that would do nothing but cause upheaval and heartache?

Alaina stepped back from Titus, brushing the tears from her face. She was aware that Father stood behind her, waiting for her words. She took a deep breath and turned.

"I wish Mr. Erickson had never come."

Father was silent.

"He's a bad person." She figured that would bring a response from her father, but she saw only a flicker of sadness in his eyes. "That's how I feel."

"You have a right to your feelings."

Alaina's next comment caught in her throat.

"You are an adult, Alaina, and one thing you learn as an adult is, if you want your feelings accepted, you have to accept the feelings of others. Not agree, but accept."

"And you don't think he's a bad person."

"No."

"And you don't think the Book of Mormon is a devil book?"

"No." For some reason Father's quiet replies calmed her.

"Why not?"

"Because I have tested the words and the man, and they have come through true."

"They're not true for me."

"Have you read? Have you tested?"

New tears ran down her cheeks. "No."

Father moved into the barn. "I didn't expect that any of you would understand, but, as a man of conscience, I have to follow where I'm guided."

The meaning of Father's words pressed into her brain. "You're going to join with them?"

"Yes."

"You're going to give up Christ for Joseph Smith?"

"No."

"No?" Alaina felt like screaming, but instead her words came out fast and biting. "No? You're going to give up the goodness of truth for gold bibles and Indian prophets? For a people who were driven out of every place they lived because they believed in a false prophet and polygamy? You're going to give us all up for a stranger who doesn't even want to live with his own family? What does that tell you about his religion?"

Father waited.

Alaina's throat was dry, and there was a tight ache around her chest. She didn't want to talk anymore. She didn't want to cry. And she didn't want the feeling that Father was leaving her.

"I love you, Fancy."

A groan came up from her stomach, and she wished she had something to throw.

Father moved close and took her in his arms. "I'm not giving any of you up. Not my family and not my Lord."

"But they don't believe in Christ."

"Have you read?"

Alaina was silent. The ache was beginning to loosen from around her chest, but her thoughts were jumbled. She shoved the worry away and felt her father's arms around her. She remembered another time when he held her like this. She was twelve. She'd fallen out of an apple tree and broken her arm. There was terrible pain then too.

"Does Mother know?"

"Yes. I've told everyone."

Alaina stepped back, breaking Father's hold. "Was she angry?"

"That's not your business."

Alaina kicked the dirt. "I just don't understand."

"I know."

"Why are you doing this?"

"'Ye shall know the truth, and the truth shall make you free.'"

Alaina's jaw tightened. "You think they have the truth?"

Father didn't answer.

"This church started by Joseph Smith has the truth, and all the other churches that have been around for hundreds of years don't?"

Father looked her straight in the face. "I think they all preach some truth, but I couldn't find answers, Alaina."

"To what?"

"Questions I had."

"Like what?"

"The nature of the Trinity."

"That's Elly's question."

"Yep. Mine too," Father said simply.

"And why would Joseph Smith be able to answer that?"

Father smiled. "I don't know that you're ready for that story."

Alaina looked down at the ground, and Father reached out to take her arm. "I have to do what I think is right, Alaina, and trust that God will work out the rest."

There was a strange silence between them, and Alaina felt betrayed by Father's acceptance of a lie. He had always been her compass, the one she could utterly trust for truth and common sense.

Titus whinnied and shook his head for attention, causing Samuel to look over and smile. "I think someone wants to go for a ride."

Alaina's feelings lifted. At this moment she could think of nothing she wanted to do more than ride up into the foothills.

"I have chores."

"I'll excuse you and Eleanor from chores this morning."

Alaina looked quickly to Titus, not wanting Father to read the emotion on her face. She could sense his worried frustration, but there was nothing she could do to ease it. She had her own demons to fight.

"Everything will be all right, Alaina."

She didn't answer.

He stood quietly for a moment, then turned and left the barn.

Alaina stood still. How could he promise her that everything would be all right? Their world was shattered. She pressed her hands against her eyelids and saw thin slivers of broken glass. She also realized that Mother would never stand for it. She may have held her peace in front of the children, but she was tenacious about her beliefs and would insist that Father give up his ties with this strange religion. She would unmask Mr. Erickson as a charlatan and send him packing. For the first time in many years Alaina admired her mother's stubborn demeanor.

She gave Titus a pat and went to retrieve the things she'd thrown. Eleanor met her at the barn door as she stooped to pick up the currycomb. Her younger sister carried a food pouch, canteen, and Alaina's least favorite straw hat. She held the hat out to Alaina.

"Father says we're to go riding."

Alaina took the hat and wiped the currycomb off on her skirt, leaving a dusty streak. "If you want to," she said hopefully.

"If I want to?" Eleanor took Moccasin's bridle out of Alaina's hand and headed for the stall. "Ninny."

A smile jumped to Alaina's lips. It felt good to have her sister behaving normally. Was she playacting for Alaina's benefit, or was she really that unconcerned with Father's announcement?

Alaina threw the saddle soap and brush into the tack box, and grabbed Titus's bridle off the wall. "Elly?"

"Yep?"

Alaina stood still, fiddling with the leather straps in her hands. There were so many things to ask, she didn't know where to start.

"Alaina, I think we should saddle up and leave before Father changes his mind."

Alaina smiled. Eleanor was right. There was plenty of time to talk when they were on the Carson Road to Miller's Bend.

Before Father changes his mind. As Alaina tightened the cinch on Titus's saddle and fixed the bit in his mouth, she wondered if Father would ever change his mind about this devilish religion. She was sure he'd been blinded by Mr. Erickson's cunning words and ways. Yet it was difficult to attribute such cunning to their quiet farmhand. She pulled Titus's cinch tighter, making him snort. *Well, even the devil can appear as an angel of light.*

Eleanor moved out of the stall with Moccasin's reins in hand. "I brought bread, cheese, and dried pears."

Alaina gave a tug on Titus's reins, and the big horse followed obediently. He gave Alaina a shove, shaking his head and causing his mane to flip. "All right! All right! I'm moving."

"Bossy, isn't he?" Eleanor said, laughing.

"Guess he figures he's been around so long he can do what he wants."

They moved out of the barn, and Alaina pushed the door closed. Puffy clouds were gathering on the western horizon, and a breeze tugged at their braids and skirts.

Eleanor looked up at the clouds overhead as she swung herself into the saddle. "We'll have to watch the weather."

Alaina pulled herself onto Titus's back and secured the chin strap on her hat. "I don't care if it rains buckets." She turned her horse's head toward the eastern track and gave him a gentle nudge with her heels. Half a mile over the crest of the hill, the winding path would meet up with the road to Miller's Bend, where beautiful trees, cooler temperatures, and solitude would welcome the girls. Titus seemed to sense Alaina's excitement, moving off at an eager pace.

"Hey! Where ya going?" It was Kathryn's shrill voice calling from the raspberry bushes at the back of the garden.

Alaina didn't stop, but called over her shoulder, "We have business in Miller's Bend."

Kathryn dropped her pail of raspberries and ran after them. "What business?"

"Important business. Tell Father we'll be back for afternoon chores."

"I want to go!"

"Well, you can't."

They rode on, ignoring Kathryn as she stamped her feet and threw dirt clods at them.

CHAPTER 11

August thunderstorms were rare but not impossible in the Sierra foothills, pelting the ground with big drops of rain and whipping the pine trees into moaning response. Alaina and Eleanor stood with their horses under a canopy of low pine branches, fending off the needles and waiting for the storm to break.

The trip up the mountain had been a sacrament. For an hour neither girl spoke—Alaina working through her sadness and trying to figure out her questions, and Eleanor waiting for her older sister to express her worries about Father's newfound faith, unwilling to force the conversation and not wanting to seem too eager to share the experiences and feelings she'd been having over the past weeks. She'd had several talks with Nephi, and was astonished by the simple clarity of his answers concerning such complex doctrines as the nature of God, baptism of children, and the purpose of eternity. She was equally astonished that he had such knowledge without years of theological training. She had gone to him with an eager thirst for answers, and was grateful that he never dismissed a question as trivial or treated her like a child.

After a time of pleasant riding, Alaina began asking questions. She was not really interested in the doctrine of the Mormon Church, but was more concerned with how Father's acceptance of this strange faith might jeopardize his salvation. Eleanor answered plainly, holding back her own enthusiasm for the message while assuring her sister that Nephi was not a wicked man out to lead Father astray. She pointed out Father's common sense and his deep evaluation of anything spiritual, so that by the time they reached their stopping point, Eleanor felt confident that Alaina was calmer about Father's chances for heaven.

The two sisters sat together in a grove of pines eating their picnic and talking about more lighthearted topics such as travels to Europe, and new wonders from the mail-order catalogue. Reluctant to leave, they tried ignoring the gray clouds gathering overhead, and were caught in a downpour ten minutes into their trek home. Laughing at their own folly, they sheltered in the arms of an enormous pine, waiting for the storm to move east to higher elevations.

"I wonder if Lake Tahoe is as beautiful as they say," Alaina said through the noise of the wind.

"I think it is. Don't you remember the pictures Miss Johnson showed us?"

"Yes, but pictures never really show the true place."

Eleanor shivered as another drop of water ran down her back. "We could ride up there and see for ourselves."

Alaina raised her eyebrows. "Up to Lake Tahoe?"

"Sure. It would only take us three or four days."

"And we could eat chipmunks and wild berries to keep ourselves alive."

"Yep. And if the rain kept up, we'd have plenty of water."

Lightning flashed to the east, followed by a growl of thunder.

Alaina moved closer to her adventurous sister. "And plenty of ways to die."

"Maybe we could get Nephi to guide us." Alaina stiffened at Eleanor's suggestion. "Sorry, Laina. I just meant because he's been there, and . . ."

"It's all right, Elly."

They stood silent after that, waiting for the rain to squeeze down to a drizzle and the wind to stop snapping their skirts. Soon the clouds to the west softened into pearly eggshell, and the last of the rain was snatched up by the tallest branches of the pines. The girls ventured out onto the muddy road, shaking water off their hats and giggling. Alaina felt renewed by the soaking, and grateful for the time to think things through. Now they needed to get home to dry clothing and work. She lifted herself into the saddle as Titus shook his head, scattering water from his mane.

"Hey! I don't need another dousing, you fool horse!" she sputtered, smacking his rump good-naturedly.

Titus headed for the trees, and Alaina pulled him back just before a low branch could dismount her. "Titus, you are a monster!"

Eleanor laughed at the antics of the twosome, turning Moccasin's head toward home and leading the way. "Well, one of us can control our horse."

"Very funny."

Alaina followed Eleanor toward the brightening western sky, feeling confident that even if Father did join with the Mormons, life wouldn't change much. There wasn't a congregation nearby, or other members with whom to socialize, so Sunday worship would remain as always. The dreaded book would be set aside for the harvest and most likely forgotten by November. And, when work slacked off during the winter months, it was only reasonable that Mr. Erickson would be sent packing. Alaina smiled. The fair-haired trespasser may have thrown a few rocks in the pond, but the ripples would soon fade and the water would be calm again.

* * *

The next weeks were filled with work. Unrelenting work. Hundreds of trees were loaded with apples, and the men became slaves to the bounty. Every morning as she fried ham or stirred mush, Alaina would watch through the kitchen window as James and Mr. Erickson lugged empty crates from the barn, loaded them in the wagon, and drove them into the fields. After breakfast the picking began—ladders moved, pouches filled with apples, ladders moved again, crates loaded with fruit and stacked on the wagon. When they ran out of crates, Mr. Erickson or Father made more. One of the three would drive the wagon to Martell twice a week, where the crates were loaded on the train for Sacramento and San Francisco.

The women took care of the livestock, harvested the garden, canned and dried the produce, cooked, cleaned, washed, and mended. Alaina kept her mind out of the orchard by losing herself in the tasks assigned her. Today it was slicing apple rounds for drying. In the somewhat less stifling heat of the barn, she and Elly stood across from each other at the worktable, preparing the fruit. Outside, fifteen large racks, set up on sawhorses, awaited their toil. The girls would expertly core, then slice the apples into thin rounds, which Kathryn would take out and lay on the racks. Laying out the fruit was an easy job for the little princess, but, being a princess, she had to complain about any task given her.

"It's too hot out there!"

"It's hot everywhere," Eleanor replied, not looking up or slowing in her work.

"When can we quit?"

"When we're done."

Kathryn looked over at the waiting crates of apples. "With all those?"

"You're just stalling. Now get busy!" Alaina snapped.

"Why can't I cut?"

Eleanor fixed her younger sister with a motherly stare. "Because we wouldn't want you to slice into your hand and have all the muscles and tendons oozing out, now would we? Not to mention the blood running all over the place."

Kathryn looked like she was going to cry, or throw up, and Alaina turned away to keep from laughing.

"You're not very nice," Kathryn grumbled, coming dejectedly to the worktable and picking up a bowl of apple slices.

"Pshaw," Eleanor said, working away and ignoring Kathryn's frowning face. "I'm nice enough not to want you to lose a finger."

Kathryn stuck out her tongue, turned abruptly, and left the barn. Alaina and Eleanor shared a smile.

"She should be glad I'm not her mother," Alaina said, grabbing more apples out of the crate. "I'd have no patience with her whining and foul temper."

"It will be a hard life for her."

Alaina was again brought up short by Eleanor's compassion. While she was thinking of all the trouble and misery their little sister caused, Eleanor was thinking of the sad life Kathryn had in store for her if she didn't learn kindness and industry.

Alaina sighed and stretched her back. "I wonder how the Robinson family is getting on? I miss going over to their homestead."

Eleanor gave her sister a knowing smile. "You miss seeing Daniel."

Alaina colored. "I do not! I mean, I do, but not just him. I miss the whole family."

"I see."

"Well, I do! Don't you miss our time over there?"

"Of course. Especially Mrs. Robinson's custard . . ."

"Hmm."

". . . And Daniel's soft brown eyes."

"Eleanor Lund! You stop teasing me!"

Eleanor laughed, and dodged the rotten apple Alaina threw at her. "I just think it's time you had a beau."

"Elly! I'm only eighteen."

"Nineteen in November. Getting a bit old, Miss Lund."

"Don't be silly. I am too young for a suitor."

"Lots of girls get married at eighteen."

"Married? I've never even been courted, you silly goose. Besides, Daniel is just a friend."

"Are you sure?"

"Yes."

"Hmm." Eleanor went back to her work. "Well, there's always Markus Salter."

Alaina picked up another rotten apple and aimed it at Eleanor.

"Hey! Are you two playing in here?" Kathryn called out as she came back into the barn.

"No," Alaina said, placing the apple in the garbage pile. "We were just talking."

"About what?" Kathryn asked, plunking down the empty bowl.

"Marriage," Eleanor said simply.

Kathryn looked at Eleanor with a puzzled expression. "Marriage? Is somebody getting married?"

"Alaina."

"She is not," Kathryn argued.

"Well, someday."

Kathryn laughed. "Alaina? She's not gonna get married ever."

"She will too, Kathryn."

"Will not. She doesn't even want to. She'll be just like Miss Johnson, 'cept she won't have any money to travel."

Alaina knew her little sister was just being her petulant self, but the words still hurt, and she wondered how much of it were true.

"All she wants to do is pick apples, and she can't."

Kathryn must have sensed she'd gone too far, because she stepped back several feet, her eyes never leaving Alaina's clouded face.

Eleanor found her voice. "Take those apples outside. Now."

Kathryn heard the warning tone and ran for the door without argument.

"Sorry, Laina. I don't know why I said any of that to her."

Alaina went back to slicing. "Never mind. She's probably more right than wrong."

Eleanor recognized Alaina's pensive demeanor, so held back her words of comfort. The two worked in silence for the next hour, finishing up their task in record time. Kathryn scurried in and out with no more complaining or comment, avoiding eye contact with her two sisters and even putting a bit of effort into her work. When their mother called for dinner, the three were placing the last of the rounds on the racks. It had been a long morning, and Alaina's hands ached like someone had hit them with a hammer. When she went to wash up at the outside pump, she held her hands under the cool water for a long time, holding herself still and taking in the familiar sounds and smells of the farm. She reveled in the sweet scent of the rose-of-Sharon blossoms, water splashing from the holding bucket onto the dry ground, the distant clucking of chickens in their coop. She didn't want to think about change, or a life sometime in the future. *Let me stay surrounded by this moment.*

She heard the kitchen door clap shut, and looked up to see Eleanor coming from the house carrying two tin pails.

"We're to take dinner up to Father and Nephi."

Alaina dried her hands, put on her hat, and took one of the buckets. She lifted the cloth to see what Mother was sending. "Mmm, smells good."

"Chicken," Eleanor answered, heading off toward the groves.

"There's a lot of food here."

"We're to eat with them."

"Really? We never get to eat with them when they're working."

"They're not working the rest of the afternoon."

"They're not?" Alaina stopped. "Father never stops work during harvest. Eleanor Lund, what do you know that I don't know?"

Eleanor turned to her sister. "We're meeting them up at Niagara Falls. Father's getting baptized today."

Alaina stared at her sister as if she hadn't understood the words, her fingers squeezing the wooden handle of the dinner pail, her face draining of color.

"Baptized?"

Eleanor moved closer. "Yes."

"In the Mormon Church?"

"Yes."

"That's not possible. It's . . . it's harvest. There's too much work to do."

"Laina, you knew this was coming."

Alaina stepped back. "No. He was going to change his mind."

Eleanor turned and started walking.

"Are you going to be there?" Alaina called.

"I am."

"Eleanor!"

Eleanor kept walking.

"Elly!"

"What?" Eleanor turned abruptly, her face a wash of anger and pain.

Alaina confronted her. "How can you?"

Eleanor looked steadily at her older sister. "How can I? He's my father and he's a good man. He's chosen this for himself, and I honor him. James and Mother may choose not to be there, but I will be there." She walked to Alaina and yanked the pail out of her hand. "I'll take this. Now you can choose not to be there if you want." She walked away, leaving Alaina smarting with the sting of chastisement.

She thought Eleanor might turn and wave her forward, but the willowy fifteen-year-old was determined in her course. She kept walking, carrying the heavy pails and moving out of sight.

Alaina fought the ache of tears in her eyes. Did she honor her father more than she distrusted this church of false prophets and gold bibles?

She stood still listening to a bird's shrill call and forcing her breathing to calm. She looked down at her boots and willed her feet to move forward. Step by step she followed her sister.

The bower had been their childhood place of dreams. Shimmering green in the early enchantment of spring or wrapped in the golden fantasy of fall, it had been their place of stories and possibilities. Alaina thought of plans and adventures written in the dirt floor or whispered to the leaves. Of the laughter of happy sisters, laughter carried away in unexpected flurries of snow or on the wings of dragonflies. Of young girls with their hair undone from braids, their feet splashing in the cool water of the pond.

"Who knows, Fancy. Things may change. Things change all the time." Alaina knew their bower would never be the same—its innocence and wonder changed forever by Father's choice.

She entered the dim refuge and saw Eleanor moving to Father. He smiled at her and took the burdens out of her hands. Mr. Erickson stood beside their pond talking to a man Alaina had never seen, a tall man with a round face, reddish hair, and wearing a Sunday suit that didn't fit. His shirtsleeves protruded three inches past the dark cloth of the suit, and the pant bottoms showed the top of his boots. Alaina was shocked to see that Mr. Erickson's boots were off and Father's as well, as were their socks. She had never seen her father barefooted before, and was feeling awkward about the odd scene when Father looked up and smiled at her. Eleanor smiled too.

"Come to see me get wet, did ya?"

She moved to him and gave him a hug. Tears sprang into her eyes, and she held him a moment longer, trying to control her emotions. Father seemed to understand, and gave her a squeeze.

"I promise not to grow horns or get more than one wife," he whispered in her ear.

She smiled and brushed the tears away as she looked up into his face. He gave her a wink and turned his attention to the stranger.

"Mr. Bates, these are my daughters—Alaina, my eldest, and Eleanor. Girls, this is Mr. Bates, come all the way from Placerville to help with my baptism."

"Glad to meet both of you," he said, shaking their hands in turn. "Isn't it a banner day? It certainly is."

"When did you get here, Mr. Bates?" Alaina questioned, the thought popping into her head unexpectedly.

"Came up from Sutter Creek about an hour ago. Stayed over at the hotel last night. Very nice place, it certainly is." He reached over and patted Samuel on the shoulder. "Now, Brother Lund, there are just a few more questions I have to ask you, then we can get on with the baptism. If you ladies will excuse us." He and Father moved over to sit on a log at the edge of the trees, leaving the others alone.

Alaina had been avoiding Mr. Erickson since coming into the bower, but now she glanced over and found him watching her intently. She didn't look away, and he didn't either, his face an unreadable mask. His pale blue eyes spoke neither joy nor guilt, while she knew her eyes expressed accusation and loss.

Eleanor took her hand, and Alaina turned. "I'm glad you came." Alaina didn't answer. "Are you all right?"

"No." She looked over at Father and Mr. Bates. "Who is he?"

"I don't know. Someone from the church in Placerville. Maybe he's the minister."

"Branch president," Nephi said, walking over to the girls.

"President?"

"He leads the church in Placerville. Like a minister I guess. Father of the flock."

Alaina thought of Pastor Wilton with his imposing stature and strong rolling voice, and wondered how this gangly man with his silly voice and too-small-suit could gather any manner of congregation.

"And he'll be baptizing?"

Nephi shifted. "Actually, I'll be baptizing."

Alaina was stunned. "You? Are you a minister?"

"No, but I hold the priesthood."

Alaina looked at him as if he were mad. "Where did you study?"

"We don't go to school to get the priesthood. Every young man from the age of twelve—"

"Twelve? You get the priesthood when you're twelve?" She wanted to run over to Father and plead with him not to associate himself with these strange people. She was so wrapped up in her concern that she jumped when Eleanor spoke.

"Alaina, how old was the boy Jesus when He was found preaching in the temple?"

She answered without thinking. "Twelve."

"Twelve. Don't you find that interesting?"

"But, that was Jesus, Elly, not Mr. Erickson, or a bunch of unlearned children."

Eleanor smiled. "And how much schooling did Peter, James, and John have?"

"Are you comparing Mr. Erickson to the holy Apostles?"

"No, Laina, but Jesus blessed them with the priesthood to preach and baptize in His name, and they were unlearned fishermen."

Alaina looked at Eleanor with new eyes, seeing the strength and peace of one well beyond her years. "Do you believe them?"

Eleanor looked over at Nephi. "I do."

Alaina saw tears come into his eyes, and he lowered his head. She suddenly felt like a stranger, alone in her beliefs and understanding. She gripped Eleanor's hand tightly. "Are you being baptized today?"

"No. Not today. I'm not ready."

Father and Mr. Bates stood up and shook hands, and Alaina had no more time to ask questions or protest.

Father came over to Nephi and thumped him on the back. "Well, I guess they're gonna let me in."

Nephi smiled. "I never had a doubt."

Mr. Bates stepped up next to Samuel and looked around at all of them. "Now, let me tell you a little about what we're going to do. First Elder Erickson . . ."

Elder? Alaina was unsure how this new title made her feel.

". . . will take Brother Lund down into the water. In The Church of Jesus Christ of Latter-day Saints we baptize by immersion, just the way Jesus was baptized. After the baptism, Elder Erickson and myself will confirm this good man a member of the Church, and confer upon him the gift of the Holy Ghost. A great gift, it certainly is." He paused and wiped his round face with a handkerchief. "Brother Lund, do you have any questions?"

"I don't think so, Mr. Bates."

Alaina searched her father's face, but he just smiled back innocently as though he'd been getting baptized every day of his life.

"If I could borrow your Book of Mormon, Samuel, I'd like to read a short passage before we proceed."

Father went to a carry sack and brought back the small black book Nephi had given him only a month ago. It looked much used for a book recently received.

"Thank you, Samuel."

Mr. Bates opened the book near the front and thumbed through a few pages. Alaina could tell it was familiar text to him as he found the passage easily.

"I wish to read from Mosiah chapter eighteen, but first a little background. Alma the preacher escaped from the court of the wicked King Noah and went out into the wilderness to teach."

Alaina's mind wandered, as she judged it to be a very weak sermon already, and wondered if "King Noah" was the prophet Noah of the Old Testament.

"I'll begin reading with verse five." He dabbed at his face and stood straight. "Now, there was in Mormon a fountain of pure water, and Alma resorted thither, there being near the water a thicket of small trees . . ."

Alaina looked around. Except for bigger trees, their bower could be that place.

"And it came to pass that as many as believed him went thither to hear his words . . ."

Father, Eleanor, Mr. Erickson.

". . . Yea, all were gathered together that believed on his word, to hear him. And he did teach them, and did preach unto them repentance, and redemption, and faith on the Lord."

These sound like words from the Bible.

". . . And now, as ye are desirous to come into the fold of God, and to be called his people, and are willing to bear one another's burdens, that they may be light; yea, and are willing to mourn with those that mourn; yea, and comfort those that stand in need of comfort, and to stand as witnesses of God at all times and in all things, and in all places that ye may be in, even until death, that ye may be redeemed of God . . ."

What a perfect description of Christian faith. Alaina frowned. *But Mormons don't believe in Christ.*

". . . Now I say unto you, if this be the desire of your hearts, what have you against being baptized in the name of the Lord, as a witness before him that ye have entered into a covenant with him, that ye will serve him and keep his commandments, that he may pour out his Spirit more abundantly upon you?"

Father looked over at Mr. Erickson.

"And now when the people had heard these words, they clapped their hands for joy, and exclaimed: This is the desire of our hearts."

There was a sweet stillness in the bower that wrapped itself around Alaina's heart. She had never heard the scriptures read with such loving simplicity, and she marveled that she had thought Mr. Bates's voice silly.

Mr. Erickson moved down into the crystal pool and Father followed. They smiled at each other as Nephi took her father by the wrist and then raised his right arm into the air. His voice came clear and strong. "Samuel Lund, having been commissioned of Jesus Christ, I baptize you in the name of the Father, and of the Son, and of the Holy Ghost. Amen." He put his right hand on Samuel's back and lowered him into the water.

Again the simplicity touched her, and when her father came out of the water, there was a rush of emotion that made tears jump into her eyes. She looked over at Eleanor and saw that she was crying too. Father stood for a moment, his eyes wide with wonder, then, with a whoop, he gave Nephi a hug around the waist, picking the sturdy young man off the ground. He put Nephi down, and turned his attention to his laughing daughters. Before they knew it, Father was out of the pool and hugging both in a wet embrace. Alaina didn't care if he was baptized. It was a good moment—a good feeling.

Mr. Bates came over to shake Father's hand as Nephi climbed out of the pond. Alaina moved out of Father's embrace and went to him. He looked at her uneasily, but she extended her hand.

"Thank you, Nephi," she said stiffly. "That was . . ."

He took her hand and held it between both of his, making her forget what else she was going to say. He was looking at her as no one had ever looked at her. She was also aware that he still held onto her hand. When Eleanor approached with a blanket, he let go and busied himself with wringing out his shirt.

"Here's a blanket, Elder Erickson," Eleanor said, smiling. She took his arm, her happiness fading into reverence. "That was very powerful. You were . . ."

He lowered his head and concentrated on wrapping the blanket around himself. "It really doesn't have anything to do with me."

"Well, it has *something* to do with you," she said with a grin.

Samuel Lund came over to the group, rearranging his blanket as he came. "I feel like a baby in this thing!" His face brightened. "I guess I am a baby! Newborn and clean!"

The three laughed at his bright expression, and for the first time in a long time, Alaina saw no tiredness in his features.

"Mr. Bates says it's time for the confirmation. You girls are to sit on the log over there," Samuel said, and he winked at them as they all moved over to the edge of the bower. The afternoon sunlight played its way into the grove, dappling the ground with brightness. Father handed Eleanor his blanket, and Alaina reached out and took Nephi's. The girls sat on the log, watching with interest as Father kneeled down, Nephi and Mr. Bates standing on either side of him. They laid their hands on Father's head, and after a moment Mr. Bates spoke.

"Samuel Lund, by the power of the holy Melchizedek Priesthood which we hold, we lay our hands upon your head and confirm you a member of The Church of Jesus Christ of Latter-day Saints, and say unto you, receive the Holy Ghost."

Alaina felt a tingle move through her arms and into her fingertips. She looked quickly at Eleanor, who smiled and took her hand. The minister went on to give her father a blessing that seemed to come from heaven itself. *What is this church?* Alaina had come to the bower full of sorrow and anger, yet now she felt peace. When the blessing ended, she watched her father stand and shake the hands of the two men and thought it was probably the deep love she had for Father that made her trust his decision.

Samuel came over and gathered her in his arms. "I'm glad you were here."

"I still don't understand, but I love you."

He gave her a squeeze. "Well, that's good."

Eleanor came to them, and he held her close as well.

"I guess I'm on the path now, Miss Eleanor."

"An infinitely fine path, Brother Lund."

Father chuckled and picked up his blanket. "And now," he said, including everyone, "should we eat dinner while Nephi and I dry off?"

"I'm as hungry as Titus," Eleanor announced.

"Oh dear! Then there may not be enough for the rest of us," Father kidded.

Alaina laughed at her dear ones and went to get the food pails. She looked over her shoulder to see Nephi rewrapping the blanket around him and running his hand through his hair. The feelings and notions she had about him were a jumble. On the one hand she knew he was a fine person who loved the farm and cared deeply for her father, but on the other hand there were too many unanswered questions about his background. The mysterious reason that had sent Mr. Nephi Erickson into their lives needed to be unraveled before she could decide if she truly trusted him.

She straightened her back and walked over to the chattering group of believers, bringing food and a renewed dose of skepticism.

CHAPTER 12

"Again, the devil taketh him up into an exceeding high mountain, and sheweth him all the kingdoms of the world, and the glory of them; And saith unto him, All these things will I give thee, if thou wilt fall down and worship me." Pastor Wilton leaned over the pulpit, fixing the congregation with a stern gaze. "All the kingdoms of the world—all the wealth of nations. Silver and gold bibles . . ."

Alaina jerked in her seat. *Did he say gold bibles?*

". . . the glory of kingdoms. For what, my friends, would you sell your soul? For what would you fall down and worship the devil?"

Alaina looked over at her mother, who was nodding in agreement, then past her to Eleanor, but her sister was standing up and moving down the row.

"Elly! Where are you going?" Alaina hissed.

Eleanor didn't stop.

"The devil can send forth false prophets and false bibles."

Father reached over and took Alaina's hand. She looked at him and he smiled. In his hand was the Book of Mormon that Mr. Erickson had given him. *He brought that book into church?* Alaina looked up to find Pastor Wilton pointing at her. She turned in her seat to search for Eleanor and found her standing next to Nephi at the back of the chapel, motioning for her to come out. Someone was calling her name, but Elly's lips weren't moving. How odd.

"Alaina. Alaina." Someone was shaking her arm. She looked over to see Joanna Wilton frowning at her. "You dozed off, silly goose."

Alaina blinked and tried to clear her mind. Where was she? She looked up to see Pastor Wilton in his preaching robes. *I fell asleep in church, sitting right next to the pastor's daughter!* She sat up straighter and took off her gloves, fanning her face with them.

"Marvel not at this: for the hour is coming, in the which all that are in the graves shall hear his voice, And shall come forth; they that have done good, unto the resurrection of life; and they that have done evil, unto the resurrection of damnation."

Joanna sighed and took Alaina's hand.

Pastor Wilton was preaching a strong sermon on the deception of the devil. It was the Sunday after Father's baptism, and Alaina wondered if the good minister's words were inspiration, or worry over a dwindling flock. She looked over at Eleanor who smiled her "secret smile," and went back to listening intently. Elly's face was such a contrast to Joanna's, which looked as if she were in mourning. Indeed, when the service ended and they were moving out of the chapel, her friend couldn't wait to confess her melancholy.

"My heart is breaking for you, Alaina. I thought Mr. Erickson was a decent fellow," Joanna said.

Alaina smiled. "He is a decent fellow."

Joanna pulled her away from the other worshipers exiting the church. "How can you say that? He tricked your father into leaving the truth."

Eleanor, who was passing by, stopped at Joanna's side. "Joanna Wilton, you know my father. He doesn't get tricked into anything."

Joanna gave her a dismissive glance. "You obviously don't know the power of the devil, Eleanor Lund."

"And you do?"

Joanna narrowed her eyes at the slender girl. "I'm the daughter of a minister, and as such I've heard many tales of wickedness and false teaching."

Eleanor gave her a scathing look. "Well, none of that has to do with my father, or Nephi Erickson."

"You are too young to grasp how awful this is," she answered, turning her attention back to Alaina and effectively snubbing Eleanor's response.

If Mother hadn't come up at that moment, Alaina was afraid Eleanor would have said something drastic, or at least embarrassing.

"Girls, we've been invited to the pastor's home for dinner. Please keep Kathryn with you."

"Yes, ma'am. Where's James?" Alaina asked.

"He's gone off with a friend from school. I will see you at the pastor's home in one hour. Please be punctual."

"Yes, ma'am."

Mrs. Lund turned and moved back into the chapel to help straighten hymnbooks.

The three girls stood in awkward silence, watching the released congregation milling about in front of the church. Markus Salter started to come over to say hello, then changed his mind and waved. Alaina and Eleanor waved back; Joanna only smiled.

"Why don't we take a walk by the creek?" Joanna offered. "It may be a bit cooler."

"What a good idea," Eleanor answered, knowing that Joanna did not intend for her or Kathryn to tag along.

"Well, I . . ."

Alaina jumped into the fray. "What a good idea! Come on, we'll find a shaded spot and dunk our feet!" She started toward Badger Road, but Joanna held her ground. "Alaina, I wanted to talk to you."

"Of course we'll talk! Come on, silly."

Joanna stood a moment longer, then grudgingly followed the departing sisters.

A walk by the creek was a good idea. The oak trees would provide welcome shade, and the sound of water tumbling over the rocks might distract their disagreement. A quarter of a mile from town the four girls found a secluded spot where they could take off their shoes and socks, hitch up their skirts, and go wading. Kathryn wandered in the shallows looking for tadpoles, Eleanor sat on a rock making reed bracelets, and Alaina practiced skipping stones. Joanna's frowning expression softened into its familiar gaiety, and worry over happenings beyond their control gave way to cool water and friendship. When Joanna did bring up the subject of Samuel Lund's baptism, her tone held none of its earlier drama.

"You know, your father came to see my father right after the baptism."

Alaina looked up. "Did he?"

"The day after. He was on his way to Martell and stopped with the news."

Alaina smiled. "Bet your father was shocked."

"We all were. I mean it's not like going back to being a Presbyterian, is it?"

"No."

"He seemed glad about it . . . the baptism."

"He is."

Joanna pressed her lips together, and Alaina could tell she was trying hard not to blurt out some call to repentance. Finally, Joanna's desire for information drove her back to the conversion.

"And Mr. Erickson did the baptizing?"

"Yes."

"But he's not a minister, is he?"

Alaina looked to Eleanor for help.

"He's an elder," Eleanor said simply.

"What does that mean?" Joanna asked.

"He holds the priesthood. All worthy men in the Mormon Church have the priesthood."

"All the men? Why would they all need the priesthood?"

Eleanor shrugged, and Joanna pressed her point. "If they all have the priesthood, then who leads the congregation?"

"One man called a branch president or bishop."

"And where is he schooled?"

"He's not."

Joanna's eyebrows lifted. "He's not schooled?"

"No," Eleanor answered, throwing her reed bracelet into the water and watching its journey.

"And the people pay this unschooled minister?"

"They're not paid."

Joanna's lifelong perceptions of ministering were so shaken she couldn't speak. She stood watching the creek water flow past in swirls and bubbles. Her father worked for God and was paid for his labor. He was a man of intelligence who had gone to school many years to train for the ministry, for the honor to baptize, and preach, and shepherd his flock. And now, her best friend's father had joined with a sect that had no connection with the true followers of Christ, who believed the strange teachings of a man who called himself a prophet, and who had no real ministers. She shivered, even with the heat of the day.

"We should get back for dinner," she said finally.

Alaina dropped the rest of her stones into the water. "Joanna, I know how you're feeling. I felt the same way. It's a very strange religion."

Joanna looked at her straight on. "It is, Alaina, and I grieve for your father's choice."

Eleanor stiffened, and Alaina held her arm. "I know. There are many things I don't understand . . . many things I question, but I was there when he was baptized." Emotion caught in her throat as feelings of that day washed over her. "I was there, Joanna, and it was peaceful and powerful."

Joanna looked long into her friend's eyes, then turned and walked to the creek bank. "We'd better hurry, or we'll be late."

The afternoon sun was strong, making the girls squint as they came out from the shade of the oak trees. August had been hot and dry, but September was hot, dry, and dusty. A pestering breeze blew grit into their eyes and noses, forcing them to pull their hats low over their faces.

"I hate September!" Joanna complained. "I think it's the worst month of the year!"

"I had a dream once that you were married in September," Alaina said, only remembering at that moment.

"You did not."

"I did!"

"I would never get married in September!" Joanna stated.

Alaina laughed. "You were wearing a white dress with yellow rosebuds."

Joanna's face brightened. "Well, that was nice. Who was I marrying?"

"I don't remember."

"Probably Jim Peterson," Eleanor put in.

Joanna made a face. "Was I at the church?"

"No, you were at our house . . ." She hesitated. "And you ran away."

"I ran away?"

Eleanor laughed out loud. "Probably took one look at Jim Peterson in a Sunday suit, and headed for the hills."

"Eleanor Lund, you hush!" Joanna chided. She turned back to her friend. "Why did I run away?"

"I don't know. And then . . . I think I left. I went out into the orchard with Father." Alaina intentionally left out the part where Markus, Daniel, and Nephi had given her flowers. That part still unsettled her.

"You left me?" Joanna was wounded. "You left me on my wedding day?"

Alaina shrugged. "Maybe I came back. I don't remember it all. But it was only a dream."

"Well, it was a stupid dream. I'd never get married in September."

Alaina and Eleanor laughed at Joanna's serious pronouncement, and their infectious behavior soon had her giggling.

The bells in the Methodist tower signaled noon, and immediately the friends stopped laughing, lifted the hems of their dresses, put one hand atop their hats, and ran for Joanna's house.

Alaina knew that she and Eleanor would get a severe scolding were Mother to see them running in such a boyish fashion, but she also knew the icy treatment Mother inflicted on those who were tardy.

The girls came into the back porch breathless and spirited from their race, jostling each other as they removed hats and brushed dust from their skirts. Savory smells came from the kitchen to greet them, and Joanna hurriedly pumped water into the utility sink so they could clean up.

"Mmm . . . Dinner smells good," Kathryn said, washing her hands vigorously.

"Roasted chickens with stuffing. I helped Mama prepare them this morning."

"What else?" Eleanor asked.

"Elly, that's not polite," Alaina chided.

"Well, I'm hungry."

Joanna smiled. "Sweet corn, beans, mashed potatoes, cabbage slaw, biscuits, and apple Jonathan."

Alaina laughed at the expression of wonder on Eleanor's face. "Satisfied, you greedy thing?"

Eleanor nodded. "I'm surprised your mother didn't make us stay to help, Joanna."

Joanna dried her hands and passed the cloth to Alaina. "I . . . I think the grown-ups wanted to talk."

Alaina knew instantly what the talk was about and inwardly bristled at the judgments being made about Father behind his back. Elizabeth Lund was sternly faithful to her church, and her feelings about Father's baptism were obvious. Several times at night Alaina overheard Mother insisting that Mr. Erickson be sent away before he deceived anyone else. Father had answered quietly but firmly that Mr. Erickson would be staying, and that no one had been deceived.

"I think they're planning a prayer vigil to bring your father back to the fold," Joanna stated, kindness coating her words like syrup.

Alaina came back from her thoughts to stare blankly into her friend's face. Eleanor had gone quiet after Joanna's announcement, her smile fading into a reflective grimace, and Alaina found she'd lost the appetite she had only moments before. In fact, she wanted nothing more than to go back home and sit with Father in the orchard and talk.

"Shall we?" Joanna asked, smoothing her hair and gesturing toward the kitchen.

Kathryn pushed past the other girls, stepping on Alaina's toe as she went.

"Kathryn! Get back here!" Alaina warned.

"I can go first. I'm the youngest."

Alaina hesitated a moment, but good manners turned her and Eleanor into sheep, and they followed the pastor's daughter obediently.

"I don't feel much like eating," Alaina whispered to her sister.

"Well, I do," Elly replied. "I'm going to eat everything in sight, but I promise not to enjoy it."

CHAPTER 13

Kathryn was in bed with a sore throat, making the most of the chance to complain loudly and order her older sisters about. Alaina had just finished securing the wool-flannel cloth around Kathryn's neck, and was making her escape to the door when Kathryn declared loudly, "It's too tight!"

"It is not."

"It smells."

"That's the poultice."

"I hate it! What's in it?"

"Lard, turpentine, and coal oil."

"It's awful! I won't wear it!"

Alaina sighed and turned back to her cranky sibling. "You will wear it."

"Mother won't make me."

"Mother is the one who made it for you."

Kathryn shut her mouth on her next words, but her eyes filled with tears. Tyrant or not, she did look miserable, and Alaina felt a twinge of compassion. "Kathryn, I'm sorry you're not feeling well. I'll bring you some sewing cards before I start my other chores."

Kathryn wiped her eyes on the sleeve of her nightgown. "Will you?"

Alaina nodded. "And maybe some tea."

Kathryn smiled meekly. "Thanks, Laina."

Alaina moved out into the hallway, amazed at her own patience. Maybe she was growing up—after all, she would be nineteen in six weeks. Was that it? Perhaps it was the cooler weather. Several unexpected rainstorms had come the last part of September, calming the dust and the temperature. Actually, if she were honest with herself, she'd have to credit her mollified spirit to the slowing harvest, and the fact that the ache of envy she'd felt for the gatherers was unbinding itself from her feelings.

She tapped lightly on Mother and Father's bedroom door, knowing no one would be inside but obeying the caution which was never set aside. She moved into the room and over to the toy box to retrieve Kathryn's sewing cards. She smiled as she lifted the lid, opening up childhood memories: a soft clown doll with painted tears, a small stuffed dog with scruffy fur, Wonder Books, tops, James's baseball, a checkers set with missing checkers, and finally, at the bottom, the sewing cards. She lifted them out, and was surprised to find a book underneath—a small green book, the cover free of any picture or marking. As she reached to bring it out, she tried to remember a time when she'd handled it or read it as a child. No, she'd never seen this book before. She had a sudden feeling of wrongdoing, and was about to replace the book when curiosity won out. She opened the cover warily, listening for any footfall on the stairs. The pages at the back of the book were blank ivory sheets, but as she flipped through to the front, a careful penmanship showed itself. Alaina had never seen much of Father's handwriting, but recognized it at once. These weren't ledgers or numbers concerning the running of the farm, but the thoughts and feelings of her father. She was fascinated with the discovery, and would not have felt it more a treasure if she'd found a leather pouch filled with gold nuggets.

She turned the pages unhurriedly, but making sure her eyes didn't linger long enough to read any of the sentences, only catching a word or date here and there. Near the end of the writing, she saw the date July 4, 1913. How well she remembered that day, and she found herself desperately wanting to know what Father had been feeling. She took a deep breath, removed her hand from covering the page, and read.

July 4, 1913

> *Gave Alaina the news today that she would not be helping with the harvest. She took it well, though it grieves both our souls. She is a wise steward and could run this farm if need be.*

The words went on, but Alaina didn't care for any other words. She closed the book with a benediction, and gently put it back in the bottom of the toy box.

When she returned to the sick room, she found Kathryn asleep, her breathing harsh, her face chalky white. Alaina laid the sewing cards on the side table and carefully freed Kathryn's arm from a tangle of linens. The little patient moaned, but didn't wake.

Alaina looked out the window to the apple trees on the hillside. *She is a wise steward and could run this farm if need be.* Emotion rose quickly in her chest, making her catch her breath.

"Laina?" Eleanor said softly at the open door. "Mother wants to know if you're finished."

Alaina turned and put her finger to her lips. She smoothed the bed covers and moved to meet Eleanor in the hallway, closing the door behind them.

"She needed extra tending."

"When doesn't she? At least she's sleeping now."

"That will be good for her," Alaina said softly.

"Are you all right?"

"What do you mean?" Alaina asked, thinking Eleanor might be perplexed by her newly found compassion.

"You look flushed."

"I do?"

"Let me feel your forehead."

Alaina smiled as her younger sister played nurse. "Well, your head isn't warm."

"Of course it isn't. I feel fine. It's just a bit stuffy upstairs."

Eleanor took her arm. "Then it's off for our next chore."

"Which is?"

"Reorganizing the root cellar!"

Alaina laughed at Eleanor's enthusiasm. "Only you would think that a pleasant chore."

"Well, it will be cooler anyway."

The girls were on their way downstairs when they heard the rattle of a wagon nearing the house.

"Who's that?" Eleanor questioned.

"Don't know, but it can't be Father. He's not going to Martell until tomorrow."

The sisters shared a quick smile, then raced out onto the front porch just as Daniel Chart pulled his horse to a stop in front of the house.

"Morning, ladies," he said, tipping his hat.

"Daniel! What are you doing here?" Alaina asked, surprised.

"I came for breakfast."

Eleanor shaded her eyes against the sun. "Sorry, that was hours ago."

"Well, maybe I'll just stay for dinner."

"Who invited you?"

"Elly!" Alaina scolded. She knew her sister was joking, but she felt uncomfortable with the idle banter.

Daniel, on the other hand, was enjoying it immensely. "Actually, if *you're* cooking, Miss Eleanor, I think I'll be heading home."

"Can't wait to see the tail end of your horse, Mr. Chart."

Daniel fixed the lithe young woman with a bemused grin. "You Lund women are full of surprises."

Both girls started laughing, and Eleanor moved out to give the horse a rub. "To what do we owe the pleasure of your company, Mr. Chart?"

Alaina was speechless. She had never known her sister to act this way around men.

"Lumber."

Alaina turned from staring at Eleanor. "Lumber?"

"Yep. My dad sent over some end-piece lumber from our house-building. Thought your father could use it for crates."

"How nice," Alaina answered, looking into the back of the wagon.

"That is nice," Eleanor added. "Maybe you will get an invitation to dinner."

At that moment the door opened, and Mrs. Lund came out onto the front porch. She glanced briefly at her daughters, then up to Daniel.

"Mr. Chart. Is there something I can do for you?"

Alaina saw a respectful mask cover the good-natured smile as Daniel sat tall to address Mrs. Lund.

"I brought over some lumber for Mr. Lund, ma'am."

"Did we purchase this?"

Daniel hesitated. "No, ma'am. They're end pieces my father sent over for crates."

"I see," Mother said, moving to inspect the offering.

Alaina thought for one horrifying moment that Mother was going to refuse the gift and send Mr. Chart away in shame, but good manners dictated otherwise.

"Thank your father, Mr. Chart. You may take the lumber to the barn and unload it there."

"Yes, ma'am."

"Alaina, did you finish with Kathryn?"

"Yes, ma'am. She's sleeping."

"Well, that's good. Thank you."

Alaina saw relief fill her mother's face, and she realized that Kathryn's behavior was a burden Mother carried with stoic acceptance. She would have pondered more on Mother's burdens, but Daniel started the wagon to the barn, and Elly ran alongside calling out to her. "Come on, Laina! Race you to the root cellar."

Mother moved to the edge of the porch. "Eleanor Lund, stop running!"

"I can't help it, Mother! I'm just so excited to get busy on the root cellar, my feet won't stop!" She did a funny little step and kept running. "Come on, slow poke!" she called to Alaina. "I'm going to be Queen of the County Fair!"

Alaina glanced at Mother and followed after at a fast walk. She looked over guardedly to watch Daniel, noting that his gaze and smile never left Eleanor's spirited form. A momentary twinge of jealousy snaked its way into her head, a thought Alaina shook out like an old dust rag. She chided herself. Daniel was caught up in Elly's sunshine, that precious gift of spirit she possessed to lighten even the darkest day. How could she fault him for that? Alaina looked at her racing sister and smiled. A wise child soul, that's what she was, who would probably be running and skipping at eighty.

Daniel pulled back on Angel's reins, slowing the rig and allowing Alaina to catch up. "Good morning, Miss Lund."

"Good morning, Daniel."

He smiled.

"It was nice of your father to think of us."

"Oh, we think of you all the time," he said with a nod.

Alaina looked down at her boots.

"My father misses your visits to the homestead," Daniel continued.

"He does?"

"He misses your father's company."

"I'm surprised he didn't deliver the lumber himself then."

"Well, it's a very busy time right now."

Alaina chuckled. "Yes, I know. So glad he could spare you."

"Whoa, Angel," Daniel said, pulling the horse to a stop in front of the barn. "Are you?"

"What?"

"Glad he could spare me?"

Alaina swallowed. She had never had a conversation like this with a man, and she was suddenly aware of her plain work dress and unkempt hair. Her breath caught in her throat, but she forced herself to look straight into his brown eyes. "I've missed you."

Her candid answer seemed to relax him, and he smiled. "I've missed you too."

With those words, Alaina felt like the Queen of the County Fair—and she hadn't even been running.

Daniel climbed down from the wagon as Alaina went to open the barn door. She saw that there were only a couple dozen crates left, so Father would be glad for the wood. She went back out to the wagon where Daniel was loading his arms with slats.

"Can I help?"

"Sure. If you'll pile 'em on, I'll tell you when."

He held out his arms, palms up, and Alaina stacked on the wood. After accepting almost as much weight as Father could carry, Daniel said, "Whoa," and moved off to the barn. Alaina walked beside him and showed him where to stack the wood. After five more loads, they were finished.

Daniel wiped his face on his sleeve and grinned at Alaina. "Thanks for helping."

"Of course. Anything to keep myself out of the root cellar."

His grin broadened. "You'd rather have sky and wide open spaces."

"I would."

"Me too. I love working in the fields." Alaina lowered her head, and Daniel immediately saw his blunder. "Sorry, Alaina."

"It's all right."

"No it's not! You ought to be able to work anywhere you'd like."

Alaina looked at him gratefully. "Well, one good thing has happened since I'm not in the orchard."

"What's that?"

"James is."

Daniel laughed and grabbed his canteen out of the wagon.

"Oh, here," Alaina said, reaching for it. "Let me get you some water."

"Wonderful. I'll bring Angel along for a drink too."

They walked in companionable silence, enjoying each other's presence and energy. Alaina liked the quiet between them. To her it meant a true friendship and not a mere association dependent on ceaseless chatter. It was only when Alaina was filling his canteen that Daniel found his voice.

"How is your father?"

Alaina stopped pumping as images of her father's tired face and hunched shoulders paraded themselves in her mind's eye. "He's fine—tired, but who isn't this time of year?"

"And he's truly joined himself with the Mormons?"

Alaina stood still, her fingers gripping the pump handle. *Ah, here's the real reason for asking about Father. Poor Samuel Lund following in the footsteps of a false prophet.* She calmed her thoughts. *No, Daniel would never think ill of Father.* Alaina knew he admired her father's lack of guile and steady character. She grinned at Daniel's worried look.

"Are you upset with me for asking?" he asked.

"No." She handed him the canteen.

"It's just that I'm curious about it, Alaina."

"I know." She picked up the bucket to fill it for Angel. "You could always ask the man himself."

Daniel smiled. "I might."

"Father's told me some things since his baptism—times when we were out feeding chickens, or milking, or brushing down the horses—but I can't make much sense of it."

The water splashed into the bucket, and Angel moved forward eagerly. Daniel watched the mare for a moment, then turned back to Alaina. "So, what does he see in their doctrine?"

Alaina dried her hands on her apron and shrugged. "He says they have answers."

"Isn't that what other religions have?"

"He says they have different answers."

"Concerning?"

"Baptism of children, priesthood authority, the nature of God."

Daniel stood staring at her as though a unicorn had just jumped from her mouth. "The nature of God? What do you mean?"

"What He looks like. The relationship between the members of the Trinity."

Daniel's eyes narrowed. "What He looks like? How can they know about that?"

Alaina hesitated, searching his face for sincerity. "Because their first prophet, Joseph Smith, says he saw Him."

"Saw Him? You mean saw God?"

She nodded. "And Jesus."

"Saw Them?"

"Yes."

"In a dream?"

"No, actually saw Them."

"When was this?"

"Around 1820."

Daniel was shaking his head. "Less than a hundred years ago a man claims to have seen . . ."

"A boy, actually."

"A boy?"

"Joseph Smith was only fourteen or fifteen when he had his vision."

"Fifteen?" Daniel was pacing back and forth. "A boy of fifteen says he has this amazing vision, finds a gold bible, starts a church, and people believe him?"

Alaina was silent.

Daniel stopped pacing and looked her straight in the face. "And your father believes?"

She nodded.

"What do you think?"

"I don't know."

Mother came out onto the back porch, shading her eyes and staring in Alaina's direction.

Alaina waved, knowing her mother was directing her to work.

Mrs. Lund went into the house, and Alaina looked back to Daniel, his expression filled with a hundred questions. She laughed. "Talk to Father, Daniel. He'll be glad to answer your questions."

Daniel's face relaxed, and he smiled. "Oh, you can be sure of it. After harvest is over, I plan on a long talk." Angel whinnied and shook her head. "All right, we're going," he said, patting the horse's shoulder.

Alaina sighed. "And I'd better get back to my chores."

A warm breeze blew a wisp of hair into Alaina's face, and Daniel brushed it back. "We wouldn't want you to get into trouble." He turned with a chuckle and climbed into the wagon.

She shaded her eyes so she could look at him. "Tell your mother and father I said hello."

"Will do." He picked up the lines and gave Angel the command to walk on. The horse started forward, and Alaina walked beside the wagon, her hand on the sideboard.

Daniel looked at her with a serious expression. "Oh, will you do something for me?" he asked.

"If I can."

"Think about going with me to the Harvest Ball."

Alaina stopped dead in her tracks, but the wagon kept on moving. Daniel turned to look at her, a sassy gleam in his eye. He made a kissing sound to Angel, and the horse broke into a trot. Alaina stood watching the wagon move off their property, the warm sun filling her from head to toe.

Was it possible to be Queen of the County Fair twice in one day?

CHAPTER 14

Mending had to be the dreariest of all the dreary household tasks, and though Alaina's fingers were slender, she could never quite get the feel for the needle, thread, and cloth. But it was a good day for mending, had she enjoyed the activity; gray clouds sat low over the hills, sending down periodic wisps of fog to swirl among the apple trees, and rain threatened with each distant grumble of thunder. October weather was fickle, never making up its mind between wet or warm.

Alaina sat in the parlor, an oil lamp lit nearby, darning socks. A toe was out of one of her ivory stockings, and she was trying to mend it as neatly as possible so she wouldn't have a bothersome lump at the end of her shoe. An errant wind rattled the porch roof and shook the limbs of the rose-of-Sharon bush, scattering the last of the dead leaves. Alaina pulled through another stitch and dropped the needle, flexing a cramp out of her hand. How long had she been at this task? She looked over at the mending basket and found it half full. She sighed, stretched her back, and picked up the needle. From a distance came a high screeching sound that shot a shiver down her back. She stood quickly, dropping the mending onto the floor and kicking the basket as she moved to the front door. She met Mother at the bottom of the stairs.

"What was that?" Mother exclaimed.

"I don't know. Perhaps Titus is afraid of the oncoming storm."

"Go check on him."

Alaina picked up her shawl and opened the door.

"Are your sisters back from taking dinner to your father?"

"No, ma'am."

"You go find them. I'll check on the horses."

"Yes, ma'am."

Alaina raced out of the house, her heart pounding in her chest. Why was she so upset over an unexplained sound? It was probably nothing more than an owl frightened out of its daytime nap or an animal being slaughtered in the wood. She ran toward the southeast orchard, knowing that was where the men were working. *And why was Mother so upset?* She flinched as a crack of lightning split the air, and she heard again the high scream. She felt the blood pound into her neck and she stumbled and fell to her knees. A horse crashed out of the orchard and onto the road. It was Friar Tuck carrying James and Kathryn, who was hitting James on the back and screaming. The horse pounded toward her, and suddenly Alaina was afraid James hadn't seen her. She scrambled to the side of the road and yelled as he approached.

"James!"

James jerked Friar Tuck to a stop, but the horse would not stand still. Kathryn continued to sob and scream.

"Where's Mother?" James asked in a panic.

"At the house."

Kathryn was hysterical. "Let me go! Let me go back!"

"What's happened?"

"Father. He's fallen," James snapped.

Fallen?

"I'm going for Dr. McIntyre."

"James, I wanna be with Father! Let me down!" Kathryn wailed.

"Kathryn, shut up!" James kicked Friar Tuck, and the horse jumped forward. Another scream from Kathryn was ripped away as the forceful animal shot toward the house.

Alaina turned and ran in the direction they had come. *Fallen? What does James mean? Why was Kathryn screaming? Where was Eleanor?*

Alaina pressed, panic-stricken, into the grove, branches slapping her face and tearing at her hair.

"Elly! Elly, where are you?"

Another crack of lightning came, and the trees lit up with white fire. For a moment Alaina could not see where she was going.

"Father!"

Suddenly she heard his voice. "Alaina, over here."

A hand grabbed her wrist and dragged her forward. She stumbled, and the strong hand pulled her to her feet.

"But, James said you'd fallen."

"He has fallen. He's over here."

Alaina focused on the person pulling her. It wasn't Father. It was Nephi.

"What are you doing?"

"Taking you to your father."

"Where's Elly?"

"With him."

She heard the hiss of rain as it began falling among the trees.

"You're hurting my wrist."

Nephi's grip immediately relaxed, but he didn't let go of her. They passed apple crates, ladders, dinner pails; then she saw Eleanor sitting on the ground next to Father. Alaina pulled her wrist out of Nephi's hand and moved over to them. She sat down, unable to take her eyes off Father's chalky-white face.

"Father?"

He didn't move.

She put her hand on his chest. "Father?" She brushed the rain off his face. "He's been working too hard. I've seen how tired he's been. I've seen it." She looked at Eleanor's face, smudged with dirt and tears, then over to the nearest ladder standing tall against the tree. "The ladder didn't fall?" She heard her voice as if it came from far away.

Eleanor shook her head.

"Did he fall off the ladder?"

Eleanor shook her head again.

"Elly, talk to me."

"I think it was his heart," she choked out.

"His heart?" Alaina looked at her father closely. "But, James said he fell."

Nephi stood next to the tree with his face in his hands, and Eleanor began crying. Alaina looked at each one with confused curiosity, then she squared her shoulders and said, "Don't worry, Elly, he's going to be fine. Nephi, bring me the canteen in case he's thirsty when he wakes up."

Nephi lowered his hands and looked at her for a moment, then picked up Samuel's canteen and brought it to her. "I can give him a blessing if you'd like," he said, forcing each word through his pain.

Alaina poured water onto her apron and washed the dirt off Father's face, oblivious of the rain falling there. "A blessing for what? He's going to be fine."

"Laina, please let Nephi give him a blessing."

Alaina looked at her sister's lost expression and took her hand. "All right, Elly, if it will make you feel better."

Nephi immediately fell to his knees at Samuel's side and laid his hands on Samuel's head. "Samuel Lund, by the power of the Melchizedek Priesthood, and by the power of faith, I lay my hands upon your head and . . ." A sob stopped his words, and Eleanor moaned. Alaina squeezed her eyes tightly against their grief.

". . . and say unto you . . ."

She heard power come into his voice.

". . . if it be the will of God that your spirit linger here with us a little while to bless and comfort, may it be so. In the name of Jesus Christ, amen."

Alaina thought it was an odd blessing, but thanked Nephi for it. She looked over at Eleanor and found her staring at their farmhand in disbelief.

"Elly? Are you all right?"

"Laina, you don't understand. Father's . . ."

But Alaina wasn't interested in what Eleanor had to say, for Father had opened his eyes and she wanted to find out how he was. He smiled weakly and tears dripped slowly out of the corners of his eyes. Alaina dabbed at them with her apron. Elly put her head down on Father's chest and wept. Nephi stood and moved away.

"Hi, Fancy."

"Hi, Father," Alaina said tenderly, taking his hand. "How are you?"

"Fine. Why am I here?"

"You fell, but everything's going to be all right. James has gone for Dr. McIntyre."

"I don't need Dr. McIntyre."

"I think we should let him decide that," Alaina scolded.

Father gave her hand a slight squeeze.

"Would you like a drink of water?"

"No, thank you." He smiled. "I love you."

Alaina brushed a twig out of his hair. "I know."

He reached out his other hand. "Miss Eleanor?"

Eleanor lifted her head. "Yes?"

He looked at her tenderly. "Nothing to fear."

She nodded.

"Who else is here?"

"Nephi."

New tears welled up in Samuel's eyes. "Where?"

Nephi knelt down next to Eleanor. "I'm here, Samuel."

He looked at the young man for a long time. "Come close." Nephi put his ear next to Samuel's mouth. "You're a good man. Thank you." Nephi set his jaw against a flood of tears. "Both of you take care of the farm. You and Alaina can do it."

Alaina leaned forward. "What did he say?"

Nephi sat up and looked at her straight on. "He said . . . he loves the farm."

Alaina took in a short, gasping breath. "Well, of course. Of course he does."

Father smiled. "Tell James I love him. I'm proud . . ."

Alaina patted his hand. "You can tell him yourself."

"Be good to Kathryn."

He closed his eyes, and Eleanor sat up. "Father?"

Just then they heard Kathryn's tear-filled voice. "He's over here; he's right over here!" She came stumbling into the orchard with Mother running behind.

Elizabeth Knight Lund went directly to the side of her husband, kneeling down next to her second daughter. Eleanor put her hand on Nephi's arm, and he helped her to her feet. Alaina looked at Mother's face and froze at the picture of desolation. *Why does she look like that?* Kathryn sat at Father's feet, holding onto his boots.

"Is he so sick, Mommy? Is he so sick?"

Elizabeth moved closer, placing her hand gently on her husband's face. "Samuel? Samuel, it's Lizzie. It's Lizzie."

Samuel Lund opened his eyes and smiled. "There's my beauty."

Mother bit her lip. "What can I do for you? Are you in pain?"

"No. No pain."

She kissed the palm of his hand.

His eyes filled with tears. "Sorry about your life . . . sorry."

Mother put her fingers on his lips. "You are my life."

"I can't believe you gave up everything for me."

Elizabeth Lund whimpered and leaned over to whisper in her husband's ear. "Your sunlight blinded me."

A smile brushed Father's lip as she kissed it.

Alaina stared at the two, finding it hard to recognize the woman at Father's side. Her mother had always been stoic and efficient, never overtly expressing emotion, especially to her children. But now Alaina could see that she was capable of tenderness and vulnerability, and the revelation was painful.

Father's hand brushed at his wife's hair. "My Lizzie." She laid her head on his chest, and he spoke to her in a whisper. "Love the children, Lizzie. Love them more."

A wail came up into her mother's throat that made Alaina's blood freeze.

Father was straining for breath. "It's all right, Lizzie. It's all right."

Mother looked at him, tears streaming down her face. She shook her head. "I don't know how."

Father patted her. "Your present is . . ."

She laid her fingers on his mouth. "No. I don't want to hear about that."

His breath caught. "Present . . . under pillow." His voice faltered. "Tell James I love him . . . proud . . . love you."

"Samuel, the doctor will be here shortly," Elizabeth gasped.

"Don't need . . . knew this was coming." He closed his eyes.

Mother shook his arm. "Samuel, don't leave me. You mustn't leave me."

His voice was a whisper. "Nothing to fear." Alaina heard Eleanor sob, and she felt a slight squeeze on her hand. "My Fancy."

Father's hand went limp, and Alaina sat staring at it. Time had no meaning for her. She thought she heard Kathryn crying and screaming—heard Mother's voice telling Eleanor to take the child home—felt herself lifted to her feet by Nephi—saw crates of apples—the rain making puddles on the road—her father's face white as death. She felt a grasping band of pain squeeze itself around her chest—then darkness.

CHAPTER 15

Grandma and Grandpa Lund's farmhouse in Sacramento had been newly painted green with white shutters. The colors were not to Alaina's liking. She would have chosen white with yellow shutters, and a yellow door. She stood on the porch looking out over a field of stubble. The flat barren acreage looked nothing like home, and before images of orchard and rolling hills could imprint themselves in her mind, she turned and walked into the dim dining room, shutting the door tightly. The mahogany table was laid out with the finest lace tablecloth, the cherished silver, and the heirloom china brought from England by Phoebe Smythe Castlegate, Grandma Lund's mother. There were tall silver candlesticks on either side of a huge floral centerpiece of purple irises, Shasta daisies, and golden mums. Kathryn sat under the table in her black dress, eating food pilfered from the kitchen. No one seemed to care.

Alaina walked the rooms trying to remember what she'd seen on a visit when she was six. The hallway seemed longer, the rooms brighter. She ventured into the parlor, running her hand over the cherub wallpaper and picking up a porcelain figurine from the mantelpiece. The beautifully detailed farmwoman wore a work dress of brown homespun and a tan bib apron. She carried a large bundle of wheat and a scythe. Her serene face held Alaina's attention. Was there a slight smile at the lips? Was she glad because the day's work was done? Alaina knew that feeling. She set the piece back on the mantel and turned to look out the window. The sky was ivory and smooth. No storm cloud marred the flat coating, no breath of air moved the leaves. The world was held in fragile suspension.

Alaina's eyes jumped to the parlor door as she caught the slightest flounce of pale blue retreating down the hallway. Small steps plinked on the wooden floorboards, accompanied by playful giggles. Alaina was drawn to follow. *This must be a neighbor child come to see the visitors from Pine Grove.*

When Alaina reached the hall, the blue had disappeared. She moved through the empty kitchen and onto the back porch. She scanned the horizon, catching sight of the blue dress as it moved past the threshing machine and out toward the tall grass. Alaina followed. The child was moving faster now, out past the hedgerows and into the line of sycamore trees. It was hard to see in the shadows under the trees, and several times Alaina stumbled. She had no concern for the child, as she seemed to know exactly where she was going. Grandma Lund called from the back porch door, but Alaina ignored her. There was urgency in Grandma's voice, but Alaina didn't care. She was determined not to let the blue dress out of her sight. Down an old drainage canal, along rows of sorghum, the little child now turned back toward the house. *Was this a game?*

Suddenly Alaina knew where the child was going, and her skin turned to ice. She willed herself to stop, to turn and follow her grandmother's voice to the safety of the house, but the soft blue pulled her forward. Within a stand of oaks, black iron fencing shoved through the dry ground like ancient spikes, daring men to pass beyond the boundary and disturb the stone crosses and cold statuary. Alaina shoved open the iron gate, the screech of metal making her grit her teeth. She walked numbly through the tall weeds, running her hand over the marble headstones: *Martin C. Lund—Precious Child; Robert Lund—In the Hands of Jesus; John Lund—Father and Friend.* The child was sitting on a stone planter looking at a grave: *Mary Margaret Castlegate Lund—Beloved Wife and Mother.* Alaina glared at the headstone. *How was that possible?* She looked back to the house searching desperately for her grandmother at the back porch door, but she wasn't there. The smell of fresh-turned earth made Alaina's stomach lurch, and she went down on her knees in pain. They were dead. Grandma and Grandpa Lund were dead. She couldn't be at their house. There was no one calling her name. The child turned from the grave to look at her, and Alaina pushed backward frantically, trying to get to her feet and escape the madness.

"Hold her, young man."

Alaina clawed the air and shoved with her feet. There was a person behind her—arms around her waist. She couldn't breathe. She stopped struggling as her stomach lurched again, throwing up its contents onto the bedspread.

"I think you can let her go now."

The arms relaxed, and Alaina felt herself laid back against soft cool pillows. There was pressure against her wrist as the stench of vomit stung her senses. She groaned and tried to speak, but a cold cloth was laid on her head, and she forgot the words she was trying to say.

"Eleanor, take the soiled linen."

Elly?

The weight of the bedspread was removed.

Elly?

The child in the blue dress stood on the low crossbars of the black iron fencing, her cherub hands clutching the pointed spikes, her forehead pressed against the black metal. Alaina reached out to her.

"Alaina?" A hand took her hand. "Alaina, I want you to open your eyes."

She would never open her eyes again.

"Open your eyes."

She groaned. *Why wouldn't this voice go away?* The rumbling words seemed to have power over her body. Her wrist was tapped several times.

"Open your eyes."

She gritted her teeth against the suggestion, but her eyes opened.

"Good girl." The voice spoke to someone else. "Hand me that wet cloth."

Cool water was pressed against her mouth, and she sucked involuntarily at the moisture.

"Good girl."

The hand let go of her hand, and another cloth was laid on her head. Alaina knew her eyes were open, but all she saw was the bedroom door. Her bedroom door. There were illusive images swirling at the back of her head—images that came clearly for a moment but scattered before she could make sense of their meaning: a basket of mending, a green farmhouse, a stalk of wheat, crates of apples. A band of pain tightened around her chest, and she couldn't get air into her lungs. Apples.

"Sit her up, Mr. Erickson!"

Alaina was pushed into a sitting position, and air filled her lungs. *Apples.* The day slammed into her.

"No!" She went to jump from the bed, but hands grabbed her and held her down. "No!" She broke free from the restraint and headed for the door.

"Laina! Stop!"

Elly?

Her hand wrenched at the door handle, but she didn't go out.

"Laina, it's Elly."

"I . . . I have to see Father."

"Alaina, he's gone." Eleanor came to her side. "He's gone."

Alaina glared at her younger sister. "Where did you take him?"

Strong hands took her by the shoulders and turned her around. She looked up into the face of Dr. McIntyre and smiled at the soft fringe of white hair that rimmed his head like a halo. Good Dr. McIntyre. Kind Dr. McIntyre.

"Alaina, your father is dead. He had a heart attack."

She stood staring at him. "I know that. Where did you take him?"

The gentle man looked straight into her eyes. "He's in the wagon downstairs. I'll be taking him into town."

"I'm going with you."

"I don't think . . ."

"I'll drive the wagon. I always drive the wagon." She looked to the window where Mr. Erickson was standing. "It's getting late. We'll want to go before it's dark."

Eleanor took her arm. "Alaina, James can drive the wagon."

Alaina pulled away. "No. I'm the eldest. It's my job." She moved to the dresser and brought out her leather riding gloves, slipping them on and smoothing her rumpled skirt as though she were going to town for clothespins. "Dr. McIntyre?"

"Only if your brother or Mr. Erickson rides with you."

"James needs to stay with the family." She turned and moved to the door, stopping beside her younger sister. "Stop crying, Elly. You need to take care of Mother and Kathryn. Can you do that?"

Eleanor nodded, brushing tears away with the palms of her hands. "Are you all right, Laina?"

Alaina's stomach lurched. "No," she snapped, clamping down on her emotions. "I don't think we'll ever be right again. Oh! My hat!" She snatched her hat from the bedpost and went to the door.

Eleanor took her hand and leaned close. "Laina, you don't have your shoes."

"Well, where are they? And why are you whispering, Elly? They're only shoes."

Eleanor looked over at the doctor, who leaned down and picked up the shoes from under the bed.

"These are yours."

Alaina moved to take them. "Yes, sir. Thank you."

"Are you sure you're strong enough to drive . . ."

"Yes, sir. I'm fine."

James stood beside the wagon, holding Father's hand, and staring blankly at the still face. Alaina marched through the front door, shoving her hat onto her head and securing it with a hat pin.

"I'm driving Father into town," she announced.

"What?"

"Dr. McIntyre is taking—"

"I'm driving."

"No, you're not." Her voice was harsh, and Moccasin stamped and shook her head.

James clenched his jaw. "I'm the man of the house now."

"Then do what you should do. Stay and take care of the family." She didn't want to look at him because she saw too much of Father—dark hair, green eyes.

James kept ahold of Father's hand. "You can't go by yourself."

Alaina lifted herself into the seat and began putting on her shoes. "Mr. Erickson is going along."

James stared at her. "What's wrong with you?"

Alaina didn't answer.

Dr. McIntyre and Nephi came out of the house. Nephi went immediately to climb into the wagon, while Dr. McIntyre stopped to speak with James.

"Rest easy, James. I'll take good care of him."

"Yes, sir."

The kindly man placed his hand on James's shoulder. "I've given your mother and younger sister a sedative. They should sleep til morning."

"Yes, sir."

Dr. McIntyre put his bag into the wagon.

"Sir?"

"Yes, James."

"What's wrong with my sister?"

Dr. McIntyre looked at Alaina, who was aggressively lacing up her boots. "She'll be all right. I'll keep my eye on her." He climbed onto the back of his horse and smiled tiredly at James. "Thanks for taking care of Forrest. You sure have a way with horses."

James put his head down. "You're welcome."

Eleanor came out of the house with a shawl. She handed it up to Nephi, and Alaina glanced over.

"For you, Laina, in case it's colder later on."

Alaina tapped the lines on Moccasin's rump. "Walk on!"

The young horse lurched forward, pulling the wagon away from the house. James held onto Father's hand, refusing to let go until the wagon reached the front gate. He stood with his hat over his heart as the foursome moved off down Cold Creek Road. Eleanor stood on the porch carrying a weight that a fifteen-year-old should never know. She watched the sun slide behind the row of sheltering pines, then turned abruptly, jumping from the porch and running for the solace of Niagara Falls.

CHAPTER 16

Work. It was their saving grace. Everyone worked all day and well into the evening—never stopping, never thinking. They wore black, and they worked. James, Nephi, and Alaina worked in the orchard. The harvest was slowing, but the leisure of winter was still weeks away.

Samuel Lund was given homage by their toil, and Nephi knew Samuel's final wish, that he and Alaina work the farm, would be fulfilled. He was astonished at Alaina's ability and stamina. She never slacked or complained, even when he witnessed the pain that knotted her arms and shoulders. She worked without thinking, the motion and consistency of her toil automatic: the last of the apples stripped from the trees, canvas bags filled, ladders moved, crates loaded, fruit transported to Martell and off by train to Californian or eastern markets. Alaina didn't care where the fruit went after it left her hand. The work was all she wanted. She ate only because it gave her the ability to work. Red apples kept her alive during the day, and Father's green book under her pillow took her through the night. She had never read more than the one entry, but that was sufficient. When the harvest was over, she would claim the farm as Father intended. She would claim the farm and work it until the day she died, and there would be no spouse to say she had to be buried in the Methodist cemetery—no spouse to keep her body from its true resting place on the hillside overlooking the groves.

In a few days she would be nineteen, but she already felt old. The Harvest Ball had come and gone, but gaiety and color were no longer a part of her endowment. She wore black, finally understanding its meaning.

Everyone at the funeral wore black. The Methodist chapel was filled with an outpouring of dark sentiment, except for the blue ribbon in Lela McIntyre's hair. Alaina was offended by the color; it hurt her eyes and distracted her grief. If she didn't look at it, she could withdraw into the somber unity of the congregation and give away some of her pain.

Fredrick Robinson stood at the back of the chapel during the service, weeping like a child. Several times Alaina saw him move outside into the sunshine until he regained his composure. Nephi sat with Daniel. Joanna sat with her mother across the aisle from the Lund family, glancing over so often that Alaina grew irritated at the intrusion of her offered pity. Joanna looked terrible in black. It turned her hair coppery and her skin sallow.

Pastor Wilton spoke words, but there was no comfort. Others seemed buoyed by the tender expressions, but Alaina thought only of building crates and moving ladders. Her mind was locked against the occupation of the cemetery, and she met condolences after the services with stoic detachment. Even when Daniel had held her in his arms for a long time, she set her jaw against emotion.

"Miss Lund, the crates are full."

Mr. Erickson's voice came gently up into the branches of the tree, and she looked down at the apple in her hand before placing it into the bag.

"Let me finish this tree. We can make cider."

"Yes, ma'am. I'll ready the wagon."

She watched him pick up the crate and move toward the wagon. He was a good worker. Maybe she'd keep him on when she ran the farm.

School had started, and Eleanor and Kathryn were unwilling attendants. While both girls liked school, their minds and feelings were preoccupied with their life at the farm. Mother wanted to keep both at home, but Alaina put her foot down. The garden was harvested, except for the patch of Hubbard squash, and the girls could manage that work and other farm chores before and after school. Alaina was determined that Eleanor's brightness would not be sacrificed to the current situation, and Kathryn was sent to school to keep her busy and out of the way.

Alaina put the last apple into her bag and carefully climbed down the ladder. There was a cramp in her right hand, and she flexed her fingers hoping to relieve the pain. She turned to see Nephi watching her. He moved forward to heft another crate of apples.

"Sling that bag over my shoulder. I'll take it to the wagon."

She did, grateful for the help, and grateful that he didn't say anything about her physical weakness. She picked up the lunch pails and followed his blue shirt to the edge of the grove.

"We're getting four cents a pound for these apples," she said, lifting the pails into the back of the wagon.

"Yes, ma'am. Top money."

She wiped her forehead with the sleeve of her dress and took a drink from the canteen. It was odd how Mr. Erickson had begun addressing her as a married woman. It suited her because it kept their dealings as business, and their stations clearly defined. His presence also suited her, as he was quiet when they worked together, never intruding on her solitude with unnecessary talk. There were times she wanted to ask him about Mormon heaven and how he thought Jesus would sort out all the sheep and the goats, but work always seemed more important than words, and Alaina was desperate to avoid any pain, which would bring up a show of emotion. She also feared that once the gates of doubt concerning her father's decision to join the Mormon Church were opened, the bitterness she'd been harboring would start and never stop. She knew that Mother blamed Father's death on his spiritual betrayal, and she wondered if Father's death was God's way of saying he'd been wrong about his baptism. Her father's conversion lay at the feet of Mr. Erickson, and Alaina was sure his thoughts must be fettered with remorse for giving her father that wicked book. She clamped down on the resentment that came into her mind as he arrived with the final crate of apples. He placed it in the back of the wagon and shoved the tailgate closed. Alaina climbed up into her seat without speaking.

The days were much shorter now, nightfall pressing down before chores could be finished. As soon as the sun dropped below Morris Hill, the air turned cool, intensifying the musty smell of dirt and decaying leaves. Alaina fetched her father's jacket from under the seat, wrapping herself in its warmth. The rig moved forward as Mr. Erickson guided Friar Tuck over the rutted trail.

She was tired and wanted this pain in her chest to go away. It wore at her like a mewling child—a thing she could not put down or abandon—and had become a burden that made her thoughts bitter and her heart unapproachable. She put the sleeve of Father's coat to her face and breathed in the fading smell of him. She looked over at Mr. Erickson, tightening her jaw against the bitter words that pressed the back of her throat. Part of her wanted him to go away. Part of her wanted him to stay and share the devastation of her father's absence.

"Mr. Erickson?"

The harshness of her voice made him jump.

"Yes, ma'am?"

"Is my father going to hell?"

She watched as anger tightened his mouth and made his hands grip hard on the reins.

"Why would you ask that?"

She sat silent, not knowing, just wanting the pain to go away.

His eyes narrowed. "Answer me." The harshness of his voice jarred her thoughts.

"My mother says he's lost salvation."

"And you believe that?"

She couldn't answer.

"Do you? You know what kind of a man he was." Pain washed through his anger. "You know how generous of spirit." He pulled Friar Tuck to a stop, set the brake, and turned to look at her straight on. "What kind of God do you believe in, Miss Lund? What kind of God would not welcome your father with open arms?" His voice choked with emotion. "Because he joined the Mormon Church, do you think God punished him?"

Alaina felt as though her darkest demons were being ripped out of her soul.

"That wicked Mormon Church has sent him to hell. Is that what you think?" Mr. Erickson's face was fierce, and his blue eyes penetrating. His words pressed against the canker in her spirit, forcing poison to rush into her mouth.

"Yes! Yes, that's what I think!" Tears coursed down her face, the weeks of grief released in an agony of senseless words. "He read that book and it changed everything! It changed everything, and I don't know if he's saved." She found it difficult to breathe as words forced through her tears. "He's lost to us because of that false book!"

"Have you read it?"

"No!"

"Then how can you judge if you haven't read it?"

Alaina wiped angrily at the moisture on her face, moaning as another wave of pain washed over her. "Why did you come? Why did you come here and take away my life?"

Nephi turned his face from her.

Alaina's stomach cramped, and she leaned forward. "I miss him. I miss him, Nephi. I miss him." She rocked back and forth, unable to stop the grief. Through her sobs she heard Nephi crying, and she looked over to see him with his head in his hands. Alaina felt a stab of regret. How could she have said such terrible things? She didn't believe as her mother. She didn't believe Mr. Erickson was a wicked person. She looked at him with pity. This man had loved her father, had shared days in the orchard, conversation, and friendship. He'd been silently grieving through all this time without a friend or sibling with whom to share his sorrow. She slid over next to him, gripping his shirtsleeve.

"I'm sorry. I'm sorry, Nephi."

He pulled her to him, wrapping her in his arms and laying his head on her shoulder. Anguish shook his frame as he clung to her. Alaina cried with him as images of her father squeezed themselves, unwelcome, into her mind.

Darkness deepened around them as their tears subsided and the pain eased, scrubbed raw and clean by the release of emotion. Nephi pulled away from her, keeping his head down. He wiped his face with his shirtsleeve and tried not to think about the awkward silence between them. A wisp of wind blew across their faces, blessing them with the pungent smell of freshly picked apples. A lost moment of summer momentarily embraced their senses and promised recovery to the wayfarers. Nephi held the reins loosely in his hands, unwilling to move the rig forward. He wanted to talk to her, but it was difficult. For weeks he had honored her grief with silence, and he worried what words might do to that agreement.

When he did speak, his voice was low and husky. "You could run this farm, you know."

It was not what Alaina had expected him to say, and she sat staring at her black skirt, unable to respond.

"Your father had every confidence in you. He hated that you couldn't work with us in the groves."

If there were tears left she would have shed them now, but they were gone. She sat in the darkness and breathed in the smell of the trees.

"Thank you."

Nephi put his hand over hers. "Alaina . . . I'm sorry I took your life away."

She shook her head. "I was . . ." The words caught in her throat. "I'm sorry I said those things."

"But, if it wasn't for me . . ."

"No. It's not true. My mother forced me out of the orchard. You had nothing to do with it."

He took a deep breath and slid his hand off of hers. Feeling the chill of the evening, Alaina put her hands into her pockets and moved back to her place.

"Will this pain ever stop?" she moaned.

"I don't know." He looked her straight in the face. "I don't know."

"You've never lost anyone before?"

"Not to death." Nephi thought of the estrangement from his father. He thought of being so angry with his father's first wife that he'd thrown a wrench through the window of the family's hardware store. The woman had a bitter tongue, and Nephi had had enough of her poisonous words against his mother. His father had insisted he apologize or no longer be considered a son. Nephi had walked out of the hardware store without speaking. Yes, his father was still alive, but lost to him.

It would have been a balm to share these wounds with Alaina, but even though plural marriage was no longer part of the culture, its threads twisted through the lives and hearts of all who had been touched by the sacred principle, including himself. It was a concept Alaina would never understand, so he kept the past in the past.

Nephi undid the brake. "Poor ol' Tuck. Probably wondering what's keeping him from supper. Walk on!" He tapped the lines and the faithful horse started forward.

Neither spoke as the ride home continued—Alaina trying to sort through the thoughts and emotions pressing in on her, and Nephi lost in the smell of her hair and the feel of her skin. He loved her. It was painful to admit, but it was plain fact. He'd been attracted to her from that first day when she'd dumped water on his boots, and over the months his feelings had gone from interest and amusement to admiration and deep caring. His pain was not only the loss of her father, but also the distance that kept him from comforting her. He ached to hold her in his arms and tell her how he felt, but he knew she thought of him only as a farmhand and would never consider his advances, especially because he was a Mormon with beliefs she found impossible to accept.

Growing up in Salt Lake City among people who had been beaten by mobs, driven from cities, and denied the rights of citizens, he knew of the distrust of the outside world. It had marked his life with separation and sorrow. As he glanced over at Alaina, he realized her distrust touched not only his life, but also his heart. How heart-wrenching that one thing he cherished estranged him from the other he loved. He looked up at the first stars appearing in the purple sky and tried not to think of her nearness, but now that he'd held her in his arms, he knew he would long to do so every time he saw her. Maybe it would be better if he moved on. The harvest was almost ended, and surely Alaina and James could take the farm through the winter. He felt sadness settle on his heart when he thought about leaving. Where would he go? Placerville? San Francisco? Prospects of the big city did not entice him. Maybe Lake Tahoe—perhaps he could find some employment there that would take him through the winter.

His eyes were drawn back to Alaina, and his heart ached at the sight of her looking like a little girl in her father's large work coat. She turned her face to him, and he looked quickly away.

"Do you truly think I could run this farm, Mr. Erickson?"

The proper distance between them had again been established.

"I do, ma'am."

She undid her braid, releasing the dark hair to fall softly around her shoulders. An owl screeched far away, and Alaina drew the jacket close around her.

"My mother would never let me. It wouldn't be proper."

"She might give up her ideas of what's proper and what's not if she was in danger of losing her home."

Alaina pondered this. Perhaps Mother was caught. James wasn't up to the task, and they couldn't afford someone to manage the entire farm. In a few days she'd be nineteen and old enough in age and wisdom to tell her mother her decision. She smiled into Mr. Erickson's blue eyes, grateful for his simple support.

"I know my father cared for you, Mr. Erickson. He told me once he'd tested your character and found it true."

Nephi attended to his driving. After a time he spoke, unsure of the steadiness of his voice. "That means a lot to me. Your father was a man to admire."

Alaina felt the intensity of emotion and took a deep breath. "He was."

"I remember him singing. He was always singing when he worked."

Alaina smiled. "Songs of the kingdom."

"He's probably up there singing right now."

Alaina caught her breath. "Do we sing?"

"What?"

"In heaven. Do we sing?"

"Of course."

Alaina was silent.

"But I don't know about playing harps," Nephi said with a soft smile.

Alaina nodded. "What else?"

"What else do we do in heaven?"

"Yes. What is my father doing?"

Nephi tried to gather his thoughts. These answers were important to her and needed consideration. He could feel her watching him. "He's visiting with family."

"Who have died?"

"Yes."

"Like his mother and father?"

"Yes."

She answered quietly. "He would like that. What else?"

"He's learning."

"Learning what?"

"Everything . . . math, science, music, love."

Alaina's brow furrowed. "Why?"

"Mormons believe that love and learning go on into the eternities."

"Why? Well, love I understand, but why learning?"

"So we can someday create our own worlds."

Alaina stared at him. "You actually believe that?"

One corner of Nephi's mouth rose slightly. "Yes." He saw the puzzled look on her face. "Of course, you're starting way at the end of the doctrine, Miss Lund. Maybe we'd better go back to faith, repentance, and baptism."

"Hmm . . . Maybe, but not tonight."

They had reached the house, and Nephi brought the rig to a stop. "I'll take care of Tuck tonight. Why don't you go in to supper?"

Alaina wanted to argue, but exhaustion was seeping into every muscle and bone. As she pulled the dinner pails from the back of the wagon, she thought of a deal that would help her save face. "All right. You take him tonight, and I'll do the next two."

"Fine by me," he answered, tipping his hat.

He'll make me stick to it, too, Alaina thought ruefully.

Nephi moved the wagon toward the barn. "I'll unload the crates for cider," he called back.

"Thank you."

She stood on the porch, looking up at the clear night sky, the joints in her hands predicting a coming storm. The autumn rains had begun, and Alaina imagined the craggy peaks of the high Sierras covered in snow, the waters of Lake Tahoe still and gray as giant thunderclouds growled overhead. Snow in the mountains would soon mean much colder temperatures in the foothills—frozen fingers milking in the morning, mud and ice at the bottom of her skirt, barren trees. The season of life would give way to the season of death. She shook away her melancholy and thought about creating worlds and learning forever. She knew one person who would find that heaven—Philomene Johnson.

She smiled at the sparkling stars and imagined her father sitting down at Grandma Lund's mahogany table with the lace tablecloth, having pot roast and laughing about the antics of his youth. *Do we eat in heaven?* She'd have to ask Mr. Erickson if there was any Mormon doctrine about eating in the hereafter.

She opened the front door and the savory smell of chicken and dumplings greeted her. She felt peaceful. Tomorrow the pain and sadness might return and follow her around like a lonely puppy, but tonight she felt peaceful. She moved toward the kitchen to the sound of pots and pans and Kathryn reciting her times tables.

CHAPTER 17

Markus Salter stood on the Lunds' front porch holding a bag of saltwater taffy. He shifted from foot to foot, rubbed his dusty shoe on his pant leg, and looked toward the front door for the hundredth time. Even the cool weather of November could not ease his discomfort as he fiddled with his tie and wondered if it would be impolite to sit down. He wasn't used to wearing his Sunday suit on a Saturday—his large frame more comfortable in work pants and homespun—but this was a special occasion and required Sunday best. His brown hair was brushed back and secured with McFister's Deluxe Hair Pomade. He felt like a dandy, but the style actually complemented his soft features and made him look older. He had inherited his father's burly frame and brown eyes, but his mother's cherub face and shy demeanor. If he was ever in a fight, those betting on Markus Salter would not be paid, and if he was ever in a science competition, those betting against him would feel lighter pockets. He'd actually been hired at the new power station at Electra, which was beginning to bring electrical lighting to the towns of the Sierra foothills. Had his personality permitted, Markus might have felt proud of his position, but like everything else life offered him, he accepted it with humility.

Alaina sat at the top of the stairs, catching glimpses of her childhood friend through the front window as he paced the front porch. She felt awkward and embarrassed, like she had in grammar school when she lost the spelling bee or spilled milk on herself. Though other girls had become young brides, Alaina knew she wasn't ready for courtship and marriage. Yet here was Markus Salter standing at her front door with a bag of candy.

"What are you doing?"

Alaina jumped. She looked around to see Eleanor at their bedroom door.

"You scared the wits out of me!" she whispered gruffly.

Eleanor crept out into the hallway and came to sit beside her sister.

"Sorry, but what are you doing here?"

"I can't go, Elly."

"To town?"

"I can't."

"Are you sick?"

"I am."

Eleanor put her hand on her sister's forehead. "You're not fevered."

Alaina brushed her sister's hand away. "Not that kind of sick, you goose."

Eleanor looked out to the porch and saw Markus open the bag and sneak out one of the wrapped candies.

"It's only Markus Salter."

Alaina glared at her. "It is not Markus Salter. It is Markus Salter come courting. It is Markus Salter with a bag of candy."

"Leave him out there long enough, and there might not be any candy."

"Elly!"

"Sorry, Laina."

"I don't want to do this."

Eleanor took her sister's hand. "Then don't. I'll go downstairs, accept the candy in your behalf, and then I'll tell him to go away. 'So sorry, Mr. Salter, but my sister is unable to attend today's recital with you because she is too young to be courted and would rather toss horseshoes with you than be your bride.'"

Alaina shivered and was about to chastise her giggling sister, when Mother suddenly appeared at the bottom of the stairs.

"Alaina Lund! What are you doing there?"

Alaina stood up. "I . . . I was . . ."

"Where are your manners, to leave Mr. Salter standing forever on our porch? I called you fifteen minutes ago."

"Yes, ma'am. I just need to get my coat." She came quickly down the stairs, grabbing her coat and Father's soft winter scarf off the coat rack. She opened the door and stepped out onto the front porch before Mother could say anything more to her.

Markus turned toward the house as soon as he heard the door open. His face was flushed, either from the cold or with expectation.

"Hi, Alaina."

"Hi, Markus."

"Here, let me help you with your coat." He debated what to do with the bag of candy, finally deciding to set it on the porch floor. By the time he looked up, Alaina had finished putting on her coat and was wrapping the scarf around her neck.

"Oh, sorry."

"Excuse me?"

"I didn't get to help with your coat."

"Oh, that's just fine. I've been putting on my own coat for a long time."

Markus looked puzzled. "But, I'm supposed to . . ."

Alaina pointed to the bag of candy. "Is that for me?"

Markus looked to where she was pointing and brightened. "It is!" he answered, picking up the bag so quickly that a few pieces scattered across the porch. "Oh, no!"

Alaina went to retrieve them. "It's all right, Markus," she said laughing. "They're wrapped. No harm done."

He had a sick look on his face as he held out the bag to her. "Saltwater taffy from San Francisco."

Her heart softened as she realized the difficulty he was having. She smiled at him as she took the offering. "Thank you, Markus. This is very nice."

Hopefulness brushed his face. "I guess we should go or we'll be late."

She put the candy in the pocket of her coat, and walked with him to the carriage. He helped her in and raced around to the driver's side, slipping on the frosted ground and nearly falling. He hefted himself onto the seat and took up the reins.

"Are you warm enough?"

"I am."

"Because I have a blanket."

"I'm fine, thank you."

"All right then." He slapped the reins on the stallion's rump, and they started forward.

It was odd to be sitting in a carriage with Markus Salter. When she looked at him she could only think of their school days together when many of the children called him Salterpepper; when the teachers sat him in the corner for his refusal to stand at the board and solve arithmetic problems; when he'd stumble over his feet and fall down on the activity field. She didn't know what to say or how to feel. She figured Markus was feeling the same as they rode silently on their way to town. When they passed the Robinson homestead, Markus gathered enough courage to ask a question.

"Did you hear that Mr. Greggs is gonna try and get a regular baseball team going next spring?"

"I didn't. That would be a fine thing."

"It would." Silence again. "I might play, if I can find the time for practice."

"That's right. You have your new job at the electricity plant."

Markus nodded and smiled. "And even as much as I love baseball, a man has to put first things first."

Alaina's stomach lurched. He was a man. Little Markus Salter, who once got his head caught in the stairwell railings at school, was a man, and he was trying to convince her of his steadiness and integrity; he was trying to show her that he'd be a good husband and treat her well. Alaina felt a chill run down her spine, and she hunched into her coat. Immediately Markus reached under the seat with one hand, retrieved the blanket, and laid it across her lap.

"Weather's turned mighty chilly."

Alaina didn't want to talk anymore, so merely grunted a reply.

Markus had spoken more words to Alaina in the last few minutes than he had the entire time at school, and was worn out by the effort. He was perfectly content to let the rest of the trip pass in silence, hoping he'd made a good enough impression with the candy and the comment about his work ethic, though he worried that she might take it as boastful.

The pale November sun offered little heat as it slid behind the tops of the trees. Bereft of summer glory, it descended into its western

175

slumber early. Here it was only four o'clock and already into gloaming. The setting sun made Alaina sad, and she sat stiffly, trying to figure out what her life would be. She'd had such high hopes when she'd gone to Mother with Father's journal, expressing her desire to run the farm—desires that were shredded with Mother's clipped and certain words.

"It is his writing. Of course it's his writing, but that is not the point. He may have had confidence in your ability to work the farm, but that does not give you ownership."

"But his words say I could run this farm if need be. That seems to be giving me ownership."

"It is not a woman's place."

"Well, you have the deed. Are you going to run the farm?"

Elizabeth Lund looked her haughty daughter in the eyes. "Alaina, please take that tone out of your voice."

Alaina was shaking with emotion, but had tried to steady herself. "We can't afford to hire anyone. I know everything about this farm. I've been helping Father since I was twelve."

"That is not the point. Now if James . . ."

"James! James can't run this farm!" she growled with frustration. "The point is that we'll lose the farm because I'm a woman and not a man!"

"It is not proper for a woman to own or run a farm."

Alaina felt the hot sting of tears in her eyes and brushed away the feminine weakness with distaste. "So, if I were married, my husband could run it?"

Alaina had said it flippantly, and in haste, but Mother's silence indicated she was considering the option. Alaina's skin flushed hot with the thought of being married, of sharing the farm and her bed with a stranger. Her mind flew from the idea like a pheasant scared from cover, and she tried desperately to think of what Father would want her to do. Images of the farm being turned over to someone else—of another family living in the rooms of their house, walking their groves, and picking their fruit—grated her senses and caused her anger to fix on a grim resolution. If being married were the only way she could control the farm, then that was what she would do. The coupling would have nothing to do with sentiment or affection, but exist only as a transaction of necessity.

Alaina looked steadily at her mother and spoke softly and without rancor. "If I were married, would you give us the deed to the farm?"

Elizabeth Lund searched the face of her daughter, expecting to see a flicker of weakness or doubt. She saw only the determination of a person she had never understood. What was her passion for the land, her resistance to manners, her lack of obedience? Mothering had been a difficult task for Elizabeth Lund, and this child tested her commitment at every turn. She looked into her daughter's eyes, seeing the defiance, a defiance which fixed her unwilling response.

"Yes. If you marry, the deed will go to your husband."

Alaina accepted the edict without emotion, turned, and left the room. Her mother never saw Alaina's tears, or the green book clutched to her chest.

"Whoa, Manasseh."

Markus's gentle voice brought her back to the carriage and the cold night. She looked up to see the stone steps and columns of the new high school. Sutter Creek had won the bid to house the new school from the county seat of Jackson, which had caused quite a stir for many months before and after. Alaina found it funny that several women's groups had worked tirelessly to get the idea of a high school into the minds of the city planners and finally onto a ballot, only to be left out of the final decision because of their inability to vote. Perhaps she would join Philomene Johnson's endeavors for women's suffrage and fight to get women the vote. Perhaps that would lead to a day when her mother would accept that women could own property and run their own farms.

Carriages were arriving at the front of the school, as well as several automobiles. One of the sputtering inventions pulled next to their carriage, causing Manasseh to shriek and bolt sideways. Markus controlled the beast with a strong hand and reassuring words while Alaina glared at the driver. She much preferred horses, and knew Friar Tuck would win in a race against one of the dreadful machines, hands down.

"I wonder what Mr. and Mrs. Hawkins are going to recite tonight." Markus said. He had hitched Manasseh to a post, and stood on her side of the carriage, offering his hand to help her down. Alaina took it reluctantly, noticing that several of those moving toward the high school turned to glance in their direction. Mason Clark, one of

Markus's friends from school, set a course in their direction. Alaina's feet had barely touched the ground when Mason grasped Markus by the hand and thumped him hard on the back.

"Hello, friend! Heard about your job with the electricity company. Congratulations!" He tipped his hat to Alaina. "How are you, Miss Lund?"

"Fine, thank you, Mr. Clark." Alaina didn't like the way he was grinning at her, and was glad when he was called away by two other young men.

"I'll talk with you later, Markus," he called back.

Talk with him later? Alaina was sure she'd be a topic of that conversation, and she didn't like it. Why had she come? She didn't want to be seen on the arm of Markus Salter—not that he wasn't a fine young man—but because the sighting would indicate an attachment. Talk would flow among those attending the recital, and assumptions would become gossip, embellished and twisted with individual hope or prejudice.

"Do you think Mrs. Hawkins will recite 'The Chambered Nautilus'?" Markus asked as he offered her his arm. "Build thee more stately mansion, O my soul . . ."

Alaina smiled to think of big Markus Salter enjoying poetry. She took his offered arm with a calmer spirit, deciding that longtime friendship was not a bad hook on which to hang a relationship. It was also nice to think that he'd be living in Electra during the week and she'd only be bothered with him on Sundays.

With the coming of fall, girls' and women's dresses had turned to darker colors, making Alaina's black not so noticeable, yet she could still feel curious eyes on her as she and Markus walked into the crowded assembly hall.

Royal blue bunting draped across the arch of the stage, and a painted landscape drop hung against the back wall. It seemed to be a picture of an English countryside, complete with sheep and shepherds and a castle in the distance. Front and center on the stage was the wooden stand for the performers, flanked by two lovely potted palms. Alaina figured the Sutter Creek Cultural Committee had secured the plants from the hotel, with sober assurances that they'd be returned safely.

"Alaina!"

She heard Joanna calling her name from a distance, then twice more as she drew closer, moving her way through the crowd and waving. Alaina was chagrined, and felt her face heat with embarrassment. The last thing she wanted was to have more attention drawn to herself and her escort. Markus took Joanna's approach with only a slight indication of discomfort, even raising his hand to acknowledge her calls.

Joanna took her friend in a genuine embrace, which evaporated some of Alaina's anger, and when Joanna stepped back to smile at her, Alaina saw tears in her eyes.

"Hi, Alaina."

"Hi, Joanna."

"I'm so glad to see you here." She glanced up at Markus. "Good evening, Mr. Salter. I hope you're taking good care of my friend."

Markus blushed. "Yes, Miss Wilton."

People quickly began taking their seats as Philomene Johnson crossed the stage to the speaker's stand. Joanna gave Alaina's arm a squeeze and whispered to her. "I'll see you after the recital. We have so much to talk about."

Alaina watched her friend move back through the crowd and sit down next to Jim Peterson, Maddie Cross, and Daniel Chart. Alaina felt loneliness wash over her. Why hadn't Joanna invited her and Markus to sit with the group? Is this what courting brought? A separation from youthful camaraderie? She didn't like it.

Markus gently touched her arm. "Shouldn't we find a seat?"

She pulled away. "Of course. Unless you want to stand in the aisle during the performance." She knew the words were too harsh as soon as they flew out of her mouth, but Miss Johnson was rapping the "call to silence" gavel, and there was no time for an apology. The pair found seats quickly, trying to focus on the stage and not on their awkward feelings.

Miss Johnson was tall—tall and somewhat plain—but her voice was low and pleasing and her figure striking. She wore a tan suit with brown accent which complemented her rich brown hair and brown eyes. She presented an assured demeanor which Alaina had always admired, and she gracefully took what life gave her and offered back an improvement on the bargain. She had enriched the life of every student privileged to be in her nest of scholarship, and when Alaina glanced over at Markus, she envied Philomene Johnson her freedom.

It was a pleasant time in spite of the circumstances, and Alaina found herself getting lost in Mr. and Mrs. Hawkins' polished presentations. Mrs. Hawkins did indeed recite "The Chambered Nautilus," along with "A Psalm of Life" by Longfellow and a few quaint pieces by a new authoress, Emily Dickinson. Alaina had never heard any of her work before, and found it charming, if a bit odd.

Mr. Hawkins was a powerful speaker whose presence and command of voice completely captivated his audience. When he recited "Columbus Addresses King Ferdinand," he became the embodiment of the seafaring adventurer. His listeners felt a chill when he spoke Mr. Poe's "The Haunted Palace" and read "The Masque of the Red Death." But it was his rendition of Joseph Drake's poem "The Flag" which brought the audience to its feet. Alaina stood and clapped with everyone else, insisting on an encore. After taking a long drink of water, the gifted orator graciously accepted the request.

"Dear friends, you are too kind. My wife and I are honored to come to your delightful town. We thank Miss Johnson and the cultural committee for deeming our talents sufficient to share." Another round of applause followed, to which Mr. Hawkins smiled and gave a slight bow. "Now, if you will kindly be seated, I will recite a piece in honor of your beautiful countryside. It is from the renowned pen of Sir William Cullen Bryant." More applause. Alaina loved Bryant and wondered what piece the orator would choose: "The Song of Marion's Men," "The Death of Lincoln," or perhaps "The May Sun Sheds an Amber Light." Mr. Hawkins began the first lines, and her heart froze.

"*Come let us plant the apple tree. Cleave the tough greensward with the spade . . .*"

These beautiful words were bitter and painful to her ear, and she tried to block out the voice, tried to take her mind away from the images they created.

"*. . . when from the orchard-row he pours its fragrance through our open door; a world of blossoms for the bee, flowers for the sick girl's silent room . . .*"

Alaina felt tears burning at the back of her eyes, and gripped the seat of her chair to stop the flow. Markus glanced over and gave her a smile, oblivious of her agony.

"*. . . and when, above the apple tree, the winter stars are quivering bright, and winds go howling through the night . . .*"

Alaina wondered how many steps there were to the door. Would anyone notice if she crept quietly to the peace outside the lecture hall?

"*. . . who planted this old apple tree? The children of that distant day thus to some aged man shall say; and, gazing on its mossy stem, the gray-haired man shall answer them. A poet of the land was he . . .*"

Alaina stood. She gritted her teeth and shoved by Markus as silently as possible, her body drawn to the door. A few people glanced at her, but, to her relief, most of the attention remained fixed on the stage. She slid into the dim hallway, closing the door on Mr. Hawkins's captivating voice and painful words, and cried. Unstoppable tears coursed down her cheeks while gouts of pain heaved from her chest. Frantically, she looked for a place to hide herself. She ran down the hallway, out through the front doors, and into the night. It was cold, and she'd left her coat on her chair, but she didn't care. The cold air took away her panic, and she sucked it into her lungs like medicine. The dam had broken. This was the release of grief. She saw a few people approaching the school, and she turned quickly, moving out toward a grove of oak trees. It was only seven o'clock, but the light was gone. She stumbled several times, but did not stop, willing herself forward, away from the school, away from circumstance. She reached the trees and slid down to her knees in their shelter. There was no turning back from this pain. It was the price for refusing emotion when she drove her father's body into town, for refusing tears at his grave, for refusing comfort to Eleanor and Kathryn. Her body shook with rage and pity. She wanted to scream at God for taking her father away. Didn't He know the anguish that had forever twisted her spirit? The anguish that had injected so much fear into her heart that she would never love again? Into her mind came images of the cemetery and the granite head-stones, and she felt her mind slipping down into the rotted earth.

Large hands wrapped themselves around her upper arms.

"Alaina?"

The large hands lifted her. Maybe they would take her to the edge of a cliff and fling her off. She didn't care.

"Come on, sweetheart."

The voice was low and loving. She stood on her feet, unable to move.

"You've had a rough time of it, haven't you?"

She nodded as the tears kept flowing. A hankie was pressed into her hand, and she turned, looking up into the face of Fredrick Robinson. She laid her head on his chest and cried tears of release. The big bear of a man cried with her, and somehow it eased her sadness. He held her gently and patted her back.

"Not fair to take such a good man. Not fair."

Alaina groaned.

"Left a big hole in our lives."

Alaina breathed out. "It's not fair."

"No, it's not."

She stepped back, wiping her face and noticing for the first time that Daniel stood a few paces behind his father, holding her coat. She felt a flush of embarrassment as she saw the look of pity on his face. He stepped forward, giving his father the coat. Mr. Robinson held it out to her.

"Here, let's get you into this."

She held out her arms like a child, and he slipped it on. When she turned around, he handed over her father's scarf. She looked back to the school where she saw some people climbing into carriages and others moving off into the night toward home.

How long have I been out here?

"I need to find Markus."

"No such thing," Mr. Robinson said, taking her hand. "We told Mr. Salter we'd be taking you home, as it was out our way. Hope we didn't overstep ourselves."

Alaina felt such relief that she smiled at him through her tears.

"I'd be grateful for a ride home." She put Father's scarf around her neck and began walking. "Oh! Joanna said she wanted to talk to me."

Daniel cleared his throat. "She told me to tell you she'd come out to the farm in a few days to visit. That way you'd have more time for gossip."

Alaina nodded her head. Another burden lifted.

A brisk wind blew down the hillside and snapped at her skirt. She moved ahead, flanked by these two good men, neither of which asked if she were cold or if she needed a blanket. That suited her just fine, and even though she wiped away a few more tears, she felt stronger than she had in a long time. She had work to do to keep the farm. Her commitment set her feet on a path, and even though she did not know where that path would lead, she would not forsake her promise.

CHAPTER 18

The sun was so hot Alaina had to reposition her umbrella to shade her face. *Unusual weather,* she thought as she stood on the porch pouring lemonade. Joanna Wilton sat quietly across from her, eating gingerbread. She'd come for a visit wearing an ugly burgundy dress. *Why would Joanna wear such a color?* It clashed with her hair and made her skin look like pasty chalk.

Kathryn came out of the house with sewing cards and sat down on the front step to play. Alaina watched as she threaded the large needle with thick green yarn and picked up the card to begin sewing.

Mr. Erickson drove by in the wagon. He was taking crates of apples to be stored in the root cellar. Along with the ones in the shed, they would supply their fruit for eating and cooking during the barren winter months.

Small brown birds hopped around on the porch waiting for crumbs of gingerbread. If Eleanor were here she'd be feeding them off her plate. *Where was she anyway?* As if summoned, Eleanor came out of the house with a bunch of white material. She sat on the step next to Kathryn and began rolling the narrow strips of fabric into little bundles. Alaina figured they must be bandages for the new hospital.

She heard a horse whinny in the distance, and all the ladies turned to look in the direction of the front gate. A young man was coming for a visit. Alaina waved, and even though the fellow was a ways off, he saw the salute and waved back.

She wished she wasn't wearing black, then chided herself for the disrespectful thought. Was she so frivolous as to wish for bright colors to take her thoughts away from honoring her father? And what was a young man doing here in the middle of the afternoon when there was work to be done? She shaded her eyes against the sun to watch as he passed through the front gate. He certainly was handsome. She looked quickly to Joanna to see if she were reading the emotions on her face, but her friend was watching the man's approach with interest.

Alaina's skin felt clammy. She pressed the cool glass of lemonade against her cheek, looking skyward to see if there was any chance for clouds to cover the merciless sun. Her heart raced as she caught a flounce of blue out of the corner of her eye. She jerked her head to the side and saw only the dead leaves of the rose-of-Sharon bush twitching in a dry wind.

Someone was singing—songs Father used to sing. This was not to be tolerated. Why would Nephi do such a thing? She jumped from the porch, accidentally kicking Eleanor's white bandages into the dirt. She would give Nephi a piece of her mind. Didn't he realize how painful it was to hear those hymns? *Someone is still singing.* Her stomach knotted in anger as she ran toward the root cellar. She slowed as she neared the barn, surprised to see the stranger's horse tied to the corral post. The young man stood quietly watching the antics of their new colt and did not turn at the sound of her footsteps. She joined him at the gate.

"Think I'll call him Titus."

She looked over at the tanned face of the lanky young man, and smiled. "It's a fine name."

"Yes, ma'am." He smiled back. "Your farm is doing well. You both should be proud."

"Yes, sir."

A cool wind blew across her face, and she looked out over the meadow covered now in white and blue lupine. The apple trees were in full bloom and would bring in a banner crop this year.

They stood together, content with silence, watching Titus buck and kick.

She could smell bacon, and turned her head toward the house. The pictures faded as she felt the soft coolness of the pillow against her cheek. *No! Don't wake up! Go back to the dream.* She squeezed her eyelids tightly shut, hoping to bring back the images, but they were gone. Alaina groaned and rolled onto her back. She took a deep breath. *Let me at least hold on to the feeling.*

"Morning, Laina," Eleanor said softly.

Alaina opened her eyes. "Morning, Elly." She sat up. "What time is it?"

"Seven."

Alaina started. "Seven? It doesn't look like seven."

"Fog."

Alaina jumped out of bed. "I was supposed to start the stove this morning."

"Mother's done it."

Alaina sat back onto her bed. "I'm so tired of being in trouble."

"I know. I'm sorry."

"It's not your fault, Elly."

"Well, she never really gets that angry at the rest of us. It's like you're the whipping boy. You and Nephi." Eleanor took her hand. "Just remember that the grief has changed her."

Alaina flinched at Eleanor's assessment, but it was true. She was aware of Mother distancing herself from others, of seeing her face chalked with smoldering anger when some intrusion took her from a faraway thought. She often found Mother mumbling to herself, or rewashing dishes that were already clean, or wandering aimlessly in the shed. Alaina shook her head. And when it came to Mr. Erickson, Mother seemed offended by his very presence, finding every opportunity to fault his work, or his person. Alaina had a strong feeling that the Utah boy would be sent packing as soon as the necessary farm repairs were done in preparation for winter.

Eleanor left to help in the kitchen, and Alaina stood, quickly stripping off her nightgown in hopes of tossing away the melancholy that was sitting on her shoulders. She washed and dressed, and thought about the day of work, the blessed routine that assured her survival. The bedroom was cold, the day somber, and the muttering of her youngest sibling irritating.

"Kathryn, get up. You're going to be late for school."

"You can't tell me what to do," Kathryn mumbled.

Alaina pulled the covers off the little churl, and went to find her boots.

"I'm telling Mother!"

"Go and tell her. You'll have to get up to do it."

Kathryn growled at her tormentor, and Alaina went out to sit on the stairs to put on her socks and shoes. Her hands ached as she laced her shoes up, and she glared out at the heavy fog, holding it responsible for her physical pain.

The smell of bacon brought her thoughts to the present and the remembrance that she was hungry. She would eat a huge breakfast, endure Mother's disjointed words, and go to work.

* * *

Fog covered everything. The groves had disappeared, along with the shed and the house. It was eleven o'clock in the morning, and yet it was like being inside a dimly lit marble tomb.

James and Alaina worked inside the phantom barn, tendrils of mist swirling around their feet. He was busy nipping the horses' hooves and filing them into perfect shape, while Alaina brushed their coats to a healthy shine. She smiled to think that Father would be proud of their efforts.

"You're making a fool of yourself, you know," James said, removing mud from Moccasin's fetlock.

Alaina gripped the currycomb, but didn't speak. James's voice had a way of irritating her, especially when he came out with pronouncements he felt no one should question.

"Putting out word that you're receiving suitors."

"I did no such thing."

James scoffed. "You told Joanna Wilton about your deal with Mother."

"Joanna's my best friend."

"And just the person to tell if you want the county to know."

Alaina felt the pain of embarrassment as she imagined people talking about the "Lund family situation," and she hated James for not understanding or appreciating her sacrifice.

"And what good does it do to be courted by Markus Salter? He doesn't care anything about farming."

Alaina glared at her younger brother. "That's not the point. The farm would belong to us."

"So, you'd work the farm, and what would he do?"

"Work at the electricity plant."

"In Electra? Not much of a marriage."

"And what are you going to do to save the farm?"

"Nothing."

Alaina stared at him. "Nothing?"

He shrugged. "What can I do?"

"You can talk Mother into letting me run things. I'm sure she would listen to her favorite."

Now it was James's turn to glare. He hated the insinuation that he was controlled by his mother's possessive nature. With Father gone he found it unbearable to be surrounded by women who couldn't understand his feelings. He looked at her straight on. "Maybe I don't think you should run the farm."

She stopped brushing. "Well, I don't care what you think. Father knew I could run it."

"I didn't say *could* run it, I said *should* run it. It's not a woman's place."

Alaina really wanted to throw the currycomb at his head, but held her temper. If she lost control, James would only say she was throwing a woman's tantrum. Titus shook his head, and she went back to brushing. There was an ache of unreleased anger in her chest, and she focused on her work so she wouldn't scream.

"It's just improper for you to be selling yourself as a bride. Why don't you take out an ad in the *Sentinel*? 'Wanted: husband for desperate farm girl.'"

Why couldn't he just leave it alone? She had always known James to be unfeeling, but right now she could use compassion and support. Why hadn't he inherited more of Father's kindness? He continued talking, but she wasn't listening to him anymore. Her mind caught on a time when she was a girl, walking with Father in the apple groves; he was teaching her about pruning and difking and harvest. She laid her head against Titus's neck and felt the familiar warmth and softness.

"James, remember the first time you rode Titus?"

James stopped talking, surprised by the gentleness of his sister's voice, and unsure of her intention.

"You were five or six, weren't you?"

"I was four."

Alaina smiled. "Four years old, and you sat on top of this huge horse like you were the mayor of the county fair. I remember the look on Father's face as he walked you around the paddock."

James hesitated and cleared his throat. "What made you think of that?"

"I don't know. It just popped into my head." She patted the big horse's neck and continued brushing. "I remember Father telling Mr. Regosi that you could ride any horse he had in his stable. That was when you were about eleven or twelve."

"Mr. Regosi wanted me to work for him, but I had to work the farm."

Alaina glanced over at her brother, understanding a bit of the resentment he carried around. "It would be nice to do exactly what you wanted to do, wouldn't it?"

"Yeah."

There was silence for a long time as they worked. Finally James finished with Moccasin and led her into the stall. He put away the tools and held the box lid open for Alaina to put away her brushes and combs. She retied her braid as they moved outside.

"Alaina?"

"Yes?"

"I guess you don't get to do what you want to either."

She stopped to look at him. "No, I don't."

He nodded, and the two headed for the house to wash up. Mother met them at the back porch door, holding a basket.

"James, I need firewood cut, and Alaina, see if you can find a dozen eggs." She held out the basket, and Alaina took it.

"Yes, ma'am."

She and James shared a look, which indicated a spark of sibling camaraderie, then turned toward their assigned tasks. Alaina moved along carefully to the chicken coop, as the fog distorted everything and made it difficult to calculate distance. She was muttering to herself when she heard the sound of hammering. She looked up from concentrating on her murky path and fell over the grain bin. She tumbled into the dirt with a guttural bark. The hammering stopped.

"Who's there?"

She froze at the sound of Mr. Erickson's voice, chiding her clumsiness and rubbing her shins.

Nephi appeared through the mist. "Are you all right?"

"Stupid fog."

He helped her up without expression or comment, for which she was grateful.

"Mother sent me for eggs."

He walked with her toward the gravelly throated clucks. "You won't have much luck. I've been repairing their coop most of the day, and they're not happy."

Alaina opened the door of the pen and moved toward the henhouse, while Nephi climbed the ladder to the roof. When Alaina moved into the interior of the little shed, she noticed immediately the gaping hole directly over the nesting area. She could see Mr. Erickson through the opening as he laid down a long, narrow board and began nailing it into place. Some of the hens squawked and flapped their wings, while others were so distraught they flew frantically from place to place. She clucked to them reassuringly, but they would have none of it. *Stupid chickens.* She went about her business quickly, found four eggs, and felt grateful to rush from the coop without major injury.

Nephi had come down the ladder to fetch more wood, and he stood smiling at her. "Tough work, but someone has to do it."

"Not funny," she replied, brushing fluff off her dress. "You could have stopped hammering for five minutes."

"And run the risk of being caught loafing?"

Alaina noted Mr. Erickson's immediate change of expression as he realized how his words indicated Mother's tyranny. He stammered an apology, but Alaina stopped him short.

"It's all right, Mr. Erickson. I understand."

Nephi shook his head. "No, ma'am. It doesn't give me leave to complain. She's my boss, and your family's been good to me."

Alaina knew this wasn't true. Eleanor was a genuine friend, and Father had cared deeply for him, but the others in the family paid him little mind.

"Well, you can be perfectly frank with me, Mr. Erickson, as I think she treats you badly."

He looked down at his boots. "She's carrying a weight of worry and sorrow."

"That's no excuse. Besides, she wouldn't have a weight of worry if she'd let me run the farm," Alaina snapped.

"That's the soul of truth," Nephi said, picking up several more boards and moving to the ladder.

Alaina was surprised by his simple affirmation. "It would just be so much better if I could take over the farm without . . ." Now it was Alaina's turn to cut off her thoughts. Her face flushed as the words *marriage* and *husband* skipped about in her brain.

Nephi looked at her with compassion. "Without having to be married?"

She looked at him briefly, then away. "Yes."

"Is there . . ." He hurriedly set the boards on their ends, and cleared his throat.

"Is there what, Mr. Erickson?"

"Nothing . . . I . . . I was . . ." His words tumbled over each other as he kicked at the dirt. "It's none of my business."

The fog thickened between them, and Alaina could not see his face clearly. It made her uncomfortable to imagine him thinking about her situation. She was embarrassed that he spent any time at all concerned for the decision she would be forced to endure. Was he worried if he'd have a job when she and her husband took over the farm? The intrusion into her privacy made her bristle.

"I will do what I must to save the farm, Mr. Erickson. Even marry a perfect stranger if need be."

His face became a stoic mask. "Yes, ma'am, I'm sorry. It really isn't my business."

"No, it isn't."

An image of last night's dream came unexpectedly into her mind, and she held back the rest of the reprimand. She was again standing next to the lanky young man with the green eyes, and together they were watching the beautiful colt in the paddock.

"Think I'll call him Titus."

"It's a fine name."

"Yes, ma'am. Your farm is doing well. You both should be proud."

Alaina stood staring at Mr. Erickson as he picked up the boards and began climbing the ladder to the roof of the chicken coop.

Both? You both should be proud? Who was the young man talking about? She began backing away through the fog.

"I . . . I need to get these eggs to Mother."

"Yes, ma'am," came the specter voice.

"I'll send Kathryn for you when dinner is ready."

"Yes, ma'am."

Alaina turned and carefully made her way toward the house. Fog swirled about the bottom of her skirt, and she felt unsettled and disoriented. She kept pushing from her mind the words of her dream. *"You both should be proud."* She pulled her shawl tightly around her shoulders and tried to think about chores and dinner, but it was no use. The impression kept tugging at her thoughts like a child—the clear, persistent impression that the young man in her dream was talking about the stranger from Utah.

CHAPTER 19

Melancholia was a thief of content for many in the early 1900s. Doctors weren't sure what to do with women who suffered with the malady, considering it to be a weakness of character or lack of spiritual faith. Men prone to the sickness attempted to cure it with drink. Society accepted appropriate sadness, but extended grief was meant to be swallowed up in earnest labor, or in the loving arms of the Lord.

Elizabeth Lund sat staring at herself in her bedroom mirror, not recognizing the face that looked back at her—the dark smudges under her eyes, the dull brown hair, the lifeless gaze. She was beginning to resemble a tired farm woman, and that frightened her.

She picked up the hairbrush and began methodically pulling it through the broken strands of her hair. Perhaps if she did a hundred extra strokes, the shine would return and Samuel would come braid it for her. She looked again at the face and scowled at the addition of tears. What an ugly, pitiful creature. She pinned her mother's cameo at the throat of her black dress and decided that she would not work today. Her mind thought of servants and carriages. Perhaps she would take the carriage into town and visit with her friend Regina Caulfield. Regina's father was a successful businessman just like her father, making Regina an appropriate companion. Perhaps they would frequent the new Marshall Hotel and evaluate the afternoon tea or the handsome young waiters. She would wear her light-blue gauze dress . . . *forty-three, forty-four* . . . someone was counting . . . and her blue satin slippers . . . *forty-eight* . . . perhaps Father would buy her a new dress. *Perhaps if I went home, Father would forgive me and let me sleep in my own bed.*

"Good morning, Miss Knight."

"Good morning, Ester. Has my father gone down to breakfast?"

"Yes, miss. He's in the solarium."

"Oh, Ester, don't forget to turn my mattress today."

"I won't, miss."

He'll be reading the paper and worrying about tin or coal or cattle.

"Good morning, Father."

"Good morning, Elizabeth. Getting a late start this morning?"

"Yes, sir."

"I have news for you."

News? I want nothing to do with news, unless he has a new suitor for me.

"Salmon, miss?"

"Yes, Mr. Latham, and a boiled egg. Oh, and tea, not coffee."

"Yes, miss."

"I'm sending you on a trip."

"Pardon, Father?"

"Elizabeth Louise Knight, pay attention! A trip! I'm sending you on a trip."

"To Europe?"

"No, not to Europe. You're going up to San Francisco."

"San Francisco? That rough wilderness? That desolation?"

"Stop being dramatic. It is far from a wilderness. Ida is not well, and she needs a family member at her side."

"She has Cedrick."

"Cedrick is busy at the bank."

"Well, Mother could . . ."

"No. Your mother is too fragile for such a trip."

"Well, I'm fragile."

"Elizabeth, there will be no argument. I have wired Cedrick, and they will be expecting you within the week."

"Your breakfast, miss."

"Take it away, Mr. Latham. I'm not hungry."

Seventy-one . . . seventy-two . . . The counting stopped. Someone was knocking on a door. "What? Who's knocking?"

The bedroom door opened. "Mother?"

Elizabeth frowned at the girl at the door. "What?"

"It's Eleanor, Mama."

"So?"

"I just wanted to let you know that Daniel Chart is here."

The woman in the mirror frowned. "Daniel Chart? What do I care?"

"Did you wish to speak with him?"

"About?"

"Taking Alaina out for a ride."

The back stiffened. "Of course not. Now leave me alone."

"Yes, ma'am." The door closed.

"What did she say?" Alaina whispered as her younger sister emerged from their mother's bedroom. Eleanor stood with her back against the door, staring down at her feet.

"Elly?"

"She doesn't care."

Alaina took Eleanor's arm. "Was she dressed?"

"Yes." She looked into Alaina's face. "She was brushing her hair."

Alaina set her face against emotion. "And she said I could go riding?"

"She doesn't care."

Alaina looked at the closed door. "Well then, if she doesn't care, then I don't either." She turned and headed downstairs. "I'm going riding with Daniel."

Eleanor looked to be on the verge of tears as she followed her sister.

Alaina stopped at the coat rack, grabbing her coat and her father's scarf.

"Alaina?"

"What, Elly?"

Eleanor stood on the bottom step watching her older sister intently.

"What?" Alaina snapped.

"I . . . What . . . what if she doesn't come down again this morning?"

"Then ready things for dinner, and I'll be home at noon to help you." Eleanor nodded.

"You'll be all right." She moved to leave, and Eleanor caught her wrist. "Do you like Daniel enough to . . ."

"To what?"

"Marry him?"

"It doesn't matter what I feel."

"Of course it does." Eleanor's blue eyes fixed on her sister, trying to read any hint of emotion.

"No, it doesn't, Elly."

She moved by Eleanor and out onto the front porch. Daniel stood beside his family's well-used carriage, looking off to the west. He turned when Alaina came out.

"So?"

"Mother told me to go and have a wonderful time and not worry about a thing," Alaina said sarcastically, climbing quickly into the carriage without assistance.

Daniel climbed into the rig and took up the lines. "I thought we'd head toward Miller's Bend."

"Fine. Anywhere but here."

Daniel gave Angel the command and the mare started forward.

It was cold. The clouds were heavy and dark, and the wind blowing down the hollow was marked by mountain snow. The dead leaves of the apple trees scattered with every angry blast, and Alaina felt like crying. She pulled Father's scarf around her face and moved closer to Daniel for protection.

"Maybe a ride wasn't such a good idea," he said, looking at her red face.

She shook her head. "I'm glad to be out of the house. I wouldn't care if it was a blizzard."

Daniel looked over at the gathering darkness to the west. "You may get your wish."

Alaina put on her wool gloves. "How's the house coming?"

"We've moved into all but three rooms, and the roof is done," Daniel said proudly.

Alaina smiled. "Just in time."

"Mother wouldn't tolerate a leaky roof."

"Of course not."

"And I understand you had a big crop this year," Daniel said with a note of pride.

"Second biggest yield in the county," she answered, lowering her head against a biting gust.

They were silent for a time, waiting for the weather to moderate. Finally the wind slackened, and they could breathe normally.

"You both should be proud," Daniel said.

Alaina started. "What?"

"You and Nephi, proud for bringing in such a big harvest."

She shook her head. "Everyone helped . . . except Kathryn and Mother."

Daniel smiled. "Very modest of you, Miss Lund. And how's Nephi doing?"

Alaina hunched into her coat. "Fine, I suppose."

"You suppose?"

"I don't see him much."

Daniel gave her a sidelong glance. "You live and work on the same farm, and you don't see him much?"

"It's a big farm."

"Not that big. You must be avoiding him on purpose."

She knew he was teasing, but she was still uncomfortable. Besides, she didn't want to talk about Mr. Erickson.

"So, how was your evening with Maddie Cross?"

"Who?"

"Maddie Cross. The girl you took to the recital."

"Oh, Madeline? Actually, I didn't . . ." He noted Alaina's intense interest in his reply. "I . . . I didn't mind her company in the least."

"Oh."

"She's very intelligent."

"Hmm."

"And pretty."

Alaina was silent, resolutely considering her own plain face.

"Of course, there are all kinds of pretty," he added.

"What does that mean?"

"Well, Miss Cross may have golden hair and devilish green eyes, but I prefer dark hair, blue eyes, and good, honest features."

Alaina laughed in spite of herself. "Good, honest features? You could be buying a horse at the county fair!"

Daniel laughed with her until a sharp wind made them suck in their breath and lower their heads. They both pulled their caps over their ears, and Alaina moved right next to Daniel.

"We're crazy to be out here!" Daniel called over the moaning in the pine trees.

"Do you want to turn back?" she yelled.

"Do you?"

"No!"

The wind dropped, and Daniel put his arm around her for a quick squeeze. "You're quite the frontier woman, aren't you?"

"Let's ride to Lake Tahoe. Do you think there's snow yet?"

Daniel chuckled and dropped his arm from her shoulder. "Oh, probably only ten to fifteen feet up around Carson Pass."

"We could do it!"

"If both of us—and Angel—had snowshoes, and you packed a week's worth of picnic."

Alaina laughed. "I think it sounds wonderful to head off into the wilderness."

Daniel smiled at her exuberance as a flake of snow settled on her eyelash. She brushed it away and looked up.

"Was that snow?"

"The first flake of the season." He tapped the reins on Angel's rump, and the dutiful horse moved to a faster pace. "Let's see if we can make it to the old Pony Express cabin."

The carriage rattled along the Kit Carson track, its occupants quietly caught up in the adventure. Youthful bravado kept them from fear and wisdom, and they pushed on, defiant of the wind and increasing snow. Large white flakes swirled around the carriage, obscuring their vision. Neither had any real idea how far they'd traveled, and it was only by chance that Alaina saw the ghostly remains of the old corral.

"There it is!" she yelled, tugging on Daniel's coat.

He slowed the rig, turning Angel carefully off the main road and onto the almost nonexistent trail leading to the cabin.

"Whoa down, Angel," he said, pulling the lines.

Angel snorted and tossed her head.

Alaina looked over at the dilapidated corral. "Maybe she senses the ghosts of all the departed Express ponies."

"I'm sure that's it," Daniel said, winking.

The wind retreated, leaving the snowflakes to drift lazily and cover the barren ground and branches of the pines with a soft coating of white. Alaina felt safe and peaceful. If it weren't for the rumblings of hunger, she would have been perfectly content.

"I'm sorry I didn't pack a picnic," she said remorsefully.

"Well, good thing I did then," Daniel said with another wink.

"You did? But I thought we were going to be back by dinner."

"But I'm a growing boy, Miss Lund, so my mother made sure I had a mid-morning snack."

Alaina laughed. "Bless your mother."

The cabin came into view, and Alaina shivered. The log walls, which had long since gone from brown to silver, were still intact, as was most of the roof. There was also one small window, but no door. Hunters and travelers sometimes used the cabin for an overnight stay, but these hardy souls required no amenities. The lean-to at the side of the cabin was leaning a bit more than it should, but the ground underneath seemed fairly dry.

"Whoa." Daniel pulled the horse to a stop. "I'll unhitch Angel. Why don't you take the food and go inside."

Alaina hopped out of the carriage and opened the rig's carry box. She found the food pail and lifted it out.

"Throw me those apples out of the box," Daniel called to her.

She found six big apples and tossed them to Daniel.

"Hey! I'll have to let Mr. Greggs know he's got a pitcher for his new baseball team," he called, dropping each apple to the ground inside the lean-to.

Alaina moved into the dim cabin through the open door frame. Piles of leaves occupied the corners of the single room and hid under the dilapidated bed frame. There was a warped table against the wall, under which was a lump of deerskins. Mice scuttled out from under this as she approached, and she was glad she was not Joanna at this moment. The blackened fireplace held its share of old leaves, and mice had found a nesting area there, too. Alaina set the food pail on the old table, causing it to sway slightly under the weight.

"Not a very good housekeeper, are you, Miss Lund?" Daniel said, moving into the cabin and assessing the disheveled interior.

"It's my servants actually. So hard to find good help nowadays."

Daniel chuckled. "Well then, I guess it's up to us to get a fire started. He saw the deerskins under the table. "And fix the door." He picked up the lump of leather and shook it out. A mouse went flying, hitting the wall and falling into a ball of dazed inactivity.

"Daniel, I think you killed it."

"No such luck," he answered as the little varmint came to and scurried for a hiding place. Daniel shook his head and moved over to hang the door, matching the holes in the leather to the old nails he found protruding from the top of the door frame.

"Anything I can do?" Alaina asked, clapping her gloved hands together and stamping her feet.

"Stay warm." He stopped just before exiting. "Oh, and clean the rubbish out of the fireplace." He smiled and brushed by the door flap.

Alaina made a face and looked around for a broom. *Huh! Not likely.* She found a bare pine branch propped up in a corner, deciding from its charcoal end that it had served as an instrument to poke the fire. She was clearing out the last of the leaves when Daniel came in carrying a load of sticks and some chopped wood.

"Where'd you get the wood?"

"Chopped it."

"Liar."

"Why, Miss Lund! Is that any way to treat a fellow who's going to keep you from freezing?"

"Some hunter left it," she persisted.

"Couple of years ago, I suppose." He dropped the wood in front of the fireplace and fished matches out of his pocket.

"Matches and a picnic? You're a wonder, Mr. Chart."

"Glad you finally noticed," he answered with a smile. Within minutes a small semicircle of warmth and light radiated from the grate. The snow outside fell in a soft, white dance, the wind having died away to slight whispers. Alaina watched the circling flakes through the small, glassless window, trying to keep her mind from previous Novembers—Novembers filled with innocence and possibility. That life was gone. Marriage was in her future—and owning the farm. She would keep her mind focused on the farm, and that alone, confident she could successfully manage every aspect without interference from anyone.

The two adventurers sat with their backs against the rickety table, which Daniel had turned on its side, wedging the legs against the wall. He had stopped unpacking the food to peruse Alaina's distant stare.

He grinned. "So, where are you off to, Miss Lund?"

Alaina started. "Yes."

"Yes?"

"Did you ask me if I wanted to eat?"

"No. I wondered where you had gone," he chuckled, moving his hand in front of her face.

"I must have been daydreaming."

"That's likely." He tossed a log onto the fire and went back to the food pail. "Now let's see what we have." He pulled out a cloth and carefully unrolled it. "Ah, pork pies," he said happily. The three pies looked like crescent moons except that their flakey all-around crusts were golden brown. Alaina had attempted meat pies once, but she couldn't quite seem to get the edges to seal properly and ended up with a gooey mess all over the flat baking pan and the oven.

"Your mother is a wonderful cook," she exclaimed, her mouth watering.

"But not very good at arithmetic," Daniel answered.

"What do you mean?"

"Two people, three pies? It doesn't work out, does it?"

She shook her head, smiling. "Well, you're the growing boy. You take the extra."

"Seems fair."

"Or, we could each have one, and fight over the extra."

He handed her a pie. "I like that idea."

"And don't think you'll win just because you're bigger."

"Never entered my mind," he said, handing her a napkin.

Her eyebrows lifted. "Matches, picnic, *and* napkins?"

"I know, what would you do without me?"

"Hmm." She bit into the perfect crust and sighed with pleasure. Why couldn't she cook like this? The meat was tender, the potatoes soft but not mushy, and the gravy seasoned just right. Even cold, it was wonderful.

"Good?"

She gulped down the mouthful. "Oh! Oh, I'm sorry, Daniel. I didn't even wait for you."

He chuckled. "That's all right. Mother will be pleased to hear you liked it."

She smiled and went back to eating, glancing every now and then at her handsome friend. Did he care for her? Would he ever think of marriage as a possibility? Would he mind leaving her alone to run the farm, never actually being a complete husband but always just her friend? She hated having to think about these questions, and felt a flush come into her face.

"Raisins?"

She looked up quickly. "What?"

"Would you like some raisins?"

"Sure." He dug into the bag and brought out a handful. "You're doing some pretty serious thinking, Miss Lund."

"Hmm. It seems that's my life now—work and serious thinking."

He handed her the canteen. "How is your mother?"

She frowned at him. "What do you mean?"

"Well, it's just that I overheard Joanna telling Jim Peterson your mother was overwhelmed with grief."

"Overwhelmed with grief? Overwhelmed? My father died two months ago!"

"I know, Alaina. I'm sorry. I shouldn't have mentioned it."

"Joanna Wilton needs to keep her opinions to herself. Where would she get such an idea?"

"Kathryn."

Alaina glared at him. "Kathryn?"

"I guess she asked Kathryn at church how all of you were doing, and . . ."

"And of course Kathryn had to be important and make up a big, tragic story."

There was silence between them.

"Well, I'm glad then," Daniel said finally.

"Glad?"

"That things are not like they were painted."

"No, of course not," Alaina managed. "We're all doing fine." A tear slid down her cheek.

"Alaina?"

Alaina swiped the tear away. "I'm just angry. I hate people talking about me, about us. I hate Kathryn for telling tales. I hate . . . I hate being alone." More tears began to fall.

Daniel moved close and took her hand. "I hate that you feel alone." He brushed hair away from her wet face. "I care about you, Alaina. What can I do?"

She sat stoically, feeling the warm pressure of his hand.

"Marry me." She said it flatly, without emotion. There was complete silence except for the slight flapping of the deerskin door. She would not meet his gaze.

"Alaina?"

"What?"

"Do you mean it?"

"Yes."

"But you don't love me."

Her words caught in her throat. "Not . . . not like that, but maybe I could someday."

He stood abruptly and paced the floor.

She looked at him sadly. "Are you angry with me?"

"Not with you. I'm angry with your mother for forcing you into this situation, forcing you to choose a husband out of desperation. I'm angry because if things had been normal, we might have come to love each other."

She sat staring at him. "Things aren't normal."

Daniel looked into her eyes, seeing only sadness and grim determination. "No, they're not." He missed the girl of dreams and imagination—the girl he could tease and talk to. He kicked the pile of firewood, glaring at the scattered pieces and wishing for different feelings. He wanted a friend, not a wife, and he didn't know if he could build on this unsure foundation.

"You must find me pathetic," she said, folding her arms around her bent knees.

"No, I don't. I hate what you're being forced into. Why can't you just own the farm? You run your place better than ten farmers I know."

"Oh, yes, and you should have seen the looks they gave Nephi and me when we took our produce into Martell."

"Oh, just tell 'em to jump in the creek."

She smiled weakly. "I wish it were that easy."

The wind picked up, blowing the deerskin out horizontal from the door and drifting snow into their sanctuary. Alaina wrapped

Father's scarf more tightly around her neck. "We'd better go before the snow gets too bad."

She moved to stand, and Daniel offered her his hand, pulling her up easily. She stood in front of him feeling young and foolish. He was too close, and he was still holding onto her. She stepped back.

"Alaina, I . . ."

She looked into his eyes and saw pain and confusion. "It's all right, Daniel," she whispered, trying to keep the tears out of her voice. "I'm glad you're my friend."

"I wish I could be . . ."

She put her fingers on his lips. "We'd better go." She turned away, moving to clean up the picnic remains. Gray cold seeped in through the open windows, sending a shiver down her spine. She was pathetic. She knew she was pathetic, but there was nothing she could do about it. Insisting circumstances had trapped her in a sad inevitability, and as much as she may have wanted to, she could not think about escape, only resolution. A dreary silence separated the two friends as Alaina packed the food and Daniel put out the fire. When he went to hitch up Angel, Alaina righted the table and looked around at the bleak cabin.

"Things change, Fancy. Things change all the time."

Well, she knew one truth for sure: she had made a fool of herself by proposing to Daniel Chart, and their friendship would never be the same again.

She moved out into the wind, put the food pail in the carry box, and climbed into the carriage, praying that the ride back to the farm would be swift and silent.

CHAPTER 20

The slight snow of the week before had vanished immediately, the weather moderating back to mild days and chilly nights. These were the warning days for the coming of winter, and Alaina now focused on pruning the trees, preparedness, and tallies. Alaina sat at the kitchen table with the ledger book assessing the farm totals for their labor. Through the agricultural cooperative they had sold 11,000 pounds of apples at 4 cents a pound, and 3000 pounds of pears at 6 cents a pound. In local markets they'd done well with weaner pigs, ducklings, potatoes, butter, and timber. Even with expenditures, including paying Mr. Erickson 85 dollars for his labor, they had made a good profit.

Alaina stretched her back and looked out through the kitchen window. Father would be proud; they had done well. Very well. She smiled at the now-barren hillsides, thanking the land for its bounty. She calculated again their readiness for the winter months: onions, potatoes, carrots, squash, and apples were stored carefully in the root cellar; and jars of beans, tomatoes, and fruit were in the pantry, along with bags of flour, cornmeal, dried peas, apples, pears, and store-bought dried beans.

There were bales of cut hay and dried corn in the barn to keep the livestock healthy through the winter. Eggs, milk, butter, bacon—the bounty was endless.

She was brought from her thoughts by a commotion at the back of the house. Eleanor came stomping up the porch steps, snapping at someone and throwing the empty grain bucket. Alaina jumped when the bucket hit the side of the house, then clattered away onto the hard ground.

What on earth is the matter with Elly? Her sensitive younger sister had been in a quiet mood ever since Mother started behaving oddly, but it had been a long time since she'd been angry. Jess Drakerman was the last to experience her wrath years ago when he tried to kiss her one day after Sunday School classes. Eleanor had punched him hard in the stomach—not a little, girly shove, but a knock-the-breath-out-of-you hit. Jess had doubled over in pain as his friends took off in fright. Eleanor had to sit in Pastor Wilton's office for an hour. Alaina remembered peeking in at her through the window and being shocked by Eleanor's unrepentant demeanor. That day Alaina felt like they truly had some similar traits, but Eleanor had never shown those character flaws again—until now.

Alaina turned quickly to watch as Elly came into the kitchen, pushing Kathryn in front of her. Kathryn's mouth was set in a horrid frown, her eyes glowering. She saw Alaina and started to say something, but Eleanor pulled her braid.

"Don't say anything! Don't even open your mouth!"

Alaina stood up. "For heaven's sake, Elly! What's happened?"

Eleanor growled, "I can't believe we come from the same family!" She paced the kitchen as though the soles of her shoes were hot. "I can't believe that a sister of mine could be so downright mean."

Kathryn's fists were clenching and unclenching. "Where's Mother?" she hissed.

"She's sleeping."

"Well, I'm going to tell her." She turned to march down the hallway, but Eleanor pushed her back.

"You stay put."

Tears welled up in Kathryn's eyes. "I'm telling."

"No, you're not. And stop crying."

"Eleanor, what happened?" Alaina asked again.

This time Eleanor stopped and looked at her older sister. "She told Mr. Erickson we hate him. She told him that Mother hated him most of all and was going to send him away as soon as the threshing machine was fixed. That he was a low-down skunk who should go back to Utah with all the other skunks."

Alaina turned to look at Kathryn. "You didn't."

"Oh yes, she did," Eleanor said sharply. "I was passing by the barn door and heard her yell every word. She would have said more, but I grabbed her out of there."

"Kathryn, why would you say such things?"

Kathryn crossed her arms and glared at Alaina defiantly.

"Answer me."

"I don't have to answer you."

Alaina fixed her with a hard stare. "I am just about to take the switch to you."

Kathryn flinched and stepped back. "You can't. You'd be in trouble."

"I'll be in trouble then."

Kathryn swallowed and bit her bottom lip. "I only told him what's true."

"That we hate him?"

"Yes."

"But we don't."

"Well, Mother does."

Alaina took Kathryn by the arm, moving her to the table. "Sit down." She was trying very hard not to lose her temper. "Kathryn, do not speak for someone else. Do not make up tales . . ."

"But I didn't make it up!" Kathryn protested. "Mother was talking to herself when she was braiding my hair. I heard her say it."

"That she hated Mr. Erickson?"

"Yes."

"And she was going to get rid of him?"

"Yes."

Eleanor snorted. "And she called him a skunk?"

Kathryn looked at the floor. "Well, I sort of put that in. She said liar, but I thought skunk sounded a lot better."

Alaina and Eleanor shared a look of disbelief. Why would Mother voice such thoughts? It was obvious the normal restraints of manners and good breeding no longer had meaning for Elizabeth Knight Lund.

Alaina turned her head and fixed Kathryn with an angry glare. "There is only one skunk here, and that's you, Kathryn Lund. What you did today was low and mean."

Defiant tears sprang into Kathryn's eyes. "Mother said Mr. Erickson brought a bad spirit here."

Alaina pulled her up by her arm. "Stop talking!"

"Ow! I'm telling Mother!"

"You will be quiet! You will go to your room, and you will stay there all day. You will not bother Mother, and you will not get any dinner." She took a breath and eased her grip on Kathryn's arm.

"I thought if I told him, he might go away, and then Mother would get better," Kathryn yelled.

"You are a little girl, and it is not your place to tell anyone anything. Do you understand me?"

Some of the defiance drained from Kathryn's face. "I . . ."

"Do you understand me?"

"Yes."

"Elly, would you take Kathryn to her room? I need to speak with Mr. Erickson."

"Gladly." Eleanor grabbed Kathryn's hand and dragged her down the hallway.

"No dinner?" Kathryn pleaded with Alaina.

"No dinner."

Alaina caught a faint whimper from her youngest sister, but no open protest. She moved to the back porch, grabbing Father's work coat and throwing it on. Not long ago she'd had to do her own apologizing to Mr. Erickson for mean words, but this was more than spilled anguish—Kathryn had coldly and maliciously imparted words she'd heard from Mother, words which should never have had utterance.

Alaina tried to calm her emotions before finding their farmhand. It wouldn't do to go ranting on about Kathryn and her nasty temperament when all that was needed was a genuine apology. *What must he think of us? It's a wonder he just doesn't wash his hands of this cantankerous family and head off to more genial employment.*

She passed by the corral where Titus was having a morning stroll. He whinnied, and Alaina laughed.

"No, I don't have carrots, you greedy horse."

She shoved aside the barn door and called out Mr. Erickson's name, but her voice only echoed in the stillness, and no response was returned. She noted the unstacked hay bales, and figured Mr. Erickson had left his job immediately after Kathryn's revelation. She turned toward the shed, moving quickly over the frosted ground. She entered the dim, familiar interior of the shed and could hear Nephi moving about in the back room.

"Mr. Erickson?" The movement stopped. "Mr. Erickson, may I speak with you?"

There was a moment's pause, then the door to the room opened. Alaina stepped inside, blinking at the brighter daylight coming through the window. Nephi stood quietly, not wanting to look at her. She saw the carry sack on the bed and the shirt in his hand.

"What are you doing?" He didn't answer. "Mr. Erickson, are you leaving on the word of a foolish little girl?"

"No, ma'am."

"Then what?"

"I think we know . . ." He stopped abruptly. "It's just time, that's all." He turned and threw the shirt into the sack.

Alaina felt panic move down her spine. Where would he go? Yes, he had a little money, but that wouldn't last long. Besides, winter was moving in and farms would not be hiring again until spring. "Did you finish the threshing machine?"

"I beg your pardon?"

"The threshing machine. Did you finish repairing it?"

"I don't . . . no, ma'am."

She brushed errant wisps of hair away from her face, and stood straight. "So, you're just going to take off and leave us with a broken machine? And what about those bales of hay you left in a heap in the barn, and the barn roof that needs repairing, and the livestock to feed, and the last of the pruning?"

Nephi looked up, and Alaina was shocked by the pained expression on his face.

"Do you think I want to leave?" he asked bitterly.

She steadied her voice. "No."

"But it's not up to me."

"Nephi, you know my sister, she's a . . ."

"She was only repeating what your mother said."

"Oh, yes, what my mother said! And we're all listening very carefully to what Mother says these days, sitting in her room brushing her hair all morning, counting the strokes, and talking to servants she had when she was a young girl."

"Alaina, she lost her husband."

She looked at him fiercely. "So? I lost my father! You lost a friend!"

"It's not the same." His voice was wrapped in empathy, but his compassion did not temper Alaina's resentment.

"Well, life moves on, doesn't it? And while she sits there, lost in grief, the farm is in jeopardy, and I have to . . . have to . . . and now you're going to leave me with a broken threshing machine and half the orchard still in need of pruning."

Her face was set hard against tears, daring him to pity her or question her resolve. He stood watching her for several moments, then turned and dumped out his carry sack onto the bed.

"I'll stay until those jobs are done."

Alaina felt the weight on her shoulders lift.

"I have something for you," he said quietly, rummaging through his few belongings and bringing out a small wrapped package. Tentatively, he handed it to her. "I was going to mail this to you."

She gave him a puzzled look.

"It was for your birthday. I know it was a week ago, but I . . . well, you didn't seem to want a celebration or anything, so I was afraid . . . Anyway, here it is."

Alaina looked down at the small parcel in her hand. It was wrapped with store-bought paper and ribbon—Victorian pink roses and ivory ribbon—just the kind of present Joanna Wilton would treasure. Alaina realized she hadn't said anything for a while, and quickly gathered her thoughts before speaking. "Thanks." She looked at him guiltily, surprised at the distant quality of her voice. "I'm sorry, Nephi, this is very thoughtful of you. May I open it?"

He nodded, and Alaina began at once to remove the ribbon and wrapping. She shoved the remains in her apron pocket and opened the small box. Her eyes widened.

"Oh!" She caught her breath as she lifted out a large silver portrait locket, letting it twirl on its sturdy chain. The precious metal was crafted in a beautiful design of delicate ivy. She was stunned. "Nephi, where in the world did you . . ."

"It was my mother's."

She came abruptly out of her reverie. "Oh, Nephi, I can't accept this." She held out the piece of jewelry to him, but he shook his head.

"I want you to have it."

"But, it's your mother's. Why would you . . ."

"Alaina, I want you to have it." He said it with tender finality, his blue eyes pleading silently that she not reject the offering.

She looked back at the locket and gently gathered it into her hand. "It's the most beautiful thing I've ever seen."

Nephi smiled. "Aren't you going to open it?"

Alaina was surprised. "Are there pictures?"

"Well, it is a portrait locket."

Alaina found the delicate clasp and gently opened the treasure, feeling the raised ivy against her fingertips. She stood transfixed, gazing at her father's face—his face exactly. The ink portrait was perfectly done, exquisite in detail and form. In the opposite frame was a summer apple tree, full leafed and filled with apples. She couldn't breathe. "How . . . how?" A release of tears coursed down her cheeks. "How did you do this?" She brushed the tears away so she could see his face.

"Eleanor brought me a photograph."

"It's his face," she said in wonder. "It's his face. And look at the apple tree. I had no idea you could do this."

She looked at him with tenderness and affection.

"I'm glad you like it."

"Oh, Nephi, I . . ." She moved to him, wrapping her arms around his neck. A soft moan came up into his throat as he pulled her close. He had often thought of holding her this way, but now that she was actually in his arms, he didn't know what to do. He didn't want to offend her by holding her too close, or for too long, but he also knew he never wanted to let her go.

Alaina put her hand on his arm and stepped back awkwardly. She avoided looking into his eyes, focusing instead at the locket in her hand. "It's the most handsome thing I've ever had."

"Would you like to put it on?"

She hesitated, then looked into his eyes. "I can't. I'm sure Mother would never let me keep it." She took the box out of her apron pocket and placed the locket back inside. "You understand, don't you?"

He nodded. "As long as you're going to keep it."

"Forever," she said. "And you're going to stay with us?"

"For a while," he answered.

They were still standing close, and Nephi reached out to take her hand.

"Laina! Laina!" Eleanor's frantic call shot through the reverie, causing both of them to start. Alaina spun around, shoving the box into her pocket and moving quickly out of the shed.

When she emerged into the cool morning light, she saw Eleanor running toward the barn. Alaina followed, calling Elly's name.

Eleanor stopped and ran back to the shed. As she neared, Alaina saw anger and frustration on her face.

"Elly, is it Kathryn?"

"Mother," Eleanor panted. "She's out by the main gate."

"What is she doing out there?"

"Don't know . . . saw her from . . . bedroom window." Eleanor put her hands on her knees, gulping air into her lungs. "Maybe she's walking to town."

Nephi had come out of the shed, catching the last of the conversation. "Who's walking to town?"

Alaina moved off toward the barn. "Mother."

Nephi followed. "On the main road?"

"That's what Elly says."

"I'll take Titus and bring her back."

Alaina's temper flared. "No! I'll take Titus and bring her back!"

"She may not want to come," Nephi answered calmly.

Alaina checked herself, seeing the wisdom in his offer. "I'm sorry, you're right."

They reached the corral and Nephi whistled to Titus. The big horse trotted to them and Alaina slipped a lead rope over his head as Nephi mounted from the fence. He shaded his eyes, looking out toward the main gate.

"Can you see her?"

"I can't. Maybe she's already on Cold Creek Road."

Alaina held the paddock gate open and Nephi urged the dutiful horse out onto the track.

"She's not going to like your interference," Alaina called after him, but Nephi only shrugged and urged Titus to a faster pace.

* * *

Alaina was right. Elizabeth Knight Lund had not liked his inter-ference. She was on her way to Sutter Creek to visit her husband's grave, and was incensed that her farmhand insisted she come back to the house. Nephi finally picked her up, shoved her onto the horse, and mounted quickly before she could think to jump down. She had fired him on the spot, spitting out hateful words and ordering him to leave the property before nightfall.

Alaina lay in bed, grateful for the cold night air coming through the open bedroom window. For some reason it calmed her fretful thoughts as she listened to the soft snores and breathing of her sisters, and the stomp of feet coming from Mother's room.

Mother had been pacing for an hour, muttering to herself and occasionally throwing something. Several times Eleanor had turned in her sleep, moaning, but had never come awake. Alaina, on the other hand, had come fully awake the moment Mother started wandering. Alaina was tired and her nerves were worn, but she could not seem to block out the measured footsteps. She held her locket under the covers, gently rubbing her finger across the ivy decoration and imag-ining the dear pictures inside. She closed her eyes, willing sleep to come, willing herself back to the dream of the young man at the corral. Slowly, a shadowed heaviness pressed on her body, and she started to drift. She was walking toward the barn and could see the colt bucking and kicking in the corral. The day was hot. She moved beside the young man, and the familiar feeling of comfort and peace washed over her.

"Think I'll call him Titus."

"It's a fine name."

"Yes, ma'am. Your farm is doing well. You both should be proud."

She looked out over the meadow of blue and white lupine. *"You both should be proud."*

A loud crash made Alaina bolt upright in bed. She looked over at Eleanor, who was groggily trying to untangle herself from her sheet. Alaina jumped out of bed, gently taking Eleanor by the arm.

"I'll check, Elly. You go back to sleep."

Eleanor looked at her blankly.

"Go back to sleep."

Alaina crept along the darkened hallway to Mother's bedroom.

The pacing had stopped, but when she pressed her ear against the door, she could hear muttering. She slowly opened the door and found Mother sitting on the floor, a patch of moonlight revealing the broken shards of her water pitcher. Elizabeth Knight Lund was staring at the pieces but not attempting to pick them up.

"Ester, you need to clean this mess immediately. And have you ironed my green frock?" She was so intent on giving directions to her imaginary servant that she didn't register her daughter's approach until Alaina stood beside her. She turned quickly, glaring at Alaina without recognition. "Are you finally here?"

Alaina reached out her hand. "Mother, get off the floor."

Mrs. Lund stared at her for a moment and then stood without help. "What are you doing out of bed?"

"I came to see what was broken."

"It's nothing. Just a pitcher. I'm perfectly capable of taking care of it myself."

Alaina bent down and began picking up the pieces of the smashed pottery. "I doubt that."

"What did you say?"

"I said I doubt you could take care of this yourself."

"Alaina Lund! Where are your manners?"

"Oh, now you recognize me."

"And who gave you permission to come into my room?"

"I wanted to make sure you were safe."

"Of course I'm safe. Go back to bed."

Alaina gathered the last of the broken pieces and deposited them in the trash bin. She stopped at the door and turned back to her mother.

"I've asked Mr. Erickson to stay on for a while."

Elizabeth Lund stiffened. "He will not . . ."

"He has given his word to complete certain tasks before leaving, and I will not allow him to back out on his word."

Mother put her hands on her hips. "*You* will not allow? What do you have to say about it?"

"I have everything to say about it because I'm the only one who knows what's needed to keep this farm running."

"Then hire someone else. I will not have that evil person near me."

"Then I suggest you stay out of his way."

Elizabeth Lund looked as though someone had just slapped her across the face. "He's deceived you too, just like he did your father."

Alaina moved toward her mother with such anger that Elizabeth stepped back.

"My father was not deceived."

"He was! That devil boy came here to bring lies and deception, and Samuel listened to him. Samuel listened to him, and . . . we should have sent the liar away when he first started preaching his wickedness."

Alaina was stunned by the virulence of her mother's words and feelings, and she knew nothing she could say would pierce her armor of delusion. She turned and walked to the bedroom door, pausing only long enough to look at her mother directly. "Mr. Erickson will stay until his work is finished. He will not speak to you, or preach to you, or indeed even look at you. I will so direct him. But you are not to speak to him either. If he does not finish the work he needs to finish this year, the farm will not flourish next spring, and I won't let that happen."

There was such finality in her voice that Elizabeth Lund only stood silently with her lips pressed together and her eyes narrowed. Taking that look as an acknowledgement of defeat, Alaina left the room, closing the door firmly behind her.

CHAPTER 21

How comforting and familiar to stand in the ordered peacefulness of her old classroom watching Philomene Johnson erase the blackboard and listening to her low, steady voice.

"The time is soon coming, Alaina, when the law will not tolerate inequality. But it is the people for whom I worry." Miss Johnson finished cleaning and turned to face her former student. She smiled. "People have a hard time accepting change."

"Because change is painful."

Her teacher nodded. "Indeed. But, it is also exhilarating and liberating."

Alaina smiled at Miss Johnson's enthusiasm but inwardly doubted. She found change neither exhilarating nor liberating.

"So, I understand your farm did well," Philomene said, indicating that Alaina should sit.

"Very well, thank you," Alaina answered, sitting at one of the student desks and remembering the hardness of the chairs.

"I expected as much," Miss Johnson replied, picking up her well-worn leather case and filling it with work booklets. "You were a good student, Alaina, but I always knew your genius lay in the seed and furrowed row."

Alaina bit her bottom lip to keep her emotions in check. Why couldn't everyone be as open-minded as Miss Johnson? Just because someone was born a female, did it mean she couldn't plant and harvest as effectively as her male counterpart?

"Won't do much good to be a genius at farming if I lose the farm."

Miss Johnson stopped working. "Is that a possibility?"

Alaina nodded, hesitating to reveal the reason she had come to her teacher in the first place. "I suppose you've heard the rumors," she said slowly.

"I have," Philomene said, watching Alaina's face closely.

"Well, they're true. My mother will not let me own the farm."

"And she doesn't wish to hold it?"

"She believes it's not a woman's place."

"And you fault her for that?"

Alaina hesitated before answering. She'd figured with Miss Johnson's involvement in women's suffrage, she would immediately see the injustice. "It's such old thinking."

"But that's how your mother was raised, Alaina—a marked distinction between men's and women's responsibilities. Especially in her life of privilege." She noted Alaina's hard expression. "She cares for you though, make no mistake."

Alaina felt her stomach tighten. "She's never shown it."

"Perhaps not in affection, but you must remember proper families do not make an outward show of their emotions."

"Or any show—not to her children anyway."

"It is a sad reflection of the culture." Miss Johnson secured the latch on her bag, appraising the sullen face of her student. "Do you remember your first day of school with me in Pine Grove?"

Alaina nodded, wondering why her teacher had changed the subject.

"Your mother brought you in, and then she sat at the back of the classroom the entire morning. Do you remember that?"

Alaina shook her head. She had been so caught up with the other children, her teacher's voice, and the bookshelf full of books, that her mother had disappeared from thought.

"She left at recess, but before going she spoke to me of her hopes and concerns for you. And even though she came from a culture where teaching women was not valued, she knew education would be important to you."

Alaina was unwilling to give up her bitter feelings. "Why? So I could darn a better sock? If she valued my ability she would let me run the farm. I think she wants nothing more than to sell the farm and move back to Los Angeles."

"To live with your grandparents?"

"I think she'd go in a moment, if they'd forgive her."

"So?"

"So, if I marry, then Mother will give the deed to my husband."

Miss Johnson sat down, an inscrutable look washing over her face as her thoughts turned inward. Alaina knew the look well. It meant Miss Johnson was carefully evaluating a response.

After a long silence, her eyes came to rest on Alaina's face. "So, what are you going to do?"

"I . . ." Alaina was at a loss. This was not the answer she expected. She looked into her teacher's steady gaze, trying to read the emotion, trying to find some direction. She found only the question. "I don't know," she answered softly. "I don't know what I'm going to do."

Philomene sighed, a tenderness pulling the corners of her mouth into a slight smile. Alaina loved that face: so honest, so caring. Philomene leaned forward, clasping her hands in front of her.

"I think you do know, Miss Lund."

Alaina stiffened. Her mind could see only blue sky, and meadows, and apple trees. Her eyes filled with tears. "I don't want to lose the farm."

"Of course you don't. Then what is the solution?"

"I auction myself as a bride," Alaina said bitterly.

Miss Johnson chuckled. "Well, that's one way to look at it." She stood and moved to Alaina, handing her a handkerchief. "Or, you find a man on whom you can rely. A man you can trust. A man who will be protective of your feelings."

Alaina felt her fears backing away. She had only thought in terms of a business partner or a Knight Royale. Miss Johnson was giving her another choice, a way of looking beyond the ledger book and the romance. Was there someone she could trust?

"All loves are not Romeo and Juliet, Alaina, and thank heavens for that. It makes for a fascinating night at the theater, but it is too intense for everyday living."

Alaina took a deep breath and wiped her face. Miss Johnson smiled at her and sat down to take her hand.

"And some loves—some of the best loves—begin with a shared commitment."

Alaina could tell by the rich emotion in Miss Johnson's voice that she'd had a love like that, a platonic love that complemented her singleness and enriched her life.

Alaina looked into the eyes of her teacher and saw truth and comfort. "Thank you, Miss Johnson."

"This is a difficult thing you have to do, Alaina."

"I know." Alaina smiled. "But the outcome lives in my attitude."

Miss Johnson gave her a crooked smile. "How often my words come back to haunt me."

There was a sharp rap at the door, and both women jumped.

Alaina stood quickly. "Oh, that's probably Mr. Erickson. I told him to come here when he finished delivering the lumber and picking up supplies."

Miss Johnson moved to open the door, and Alaina, feeling like a schoolgirl, followed closely behind. She caught her foot on the leg of a desk and stumbled.

"Are you all right?" Philomene asked lightly.

"Fine. I'm fine," Alaina answered, trying to compose her ruffled dignity.

Miss Johnson opened the door to find the Lunds' farmhand reading the placard that sat above the entrance to her classroom.

"The glory of God is intelligence, or, in other words, light and truth," Philomene recited. She smiled at the puzzled look on Mr. Erickson's face when he turned to her. "I thought you might find that interesting, Mr. Erickson." She extended her hand. "I am Philomene Johnson."

Nephi shook her hand politely. "Alaina speaks of you highly, Miss Johnson."

"Well, that's a relief. Come in, come in, Mr. Erickson. You can wait with Alaina while I finish packing, and then we can all walk out together."

Alaina was still trying to figure out why Nephi would find the saying outside their classroom of any special interest. "Do you know our class motto, Mr. Erickson?"

Nephi nodded. "I do."

Miss Johnson smiled at Alaina and continued packing. "Our class motto is from the Mormon Book of Commandments," she said simply.

Alaina was stunned. "It is?"

"I have a friend who belongs to the Mormon congregation in Placerville, and she suggested it as something I might like." She smiled at Nephi. "I like it very much."

"Have you read all the book?" he questioned with interest.

"I have, Mr. Erickson, as well as the Book of Mormon." She finished packing her belongings and secured the latch on her case. "Only ignorance is to be feared, Mr. Erickson."

"Yes, ma'am. But, please call me Nephi."

"I, Nephi, having been born of goodly parents . . ." She winked at him and put on her coat.

"And how did you find the book?" he asked, picking up her bag. The two of them walked off together like old friends, Alaina tagging along behind, trying to make sense of their conversation.

"Either it is a true book of scripture, or it is one of the most brilliant books ever written."

"And I can tell you are a reader of books," he complimented.

"Well, Nephi, I have four passions," Miss Johnson stated. "Reading, teaching, travel, and my roses."

"Wonderful things," he said, opening the door for her.

"And each passion teaches me a great deal about life."

"I would imagine."

"And what are your passions, Mr. Erickson?"

Nephi's blue eyes widened, and his cheeks flushed with color. He looked quickly over at Alaina, then away.

Philomene Johnson watched him out of the corner of her eye and smiled. "Sorry, Nephi, not a fair question on my part. I shall change the subject. You realize, don't you, that the Mormon people have a rich heritage in this part of the country?"

"The Mormon Battalion?"

"Yes, that indeed. And the discovery of gold at Sutter's Mill, and the formation of the Kit Carson Trail."

Nephi marveled at her expansive knowledge.

"It seems faith, Mr. Erickson, has carried your people through many adventures."

"I don't know if we'd consider them all adventures," he said quietly.

"Rightly so," she answered, taking his arm as they moved down the stairs. "And has your family been affiliated with the Church for a long while, Mr. Erickson?"

"Yes, ma'am. My grandfather's family joined the Church in Denmark in 1839."

"And immigrated to this country?"

"A year later. My grandfather was nine years old when they came."

Miss Johnson stopped and looked at Nephi with admiration. "Brave people, Mr. Erickson. Brave people to come all that way for a new, untried religion."

"Yes, ma'am."

They began walking again. Alaina didn't move for a moment, stunned at the story she was hearing. She had never considered asking Nephi about his history. Miss Johnson's voice broke into her wandering thoughts.

"And your mother's family?"

"The Keels. They joined in Ohio, just after the Church was organized."

"So, some of your people actually knew the Prophet Joseph Smith?"

"Yes, ma'am."

"What a fascinating heritage, Mr. Erickson. Fascinating." They had reached the front doors of the school. "I would be pleased if you'd come share more stories, Nephi, anytime you'd like."

"I would be glad to, Miss Johnson." He wondered what her views would be on plural marriage, the Manifesto, and Utah's bid for statehood. Seven hundred miles separated Utah from this part of the world, but suspicion and prejudice had a long reach. As he looked at Philomene Johnson's open face, he doubted that intolerance controlled her thinking. He smiled as he held the door open for the two women. A stiff gust of wind blew in, catching them unawares and causing the women to grab for hats and scarves.

"Now, here's a mean fellow," Philomene complained, pushing her way outside. "Why doesn't he go back to his snow cave where he belongs?"

Alaina smiled at remembered stories of winter fairies, ice trolls, and snow elves, all sprouting from the splendid imagination of her dear teacher. How remarkable it was to sit around the warm cast-iron stove in the little schoolhouse in Pine Grove, having their minds and hearts filled with the wonder of words. Alaina had mourned when Miss Johnson was promoted to the big school in Sutter Creek, and anxiously counted the months until she moved into the upper grades.

Another callous gust of wind pulled Alaina's scarf from around her neck and sent it tumbling down the front steps. Nephi ran after it without hesitation, bringing it back and handing it to her unceremoniously.

Miss Johnson held out her hand to him. "Well, Nephi, it was a pleasure meeting you. You seem like a very reliable young man." She moved over to Alaina and gave her a hug. "You will find the strength and good sense to figure it all out. I know you will." She gave her an extra squeeze, then stepped back and picked up her case.

"We could drive you home," Nephi offered.

"Oh, no thank you, Nephi. I must have my daily walk. I go to Belgium next summer and must be fit. Besides, you two should be on your way, or you'll freeze halfway home." She gave Alaina a pat on the arm and moved off down the steps. "Be brave, young people! All things are possible to them that believe!"

They stood watching her until she reached Mill Road and turned toward town, each unwilling to break the positive mood left by the irrepressible educator. Suddenly another sharp blast of wind swept across the cold marble steps, causing the two to grab tightly to their coats and race off toward the wagon.

"Did Mr. Park give you a fair price for the timber?" Alaina shouted as she ran.

Nephi nodded, holding onto his hat. "He did. Fifteen cents a board foot."

"Did we have one hundred board feet?"

"A little over," Nephi yelled, reaching the wagon and untying Friar Tuck from the post.

Alaina shoved her wool gloves onto her hands and reached up stiffly to pull herself into the seat. She looked at the supplies in the back of the wagon. Nephi must have taken care of that job after dropping the timber off at the mine. She was grateful for his industry and foresight because she did not want to stop again. All she wanted was to be home out of the cold.

Nephi pulled the blanket out of the carry box and laid it over their legs. "Walk on, Tuck!" He snapped the lines lightly on Tuck's rump. "Come on, champ! Get us home fast."

Tuck moved easily into a trot, and Alaina felt the wind sting her uncovered ears. She pulled Father's scarf up around her face and over her ears, growling at the merciless weather. *At least the apples will have a great set if these temperatures persist*, she thought to herself.

They passed the cemetery where Alaina had spent an hour earlier that day cleaning Father's grave site. *Is he truly gone?* She talked to him every day, asking questions and sharing problems. Sometimes she felt as though he were nearby listening—other times she knew she was talking to the pot of soup or the rug on the parlor floor. Where was the father she loved so much? Did he watch as they harvested the apples? Did he sense her grief?

She pulled her mind away from the unknown realm and tucked the blanket close. It would do no good to wander in shadows and avoid the business of living. Miss Johnson had said it was a difficult thing she had to do, and that was plain truth, but difficult or not, she would take her teacher's words of wisdom and figure out her life.

During the ride home she kept edging closer to Nephi for warmth, until their shoulders were touching. She didn't care if he thought her forward. She was cold and tired. So tired. Her mind wandered past frozen apple trees and English castles and golden bibles. Snow elves danced around her feet, and Joanna took her hand and walked her into the church. She had on a white dress with yellow rosebuds. *Why am I wearing Joanna's dress?* The wind blew outside the chapel windows, making them creak and groan. Titus ran in the corral, and the green-eyed young man smiled. Warm arms wrapped around her, and a soft voice whispered in her ear. "Alaina, you're home." She felt a shake. "Alaina."

She looked into the face of Nephi Erickson. "We're home?"

"Yes, ma'am."

She sat straight. Her mind and hands felt numb. "Already?"

He smiled as she clumsily climbed out of the wagon. "You've been asleep an hour."

"I slept sitting up?"

"Yes, ma'am."

She moved to the house. "I'll see if they have supper on. We'll bring you something."

He chuckled kindly at her stupor. "Thank you." He gave a command to Friar Tuck and the horse headed for the barn.

Alaina stood on the porch watching him and trying to clear the fog out of her brain. When she had opened her eyes, had Mr. Erickson been about to kiss her forehead, or had she been dreaming?

CHAPTER 22

Elizabeth Lund sat in the parlor knitting. Kathryn, at her feet, played mumbly pegs, and Alaina waited at the window for Markus Salter to arrive.

"Should I put the rolls in to bake?" Eleanor called from the kitchen.

"Not yet!" Alaina returned. "When I see his carriage at the front gate."

"Do not shriek at each other like scullery maids," Mother snapped.

Alaina sighed and walked to the kitchen. She stood in the doorway watching Eleanor set plates and align the silverware.

"Should I put Mr. Salter at the head of the table?" Eleanor asked.

Alaina shook her head. "Mother at the head, Mr. Salter at the foot. I will sit to his right, you on his left. Kathryn at the left of Mother."

"And James?"

"James isn't coming," Alaina said with an edge to her voice. "He has taken Lois Drakerman to a moving picture show in Jackson."

"I want to see a moving picture show," Eleanor replied. "Don't you wonder how it works? It's like magic."

Alaina rearranged the napkins and set the glasses. "Will the ham be done?"

"I hope so," Eleanor said, lifting the roasting pan out of the oven and setting it on the sideboard. "I'm putting in the rolls."

"Fine." Alaina shrugged. The rolls could burn or be stone cold. What did it matter to her? Out the kitchen window she watched the pale rim of yellow on the western horizon broaden and darken to purple. "Mr. Salter is late."

Kathryn came into the kitchen and took a hard-boiled egg out of the icebox.

"What are you doing? Give me that!" Alaina demanded, reaching for the egg.

"I'm hungry."

"Well, put it back. We're eating supper soon."

"When?"

"When Mr. Salter arrives."

Kathryn began laughing.

How odd. Alaina stared at her youngest sister. "Why are you laughing?"

"Well, I might starve."

"Oh, for goodness sake, he's not that late."

Kathryn laughed harder.

"Stop that! I mean it, and hand me that egg."

Kathryn hid the egg behind her back.

"Kathryn Lund! What's gotten into you?" Alaina turned to look at Eleanor, who covered a smile with her hand. "Elly?"

"Sorry, Laina," Eleanor said, trying to contain herself. She turned her back on her older sister and burst out laughing.

What was going on? Elly never laughed at her. Alaina felt her body flush with heat. "He's not coming, is he?"

Eleanor shook her head.

"He doesn't want to be my husband."

Eleanor shook her head again.

"How do you know?"

Eleanor turned around and brought a piece of paper from her apron pocket. "He sent a note." She held it out and Alaina snatched it.

"A note? He sent a note?"

Kathryn recited, "*Dear Miss Lund, I do not want to marry you, but I will send some saltwater taffy tomorrow.*"

Eleanor wagged her finger. "Now Kathryn, don't be mean."

Alaina kept looking at the writing, trying to make sense of it.

Mother walked into the kitchen carrying a vase of yellow roses, which she placed on the center of the table. "Does she know?"

Eleanor nodded, a look of sadness in her eyes.

"Good then," Mother continued, "my patience was wearing thin. Now I can sell the burden and be done with it."

Alaina glared at her mother. "You can't do that!"

"Oh, but I can. It doesn't seem as though there's a husband in the cards for you, Miss Alaina, and that was our agreement."

"I told you she'd never be married," Kathryn said smugly. "Now we can go live in a big house and have servants!"

Eleanor set the ham on the table, tears washing her face. She gave Alaina a wounded look and intentionally tipped over a wine glass, spilling red wine all over the white tablecloth. "I trusted you. I trusted that you would make everything better."

"Elly, I tried!"

"No! No, you didn't!" She pulled Father's Book of Mormon out of her apron pocket and flung it at her.

Alaina went to take her younger sister's hand.

"Don't touch me! Don't talk to me!" Eleanor wrenched away and ran out the back door into the darkening night.

"Elly! Elly!" Pain was pressing down on her chest, and she found it hard to breathe. "I tried! I did try!"

A soft whimpering voice came to her ear. "*Try . . . did try.*" She opened her eyes onto darkness. A weight of sorrow pinned her to the bed, and she lay still, tears dripping from the corners of her eyes. "I tried," she moaned, turning onto her side and wiping the tears off her face. *Why won't these dreams go away?*

Slowly she sat up, looking over at her sleeping sisters. Her body felt clammy, and there was a pain in her stomach that made her wince. *Why won't these dreams go away?* The nightmare images flashed again into her mind: the look of sadness on Eleanor's face, the note of rejection, the vase of yellow roses. Alaina abandoned the warmth of her bed and went to the window, laying her head on the cold glass. Moonlight washed the barren meadowland, and she saw the flick of a fox's tail as it moved through the dry grass.

She would not lose the farm. She turned and crossed to the door, opened it quietly, and moved out into the dark hallway. She ran her hand along the wall until the break came, then reached down to grasp the stair railing—one careful step after another to the rug at the bottom of the stairs, turning and moving to the kitchen, past the kitchen table devoid of plate or silverware, and out onto the back porch. Here she paused for a moment at the rack of coats, running her hand along the blue scarf she had so often seen her father wear when he was milking or repairing fence posts or hauling hay. She slid it off the hook and wrapped it softly around her neck. She put on her coat, shoved her feet into Father's work boots, and went out the back door into the cold night. The quiet chided her clumsy footsteps, but she didn't care. She held her coat together at the chest, and trudged past the barn where she heard mingled sounds from the livestock. She thought of Friar Tuck and Titus, of the milking to be done in a few short hours, of the unexpected brood of piglets. And then the shed was in sight, a swath of white in the dark.

She pushed back the shed door and breathed in the smells of apples and leather, slowing as she drew near Mr. Erickson's bedroom. Her blood pounded in her ears and she felt sick, but there was no turning back. She laid her hand on the rough wood of the door and tried to still her breathing. She rapped sharply and instantly heard movement, then a pause. She rapped again.

"Yes?" came Mr. Erickson's ragged voice. "Yes? Who is it?"

Alaina spoke firmly. "Alaina Lund."

There was only a moment's hesitation until she heard the latch click and the door open. Nephi stood in the partly opened doorway with a blanket around his waist, his sandy hair disheveled and his eyes wide with concern.

"What is it? What's wrong? Is it your mother?"

This was the moment. She could step back now. She could say it was all a mistake; she could assure him that everything was fine and she was sorry to disturb his sleep. This was the moment.

"I need to speak with you."

She saw his eyes flicker from her face to her boots and back again. He ran his fingers through his hair and opened the door for her. She had been in this room not long ago, but the intimacy of moonlight and her purpose made her uncomfortable, and she found she could not force herself to look at him.

"If you'll turn around, I'll put on some clothes," he said quietly.

She turned without speaking and heard the rustle of clothing as he put on a shirt and a pair of pants.

"I'm dressed," he said, and she turned back to face him.

"My mother is going to sell the farm, Mr. Erickson."

Nephi lowered his head and an angry growl came up into his throat. It startled her.

"Sorry, ma'am, but it makes me mad. I thought you two had a deal."

Alaina's voice was thick with emotion. "Well, I don't seem to be doing my part."

He let out an exasperated breath. "What does she expect from you?"

"To be a proper lady, to beg for a husband, to move to China. I don't know."

There was silence between them as Nephi tried to figure out why she was there, and Alaina tried to find the words for her pathetic situation.

"Would you like to sit down?"

"No. No, thank you. It's bad enough I get you out of bed in the middle of the night."

"It's all right. I can tell you're upset about something."

She kicked the leg of his bed and wrapped her arms across her chest. "I am upset. I am." She kicked the bed again. "I'm supposed to fix things for everybody, and I don't know how to do it. How do I keep Mother from selling the farm? What man would even consider marrying me as a business arrangement? What man would sell his soul for a few acres of land? Would anyone take on such a situation for friendship alone?"

"Alaina, why did you come here?" he asked simply, stopping her next sentence.

She stood staring at his partially shadowed face, his blue eyes illuminated by the moonlight. "I . . ." She pressed her lips together to keep them from trembling. "I can't lose the farm, Nephi. I can't." A tear slid down her cheek.

He wanted to take her in his arms, but he knew that wasn't what she wanted or needed. He stood relaxed, willing his body not to betray his heart. "What can I do?"

She met his look with determination. "Marry me."

She saw his eyes flash, and knew her proposal was not what he expected from her. What did she see in those eyes now fixed on her? Confusion? Pity? Tenderness?

It seemed hours before he spoke. "Do you care for me?"

She was glad he had not said "love," and she considered her reply carefully. "I do care for you. I believe you to be honest and a hard worker." He smiled, and the awkwardness retreated a bit. "My father trusted you, Mr. Erickson, and my father was a good judge of character."

Nephi sat down on the edge of the bed with his elbows on his knees and his hands together. Alaina thought for a moment that he might be praying, but he looked at her solemnly. "This is a hard thing you're asking."

"I know," she replied, her emotions going numb. She wasn't angry, or sad, or embarrassed—just numb. She had spoken the words, and she would calmly wait for the answer. She avoided thinking about the outcome, whatever Mr. Erickson's decision.

"I worry, Alaina. What sort of life will it be for you?"

She thought of the portrait locket under her pillow and the words of Philomene Johnson. *"A man who will be protective of your feelings."* She gave him a genuine smile.

"I don't have an answer for you, Mr. Erickson. Do any of us have a promise of what our lives will be? But I do believe that my life will be better here than anywhere else. If we were married, you would hold the deed and we could run the farm together."

Nephi's heart ached at the coldness with which she viewed their future. There was no indication of joy or anticipation, but then, of course, that was to be expected; she cared for him, but she did not love him, and she was being forced into a situation where she had to consider the most sacred connection between a man and a woman with her mind alone. He had anguished when Daniel and Markus had courted her, and dreaded the day he might have to watch her wedded to another man. And as much as he admired Daniel Chart, it would have been impossible to stay on at the farm if his handsome friend had become Alaina's husband.

Yet, as she stood stoically waiting for his reply, he realized he'd been given a gift. He'd been praying for her to see him differently, and even though this wasn't exactly what he'd had in mind, it was still a gift. She'd said nothing about his religion or how it might affect their relationship; obviously it didn't matter to her as much anymore. And what of his desires for eternal marriage? Was he willing to give that up for someone of another faith who didn't love him? An ache took hold of his heart as he looked at the dear young woman standing in front of him in her father's boots. *I love her. Can I abandon her to sadness?*

He stood and moved to her, taking her hands. He waited until she looked into his eyes. "Yes. I will marry you."

Her hands gripped his tightly, and unbidden tears ran down her cheeks. "Thank you, Mr. Erickson."

Nephi smiled. "I think you may want to start calling me by my given name, Miss Lund."

She smiled back, and ran her coat sleeve across her face. He could see that any reserves of strength she had were gone, and he resolved again to help her through this hard time.

"Go back to bed, and don't worry about milking, I'll take care of it this morning."

She nodded, turned without speaking, and walked through his bedroom doorway out into the shed. He followed her to the outside door.

She turned to him. "Go back, go back! It's freezing out here, and you have bare feet. We'll talk later today."

He hesitated. "Alaina, if you want to change your mind, I'll understand."

"Thank you, Mr. Erick . . . Nephi, but my mind is made up." She shoved her hands into the pockets of her coat and moved back toward the house.

He watched until she disappeared around the corner of the barn, amazed at how life could change in an instant. Doubt flickered across his mind as he thought of his father. What would Father think of his hay-headed son running off to California and getting trapped in a loveless marriage? *No, not trapped, and not loveless.* Nephi shook his head. He was a man now and not reliant on his father to chart the course of his life. He had made a deliberate decision, and though he knew things might prove a test, he was willing to accept it. He smiled. It was more than just acceptance; he truly found joy in the prospect. Alaina was one of the most remarkable women he had ever met. He looked up at the star-filled sky and felt a quiet peace come over him. His heart lifted and he felt like hollering, but knew his voice would carry all the way to Pine Grove on the stillness of the night. He offered a prayer of thanks for the assurance he now felt that God was aware of him, that he would have help determining the direction his new life. *"Please God first and yourself second,"* his mother had always taught him. It was wise counsel. He closed the door of the shed and moved back to the solitude of his room.

Alaina moved slowly by the corral, running her hand along the smooth rails. She saw Titus as a young colt, and the green-eyed young man watching as the beautiful horse bucked and kicked. She saw the meadowland filled with blue and white lupine, and the delicate blossoms on the apple trees. The numbness drained away and she felt calm. She knew she had been guided to the right road, and somehow she would find the strength to walk it.

CHAPTER 23

The chapel was cold. Pastor Wilton had started the stoves earlier in the morning, but they were just beginning to take the chill from the first three rows of pews. Alaina sat at the front of the chapel with a shawl pulled around her and her coat draped over her shoulders. Her face was drained of color, and she kept worrying a dirt spot on the sleeve of her white, summer dress. Why had they arrived so early? She looked over at Eleanor curled up under her own coat on the second pew, sleeping soundly. She was using her shawl for a pillow, her dark hair a contrast to the pale gold yarn. Alaina noted her fifteen years with envy; Elly's life still had choices. She growled at herself, stood up, and walked to one of the warming stoves, vowing that she would not rethink her decision. She had made that same vow many times since the sun rose over the eastern hills that day.

She and Nephi had not spent much time planning for this day. The two things discussed were the date and who would perform the service. Alaina had offered Nephi the chance to have Mr. Bates come down from Placerville, and although he appreciated her consideration, he knew it would be one more heartache in her life. So, in the end they'd agreed on Pastor Wilton. She never knew the many nights Nephi spent before the wedding on his knees asking his Father in Heaven to calm his spirit and hallow the decision.

The door to the pastor's prayer room opened, and the reverend and Nephi emerged, each man dressed for Sunday and carrying an air of solemnity. Alaina tried to read the look on Nephi's face, but his head was down and in shadow.

The main door into the chapel opened, and Joanna Wilton entered, followed closely by Fredrick and Edna Robinson and Daniel. Alaina's heart jumped, and she found her feelings torn between gratitude and embarrassment. She avoided looking at them by taking off her coat and staring at the dirt spot on her sleeve. From the corner of her eye she saw Eleanor sit up and attempt to compose herself. Eleanor would be the only family member in attendance.

Joanna went immediately to her father. "Why is it so cold in here?"

Pastor Wilton smiled. "It's a cold day, daughter. Don't worry, it will warm sufficiently for the ceremony."

Joanna moved to Alaina. "But the bride is freezing."

It was the first time the word *bride* had been said, and Alaina felt a chill of apprehension. "I'm fine Joanna, really."

Joanna wrapped her arms around her friend and whispered in her ear, "I know you. You are not fine, but you'll make the best of things." Her eyes were shiny with tears, and Alaina had to clamp her jaw against emotion.

Joanna whispered again. "Will your mother be here?"

"No."

Elizabeth Lund was probably still in her bedroom, wearing the dressing gown that had been Father's final gift, and brushing her hair.

"You must come to Alaina's wedding," Eleanor had pleaded, taking the brush out of her mother's hand.

Mrs. Lund narrowed her eyes and glared at her middle daughter. "Give it back."

"No. I want you to listen to me. Alaina is doing this for all of us. This way we can keep the farm. It was your agreement."

Mrs. Lund scoffed, "Why do you care so much about the farm?"

Eleanor stared at her mother's mocking face, and held on to compassion. She knew that Mother's mind was wandering—trying desperately to find solid ground, or at least a refuge from grief. She knew her times of strength and clarity were few. More and more of Elizabeth Lund's thoughts centered on a different life, a life of abundance and freedom, a life where pain was kept at bay. She preferred shelter there and resented anything that turned her sight to leafless trees and barren meadowland.

Eleanor knelt down and took her hand. "Mother, this is our home. We were all born here."

Mother's eyes snapped. "I was not born here." She took the brush from Eleanor and laid it on the table. "Besides, there was the agreement."

"But Alaina's kept the agreement! That's why we're having a wedding."

Elizabeth Lund stood and moved to the window. "Kept the agreement? No, Miss Eleanor, she has not kept the agreement."

"But she has."

"No. The boy from Utah is not an acceptable choice. I have told her this time and time again, but she is defiant. The man killed my husband, and now he wants to steal the farm."

Eleanor stood, and her voice took on an uncharacteristic edge. "Mr. Erickson had nothing to do with Father's death. Father's heart was sick long before Mr. Erickson even arrived." Her voice softened as she watched her mother drum her fingers on the windowsill. "Mother, please listen to me. You have to come back to us. We need you. Do you think we're not all grieving—that Alaina isn't grieving?"

"You know nothing about it."

Eleanor had no words for this. It was true: she could not feel exactly what her mother was feeling. But she did know pain—pain so intense that at times she had to stop what she was doing and walk off into the fields until she could breathe again. She moved to the door, turning back to watch as Mother laid her forehead against the smooth glass of the window, a dark figure against the pale light of morning.

"Well, Mother," Eleanor said firmly, "Alaina will be married today, and you will have to keep your word." She moved quietly out of the room to find Alaina in the hallway. Her face was chalk white, and Eleanor knew immediately that she'd heard every word. She'd taken her sister's hand, and the two had walked back to their bedroom to finish getting dressed for the wedding.

Alaina's thoughts cleared and she turned to find Nephi standing beside her. Mr. Robinson was patting him on the back and offering advice. "You look a bit nervous, lad. Not to worry. There's only a few words you've got to remember on your own." The big man then turned to her and took her hand. "You're as pretty as sunshine." Alaina smiled at his genuine kindness. The next moment she was gathered into his arms and lifted off the floor.

"Oh, Fredrick! Put her down!" said Mrs. Robinson in a small voice. "You'll rumple her dress before the ceremony."

But Alaina laughed, and felt the cold of morning pushed back. "No, it's all right, Mrs. Robinson. I don't care about my dress!"

Mrs. Robinson laughed then too and slapped her bear of a husband on the arm. "Just don't break her."

When Mr. Robinson put the bride back onto the floor, Alaina was rosy cheeked, and everyone was smiling, even Pastor Wilton.

"That was for asking me to give you away," Fredrick said heartily. "It's a great honor."

She gave him a squeeze, hoping the gesture would tell him what words could not.

The church door opened again, and everyone turned to watch as Philomene Johnson came into the chapel. She observed the happy gathering and smiled at the unexpected atmosphere. All her students were precious to her, but some distinguished themselves by their valiant struggles. Life was meant to be a prudent teacher, and either you conquered or were conquered by its tests. Some of her students had faced trials far less challenging than Miss Lund's, and had abandoned themselves to drunkenness or a cold heart.

Alaina approached her teacher timidly, a look of wonder on her face. "You came to my wedding?"

Miss Johnson smiled. "Since I've been praying for it, I thought it appropriate I attend. These are for you." She held out a small bouquet of white carnations, tied with a pale ivory ribbon. "They're from my hot house. Not very elegant, but flowers nonetheless."

Alaina was overcome by her thoughtfulness. She embraced her teacher tenderly. "I love them, and I love that you're here."

Nephi came to stand with Alaina, reaching out and taking Philomene's hand. "Welcome, Miss Johnson. Thank you for coming."

"Actually, I must thank you, Nephi. It is always a pleasure to be a witness to selfless nobility."

"Hello, Miss Johnson," Eleanor said quietly. She had edged her way around several pews and was now standing beside her teacher, nervously shifting from one foot to the other.

Miss Johnson put an arm around her shoulder and pulled her close. "Miss Eleanor! How is my scholar?"

Eleanor smiled and blushed. "I'm fine, thank you. I'm the maid of honor."

Philomene held out another bouquet of flowers—smaller, and with a gold ribbon. "Then these are for you."

Eleanor's eyes widened. "Oh, they're so pretty . . . and the ribbon matches my shawl!"

"Lucky chance."

"Thank you, Miss Johnson."

"Well, the maid of honor is an important calling, and I know your sister is glad to have you near her side." She looked earnestly into the young girl's face and knew she understood the responsibility.

As everyone greeted Miss Johnson and began talking amiably with each other, Alaina couldn't help but notice that Daniel stood a little off to the side of the group, his expression unreadable. She knew this day was not easy for him. Did he regret not saying yes to her proposal and working out the emotional issues later? Or was he, like she, mourning the loss of friendship? He would still be her friend, but only through Nephi. There would no longer be conversations with just the two of them, no more shared secrets or teasing, and certainly no more opportunity to establish a closer companionship. She caught his eye and smiled at him.

He smiled back, and she moved to him. "How are you?" he asked softly.

Alaina hesitated, not knowing what to say.

"I'm sorry, Alaina. That was a stupid question."

"It's all right, Daniel. I just wish I knew how to answer."

There was an awkward silence as each tried to think of appropriate conversation. Daniel glanced over at Philomene Johnson. "Miss Johnson is an amazing woman."

"She is. It's a shame you were never able to have her as a teacher."

"She seems to like Nephi."

Alaina chuckled. "Oh, they're old friends. One meeting and you'd think they'd known each other for years."

"He's a good man, Alaina. I know he'll treat you kindly."

She felt tears pressing at the back of her eyes, and she looked down at the floor. Her voice was ragged when she spoke. "Thank you, Daniel."

Pastor Wilton moved over to them, speaking to Alaina as he came. "We are ready to begin, Miss Lund. Are you expecting anyone else?"

She looked over at the small group of people who were dear to her and smiled. "No, I think we have everyone." She straightened her shawl, brought her bouquet of carnations to her face, and breathed in the delicate smell. *November eighteenth in the year of our Lord 1913, Alaina Kay Lund and Nephi Erickson become husband and wife.*

Mrs. Nephi Erickson. How odd. She didn't even know if he had a middle name. She looked to Miss Johnson and found her smiling a calm smile. Alaina tried not to think about the cold ache in her stomach, or the desire to run out through the front doors into the brilliant blue sky. She looked to Pastor Wilton who was nodding and motioning her to the altar area. He held out his hand to Nephi, who came to stand beside his bride. She could sense him trembling, and agonized that the only emotion he could feel on their wedding day was fear.

Pastor Wilton lifted his voice. "Friends and neighbors, I think we are ready to begin. Who is standing up for Alaina Lund?"

"I am, Pastor," came Eleanor's reply.

"Then come and take your place beside her. And who for Nephi Erickson?"

"I am," Daniel answered as he crossed to his place. He and Nephi shared a handshake.

"And who giveth this young woman to be married?"

Fredrick Robinson rose from his seat. He cleared his throat, began to speak, and then stopped as emotion overcame him. Mrs. Robinson handed him her lace hankie, and he pressed it to his eyes. Everyone smiled at him, not minding the wait.

"Sorry. Sorry about that," he said finally, standing straight and handing his wife her hankie. "I, Fredrick Robinson do proudly give . . ." A tear ran down his cheek. "I give this sweet young woman to be married." He beamed at her, and she felt a tear run down her own cheek. She brushed it away and turned back to Pastor Wilton, who began speaking words that were nothing more than a jumble of sound. Her head felt hot, and her legs were shaking. Was she going to faint at her own wedding? Nephi moved close and put his arm around her waist. She was so overwhelmed by the moment that she didn't notice the door open slightly and her brother James slipping in to stand at the back of the chapel.

Pastor Wilton's voice continued on. ". . . to love, honor, and obey from this day forward until death do you part?"

Nephi gave her a small squeeze, and her voice somehow responded, "I do."

Was that right? Had she said the right words? She put the flowers to her face and tried to breathe in their sweetness. Surely if she'd said the wrong words they would have stopped the ceremony and corrected her. She mouthed the words again—*I do, I do, I do*—and then heard them repeated aloud by a man's voice. She looked over to see Nephi, a slight flush on his cheeks, staring up at Pastor Wilton. Nephi's arm left her waist, and he turned to Daniel Chart. Daniel handed his friend a ring, then smiled at Alaina, but she only blinked. *This is stupid! This is the only wedding I will ever have, and I'm missing it!* She took a deep breath and forced her mind to slow down. Her legs stopped shaking, and she found that Pastor Wilton was no longer speaking a foreign language. Eleanor reached over and took her bouquet.

"Now, Mr. Erickson, if you will take your bride's hand."

Nephi reached down and gently took Alaina's left hand. *Where did he get a ring?* She was amazed to see a simple gold band and to feel the warmth of Nephi's trembling hand on her hand. She looked into his face, and he was smiling. She smiled back, and his hand stopped trembling.

"Please repeat after me, Mr. Erickson. With this ring . . ."

"With this ring . . ."

"I thee wed."

"I thee wed."

"This ring is a symbol . . ."

"This ring is a symbol . . ."

"Of my endless devotion."

"Of my endless devotion." He smiled again and slid the ring onto her finger.

Then Pastor Wilton spoke more words that she didn't hear. She was staring into Nephi's blue eyes and thinking about days in the orchard together. He was a good man, and so kind to marry her with only a slight friendship on which to tie their lives.

"I now pronounce you husband and wife." There was a pause. "You may kiss your bride, Mr. Erickson."

Those words she heard clearly, and her breath caught in her chest. She hadn't even thought about the tradition. She and Nephi hadn't talked about this. He probably didn't even want to kiss her. Nervously she glanced at his face as he leaned forward, kissing her softly at the corner of her mouth. It was the first kiss she'd ever received, and a chill raced from the top of her head into her fingertips. She gripped his hands tightly, realizing that her eyes were still closed.

Suddenly there was clapping and cheering, and she was being hugged by Eleanor, and Nephi was being thumped on the back by Mr. Robinson. Her heart felt light, almost giddy. *November eighteenth is a good day* . . . She looked down at the ring on her finger and thought it odd that she'd never had jewelry before—and now the same man had given her a ring and a locket. Her locket! She reached to the chain around her neck and drew the precious treasure out from under her bodice. Eleanor smiled, glad that her sister no longer needed to keep the piece a secret, and Philomene Johnson, who was next in line for greetings, noticed it immediately.

"How lovely, Alaina. Is it a family piece?"

"Nephi's family," Alaina responded. "And look inside." She opened the locket to reveal the cherished pictures.

"Did Nephi do these?"

"He did."

Miss Johnson looked over at Nephi, who was giving Eleanor a hug. A smile played at the corners of the astute woman's mouth. "And from the quiet heart are continents revealed."

Alaina, who had turned to be hugged by Edna Robinson, glanced back at her dear teacher. "I'm sorry, Miss Johnson, what did you say?"

"Just that I truly believe you two can have a fine life together."

Mrs. Robinson moved off to talk with the preacher, and Alaina turned and took her teacher's hands. "Do you really think that?"

"I do."

Alaina nodded, wishing the two of them could be alone to talk through her fears.

"Congratulations, Alaina."

Alaina spun around at the sound of her brother's voice. "James?" He smiled at her. "James! Did you come to my wedding?"

He chuckled. "Well, I did, unless this is some other sort of party."

"Oh, James." Tears filled her eyes and she hugged him tightly.

Everyone was captivated by the sweet moment, and it was some time before anyone could speak. Eventually Alaina stepped away from her sibling, and Nephi gripped James's hand tightly. "So glad you came, James."

James smiled timidly. "I hope you two will be happy together."

"All right! I've been waiting long enough!" Joanna interrupted with mock impatience, taking hold of Alaina's arm. "I get her all to myself for a while."

Alaina smiled at her girlhood friend, noting sadly the feeling of distance already separating them. Miss Johnson came up to speak to Nephi and James as Joanna pulled Alaina to the side.

"Married!" Joanna sighed, fixing one of the flowers in Alaina's hair. "I can't believe it. We just played hopscotch yesterday, didn't we? I thought we would stay blissfully unmarried and travel Europe together."

Alaina laughed. "You unmarried? Never."

Joanna laughed with her. "I suppose you're right." She looked at Alaina wistfully. "Oh, but it was a lovely ceremony."

"Was it? I don't remember much."

Joanna gave her friend a squeeze. "Well, you're not supposed to. You're the bride."

"Well, it would have been nice if I'd remembered to say, 'I do.'"

Joanna giggled. "You did. Nephi sort of had to squeeze it out of you, but you said it. Actually, you both looked nervous, but Daddy got you through it. In fact, I'm going to go give your new husband a few pieces of advice." She turned purposefully toward the unsuspecting groom, and Alaina worried what she would say to him.

She didn't have much time to fret about it, because Fredrick Robinson came to visit the moment Joanna left her side. He looked a bit sheepish. "Sorry that I spoiled the ceremony."

Alaina took hold of one of his big hands. "Don't be silly; it was my favorite part."

His eyes twinkled. "Oh really? I would have thought that the kiss was your favorite part."

She stepped back from him, her face filling with color, and he laughed a huge laugh that filled the chapel with gaiety. Alaina laughed with him.

"Stop that now, you're terrible," she reprimanded.

"Well, I may be terrible," he whispered, "but that kiss wasn't."

Her eyes widened at his teasing, bringing more chuckles from the big man.

"Your wife is about to come over here and drag you home if you don't behave yourself," Alaina said, trying to sound stern.

He calmed himself a little. "Sorry, sweetheart, just having a bit of fun." He smiled and patted her arm. "Thank you again for letting me stand in your father's place. I mean, not that I could actually stand in his place . . . but I . . ."

She smiled at him. "I know what you mean. Having you there is exactly what he would have wanted."

Fredrick didn't say any more, but wiped his eyes on his shirtsleeve.

Nephi came to stand beside his new bride, and from the look on his face, Alaina could tell he was overwhelmed by all the attention and well-wishing.

Daniel came up, thumped his friend on the back, and reached over to shake Alaina's hand. "Congratulations, Mrs. Erickson. Happiness to both of you."

"Thank you, Daniel . . . Mr. Chart, thank you."

Pastor and Mrs. Wilton came over with their congratulations, and the minister handed Nephi the marriage papers. Alaina smiled, thinking about another piece of paper they would soon be receiving.

"You had not mentioned if you had plans," Pastor Wilton was saying.

Alaina didn't understand what he meant. "Plans?"

"Dinner at the hotel, a short stay in Jackson."

Alaina's face colored. "Oh. Oh, no. We . . . we have to get back to the farm. There's pruning still to be done."

"Oh my," Mr. Robinson said good-naturedly. "Seems like there's no rest for you, Mr. Erickson."

"It suits me, sir," he said smiling.

Mr. Robinson laid a hand on Nephi's and Alaina's shoulders, "A perfect match, Pastor Wilton. A perfect match."

"And a blessing to each other for many years to come," the pastor agreed.

"Thank you, Pastor Wilton," Alaina said, shaking his hand. She turned to the others. "Thank you for coming. Life would be a dreary place without friends."

"And love," Edna Robinson put in timidly.

"And love," Alaina nodded.

Miss Johnson handed them both envelopes. "A small wedding present." Alaina began to protest, but Philomene held up her hand. "Never deny a gift, for its true magic is that it bestows more pleasure on the one who gives."

Alaina thanked her, and Philomene gave her a smile. "That's better." She put on her gloves. "Now, sometime this winter you two must come for dinner." She put on her coat. "I will cook rabbit stew—my great-grandpa's recipe. It came all the way from Wales."

"The rabbit?"

"Very funny, Mr. Erickson." She gave him a look as though she would jokingly hit him with a ruler. "And you can tell me of adventures of faith from Denmark." She held their hands. "Congratulations, my dear young couple. I will see you soon." She turned to leave, wishing the others well, and moving out into the bright day.

Everyone said their final good-byes, James actually giving his sister a hug before leaving. Alaina was touched by his unselfish act in attending, and she felt it an omen of how well things were going to run on the farm as they all worked together.

She looked over to Eleanor and Joanna who were whispering secrets to one another. She found that behavior very odd, as she'd always figured the two girls had never cared much for each other.

"What are you two whispering about?" Alaina asked as she approached.

"Just never you mind," Joanna said. "It's a surprise."

"I don't like surprises."

"Well, that's too bad. I'll be out to the farm to see you in a few days."

"Is that the surprise?"

"No," Joanna said mysteriously as she kissed Alaina on the cheek. "And don't wear yourself out trying to guess." She nodded at Eleanor, and moved out of the chapel with her mother.

Alaina gave her sister a searching look. "What was that about?"

Elly gave her a mischievous grin and put on her coat. "Sorry, Laina, but I'm sworn to silence." She gave her a hug. "I'll see you later."

"What do you mean?"

"I'm riding with the Robinsons."

"But why?"

Eleanor gave her a half-smile. "So you and Nephi can ride home together."

Alaina panicked. "Oh, truly Elly, there's no need. I'd rather you stayed with us."

Eleanor put her hand on Alaina's arm and whispered, "Laina, it wouldn't look right. Just drive with your husband, and I'll see you at home." With that she walked over to join the Robinsons. Mr. Robinson waved as they walked out into the afternoon sunshine.

Alaina knew that Elly was right, but she didn't want it to be just the two of them in the carriage. What would she say to him?

Pastor Wilton moved back to the prayer room, leaving Nephi and Alaina alone in the chapel. It seemed cold and echoing after the warmth of friends, and Alaina shivered. Nephi came to her with her coat and held it up so she could slip her arms into the sleeves.

"Thank you."

"You're welcome."

She looked at him steadily. "Thank you for everything."

His face flushed. "You look so beautiful, Alaina," he said, holding out her father's scarf to her. She took it, grateful for something to distract her embarrassment.

Nephi watched his wife as she wrapped the soft fabric around her neck and put on her knitted winter hat and gloves. A bit of her summer white dress showed in the break at the bottom of her coat, and he shook his head in wonder at the sight of her. She was his bride. He was a married man.

Alaina's voice broke into his thoughts. "Are you all right?"

"Fine, fine. Are you ready to go?"

She nodded, and they headed out to the carriage.

The sky was cloudless and a brilliant November blue. Alaina was surprised at how the air had warmed since their early morning ride in.

"We could stop at the hotel for dinner if you'd like," Nephi said, helping her into the carriage.

"Oh no. No, thank you," came her quick reply. "I'll fix something for us when we get home."

He climbed into the carriage feeling awkward and ill at ease. He didn't want her cooking today. This was her wedding day, and she should have something special—but he also didn't want to go against her wishes. He picked up the lines and gave Friar Tuck the command to move forward.

"I'll fix something for us when we get home." Over the years, Alaina had often heard Mother say similar words, and she was surprised at how readily she'd given the offer. There was only one problem: she cooked only what she was told to cook. She had no idea how to prepare an entire meal from beginning to end. The few times she'd attempted her own experimental dishes, they had always ended in failure.

She brushed aside the worried thoughts. *Oh well. Mother and Eleanor can do the cooking. I'll be too busy working the farm.* She glanced over at Nephi and then back at the road. Friar Tuck was setting a brisk pace, and the breeze was cold against her face, chapping her cheeks rough and red. She pulled the scarf closer around her neck and pulled her hat snugly over her ears. She employed the rest of the ride home figuring out the jobs that still needed doing before winter set in.

* * *

Nephi changed out of his Sunday clothes the moment they arrived home and went to work on the threshing machine. He liked the work and the quiet. Other than the distant cluck of chickens, and an occasional snort from one of the horses, the afternoon drifted away in peaceful silence. His stomach growled, and he realized he was hungry. He smiled as he thought of Alaina attempting to cook their first meal. He didn't care if he had to wait until supper; he knew she was trying, and he would love whatever she set before him. It was odd to think that he'd actually be sitting at the table in the kitchen.

He was jolted from his thoughts by a loud crash coming from the house. There was another crash. He moved around the side of the barn and shaded his eyes so he could see the back of the house. Eleanor was running across the yard making a direct line to him.

"Nephi! Nephi! Come with me!" She grabbed his arm and urgently pulled him toward the house.

He dropped the wrench. "What? What is it?"

Eleanor burst into tears. "It's Alaina . . . terrible . . . so terrible."

His heart lurched. Was she hurt? *Oh, please don't let her be hurt.*

They reached the house as another crash sounded. He could now hear what he assumed was Alaina shrieking. They moved into the back porch and found Kathryn huddled in the corner, crying.

"She's . . . going to kill someone," the little girl sobbed.

Another crash as he moved into the kitchen. He saw a serving plate shattered on the floor, along with pots, pans, and food. He looked up to see Alaina, her hair disheveled, her blue skirt a splattered mess. She picked up a metal colander and threw it at the door frame where Elizabeth Lund stood, frozen with fear.

"Alaina, stop it!" Nephi yelled.

She turned to look at him, her face filled with grief and anger. "Stop it? Stop it?" She picked up another plate and flung it at the wall. Kathryn screamed and Eleanor stepped back onto the porch.

Nephi ran and grabbed Alaina's wrist just before she got hold of the coffeepot.

"Alaina stop!"

She was filled with such fury that she broke his grip and went for it again. "How? How could she do it?" He grabbed her hand and her arm knocked the pot to the floor. He yanked her back, but the hot liquid splashed over her feet, causing her to scream in pain and rage.

Nephi wrapped his arms around her, pulling her back against his chest. She struggled to free herself, but he could tell the anger had taken its toll. She screamed and gasped for breath. "She sold it! She said she sold it!" She screamed again. "It's not true! It can't be true!" Great sobs racked her body as she clawed at Nephi's hands. He'd gone stiff when he'd heard the word *sold*. He didn't want to think about what it meant. He looked at Mrs. Lund, who glared at him defiantly.

"I told her you were not a suitable husband. I told her."

Alaina tried to lunge for her. "You knew before I was married . . . sold it before . . . you didn't tell us!"

The full impact of what was happening hit him, and he let Alaina go. She slumped to the ground, moaning and crying. Nephi looked into Mother Lund's worn face. "You sold the farm?"

Her back straightened, and her hand went to the cameo at her neck. "I did."

He wasn't sure of her reply. "You sold the farm?" He tried to shake reason into his head. "Why? Why would you do that?"

Mrs. Lund narrowed her eyes. "Ask her," she said, pointing at Alaina. "I told her she was not to marry you. I told her. She thought she had power over me."

Nephi looked at Elizabeth Lund's chalky-white face and red-rimmed eyes and knew that madness was staring back at him. He calmed his breathing. With this knowledge there might be a way for him and Alaina to reclaim what was theirs, a chance to bring the farm back into their hands. He spoke softly. "Eleanor, please take Kathryn and your mother up to their rooms." Eleanor didn't move, and he turned to look at her. "Please."

She looked to her elder sister. "But . . ."

"I'll take care of Alaina. Your mother needs your help."

Eleanor nodded and picked Kathryn up off the floor. She moved to her mother and took her by the arm. Elizabeth Lund turned from the chaos and followed her sweet daughter obediently.

Nephi stood staring at Alaina until he heard the bedroom doors shut, then he knelt down beside her. She had her arms folded across the seat of a kitchen chair, her head down, her breath coming in short ragged gasps. He patted her back. "It's going to be all right. Somehow we'll figure it out."

She sobbed into his arms. "She let us get married, and we didn't need . . . didn't need to."

Nephi's heart ached as he felt her regret. He lifted her up. "Come on. Let's go walk out in the orchard."

She stood for a moment, looking blankly at the destruction, then turned to find her coat and scarf. Perhaps they could walk until the nightmare ended.

CHAPTER 24

The nightmare did not end. Elizabeth Knight Lund had been perfectly sane when she'd sent a telegraph to the Sacramento newspaper advertising a farm for sale, perfectly coherent when she'd handed the deed to Mr. Blackhurst in the county clerk's office, and perfectly calm when she'd deposited several thousand dollars in the bank.

Alaina and Nephi had appealed to the county probate judge, but received no encouragement, only words of law and ownership rights. Besides, there was no written agreement between Alaina and her mother, and the law required paperwork.

Through the first days of fact-finding and struggle, Alaina fiercely held on to hope, but recently Nephi had seen a dispirited resignation engulfing her as appeal after appeal was rejected. He often found her in the barn brushing Titus, or pruning fruit trees that needed no pruning, or muttering to herself as she made bread. He waited for her to ask for an annulment, but those words never came. The newlyweds spoke only when it concerned farm work or legal issues about the land. It was nearing the end of November, and their vision of the future was narrowing.

The farm was now at rest: the fruit had been sent to market, the sap in the leafless trees had retreated to the very core of the wood, and the garden was a neglected mass of rotted vines and unused produce. The work now centered on care of the livestock and repairs.

Alaina brought a pan of biscuits from the oven and set it on the table. "Thank you for your gracious bounty, Lord," she said without thanks at all, and turned back to the stove to place ham on a platter. Kathryn grabbed a biscuit while James and Eleanor shared a look, and

Nephi sat staring at his plate. Mother was in her room, and Eleanor would take food up to her later.

Alaina put the plate of meat on the table and sat down in her place. "Nephi, you're not eating," she said, pushing the pan toward him.

Nephi glanced at her, then took a few biscuits and a slab of ham. "Thank you."

"It looks like snow is coming," Alaina announced. "Is the barn roof finished?"

"Just about," James answered. "We had to stop to make shakes. Should be finished this afternoon."

"Good." She looked at James and nodded. "Good."

They ate in silence, Alaina picking at small bites of ham and looking distractedly out the kitchen window. Finally she laid her fork on her plate and looked directly at James. "So, have you decided what you're going to do?"

"Do?"

"Where will you be going when the new owners arrive?"

Everyone stopped eating and looked at her. It was the first time she had talked about their future, and each took note of the detached, unemotional quality in her voice. Even Kathryn sensed the odd behavior of her older sister.

"Alaina, what's wrong with you?"

"Kathryn, hush up!" Eleanor snapped.

"Why? I just asked a question."

"Do not speak unless you're spoken to."

Kathryn crossed her arms and sat dejectedly back in her chair.

There was silence until Alaina spoke again. "Well?"

James looked at her straight on. "I'm not going to San Francisco with the others."

Alaina sat perfectly still. "You're not?"

James shook his head. "No. There's no place for me at Aunt Ida's. Mr. Regosi offered me a job on his ranch, and I'm going to take it."

A smile touched the corners of Alaina's mouth. "Finally a chance to work with horses. Good for you."

"Yes, ma'am," James said quietly.

"And you'll be taking our horses with you?" Alaina asked simply.

Eleanor turned quickly to James, anxious for his response. She hadn't even thought about the eventual ownership of their precious horses.

James took a breath. "I thought I would, yes."

Alaina stood to get the coffeepot and filled James's mug. "I think it's the best thing."

Nephi pushed the half-eaten plate of food away from him. His wife was talking about these painful decisions as though she were buying sugar or sacks of flour at the mercantile, and he understood, without doubt, that anguish was pouring into some dark cavern of her soul—anguish that would be meted out when life seemed fenced and quiet.

"And Eleanor, you and Kathryn are going to San Francisco with Mother?"

"We are!" Kathryn said excitedly.

"Kathryn, be quiet," Eleanor warned.

"What? I was spoken to. I can talk if I'm spoken to. You said. And we are going to Aunt Ida's to live in a big house and have servants."

Alaina sat down. "Eleanor?"

Eleanor's eyes filled with tears, and she nodded. "I would rather go with you, but . . ."

". . . but Nephi and I don't know where we are going as yet. Our options are . . . small." She looked at her husband. "We will decide in the next few days."

"Besides," Eleanor continued, caught up in the desire to share her frustration, "I have to stay with Mother. She's not well."

Alaina nodded. "I understand."

Nephi watched as his wife twisted and untwisted the corner of the tablecloth. He reached out to take her hand, but she pulled away.

"So . . . so other than Nephi and myself, we're all settled. Good. That's good." She stood up, put two biscuits and a piece of ham onto a plate, and handed it to Eleanor. "Please take Mother her breakfast. Kathryn, you will help me with the dishes, and you men better get to that roof."

They heard the sound of a carriage at the front of the house, and Kathryn abandoned her duties immediately to run for the door. "I wonder who it is."

Eleanor put Mother's breakfast on the table and hurried after Kathryn.

"Eleanor!" Alaina called, but her younger sister was halfway down the hall. Alaina sighed, took off her apron, and followed. Kathryn had swung open the front door, and Alaina could see Jim Peterson helping Joanna out of the carriage. Joanna was rosy cheeked from the ride up from town, and Alaina was surprised that she'd made the trip on such a cold day.

Joanna came to her quickly. "Isn't it a wonder that I'd come out on a day like today?" She laughed and hugged Alaina tightly. "But I had to. I just had to." James and Nephi came out onto the front porch. "And here's your handsome husband come just in time."

Joanna's innocent girlish chatter unsettled Alaina, but it took her mind off of harder thoughts, so she welcomed it.

"Good day, Mrs. Erickson," Jim Peterson said, tipping his hat.

"Good morning, Mr. Peterson. I imagine you two had to start out about daybreak."

"Yes, ma'am. First light."

"That's because of the surprise!" Joanna beamed.

"What surprise? Are you two . . . ?"

"No! Heavens, no!" Joanna said quickly—a bit too quickly for Mr. Peterson's liking. "It's your wedding present!"

"You came out in this weather to bring our wedding present?" A cold wind blew across the porch, making Alaina painfully aware that she was without coat and gloves. "Well, bring it inside before I freeze to death."

Joanna laughed. "I don't think that would be a good idea. Nephi, get her a coat, and Alaina, you close your eyes."

Alaina glanced over at Eleanor and found she was smiling almost as broadly as Joanna. She remembered Joanna and Elly's whispered conversation at the church, and knew her sister had been in on the secret from the beginning.

Nephi brought out her coat, and Alaina slipped it on.

"All right, both of you," Joanna directed Nephi and Alaina. "Both of you close your eyes."

They did as they were told, and Joanna went to the back of the carriage to secure the gift. She came around to the bottom of the porch, and Kathryn gasped.

"All right, you can look!" Joanna said brightly.

Alaina opened her eyes first to see Joanna, and then by her side, the most beautiful little horse in the world. Her heart melted as she looked at the precious face and watched the ears flick this way and that. It had come from town tied to the back of the carriage, and was obviously stimulated by the travel. It nuzzled Joanna playfully, pawed the ground, and bucked several times.

Alaina looked wide-eyed at her lifelong friend. "You bought us a horse as a wedding present?"

"I did!" Joanna said, giggling. "Aren't you going to come meet her?"

Alaina pulled herself from shock and moved down to run her hands gently over the back and rump of the chestnut filly. The coat shimmered with health, the legs long, the stance perfect.

"And, this is not just any horse," Joanna said softly.

"I can see that," Alaina answered, putting an arm affectionately around the filly's neck.

"You know that the Petersons have a horse sired by Titus," Joanna said.

Alaina nodded. "Of course. Shasta Blue Mountain."

Joanna continued, "And Shasta sired a mare for the Mattuchi family?"

Alaina thought for a moment, and began to tremble at the possibility of where Joanna was headed. "The Mattuchis' mare, Cinder."

"Well," Joanna paused as emotion caught in her throat, "this is Cinder's foal."

The strength gave way in Alaina's legs and she sat down hard on the porch steps. Nephi came to sit beside her, looking up into Joanna's face. "There couldn't be a better gift, Miss Wilton. Not in all the world."

Joanna beamed, and Alaina took Nephi's hand, saying, "No matter where we go, we'll take this horse. Promise me we'll take this horse."

"Of course," he said smiling.

Alaina jumped up and flung her arms around Joanna's neck. "I love her! You are the dearest, sweetest friend."

The horse bucked sideways, and Joanna almost dropped the lead rope.

James stepped forward. "Here, let me take her while you two cry," he said with a wink. He looked the filly over with a capable eye.

"She's a beauty," he remarked to Nephi as Eleanor and Kathryn came near to touch and admire the animal. "She's spirited, but not skittish," James went on, running his hand over her legs. "I'd give three regular mares for the likes of her."

"Thanks, James," Nephi said, admiring his brother-in-law's ability. He hadn't seen James this animated since the Fourth of July baseball game—an innocent day that seemed a lifetime ago.

They all watched as James skillfully led the little animal around the yard, and Nephi found himself experiencing an odd envy. He realized that while he was glad James had secured a place at Mr. Regosi's ranch, he was also aware that he had no place or prospects. Something had to turn up. He'd been praying every day, and he'd even written a letter to Salt Lake City. Maybe he could find work on a neighboring farm or cutting timber at Lake Tahoe. He shook the thought away. What kind of life would that be for Alaina? Somehow he would make a home for them. He watched Alaina closely as she ran beside her precious new gift, unable to imagine the grieving of a heart that saw nothing but loss and separation. Yet, for the moment, she seemed to have regained some of her youthful innocence. For the moment, there was laughter and hope.

The horse was eventually put into the paddock, and Jim and Joanna had a bite of breakfast and some hot coffee to fortify them for the ride back to town. When it was time for them to go, Joanna and Alaina stood in the yard with their arms around each other's waists, just as they'd done so often at school—each unwilling to break the grasp, each unwilling to sever the tender years of girlhood. But the soft gray clouds had turned to steel, and they could taste snow in the air.

"Have you thought of a name for her?" Joanna asked, ignoring the cold wind.

Alaina shook her head. "I'll let you know when I do." She held her friend close. "I can't tell you what she means to me."

Joanna only nodded, her heart filled with sorrow for her friend's sadness.

Mr. Peterson broke into their solitude. "Joanna, we'd better go. The storm is moving in fast."

Nephi helped Joanna into the carriage, holding onto her hand well after she was settled. "I always thought you were a little spoiled, Miss Wilton, but I was wrong. You have a wise and understanding heart."

"Thank you, Mr. Erickson." She smiled at him with genuine kindness. "I guess people can get the wrong idea about a lot of things."

Jim Peterson slapped the reins and the horse started off with a jolt. Alaina ran along with them for a few moments, holding onto the side of the rig. She was fearful of the time when she would lose the grip. When it came, she wanted to scream for Jim to stop, to take her with them. Gulping air into her lungs, she watched desolately as the carriage moved out the front gate. She shot her hand into the air for a final wave, but her friends were too far away.

Suddenly, she wanted nothing more than to see her wedding present. She turned quickly and ran all the way to the barn, bringing Titus out into the corral to meet the little darling. The big horse stood stoically while the filly pawed the ground, tossed her head, and squealed. Alaina watched from outside the paddock, filled with wonder at the gift of this perfect creature. She thought about the other horses, and their loss felt like a knifepoint in her throat. She knew James was the one person Father would trust with their care, yet knowing that did not ease her grief. She laid her head on the railing, fighting back the emotional storm that beat inside her head. Her face felt hot, despite the cold wind that was blowing. Words came raw and forced from her throat. "Father, I'm sorry. I don't know what to do. How did this happen? All your work for nothing!" She gave a strangled cry and kicked the fence.

Titus whinnied and Alaina looked up just as she bucked sideways into the patient sire. Titus stamped one of his massive feet, and the little horse bolted away, twisting and kicking, then giving a snort and racing around the corral.

Alaina laughed at the comical little thing, and some of her pain was borne away. Nephi came quietly to stand beside her. "Have you thought of a name?"

Alaina folded her arms across her chest. "I think I'll call her Miss Titus."

"It's a good name," he said simply.

Alaina nodded, and took hold of her locket. "Thank you for letting me keep her."

He looked into her dark eyes. "That's none of my say."

"Well, it might be a lot of transporting depending on where we end up."

Nephi kicked the dirt. "I truly have troubled your life."

Alaina turned to look at him square on. "Nephi, my mother had it in her mind to sell this farm no matter what. She's never felt planted here, and after Father's death . . .." She looked back at the horses. "I just think there's too much pain for her."

But isn't our marriage a burden to you? Wouldn't you rather be free to go to San Francisco, or live with Joanna, or travel the world with Miss Johnson? He wanted to ask all these questions, but wasn't sure he wanted the answers. She had never mentioned separation or divorce, so perhaps it was better if he said nothing. In the silence between them, they heard the rattle of tools in a toolbox and knew that James was coming to fix the barn.

Nephi stepped back, tipping his hat. "I will find a place to settle, I promise."

Alaina moved to put the horses into the barn. "I have no worries on that account, Nephi. You are a man of character."

James came around the side of the barn lugging tools and shakes. "There you are!" he called good-naturedly to Nephi. "Get over here and help me!"

Nephi chuckled and ran to pick up the box of tools. "I was only trying to let you build your muscles."

"Some other time. Some other time," James chided. "We'll be lucky to beat the storm."

Alaina watched the two men as they disappeared around the side of the barn, amazed at the fledgling friendship. She would never have thought it possible. *"Things change, Fancy. Things change all the time."*

She slid her hand along the filly's shiny coat and grasped the lead rope. The little horse shook her head while Titus nuzzled Alaina's coat pocket.

"No, you silly horse, I don't have carrots, but I'll give you some fresh, sweet hay." She led the beloved animals toward the warmth of the barn, sliding back the side door and stepping into the familiar surroundings. "Well, I suppose Mr. and Mrs. Erickson could always set up housekeeping in a barn somewhere."

CHAPTER 25

"Grab that lead! She's going to buck again! Don't let her run!" The baggage captain was yelling commands at his seemingly inept loaders as they tried to get the chestnut filly into the stable car. If they didn't secure her soon, the train would have a late departure—and the conductor was a man for punctuality. The trains from Martell ran into the heart of California, carrying produce and livestock every day, and the loaders were normally efficient at their jobs, but this spirited animal was testing their abilities.

Alaina could see that Miss Titus wanted nothing to do with the moveable barn filled with a half-dozen sheep, two cows, and a huge sow. The filly's eyes were wide with fright as she strained against the lead, bolting from any strange hand that tried to touch her.

"Oh, let me have her!" James yelled, losing patience. He didn't care about company policy. He moved up the plank and yanked the lead out of the hand of the burly man who had loaded all the other livestock without incident. James ignored the man's muttered curse, running his hand down the little horse's neck and speaking to her in a soft, low voice. "Hey, hey girl. Steady now." Her ears flicked, and she shook her head, but she stood still without pulling. "You're fine, you're just fine. You're going on a nice, long trip—all the way to Salt Lake City. They'll give you plenty to eat, and you'll have your own little stall." He guided her gently up the ramp, and she followed. "See, you'll have all these nice sheep to keep you warm, and that big old sow is way at the other end of the car."

They disappeared into the car, and Alaina felt the familiar twinge of fear and sadness. How she wished James could come with them to help Miss Titus through the train changes at Sacramento, Truckee, Reno, and Ogden—such an arduous trip for such an untried creature. How she wished Eleanor could also come with her. Her mind tried to grasp the long journey she was taking from familiar things. Over seven hundred miles to an unknown place, and even though Nephi had shown her the kind letter his mother had written, inviting them to come live in her small home in Salt Lake City, Alaina knew that she would be a stranger in a strange land—a nonbeliever among people who had struggled and suffered for their faith.

She shook her head at the memory of this final moment that so altered her life. Nephi had come to the back door and knocked quietly, taking off his hat when she'd come to answer.

"Nephi, you don't have to knock. Just come in." He nodded and moved past her into the warm kitchen. "I'll have supper ready in a bit."

He smiled at her. "Smells good."

"Stew."

There was an awkward silence as Nephi cleared his throat and reached into his pocket. "I was in town today and stopped by the post office." He showed her the letter. "This is from my mother in Salt Lake City."

Alaina stood silent, staring at the white envelope.

"She invites us to live with her."

"And your father?"

"My mother and father don't live together."

Alaina's head came up quickly. "Divorced?"

Nephi shifted his weight and shook his head. "No. They just don't live together. There'd be a room for you, and I'd have a bed out in the storage room."

Alaina's face flushed hot with embarrassment. How much of their situation did Mrs. Erickson know, and what must she think of such a daughter-in-law? Alaina turned, picked up a pot cloth, and lifted the lid off the stew. She stirred slowly, biting her lip, and fighting back emotion. Nephi stepped toward her and she stiffened.

"I know it's a long way from your home, but . . ." He hesitated. "I . . . I don't know what else to do."

The anguish in his voice made Alaina wince, and she resolved not to add to his grief. She put the lid back on the pot, wiped her hands on her apron, and turned back to her husband. Pain had lodged itself in her throat, but she spoke past it. "How kind. How very kind of her to offer us a place." She saw tears spring into Nephi's eyes, and she quickly smoothed her apron to stop the sympathetic rush of emotion. She vowed to keep a clear head. "Will we be able to take Miss Titus?"

Nephi wiped his eyes on his shirtsleeve. "Of course."

"Well," Alaina looked him straight on, "it's settled then. Will you take care of the arrangements?"

"I will." He took her unexpectedly into his arms. "I've been so worried."

She'd patted his back and stepped away. "I'll have supper ready in an hour. Will you tell James?"

"I will," he'd said as he left.

A train whistle blew, and Alaina looked along the platform. *Where was Elly?* Eleanor had taken Kathryn to the relief house long ago, and Alaina wanted her back. She wanted Elly's happy spirit to lift and calm her when her heart filled with fear.

Alaina repinned her hat and shoved her carpetbag with her foot. One trunk, one carpetbag, and one satchel carried all her earthly belongings. In her right coat pocket was Father's journal and her letter from Philomene Johnson, and in her left pocket, the hundred dollars Mother had given her.

She squeezed the money in her fist, remembering the harsh interchange that morning.

"I don't want this."

"I am giving you and James each money to begin your new lives."

"I don't want a new life."

Elizabeth Lund stood straight and tall, her hands clasped in front of her, her eyes turning to look out the kitchen window. "We do not always get what we want," she said, her voice full of pain.

Alaina had stared at her mother for a moment, then picked up the money from the table and put it into her coat pocket. Eleanor came into the room. "It's time, Laina," her sister said quietly.

Mother turned to look at her oldest child as Alaina buttoned her coat and picked up her carpetbag. "Alaina, I do wish you well."

Alaina stood for a moment staring at the floor. She glanced up into her mother's face. "For Kathryn's and Eleanor's sake, I wish you well too." She turned and walked out of the house. The cold November air stung her face, causing her eyes to water. She brushed away the wetness and looked over at the dormant rose-of-Sharon bush, trying to imagine it green leafed and full of delicate ivory blossoms.

As she stared at the bush, Nephi came to get her bag and help her into the wagon. He did not speak to her or ask her questions, for which she was grateful. Kathryn and Eleanor sat on quilts in the back of the wagon, and she sat on the buckboard between James and Nephi. If she looked straight ahead, she could not see the meadow or the orchard or the pine-covered hillsides.

James gave the word to Friar Tuck, and the horse started forward, the faithful companion unaware that this was more than just another trip to town. Alaina thought of Moccasin and Titus, and felt darkness press in around her. She shoved her hair away from her face. They would be all right. James would take good care of them. She thought of Miss Titus and looked back to make sure she was doing well tied to the back of the wagon. She glanced at the house and saw Mother standing on the front porch, her arms folded across the bodice of her black dress. Kathryn waved, but Mother only stood still, watching them move away.

Suddenly Alaina wanted to run back and throw herself into Mother's arms. She wanted her mother to hold her and tell her it had all been a mistake, that no matter what propriety or the law said, the family had every confidence that she could manage the farm. In return Alaina would promise to learn all of Mother's wonderful recipes, and sew all her own clothing, and never lose her temper. But the wagon had moved on, and Alaina turned her face to the road ahead, insensible of the anguish that had marred her mother's face.

Alaina suddenly looked up to see James as he appeared at the door of the boxcar, nodding to her that all was well. The burly man came up the ramp, growled at James to get a move on, and slammed the door with a bang.

"Thank you, James!" Alaina called as her brother moved down the plank.

"All aboard!" The conductor's voice lifted above all the other sounds. The loading man unhinged the plank, and he and the other loader carried it off, giving James a sour look when they passed him. Kathryn and Eleanor came running from the ticket office.

"Did they say 'last call'?" Eleanor gasped as she ran to Alaina. "Is that what he said? I thought we'd missed you!" She tossed an angry look at Kathryn and tried to calm her panicked breathing.

"Well, I couldn't help it if I had to relieve myself," Kathryn answered petulantly.

"Yes, but you didn't need to pull the chain twenty times."

"I did not pull it twenty times!"

Eleanor ignored her combative sister and turned to Alaina as the last of the boxcar doors were slammed shut. Nephi hopped off the train and came to Alaina's side. "Everything's settled." He picked up her bag, and he and James shook hands warmly.

Eleanor grabbed Alaina's hands. "Oh, please tell me it's not time!" Eleanor pleaded, her voice shaking. "Please, please tell me you're not really going, Laina. You have to stay! You have to stay with me!"

Alaina had not expected this desperate anguish from Eleanor, and it unsettled her far more than anything she could have imagined. Kathryn started crying, and James stood staring at his boots.

"Last call! All aboard!"

Eleanor shrieked, flinging her arms tightly around her older sister's neck. The train's whistle blew, and Nephi took Alaina's hand, pulling her toward the train.

"Elly, I have to go!"

"No! I won't let you!"

"Elly . . ."

"No!"

Alaina began crying, and James stepped forward to pull Eleanor back. He held her arms, but she struggled against him. "Laina, I can't go to San Francisco! I can't! I'm too afraid."

"Oh, Elly . . ." Alaina started to go to her, but Nephi held her.

"Alaina, we have to go!"

"Wait, one minute!"

"There isn't time!"

The train's engine engaged. Alaina pulled every bit of courage into her being and ran to her sister. She grasped Elly's arms and shook her. "Eleanor Lund, you listen to me. We can do this. We *will* do this. We Lund women are strong."

Eleanor stood still and looked at her. "We are strong," she said in a small voice.

Alaina smiled. "Yes, we are."

The train began to move. Eleanor wiped her face and stood taller as Alaina leaned over to hug Kathryn.

"I love you. Be a good girl."

Kathryn's beautiful little face was filled with honest grief. "I love you too."

Alaina looked squarely at James. "I'm very proud of you."

James nodded.

Steam swirled onto the platform as the train picked up speed. "Alaina, you have to come now!" Nephi yelled.

Alaina grabbed Eleanor's hand, and they ran for the train. "This parting is not forever, Elly! It's not forever!" They hugged each other quickly, then Nephi grabbed his wife and lifted her onto the moving stairs. He threw her bag onto the landing, grasped the handrail, and jumped up beside her. Steam billowed from the stack and the whistle blasted.

Alaina laid her head on the cold metal of the train and watched her dear ones disappear. She couldn't even lift her arm to wave, and she thought of Mother standing on the front porch just watching as the wagon moved away from the house.

When the train moved over the crest of the hill, Nephi took her by the elbow and led her to their seats. Fawn-colored hills and barren oaks moved by outside the window, but Alaina saw none of it. Her mind was a jumble of images from her past, a past where she had lived on a farm, a past that was a hundred years ago. *Where am I going?* Away from her home. Away from everything familiar. The circumference of her life had always been small. How would she find life outside that known enclosure? She had told Eleanor that they were strong, that they could conquer this hardship, yet she doubted every word.

She opened her locket, losing herself in the images—Father's face and the dear little apple tree. Her mind fixed on the repeated sound of the wheels on the track. She rubbed her fingers on the ivy engraving, trying to reassure herself as she had Elly that their parting was not forever . . . their parting was not forever . . . their parting was not forever. The words repeated in her mind until exhaustion overtook her and she slept.

CHAPTER 26

She was making dinner: stew, rye bread, and apple cake. She took the cake out of the oven and set it on the sideboard. Eleanor sat at the table, her head bent over her books. The sun was setting, and Alaina squinted at the rays as they shot through the tattered clouds on the western horizon. The room was bright, but there was no warmth. The sun kept flickering back and forth, back and forth. It hurt her eyes and made her head ache.

Then the train jolted and she banged her head on the window. When she opened her eyes, she was looking out at the passing ground. The movement made her sick, and she sat up, fixing her gaze on the seat in front of her.

Nephi touched her arm "Are you all right?"

She shook her head. "No."

"Would you like some water?"

She nodded.

Nephi stood and made his way unsteadily down the aisle.

Alaina looked around at the few other passengers, noting that several glanced at her, then away. She figured they had witnessed the scene on the platform in Martell and were feeling sorry or embarrassed for her situation.

She shut her eyes to block out the pain in her head, but that only brought on waves of nausea. She'd always thought a trip on a train would be a grand adventure—she now knew better. They were moving faster than she would have thought possible, at least forty-five miles per hour, and she was disappointed that instead of being excited, she was frightened and agitated.

Nephi returned with a glass of water.

"Where are we?" she asked.

"Half an hour out of Sacramento."

"Can you see any of the city?"

"Not yet. A few farms." He sat down. "Would you like something to eat?"

"Maybe a hard roll."

He brought down his bag from the storage compartment and secured the small food sack. He handed her a roll and brought out an apple for himself.

Alaina looked out across the flat fields, forcing herself not to think about the farm, or Elly, or the scene at the train station. She had to think about something else, something to keep her mind away from the pain.

"My grandpa, John Samuel Lund, came out to Sacramento on the transcontinental railroad."

"He did?"

"Yes. In 1878—from Iowa. Brought his whole family. My father was ten. They had a farm southwest of the city."

"Why'd they come way out here?"

"My grandmother, Mary Margaret, had arthritis. Grandpa figured it was drier here than in Iowa." She watched quietly as they passed a field dotted with cattle. "They grew wheat, sorghum, and chickpeas. It was a good life."

"And they're both gone?"

Alaina nodded. "My uncles too."

A purser came into the passenger car, moving efficiently down the aisle. "We'll be at the Sacramento station in fifteen minutes."

Nephi thanked him, and Alaina noted her husband's shyness with strangers. *My husband.* She understood words like *brother*, or *friend*, but this word was a mystery. Relationships only meant something when experiences and emotions gave them texture. So what did she know about this man? He was a hard worker, he stayed silent when she was thinking, he played baseball, and he never drank coffee. This man she barely knew was her husband, and she was moving seven hundred miles with him to live in a strange place. Well, a strange place to her. The only thing Nephi had said about his family was that his mother and father didn't live together and that his mother had her own little house where they would be welcome. In truth, Alaina had become numb to the vagaries of her life. Circumstance had stripped her of options, and though she knew Nephi was not trusting her with all his family secrets, she didn't care. All her weary mind craved at the moment was security—and that meant Salt Lake City. She glanced at Nephi, then back out to the passing fields. Did she really have any other choices? She wouldn't consider divorce after the sacrifice Nephi had made, and his support of her. Nephi couldn't find work around her home, and she hadn't been asked—nor did she desire—to live in San Francisco. She supposed they could have hired on with Mr. Regosi and learned to break horses. Despite all the pain, she chuckled to herself at that idea.

Nephi turned and caught the slight smile at the corners of her mouth. "Feeling better?"

"A little."

His smile broadened. "Good."

Alaina finished the last of her water and handed him the glass. "So, they have to move Miss Titus to a new stable car?" She shook her head. "She's not going to like it."

"As soon as I've moved our baggage, I'll help."

Alaina nodded. "Then how long to Truckee?"

"We should arrive about four this afternoon, if we're not slowed by too much snow. They have snow wedges on the front of the train, and there are snow sheds and tunnels all along the line, so we should be all right. Besides, I think it's been a light snow season so far."

Alaina smiled at Nephi's obvious excitement of venturing into the rugged Sierra Nevadas, and found it fascinating that he knew so much about snow wedges and snow sheds. She actually felt the thrill of anticipation at seeing these magnificent mountains of legend and folklore, and of moving over rails that had been laid by a tenacious Chinese workforce of the Central Pacific Railroad almost fifty years before. Miss Johnson had shown her class pictures of the monumental task, and Alaina never quite understood how they conquered the eleven-thousand-foot peaks, or blasted tunnels through solid granite. Soon she and Nephi would be the beneficiaries of their labor, and she marveled.

The transfer in Sacramento went well, as Miss Titus seemed not to mind the moving stable as long as she was supplied with sufficient amounts of sweet hay and coaxed in by a handful of oats.

Alaina was disappointed they couldn't see any of the city from the train yards, for she had heard the California state capitol building was magnificent and that the city had impressive stone structures—many over five stories tall—and grand homes on tree-lined boulevards. Then she thought about her plain, rumpled clothes and worn shoes and figured it was better there was no time for sightseeing. When the *Governor Stanford* pulled out of the train station a little after noon for its hundred-mile run to Truckee, she found that the excitement of moving toward the summit was pushing back feelings of fear and loneliness. Soon the train was climbing into the rolling foothills of the Sierras, and the bare deciduous trees of the lowlands gave way to yew, cedar, and pine. The day was clear, but evidence of prior storms could be seen as they moved higher. At first only patches of snow nestled in shadows and north-facing overhangs, then a milky glaze frosted the tawny carpet of fallen pine needles. When the train climbed another thousand feet, the sky turned from pale blue to vivid blue, and the forest floor shrugged on its white coat, settling into the season.

Entranced, Alaina and Nephi watched the splendor outside their window, both going for long stretches of time without moving or speaking.

Finally Alaina fell back into her seat and closed her eyes. "I can't look at another beautiful thing or my eyes will pop out!"

Nephi chuckled, standing up and stretching his back. "Good thing we're almost to Truckee then."

She sat up. "Are we?"

"I would imagine. The snowpack's been light, so we've made good time. Hey! Another snow shed coming up!"

As the train passed through the heavy-timbered building, Alaina was again awed by the skill and grit of the men who had forged this part of the line. Was anything impossible if men could do this? She looked up to find Nephi staring at her. His eyes flicked away and he stretched again.

"So, we'll be staying overnight in Truckee?" she asked.

"Right," he answered quickly. "I arranged boarding for Miss Titus at the blacksmith's stable."

He seemed nervous, and she imagined it was because they would be spending their first night alone in the same room. There had been no question after the wedding that she would continue to sleep in her old bedroom with her sisters, and he in the shed, but tonight that would change. She knew there would be no romance between them, but even sharing a room seemed an intimate thing. She wondered where they would sleep and what they would talk about as the long night dragged on. Nephi had insisted on paying for the journey, but she was sure he would not be foolish enough to secure two rooms just for sleeping. How would she change into her nightdress? The thought made her blush.

The sun was sliding quickly toward the western peaks as the train dropped down into the lovely valley that sheltered the town of Truckee. Alaina peered through the window as the main street of town came into view. It was close to the north side of the tracks and seemed to be a mixture of one- and two-story shops of wood or brick. A covered walkway fronted most of the buildings, and many people were making their way along the walkway to avoid the mud as they shopped.

The train, which had been slowing now for several minutes, began to hiss and groan to a stop. On the east end of the street Alaina saw a large three-story structure with a covered veranda. If she squinted, she could just make out the sign "American Hotel." It looked new compared to most of the other buildings, and Alaina wondered if fire might have consumed an earlier structure. On the north hillsides, sloping up behind the main street, she could see a jumble of small and large homes, and she tried to imagine how the people of Truckee existed, especially in winter when the snow could be ten to fifteen feet deep.

The train jolted to a stop, and any further questions about the residents of Truckee were set aside for the work of the moment. She and Nephi gathered their bags and stepped off the train into the bracing November air of six thousand feet of elevation. It smelled heavily of pine, and Alaina's thoughts jumped back to the ride to Miller's Bend when she and Elly had found shelter from the rain under the giant pine.

She forced her mind to the present, helping Nephi push the cart with their belongings to the station baggage room. When their things were secure, they went off to find Miss Titus.

They arrived at the end boxcar as an elderly baggage handler was guiding her carefully down the ramp; the spirited horse was doing well under the watchful care of the weather-worn gentleman. The lead rope seemed small in the man's large hand, and Alaina could easily imagine him as a miner or logger in his younger days.

"You own this beauty?" the man asked as he spied their approach.

"We do, sir," Nephi answered, handing him the claim paper and offering his hand.

The man shook it heartily. "Name's Kamp," he said, taking a close look at the paper. "Miss Titus," he repeated, reading from the form. "Good name."

"Thank you, Mr. Kamp."

"You're Mr. and Mrs. Erickson?"

They nodded.

"From here to Reno, and Ogden?"

"Yes, sir."

"Heading for Salt Lake City?"

Nephi stiffened. "Yes, sir."

"Been there on my way out from Chicago. Beautiful city. That Mormon temple is a wonder."

Nephi relaxed and smiled. "Yes, sir."

Miss Titus tossed her head, and Mr. Kamp patted her affectionately. "Seems like she's glad to be out of that box. You have a place to board her, Mr. Erickson?"

"Yes, sir. I telegraphed the blacksmiths."

"Oh, that'd be the carriage shop. Mr. Gray's place. Not far. Go down the main street here to Bridge Street, take a left, can't miss it. Don't worry, Mr. Gray will take good care of your little treasure."

"Thank you, sir." Nephi took the lead from Mr. Kamp while Alaina checked to make sure the filly's padded blanket was secure. Nephi shook the good man's hand again, and they turned to leave.

"You two have lodging?" he asked.

"We do sir, thank you," Nephi answered quickly. "And what time do you have?"

Mr. Kamp checked his pocket watch. "Near on to four thirty."

Nephi jumped. "Oh! Thank you kindly!" he said, moving quickly toward the main street.

"Lift your skirts there, ma'am! We have mud galore!" Mr. Kamp called after them.

Alaina did as she was told, and ran to keep up with her husband. "Why are you running?"

"It's a surprise."

She slipped and he grabbed her arm. "A surprise?"

The train whistle blew and Nephi moved ahead faster. "Yes, ma'am. And I hope we don't miss it."

They found the blacksmith shop and stable easily, and were reassured by Mr. Gray's competent handling of the little filly. His son took a particular liking to the chestnut beauty, promising to brush her down special and exercise her. Everything went well, yet Alaina looked perplexed when they came out of the shop.

"Nephi, why did Mr. Gray charge us three nights' keep? Won't we be picking Miss Titus up first thing tomorrow?"

From the train station a whistle blew, and Nephi grabbed Alaina's hand and began running. "Oh, no! Not two times in one day!"

"Nephi! Where are we going?"

"It's a surprise!"

"What surprise?"

But there was no time for talking as Nephi continued running all the way down Bridge Street, across Donner Pass Road, and into the train station. He claimed their two carry bags and sprinted out onto the platform, with Alaina panting behind. He found a conductor and breathlessly asked, "The train for Lake Tahoe? Has it gone?"

The conductor smiled. "Take a breath, son. It's right over there. Number 3. Leaves in two minutes."

The whistle blew, and steam billowed from the stack of the gleaming locomotive. Nephi gulped air into his lungs and turned around to find Alaina staring at him.

"You're taking me to see Lake Tahoe?" she asked, her voice ragged with emotion.

He walked back to her. "I didn't want you to miss it."

She looked at him through tears. "Oh, Nephi, I . . ."

The whistle blew again, and he motioned her toward the train. "Come on! Unless you want me to throw you onto another moving train."

She laughed, moving quickly toward the stationary giant. "No, thank you. Once in a day is enough."

She was physically exhausted, and her heart still carried a weight of sorrow and loneliness, yet somehow the wonder of what lay ahead brought a lightness to her spirit she would not have thought possible. She looked at the man striding beside her and wondered at the unexpected circumstances that had brought them together. The train whistle gave three shrill blasts and the engine engaged. The passengers safe inside Number 3 watched with critical expressions as two young stragglers came running and laughing the final ten yards to the train.

CHAPTER 27

Alaina awoke to a quiet she'd never heard before. It was odd to think of hearing nothing, but that's what it was—no animal sound, no bird song, not even a breath of wind. She turned her head to look at the bedroll where Nephi had slept and was not surprised to find him gone. He was usually up by five, and she could tell from the light that it must be nearing seven.

She lay quiet, thinking about last night's ride up the Truckee River Canyon. The fifteen-mile trip began in evening shadow, the light from the pale autumn sun lost quickly in the thick branches of the pines. The swirling crystal water of the river flowed beside the train's route, and she watched, entranced, as it made its way past the sentinel mountain peaks. A slender crescent moon rose over the eastern ridge, and as the sky darkened, thousands of stars appeared. The enchantment had drawn her, for a short time, to a place where dreams were still possible.

When they reached the stop at Tahoe City, Alaina was so tired that all she could do was follow Nephi doggedly wherever he went. He rented a small cabin at Lawson's Lodge, while Mrs. Lawson, a feisty older woman of five feet tall, was quick to point out that she could never understand why her husband ("God rest his soul") had called it Lawson's Lodge instead of Lawson's Cabins, as it really wasn't a lodge at all, but cabins. Of course, she'd prattled on, there was the main building where meals were served to the guests, but the rooms were five separate little cabins set among the pine trees—each named after a bird. Alaina had been too tired to care. Mrs. Lawson had given Nephi a lantern, and he'd guided his wife through small drifts of snow to their lodging. He'd started a fire in the little potbellied stove, thrown his bedroll out, and lain down fully dressed. Alaina covered him with a quilt and followed his example, laying her coat over the two quilts on the bed and climbing quickly under them. Nephi blew out the lantern, and they had fallen asleep to the sound of a rising wind in the pines.

She wanted to get up, but it was very cold. She could see her breath on the air, and her nose felt like a piece of ice. Quickly she jumped out from under the warm covers, putting on her coat, and wrapping Father's scarf around her neck. She sat down and put on a thick pair of socks, then her boots. She stood, stamping her feet, while she put on her hat and mittens. She drew a quilt around her shoulders and opened the cabin door. She caught her breath, not from the cold, but from the most beautiful vision she had ever seen. In the dark of last night she had not realized their cabin sat only a stone's throw away from the edge of the lake. Alaina stood, staring. A part of heaven had come down to earth. She knew God had scooped out a piece of the sky, turned it to liquid, and poured it into the deep basin between the soaring mountain peaks. She stood transfixed, her heart aching to share this rapture with everyone she loved. She grasped the quilt tightly to her chest to keep herself from weeping.

It had snowed during the night, and Alaina stepped from the cabin into the glistening wonderland, drawn to the beauty of the lake like a sick man to medicine. She didn't care about food, or the cold— in fact, nothing else mattered but standing beside the shore and gazing at the shimmering blue water.

That's where Nephi found her, sitting on a log bench and staring out across the calm water that went on for miles into the hazy distance. Her face was flushed with cold and washed by tears.

"I told you words couldn't describe it," he said quietly.

"You were right." She motioned for him to sit by her. "Look how clear it is. You can see every pebble ten feet down."

Nephi smiled at her delight, and his heart made another connection to her person.

She turned to him. "Why did you bring me here?"

He looked at her straight on. "I wanted to share it with you." She nodded, and he started to look away, but then held his gaze. "I hoped it might bring you some peace." A tear ran down her cheek, and he took hold of her gloved hand. "You've had so much trouble. I guess I wanted to take away some of the pain."

She brushed the tear away. "You're a good man, Nephi. Thank you." She looked into his blue eyes and smiled. It was comforting to have him close to her. She felt stronger in his presence—at peace.

He kept his hand protectively over hers, and she didn't pull away. In his heart there was a soft stirring of hope that someday she might grow to love him.

"Tell me about our new home," she said, looking out over the shining crystal water. Somehow she felt she could talk about the next part of their journey together.

Nephi took a deep breath, looking out at the splendor with her, knowing that the beauty of this place and the tenderness of feeling between a man and a woman were gifts from a loving God. He said a silent prayer of thanks, squeezing Alaina's hand and moving closer.

"My mother's first name is Eleanor . . ." he began simply.

ABOUT THE AUTHOR

   Gale Sears grew up in Lake Tahoe, California, and spent her high-school years in Hawaii. After graduating from McKinley High School, she went on to receive a BA in playwriting from Brigham Young University, and an MA in theater arts from the University of Minnesota. She lives in Utah, where she celebrates life with her husband George and her children Shawn and Chandler.